OATH
OF
MOONLIGHT

OATH
OF
MOONLIGHT

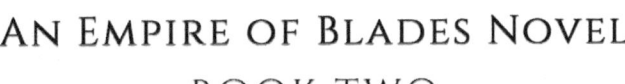

AN EMPIRE OF BLADES NOVEL
BOOK TWO

NICOLE CONWAY

BROADFEATHER
BOOKS

For Donna

N
W E
S

GAVRAL TUNDRA

WHITE WASTES

ETHALAN

ICEDRIFT SEA

WESTERN OCEAN

WHITECROWN MOUNTAINS

VORDEGA

HALONAR

DAN

VAARN

LUNTHARDA

MALDOBAR

Halfax ●

SOUTHERN SEA

Almo

RIENKA

Brazur's Point   Ipsol   Sal'Karr   Derith ●

Salodurn   Banaris

Tkyeran   Kosaar   Malis ●

Mathros   Vetharkis   Pithan   Kua Tar

Savarian Mine   Soman Taal   Esfolar

Obsidian Ridge

DAMARIA

Fallern   Faladurn

Alsferth   Ollenvale   Hallowdu

PANTHEON OF REATIA

FOREGODS

Itanus
Enais
Milontos
Vescor*

OLD GODS

Giaus
Astaris
Avgior*

LESSER GODS

Paligno
Clysiros
Undae
Proleus

GODLINGS

Ishaleon
Adiana
Tykeron
Iksoli

deceased or banished

ONE

Tonight, I would be a monster again.

Two years of biting my tongue, holding back every instinct, and trying to smother the rage that kindled deep in my chest—I couldn't bear it for another cursed second. Not when scumbags like Sulam and all the men he employed were slinking through the streets every night completely unchecked. Utter filth.

So here I was again, in the dead of the night, letting all my wicked instincts run wild.

On the surface, I couldn't let it show. I had to behave. I had to walk the line and perform just the way the Zenith's Call wanted all the time. But I couldn't let this go. I couldn't let men like that—like him—roam free without fear.

So no one, not even Roxus, knew where I was tonight. This was my secret.

And it wasn't the first time.

It had become a terrible and extremely risky habit I really needed to kick. But every few weeks, the urge grew inside me like a thorny briar until it choked out every other thought. I was a wolf pacing a cage. A black powder keg with an unlit fuse. Too long in training, honing myself for a mission that still hadn't come. Waiting, waiting, waiting.

What if I started losing my edge? I couldn't have that. And, well, this seemed like as good a way as any to keep it.

After all, I owed Sulam all the stress and strife I could inflict on him, and killing his slavers for spite wasn't exactly a bad thing, right? Someone had to take the trash out on occasion.

I just happened to enjoy it.

My pulse roared in my ears as I watched the crew of slavers unloading a group of people dressed in rags and smeared with filth. The armed guards dragged them from the back of a windowless wagon. All ten members of their cargo were bound in shackles at the wrists and ankles, strung together like a line of caught fish, and marched into the rain-dampened side street outside one of Sulam's warehouses on the outskirts of the harbor.

My fists tightened, aching for the hilts of my blades.

I'd watched his men moving new slaves in and out of the city just like this twice a week at a minimum. I'd lurked in the shadows and watched long enough to memorize their patterns and practices. Long enough to be sure there would be no mistakes or surprises. I was careful not to strike the same route twice. Careful not to leave any evidence behind.

I licked my teeth behind my lips, watching the four guards set up their perimeter around the wagon while a fifth and sixth went down the line, examining each individual in their cargo. Evaluating them for sale.

I stifled a growl.

Sulam's men were nothing if not thorough. This trade kept Sulam's coin purse lined with fresh gold and funded his vile appetite. Some went to pleasure houses or noble homes, while others were sent to work the mines. Some he even kept for his own entertainment—like Declan's little sister. He used her as collateral to keep Declan chained to that pit, fighting for his life every night.

My stomach clenched at the thought. I wouldn't say it. I wouldn't admit that this was as much for him as it was for my own sanity. Declan wouldn't like it. He'd want me to stay out of his personal affairs. I usually did. I owed him that much.

But not tonight. Tonight, Sulam would pay in coin and blood.

I couldn't kill him outright—not when he sold valuable information to the Zenith's Call sometimes. They didn't like him or what he did, but they needed what he could provide. So I couldn't touch him personally.

I could ruin his day, though. I'd settle for that.

For now, anyway.

A whistle gave the rest of the guards a signal to close up the wagon. Two of them took the driver's seat at the front and snapped the reins, starting the horses. The sound of hooves on the cobblestones was barely audible above the rush of the rain.

The wagon disappeared down the street. Gone without a trace.

Good.

I watched from my perch on a second-floor balcony, marking the bright yellow-orange outlines of each remaining guard in my heat vision. Rain dripped from the hood of my dark cloak. My thighs burned from crouching for so long, but I refused to move or even shift position. No, this had to be flawless.

Four guards left, all heavily armed. Shortswords on their hips. Leather armor with a fitted metal breastplate, gauntlets, and daggers. Two had crossbows. A third had a short whip studded with metal.

The sight of it put a cold spike of dread in my gut as he walked the line of slaves again, barking orders to the other guards. He was the one in charge—the one I had to take first.

The rest would panic without him to give directions. They'd get sloppy. Desperate.

Easy to kill.

I couldn't see their faces through the sheets of cold rain, but I could make out enough to tell that most of tonight's group of slaves were humans. There were a few elves, too—Lunthardan, most likely. Only the elves of that wild jungle kingdom had that shock-white hair. That's why they were often called Gray elves.

The captured women, children, and young men stood in a line, all tangled together in the iron chains, their feet bare and their heads bowed low. The rain poured down, soaking them through. But they didn't so much as whimper. I guess they'd already learned what would happen if they made a sound.

"Take those two girls to the Lowlamp District," the leader of the guards snarled as he stroked the whip at his hip as fondly as if it were a beloved pet. "The rest go to the stockyard."

The other three guards snapped into action, opening the locks around two of their quarry.

My hands slipped to the soft, padded leather hilts of my blades as my jaw settled into a hard clench and my pulse began to slow. Every nerve drew taut. A bowstring ready to snap.

Sulam must have paid a hefty sum to get them all the way here to the Southern Kingdoms.

Good. This would hurt more than usual.

A sudden, deep crack of thunder overhead propelled me forward. I sprang through the air, dropping the distance and landing right on the shoulders of the lead guard. The impact of my boots against his back sent him sprawling forward all the way to the ground.

He hit with a cry, and I immediately drove both my daggers through his back to the hilts—one through each lung.

A brutal twist of my blades sealed his fate, making his body writhe beneath me.

He groaned and gurgled, dying noisily as he drowned in his own blood.

The other guards whirled on me. The chained slaves screamed, scrambling together and trying to shield the children and elderly in the middle.

I stood slowly and stepped off the fallen guard, the lengths of my rain-soaked cloak whipping in the stormy night wind.

"What the—?! Who are you?!" one of the guards shouted in alarm.

I peered at him from beneath the cowl of my cloak, tilting my head up just enough that he would see the glint of my ruby-red eyes.

Just enough that he would know what I was.

"Pi ... Pitathi," he wheezed brokenly as his face paled. His hands shook as he ripped his sword free of its sheath.

The fire of crossbow strings cracked in the night. Bolts pinged off the stones in front of me. Was their aim *that* terrible in the rain? Or was it just a warning shot?

Either way, it was my cue.

I rushed forward, a streak of steel and shadow, and sprang again, kicking off the stone side of the building and arching over them. They fired more bolts, shouting and floundering as I landed in a crouch behind them and rushed in.

The second guard fell with one of my daggers through his neck.

The third and fourth threw down their crossbows and drew their swords. Sparks winked in the night as I locked blades with them, holding them at bay with one on each side. Every muscle burned with wild delight as raw energy sizzled through my body.

Throwing all my weight back, I arched into a perfect backflip and landed on my feet. Nimble as a cat—that's what Roxus said. He wasn't wrong, I guess.

I ducked and dodged, angling myself easily around the guards' wild swings as our blades hummed in the dark, whipping like tongues of silvery flames. Fierce strikes. Rigid parries.

Behind them, the group of would-be slaves was moving again. Shouting to one another. Doing something—I couldn't tell what.

It didn't matter.

One of the guards feinted to the side, just as the other drove in hard with a strike aimed at my head. I dipped back, falling into a backbend at the last second. My cheek stung as the blade grazed my cheek. Too close.

"AUGH!" A feral noise broke through the whoosh of rain as one guard was suddenly thrown back on his heels.

I gaped, sparing an extra second to stare at the chain now wrapped around his neck ... and the young Gray elven man holding it there with all his strength. One slave had worked himself to the end of the chain and was using his shackled hands to throttle the guard from behind.

Our gazes locked—his a startling riot of color even in the near-dark.

He shouted at me in a language I didn't understand.

Fortunately, the panic and urgency in his expression were easy to interpret.

I dipped to the side just as the second guard swung at me again, his blade glancing off mine with a screech of metal on metal.

Focus, curse it. I couldn't afford to get distracted.

With only one enemy before me now, I moved like a ripple of darkest shadow. Frustration and fury scorched my throat as I whirled my blades, feeling them like extensions of my own inner fire. One leg sweep put him down on a knee, and I did not hesitate.

I drove both my daggers through his chest, angled inward to pierce his heart. His gaze fixed on mine, eyes wide and horrified, as I gave them the same brutal twist I had when I gored his boss.

"Fates condemn you," I spat as the life left his eyes and his body went slack.

I ripped my daggers free of his corpse and kicked him the rest of the way to the ground. He hit the cold, wet stone with a soggy thud.

Good riddance.

My chest heaved with every deep breath as I slowly turned back to the last guard, blood still dripping from the ends of my weapons.

The Gray elven boy still had him by the neck, the muscles of his arms bulging as he kept the chokehold. The guard pitched and clawed at the chain cinched tight over his throat, his face turning from red to blue. His eyes bulged.

Then, at last, his struggling slowed. His arms flopped limply at his sides, and his expression emptied.

But the Gray elven boy didn't let go. His multi-hued eyes were wide and wild, mouth twisting in a grimacing snarl. His dark brows skewed upward as his drenched white hair stuck to his face, neck, and bare shoulders.

"Hey." I sheathed my weapons and took a few slow steps closer. "It's over. He's dead. You can let go."

The boy's gaze snapped to me, and he rasped a few sharp, frantic words that sounded like a warning. Or a plea. I still didn't know. I'd never learned Lunthardan. But sometimes, the words didn't matter as much as the body language.

So, I lowered my head and raised my hands in surrender.

"I'm not going to hurt you," I tried again, using the common tongue of the north. It was far more common among the humans in Maldobar, but they shared a border with Luntharda. Maybe I'd get lucky.

He blinked a few times, studying me as he kept that fierce chokehold on the guard. Then his shoulders went slack. His grip on the guard suddenly loosened, and the dead man flopped to the ground at his bare feet.

"Wh-Who are you?" he asked, stumbling back a step as though he couldn't believe what he'd just done.

"A pitathi," I muttered as I strode over to the fallen lead guard and began rifling through his pockets.

"That is your name?" he asked.

I snorted and shook my head. Poor guy. He really had no idea.

I'd always heard that people from the northern kingdoms didn't stray this far south often, and I guess tales of the wretched, wicked pitathi didn't find their way to those shores, either.

It would have been kinder to be cruel to him. To walk away right then and there since I was likely the only Viperi he would ever meet that wouldn't try to kill him on sight. No need to instill a false sense of trust, right?

But I just ... couldn't.

I yanked a fat velvet coin purse from the lead guard's pocket, along with a set of heavy iron keys. I tossed both to him and sighed.

"Unlock the others. You need to get out of here before Sulam sends someone to see why his shipment is late," I warned.

The boy caught the keys and the purse, but kept staring at me. His expression creased with something like suspicion. Or concern. I couldn't quite tell.

"Why do this if not to keep the coin?" he asked.

I shrugged. "Some things are worth more than gold." Things like defying the disgusting pig of a man who'd tried to put me in those same shackles years ago.

The boy arched an eyebrow dubiously. "Not much in this land, apparently."

A grin slipped across my lips before I could stop it. He caught on quickly. Maybe he'd be all right here after all.

"They don't have slaves where you come from?" I asked as I went to check the pockets of the other fallen guards. Nothing but a few coppers and four silvers, which I kept.

"No. It is against our laws. Some still try, but they risk the wrath of many crowns," he answered quietly, looking to the rest of the would-be slaves.

They were watching him like a herd of terrified lambs, waiting for any signal to run and hide. Not that I blamed them.

"Well, there are plenty of others here who would see you all back in those chains. So hurry up and let everyone go. Then take that gold and head to the temple of Undae that way. It's a big white building with stone pillars and a reflecting pool." I pointed up the island's steep incline. "They will shelter you and help you find passage back home."

He did, and I kept watch at the front of the alley the whole time. It took several minutes to get everyone unbound, and a few of the children were so weak from hunger they had to be carried. But as they filed out of the alley and into the night, I watched and kept a hand on the hilt of a dagger, just in case.

"Thank you," the boy said, pausing beside me for a moment.

I flicked him a sideways glance. He was about my age, I guess. With nothing but a pair of ripped, filthy breeches on his lean frame, I couldn't tell if he was shivering from the adrenaline rush, horror at the life he'd just taken, or the cold rain.

Either way, there wasn't much more I could do for him ... or any of the others.

Save for this.

I took off my cloak and held it out to him. "Watch your back here. You can trust the priestesses of Undae, but no one else. Find a merchant headed back to the north and barter passage as soon as you can."

I could feel his odd, multicolored gaze studying me as he took my cloak and put it on. My hair probably looked similar, although it was more of a very pale blonde than true silver like his. I was far shorter, of course, and probably not what he'd expected to find beneath the heavy dark cloak.

"I am called Aeron. Do I get to know your name?" His voice was softer. More careful.

A bit of heat tingled in my cheeks, and I bowed my head. "Violet."

He pulled the hood down low, the corners of his thin mouth hinting at the faintest tug of a smile as he nodded once. "May the gods go with you, Kind Violet."

He said it so carefully, like a prayer or a blessing. Like he believed every word and knew it would come true.

I watched him dart after the rest of his group, slipping away into the dreary night as the rain soaked through my hair and clothes and filled my boots.

Gods go with me? He couldn't have possibly known how ridiculous it was to say something like that to me. To someone the gods hated most of all because my kin had been created to spite and destroy them ages ago.

And, Fates, I hoped he never would. I hoped he and the others left for their home before they learned about any more of the horrors this place was capable of. The monsters writhing beneath these rainy streets, hungry and waiting to ensnare more innocents.

Monsters I would kill, one by one.

Er, at least I'd try ... until Roxus caught me, I guess.

Whirling on a heel, I forged down the side street through the rain and bitter wind. Drops seeped between the seam of my lips, cold, crisp, and slightly salty on my tongue. It whipped at my hair and stung my cheeks, running in chilly streams beneath my leathers without my cloak.

My pulse slowed as I let myself meld back into the fabric of the night, disappearing into the soggy tapestry of darkened avenues and shadowed alleyways. The streets slithered up the steep side of the island's only mountain, carrying me along back toward home.

I groaned at the thought. I'd been doing this for months now, and slipping in and out of my room was as easy as breathing. But I wasn't stupid. Sooner or later, Roxus would figure out what I was up to when I was supposed to be studying or sleeping upstairs. Then I'd have to deal with the consequences. His anger. His hurt and betrayal.

Just the thought of it twisted at my heart like someone trying to wrench an apple off a branch. I hated it—the fact that I would disappoint him again. But what other option was there? I couldn't turn a blind eye to what Sulam was doing. I couldn't let him hurt more people the way he was hurting Declan. The way he'd tried to hurt me.

Someone had to make sure he paid.

So, I'd make the streets run red in his honor until my luck ran out. Then I'd stand in the flames of the aftermath ... and hope Roxus would forgive me.

Two

The crack of Varren's nose under the hilt of my dagger filled the sparring room.

Gods, curse him, he was still too slow.

It would get him killed someday.

Blood dribbled off his chin as he staggered back, spitting and cursing. He shook his head, making his shaggy dark hair swish over his brow. Collecting himself.

I waited, shifting my weight and feeling the slight give of the sparring room's woven reed mat under my bare feet. It made for a softer landing—supposedly.

Tell that to all the bruises on my knees and back.

Varren's body tensed, bristling as he flexed his corded arms, probably trying to shake the feeling back into them. Veins stood out against the tops of his hands, and his fingers twitched. Contemplating. Planning.

I paced back and forth, my body humming with primal energy that made all my senses flare to life. The scent of sour sweat hung thick in the close, too-warm air. My thighs quivered with each practiced step, ankles threatening to buckle after so long on edge. Exhaustion vibrated through every part of my body.

But my pulse stayed steady. I was controlled and composed as I moved in a wide arc around him. I set my teeth against the fatigue and squeezed the hilts of my practice daggers, watching his every tiny movement—every ragged, uneven breath that heaved in his broad chest.

He'd grown in the last two years since we'd both become fully-oathed members of the Zenith's Call. Well, we both had, I guess.

Unlike me, however, Varren had gotten taller and now was easily twice my size. Stronger. More brawny. His dark hair was always messy and fell around his neck and ears, and his features had hardened with maturity. He looked much less boyish and pathetic.

Too bad he was no less stupid and stubborn.

And reckless when he got frustrated—a fatal flaw I was counting on.

Varren dove for me with his dulled shortsword again, his attack so obvious I didn't even bother with a parry. I dropped into a sideways roll and came up right beside him, driving my elbow into the side of his head at the same time I hooked a heel around his ankle. Every muscle sang in protest like a fingertip over taut resin lute strings.

But I refused to buckle.

Varren swung at me, trying to put more distance between us, but I dropped into a backbend and immediately snapped upright, twisting my foot around his.

Varren barked a cry of fury as he toppled sideways, hitting the sparring mat with all the grace of a falling tree.

I knew by the sound he made, like a dying animal groaning for breath, that it was over. I had won.

Again.

"Vedra'tavas!" he cursed in Damarian as he slammed a fist against the sparring mat.

I couldn't hold back a smirk. "Throwing tantrums now?"

Varren shot me a withering glare, face flushed and brows rumpled together. "Screw you. Just … give me a minute. I need to catch my breath."

I spun one of my daggers over my hand and twirled it through my fingers as I strolled around him in a circle. "Whatever you say," I purred. "Big baby."

"I hate you sometimes," he growled through his teeth as he wiped at his nose, smearing some of his blood over his cheek.

"No," I corrected. "You hate me *most* of the time."

He didn't reply.

We both knew it was true. He just didn't have the guts to say it out loud.

It probably should have upset me that he still felt that way after so many months of training together like this. Or, at the very least, it should have made me want to avoid him. People disliking me wasn't news, though. The other agents of the Zenith's Call had resented me the instant I crossed the threshold, and being oathed in two years ago had not changed much in that respect.

I was still a Viperi. Still evil down to the marrow of my bones, as far as they were concerned.

But now I was a *necessary* evil. A useful one.

I could live with that.

You didn't have to like someone in order to work with them. Or, as Roxus had so eloquently put it to the council of elders, "If you can't beat 'em, hire 'em."

That had been a particularly hard lesson for me to swallow at first. Of course, I'd wanted to belong. I'd wanted to fit in *somewhere*.

And if I were being honest, it was still uncomfortable to think about. It made it hard to turn my back on anyone here.

There was always that little prickle of unease in my gut, the tinge of fear that someone might have finally decided I wasn't useful enough to keep around anymore.

My mentor, Roxus, had fought tooth and nail to counter that mentality in Arx Eburna, though. He'd often made grand sales pitches to Orvana, the Mistress of the Call, on my behalf to keep her and the elders from kicking me back to the gutter my first year.

Gods only knew why they'd actually listened to him.

I tried not to think about that too deeply. My mentor was a man of many faces, many angles, and dangerous secrets. He had brought me here to the stronghold of the Zenith's Call as a half-starved, young, and practically feral street urchin. Sure, I knew how to fight, how to survive, and how to kill when necessary. But I was like a dust devil twisting wildly through the desert, directionless and flinging debris, leaving a path of destruction in my wake.

Roxus had insisted that I learn to cage that chaos. To control it. To wield it for a purpose beyond just mere survival.

And I had.

Well, I'd begun to, anyway. Last night, I'd let the dust devil toss a few things around. But my brand of chaos wasn't so easily defined ... or harnessed.

A work in progress.

The thought made me frown as I watched Varren sit there, elbows on his knees, still trying to breathe. Maybe hate was too strong a word for how he regarded me. I didn't believe for a second he would actually try to kill me if given the chance. Gods knew he could have done it during one of our countless sparring sessions and chalked it up to an unfortunate accident. No one would have questioned it too much.

Well, except for Roxus, of course.

So maybe it wasn't hatred that flared in his cobalt eyes when he slid me that sideways glare through sweaty bangs, blood still oozing from his nose down his lips. More like frustrated disgust with a sprinkle of competitive rage.

Whatever it was, Varren just shook his head and muttered another curse. We'd been at this for an hour now, and judging by the heavy circles under his eyes, he'd been on night watch duty with the Vindexori for several days running. He didn't have much fight left in him this morning.

"I have an appointment with Roxus soon. You should go eat," I huffed as I turned away. "You look terrible."

"I'm supposed to be back on guard rotation in four hours," he growled back.

I hesitated, giving him another hard look from head to foot. He was practically catatonic, sitting there staring ahead like he might collapse. A lot of good he'd be if something actually went wrong.

I pursed my lips, angling my face away so he didn't mistake my words for concern. "That's not much of a break."

"We're still shorthanded."

"Oh. Right."

The attack on this place had been a while ago—two long, uncomfortable years, to be precise—but the effects still reverberated through the ancient stone halls like aftershocks.

Many Vindexori had died the day Chrysa and her accomplice, a powerful Rajinna sorcerer, had cracked open the Vault of Whispers and nearly made off with a ledger chock-full of dangerous divine secrets. We had stopped them, of course, but Chrysa and Kalsin had not been working alone. They were backed by the Tibran Empire, sent directly here to loot our sacred vault. Defeating them had prevented a potential disaster of epic proportions.

Unfortunately, the fight had also cut the ranks here to nearly nothing. It had forced Mistress Orvana to call in temporary replacements from other strongholds throughout the southern kingdoms while we acquired and trained new prospects. Those new recruits, like Varren and me, were still finding their feet. We were considered far too green to be handed much authority.

But the scars ran deep, and healing within the order was slow. Training took time, especially when the order was very particular about who it let in. Now more than ever, they couldn't afford to get sloppy about their selection process.

They couldn't afford to make the same mistake twice.

Knowing the Tibran Empire was lurking in the shadows, eyeing all the divine power and knowledge the Zenith's Call was sworn to protect, had everyone on edge. The order had endured wars before, watching from the sidelines and pulling threads when needed ... but a direct attack?

No one had seen that coming—not even me.

And, gods, I *should* have.

The memory put a stab of sharp pain through my chest. I gripped my daggers tighter and bowed my head.

"Ugh. Forget this. I'm done," Varren announced suddenly, his tone heavy with surrender as he loosed a deep sigh. "I ... I need sleep."

My brows rose. He was actually admitting he was tired? Gods, he must have been a lot worse off than I thought.

"And a bath," I agreed, wrinkling my nose. "And food. Maybe a healer, too."

That nose did look a little crooked now. Oops.

"Don't fuss over me. It's weird," he muttered as he hauled himself back to his feet with a hiss and grunt of pain. "Curse it. I think you broke my nose."

"You said you didn't want me to take it easy on you," I reminded him, keeping a few steps between us as I followed him to the weapons rack on the far wall of the sparring room. No need for anyone to get the wrong impression—least of all him.

After all, Varren and I were *not* friends.

I did not have those. Not anymore.

"That doesn't mean I want you to break my bones." He dumped his shortsword back into a crate with the others and turned to give me a hazy, exhausted stare.

"Technically, it's cartilage—" I started to correct him.

A sudden chorus of laughter and giggles from the other side of the sparring room made us both turn.

And there *he* was.

Axien.

THREE

I was frozen.

One glance from his eerie, vibrant glacier-blue eyes was all it took.

They weren't Rienkan. Not sea-blue or rain cloud gray. No, Axien's eyes shone like fire-lit sapphires. And something about them struck me at my core, sending a surge of adrenaline through my veins. It locked every muscle in my body up as solid as stone.

My stomach soured, and my jaw tightened. My pulse skipped sloppily. Primal fear vibrated deep in my chest like someone strumming a taut bowstring.

Fear because that man always looked at me the exact same way. Like he knew something—could see something deep within me—that no one else did.

A hidden, dark truth that not even I had discovered yet.

I didn't understand it at all. Axien didn't know me, and I had absolutely no desire to know him. I could only imagine that he, like everyone else, assumed he understood everything about me simply because I was Viperi. Just a dumb, angry

little beast he liked to poke at whenever he could get away
with it.

It was stupid. Stupid and annoying.

And, gods, I *hated* it.

Nothing Axien did made any sense to me, honestly. He
had a way of always showing up to haunt my steps from afar
whenever I came to Arx Eburna, watching me with that stupid
knowing grin. I couldn't fathom why he felt entitled to
critique my performance during training exercises, either. Not
just because they were flawless—they were—but why he
thought I needed his opinions in the first place.

Then there were the names.

He insisted on calling me patronizing pet names like "darling" and "lovely." Things that sounded affectionate, but I wasn't
stupid. I was Viperi, so terms of endearment could only be
sarcastic if they were aimed my way. They were insults. His way
of throwing it in my face that I was neither darling, lovely, sweet,
enchanting, nor any of the other ridiculous names he used.

I clenched my teeth, steeling every frayed nerve and
holding his stare as he strode by. Regardless of what he *thought*
he knew about me, or what he called me, I would never be the
first to look away. I would not show weakness.

Axien's smirk widened, chin tilting down some as he
cruised past Varren and me like a lion prowling through his
domain. Power and intent in every step. Intense control. A
predatory grace he probably thought no one else had noticed.

But I did. I saw the razor-sharp edges in that infuriating,
lazy smile that dimpled one of his cheeks as he flicked his gaze
over me from head to foot.

"Good morning, Lovely Miss Violet," he purred
smoothly.

I bristled. My voice tangled in my throat, and I couldn't
even muster a convincing growl.

His gleaming eyes danced up to the top of my head. His smile widened. "Interesting hairstyle choice today."

Rage—hot and swift—swept through me.

I waited until he'd swaggered off to furiously comb my fingers through my messy, sweaty, combat-tousled hair. Gods, it was probably sticking up everywhere. Why hadn't Varren said anything?

And why did I even care?!

Varren ambled over to stand beside me, wearing a scowl like he might throw up or start swinging punches if Axien came any closer. Part of me hoped he would. It would be a good fight—quick, and Varren would certainly lose.

But it would definitely be entertaining.

After all, despite those fair half-elven features and broad, pleasing smiles ... I knew Axien was not someone to trifle with. I'd observed him from afar for two years, studying his movements and methods. The way he talked and trained with the other dextrum agents and even the Vindexori. Maybe he thought he knew something secret about me, but I saw the man behind the mask of that saccharine smile—even if no one else did.

Or maybe they did and just didn't care. The Zenith's Call needed people like him—like us. The necessary evils.

But that didn't mean I trusted him.

Nope. Not for a single second.

Because *I* was the other apex predator in this territory, and I knew better than to let him see me flinch. If he was the lion, then I was the viper poised to strike.

I couldn't hold back a soft growl of defiance when Axien finally turned his back. I snapped my teeth and swiftly put my two wooden practice daggers back on the rack where I'd found them.

"You'd think the luster would have worn off by now,"

Varren grumbled, still poking gingerly at his nose. He winced, and his eyes watered.

I frowned. "What?"

"The way they all keep fawning over him. I mean, I understood it when he first arrived. But now it's just ridiculous." Varren nodded toward Axien as a pair of giggling, young female dextrum agents approached him. They blushed and smiled sweetly, not seeming to notice the way he avoided even glancing their way when he spoke a greeting.

"Jealous?" I taunted, knowing exactly where to slide the knife to get him riled up.

Varren's face flushed as red as a radish, and he cut me a sideways glare. "Vindexori aren't allowed to fraternize within the order," he barked angrily.

I rolled my eyes. "You're so boring," I sighed.

"So are you."

"You're just saying that because I haven't murdered anyone in a while," I lied and grinned, batting my lashes at him.

The rosy color in his cheeks darkened. He scowled down at the floor, crossing his arms and avoiding eye contact.

I felt it even before I glanced back toward Axien—the intensity of his stare sent another prickle of unease up my spine. He stared at Varren as though evaluating him for weakness, jawline drawn tense, and those gleaming, frost-blue eyes unblinking.

He wasn't smiling anymore.

Interesting.

"You really have an appointment this morning?" Varren muttered sheepishly.

Changing the subject? Well, I'd just have to call that my second victory this morning.

I shrugged. "With Roxus and Mistress Orvana. Might as well prepare since that's sure to be its own form of torture."

"What'd you do this time?" His cobalt blue eyes flickered my way, and I caught a hint of concern creasing his brow.

Was that sentiment? Concern? For *me?* Ew.

I feigned an insulted gasp and put my hand on my chest. "How dare you? I'll have you know I've been perfectly well-behaved this week."

"Oh yeah? Then why do you have a fresh cut on your cheek?" he countered.

A prickle of panic tingled in the pit of my stomach, and I brushed my fingers over the mark. The place where one of the slavers got a lucky strike in with his sword last night. It had scabbed over, but it still stung a little.

Curse it. I had hoped he wouldn't notice. Or care.

"Want to kiss it and make it better for me?" I baited.

Varren rolled his eyes and curled his lip. "Forget I asked."

"I try to forget everything you say."

He gave a subtle motion, jerking his chin toward Axien as we sauntered across the sparring room toward the door. "Sooo ... any particular reason that guy keeps staring at you?"

Great. If Varren had picked up on that, then everyone else around Arx Eburna likely had, too.

I worked my jaw from one side to the other, keeping my gaze trained only on the doorway ahead. "I suspect he's just as stunned and disgusted by the sight of a Viperi here as the rest of you," I said dryly. "Or maybe just shocked that no one's killed me yet."

"He doesn't look particularly disgusted." Varren snorted and shook his head. "You mean to tell me you haven't had words with him? Not a single introduction? Not a casual chat?"

I shot him a glare of warning. Did he think he was being subtle? Idiot.

"No," I snapped.

Varren's genuine surprise was infuriating. "He doesn't visit you at home?"

Gods. I'd rip his tongue out for even suggesting it.

"No," I growled through my teeth.

"Oh. It's just ... I mean, word around the temple is that Roxus has a pretty extensive history with his tandem. That they used to be partners," he murmured, like he didn't want any of Axien's adoring fans to overhear us as we passed. "Some are even saying they were lovers. And he watches you while you train. So I just figured ..."

Hot bile rose in my throat at the thought. "Yeah. I know."

Did I ever.

While Axien had become a regular fixture in Arx Eburna, cruising through the halls with an occasional gaggle of swooning young women in tow, Axien's elder tandem had become a similar nuisance at home.

Sanja—that was what Roxus called her. He said it so warmly. Fondly. Like it was the familiar, welcome taste of his favorite wine on his lips.

My stomach curdled at the thought of her inviting smiles and airy giggles. The way she always took *my* seat at the dinner table. The way Roxus didn't make her move, or notice how she blatantly ignored me.

It had started casually. A visit here and there. A light conversation if we passed them in the halls. I'd been too distracted by snarling at Axien while he pinned me with that vulpine grin to even notice much of what they'd said.

Now, Sanja came over several nights a week, bringing bottles of fine Lunthardan liquor and charming smiles that didn't fool me for one single second. She stayed way too long after dinner, and Roxus seemed to enjoy every second of her sitting in his office, chatting and reminiscing about their past missions. Laughing. Drinking.

Always with the door closed and me on the opposite side of it.

I shuddered at the thought.

The only thread of mercy in the tapestry of that misery was she always arrived alone. Never with Axien. I wondered if Roxus knew that forcing me into proximity with him would get someone stabbed, and had already warned her off the idea of bringing him around. Or maybe Sanja was just far more interested in rekindling the flames between her and Roxus than anything else to bother bringing him.

Whatever the case, I didn't have to deal with Axien at home, in my personal space. Er, well, so far, anyway. I could only hope it stayed that way.

Stealing a glance back in Axien's direction, I caught him still staring at us. At me, specifically. The flickering magical blue flames from the sconces made his eyes gleam strangely, like they were made of that same fire, too. It put all my nerves on edge as that fear tingled in the center of my chest.

Curse it. Why? What was it about him that felt so bizarre?

I narrowed my eyes back at him and curled my lip enough to let one of my pointed incisors show.

Whatever game Sanja was playing at, coming around my home and acting so friendly, I didn't trust it. And I didn't trust him, either. Regardless of how smitten Roxus seemed with Sanja, I would not let my guard down.

Not again.

"Same time tomorrow?" Varren asked, jarring me from my trance as he held the door ajar for me on our way out of the sparring room.

I made sure to step on one of his toes as I went past. "Fine. If you're dying for another round of public embarrassment, who am I to stand in your way?"

"Pitathi brat," he rumbled bitterly.

"Human idiot," I hissed back.

He presented a fist, and I bumped mine against his. Bruised. Battered. Every knuckle sang with fresh pain from so much sparring.

Just the way I liked it.

"Stay out of trouble. I don't want to be the one tossing you in the dungeon next time you cause problems," he warned.

"No promises," I taunted, giving him a rude gesture, as I started away down the dark, cavernous hall, not looking back as I called over my shoulder. "No promises."

FOUR

I'd have to make this fast.

My fighting leathers came off like a slimy second skin. I cringed as I rolled them up and stuffed them into my haversack, leaving it hanging on a hook in the bath's antechamber. I'd deal with that later.

Fortunately, I'd brought along clean ones to change into once I'd scrubbed myself free of sweat, dried blood, and grit from the sparring room floor. Even if it was all in the name of bettering myself for the Zenith's Call, I couldn't stand before Mistress Orvana looking like I'd just crawled out of a tavern brawl. Not when she still held my fate in her hands.

One wrong step, one false word, and she'd have all the excuses she needed to toss me back out—oathed in or not.

Every part of me was aching, reeking of sweat, and trembling with exhaustion as I shuffled into the next chamber. My stomach gave a loud, long growl that echoed in the tiled room.

Gods, I hadn't packed anything to eat before the meeting. Stupid.

I took a deep breath of the steam-choked air as it rushed over me, heavy with the scent of perfumed oils and soaps.

Bundles of eucalyptus were displayed in fine porcelain pots, and oil lamps burned low and dim in the corners. Beautiful mosaics of hippocampi, fish, and twisting seaweed covered the floor—all warmed by the smoldering coals in the subfloor.

Water ran through a shallow, rectangular depression like an artificial stream through the middle of the room, filling the space with a constant tranquil gurgle. I crouched down beside it and used a long-handled scoop to pour the chilled water over my body.

I hissed through my teeth the instant it met my skin. Fates, curse it. Why did they keep it so cold? Even with the warm steam, it made my whole body shudder.

I hurried and rinsed the grime from my feet thoroughly. I soaked my waist-length hair and scrubbed my body with hand-fuls of salt and sugar-packed oils before rinsing off again. The places where I had open cuts and nicks from training stung at the contact, but none were bad enough to warrant a bandage.

Little souvenirs from Varren, mostly. I'd been forced to start sparring with him more and more since Declan was ... unavailable.

My heartbeat skipped at the thought of him and I winced.

We'd been pretty close right after I had first started living with Roxus. He'd taught me a lot when it came to unarmed combat, especially against opponents who were so much bigger than me.

Now, I only saw him a few times a month, if I was lucky.

It bothered me—a lot, actually. I didn't like not knowing what was going on with him while he was still pinned under Sulam's thumb. But as I found myself drawn deeper and deeper into the fold of the Zenith's Call, focusing on my conditioning and studies here, I couldn't check on him as often as I had before.

Nothing about his situation had changed. He still fought in that pit almost every night. I didn't see how it ever would as long as Sulam had his sister as a hostage. Declan would fight to the death to make sure Sulam didn't put a hand on her—which had been their bargain. As long as he kept fighting and winning, she would be untouched.

Or so he hoped.

I let out a breath and pushed those thoughts from my mind.

Far, *far* away.

Binding my hair up in a silken shawl, I left the antechamber through a heavy linen curtain strung across a narrow doorway. Beyond it, the soaking pool spread out between gourd-shaped pillars of pale alabaster. Thick clouds of steam curled off the surface of the still, mineral-green water, and I couldn't hold back a sharp hiss as I stepped down into it.

Hot—it was almost too hot.

My jaw clenched and my mouth twisted as all those little scrapes stung again. But as I sank down to my shoulders, my body adjusted to the heat. All my aching muscles seemed to go wobbly and limp.

I let out a deep sigh like the hiss of a kettle.

Sweet relief.

Sitting alone amidst the clouds of steam, my limbs floating in the still-hot water, I could barely distinguish the shapes of other figures soaking around the large pool, but no one approached. The only light came from flickering candles placed around the edge and at the base of the pillars. The pool was a place for relaxation and meditation. For the slow release of the day's pent-up frustration.

Too bad I didn't have much time for either today.

My gaze drifted down to the mark on my forearm, just below my elbow. A sword and crescent moon were inked into the pale white of my skin. My oathmark. My tether to the Zenith's Call.

Somehow, it felt like that mark stared back at me. Watchful. Waiting for me to fail.

I frowned.

After a few minutes, I returned to the dressing room. I ran a comb through my hair and wound it into a long, damp braid that hung down my back, then pulled on a loose, white silk tunic and fitted leather pants.

My neck throbbed, still sore all the way down to my shoulder blades, as I fastened on a broad waistbelt and matching black leather vambraces. My stomach growled angrily again as I laced up my boots.

Food. I needed to find something to eat. Maybe that was why my hands were still shaking some.

Standing straight, I checked myself over in the long dressing mirror by the door. I hadn't grown up all that much height-wise, but I had filled out into a more womanly shape thanks to two years of good food and constant training. Delthene hadn't done a great job of disguising her relief when my monthly cycles finally started last year. She had mentioned, off-handedly, that she was worried the malnutrition might have lasting effects beyond just stunting my stature.

Fortunately, I was healthy and whole. Just bruised and a little ragged around the edges. I still didn't bother with wearing rouge or perfume, no matter how heavily Delthene hinted I should.

No, this was me.

Not great. But also not terrible.

Good enough.

Mistress Orvana wouldn't be able to complain about whether or not I was presentable. Naturally, she'd find something else to be critical of, but now she'd have to get a little more creative about it.

Roxus stood, already waiting for me in Krin'Moir's sprawling central hall, his back to the towering fountain of the two draconic gods—the Viepol—with his arms crossed and expression tight with thought. Dressed in his favorite ragged longcoat, a rumpled linen tunic, and road-battered boots and pants, Roxus could have easily passed for a common vagabond. His shoulder-length brown hair was pulled into a haphazard ponytail at the base of his neck, and he wore a longsword belted low across his hips.

Interesting.

I hadn't bothered bringing any of my real weaponry. According to Roxus, it sent the wrong message when meeting with the mistress or elders. But maybe I should have ...

Hmm.

"Any idea what this is going to be about?" I dared to ask as I swaggered toward him, one hand on my hip and the other holding my haversack of dirty laundry over one shoulder.

Roxus startled some as though he'd been lost in the labyrinth of his own mind. He straightened as he looked up, casting a quick, appraising glance over me and shaking his head slightly.

"I suspect it's another mission," he replied. "Although, if she's going to the trouble of having us in to discuss it rather than just sending a missive—"

"—Then it must be something big," I finished for him, unable to keep a grin from spreading across my lips.

He made a wincing face and shrugged slightly. A cautious affirmation. "Could be. Let's just keep our heads on straight, eh?"

I grinned wider.

He must have noticed the excited spring in my step as I walked along beside him toward Mistress Orvana's office because he just sighed and shook his head. "All it takes to get you beaming is the prospect of getting to stab someone, eh?"

"And getting to see something other than these drab walls every day," I added brightly.

He laughed. "Don't get too excited. It's probably just security detail."

I pursed my lips at him sourly. "Trying to dash my dreams?"

"Only when it involves death and dismemberment."

I laughed too.

But we both fell silent as we approached the grand doorway that led into Mistress Orvana's private office. The two Vindexori keeping guard outside stopped us, questioning our intent before they finally allowed us to go inside.

My stomach was flipping and spinning like mad—half from anxiety and half from wild, primal hunger.

The smell of freshly baked curry meat pies hit me like a punch to the jaw as soon as we stepped inside. I almost came to my knees right in the doorway.

Mistress Orvana sat behind her desk, too distracted by something on her desk to even look up as we entered. But all I saw was the untouched breakfast tray beside her. My mouth watered at the silver platter stacked with hot, flaky pastries and a bottle of cinnamon-spiced warm milk. Merciful stars.

Too bad she was far too caught up in her own stuffy head to offer us any.

"You're late," Mistress Orvana observed, her tone cool and prickly. She kept her gaze fixed on a spread of paperwork strewn out across the desk before her like a mismatched patch-work quilt of ink and parchment.

"By two minutes." Roxus was grinning roguishly—a look I knew was a mask he liked to wear around her.

It kept his real thoughts, his real feelings about the things she said, carefully disguised.

Gods, I envied him that skill. I was fighting for my life just to keep from diving over her desk for a meat pie.

"You might've taken five to feed your tandem," Orvana

said, her gaze still focused on her papers. "She's drooling on my carpet."

Heat tingled in my cheeks, and I looked down at the toes of my boots.

"Have one, then. No point in letting them go to waste." She waved a hand at the platter dismissively.

I didn't like Orvana. And she didn't like me. But I was willing to bet in that moment that she didn't hate me quite enough to poison me, and dove for the platter before she could reconsider. I swiped two of the little meat-packed pastries and shoved one in my mouth on my way back to stand next to Roxus.

He just sighed and shook his head. "I doubt you invited us here to share your breakfast."

Mistress Orvana finally looked up, leveling a no-nonsense stare through the thin, half-moon lenses of her spectacles. "Indeed not." She picked up a slip of parchment; one lined with curling text, and folded it crisply before holding it out to him.

"A mission?" he asked as he took it carefully.

"One most urgent," she confirmed. "You'll need to prepare yourself. This one will take you to Levanurith."

My eyes nearly rolled right out of my skull mid-bite. Had ... had I heard that correctly?

Levanurith?

But that was all the way in Salnis. Miles to the west, beyond Rienkan borders.

My gaze swept between them, panning from Mistress Orvana's stern, earnest scowl to Roxus's eerily blank features. No smile. No frown, either.

Gods, what did that mean?

"Are we to leave immediately?" he asked quietly, folding the paper and tucking it into his coat pocket.

"No," she replied evenly. "You'll be working with another

tandem team. In this particular case, we cannot afford half-measures, no matter how thinly stretched our resources."

Roxus's head bobbed slightly. "When should we depart?"

"I'll send word once the arrangements are set. Right now, we have our contacts in the field making sure the path is made clear for you," she said, her tone precise and her words far too cryptic.

It made a rush of unease tingle up my spine.

Roxus widened his stance, his jawline going tense as he seemed to weigh his next words far more carefully. "You're talking about the Tibrans."

Mistress Orvana was the first to look away, her gaze falling to another piece of cream-colored parchment that sat right in front of her, the page still creased as though she'd only just opened it. "It will be dangerous. You will need to take all necessary precautions."

Silence hung as thick as morning fog on the dockside street. Every breath seemed too loud. Every movement made my instincts draw tighter and tighter, like a bowstring ready to snap.

Not just a mission, then. A dangerous one. One that would put us in the path of the Tibrans again.

"Care to be specific?" Roxus pressed, his tone much softer. More careful.

"It's the Moonscape Staff, Roxus," she said, matching the hushed caution in his voice. "We must see it safely delivered into the appropriate hands."

He frowned, his light amber eyes seeming to spin with dark shadows of thought. Of worry. "She's still too young for the final rite."

"We're out of time," Orvana replied. There was real regret in the way her mouth pulled into a thin, tense line, and her slender brows drew together. She brushed a few runaway locks of her graying dark hair behind her ears as she shifted uncomfortably in her fine velvet chair.

Roxus's face seemed to leech of color. But he didn't so much as breathe as we both stood, waiting for her to explain.

A few seconds of silence. Then, a heavy, defeated sigh left her lips.

"The wheels of war are turning, Roxus. We cannot afford to underestimate the powers that be once again," Mistress Orvana announced, her fingertips trailing over the slip of parchment on the edge of her desk. "We must move quickly, precisely, and discreetly."

"You think the Tibran Empire will invade Nar'Haleen," Roxus said suddenly.

The words sent a bolt of emotion through me like a lightning strike. I flinched and stared at him, desperately trying to read the hard lines of his rugged features. Was that a guess? Or something he'd heard through his own contacts?

Mistress Orvana's eyes narrowed slightly, as though she were also trying to read him, too.

Neither of us succeeded, apparently, because her slim shoulders dropped, and she sighed again.

"They are moving much faster than anyone could have anticipated and without impunity. Noltham, Braskol, and Elondia have already fallen. The dwarven houses of Whitecrown have gone silent, and Tibran ships have been spotted moving in large fleets across the western ocean," she said, slowly looking up to meet Roxus's gaze with grim resignation. "Yes, I believe they will move against Nar'Haleen, if they haven't already. You know as well as I do it takes time for word to travel this far, even from our own strongholds."

"They'd need a mighty army for a conquest of that magnitude," Roxus countered, his tone tight. Forced. Worried.

"I know," she answered quietly.

Roxus stiffened. A muscle feathered in his jaw as his gaze went cold. "Vordega?"

She nodded.

"By force? Or alliance?"

I'd never seen Mistress Orvana do anything but sneer and snarl, but in that moment, a gentle, mournful softness ebbed into her sharp features. Her lips pressed together slightly, her throat bobbing as she looked down and away. "You know Illiria better than I do."

Roxus's eyes darkened, his gaze frosty steel as his hands curled into tight, shaking fists at his sides. "Alliance, then. And an expensive one."

Mistress Orvana turned in her seat, her focus shifting to the huge, ornately framed map that hung behind the hearth on the far wall. A map of all Reatia—of all the known world. Her head bowed some, making her hammered copper earrings jingle. "We've seen tyrants come and fall. We've seen wars that spanned decades. But if half of what I am learning about this man, the new ruler of the Tibran Empire, is true ... then Gods help us."

It took everything I had not to roll my eyes at that. Like they ever did. I'd seen plenty in my sixteen years—good, horrible, and brutally violent—but I'd never seen any of the gods lift a finger for anyone.

I doubted they'd make any exceptions for Viperi.

No, I was on my own. My strength and my skills would be my only arsenal, as always.

I just hoped this time it would still be enough.

FIVE

I t made no sense.

My mind whirled, thoughts tossing like a wooden dinghy in a stormy sea, as I tried to make sense of their cryptic exchange.

Who was Illiria? What did Vordega have to do with anything? It was just a small nation in the icy waves of the Western Ocean. Surely, it couldn't have that much impact on the rest of the world.

Right?

My stomach swirled and churned, sending waves of jittery tingles through all my extremities as I tried to read between the lines of their cryptic words and meaningful glances. Later—I could question Roxus later.

I *would* question him.

But the mention of the Tibran Empire, and more specifically, of their bloodthirsty emperor, made a dark tide of dread well up inside me. Cold and abysmal, I couldn't help it. His name left my lips as a low, tight growl.

"Argonox."

Suddenly, all eyes were on me.

I dipped my head low, flushing again.

"What do you know of him?" Mistress Orvana asked.

I tensed. *Of course* she would assume I had some insight into the mind of a brutal tyrant.

"I've only heard him mentioned in passing," I replied. "They say he is monstrous. That he enslaves the peoples of the nations he's conquered and forces them to fight under his banner. Those who refuse are tortured and butchered."

Mistress Orvana's gaze was as keen as a razor's edge, sizing me up from head to toe. "So it would seem, although he does far worse than that at times," she agreed at last. "And now we must work to upend his plans before he ever sets foot on our shores. I hope you're up to such a task, pitathi."

Slowly, I lifted my head and fixed her with a stare—one I sincerely hoped smoldered as fiercely as the coals in her office hearth. Even after all this time, after everything that had happened, she still called me that word. She still expected me to cringe or falter as it left her lips. But I wouldn't.

"I will fight to my last breath," I promised.

Her smile was frosty, and it never reached her eyes. "We shall see, won't we? Go. Make your preparations. And you'd do well to make temple offerings. I don't know what gods might hear the prayers of a pitathi, but in your case ... it might not hurt to try."

"I'm not the praying sort," I muttered.

I'd never once dared to light a single candle before any of the temple altars. And not because I would have gotten stared at. To be a Viperi meant I came from a long lineage of cursed blood. My kin had been created to be instruments of vicious wrath and murder for the Dire King Zarexius centuries ago. We were the spawn of the dark god of oblivion, Vescor.

Time had not made us friendlier ... or more welcome amongst the races of the surface world. And it wasn't some grand miracle of mercy that had delivered me from them into the loving arms of the Zenith's Call.

It was pure dumb luck … and a little bit of murder.

Roxus cleared his throat as though hoping to cue a change of subject.

It must have worked, or something in his demeanor warned her not to push the issue any further, because she waved a hand as though to brush the whole topic aside.

"Do as you wish, then. But in the meantime, I have some requirements for you if you wish to take part in this mission."

Requirements?

I arched an eyebrow and flicked Roxus a sideways look.

He just shrugged.

"This will require you to move in the public eye. You're to begin instruction in social etiquette immediately. I've already appointed a tutor willing to take you on and teach you the subtleties of the social arts," she said. It was impossible to miss the sharp edge of doubt in her tone—like she had no faith whatsoever that I'd actually be successful.

"Social arts?" I frowned, looking at Roxus again.

He was grinning from behind his hand, doing a shoddy job of trying to hide it as he rubbed at his chin.

Mistress Orvana didn't so much as spare me a glance, though. "Indeed. You are skilled with a blade. No one would question that. But you lack tact and discipline in social situations. If you wish to continue your training and be invited to participate in such missions, you'll need to improve those skills, as well."

"Table manners? Curtsying?" I fumed, biting at each word.

Mistress Orvana snorted, still not looking my way as she began sifting through her papers again. "To start with. One must crawl before they run, I suppose."

Great. Just … fantastic.

I glared at her, hoping my stare might light some of her hair on fire if I focused hard enough.

It didn't.

"Your tutor will be Curator Vanora. Address her with appropriate respect, and perhaps she will be able to hammer some manners into you before the mission begins," Mistress Orvana ordered. Only then did she spare me a soul-piercing glare from behind the rim of those shining spectacles. "Do not waste her time. Or mine, for that matter. You must learn to lie as well as you fight. To charm as well as you fire your bow. Your life and those of others around you may very well depend on it."

I opened my mouth, ready to protest.

But she snapped a glare of molten warning up at me, adding quickly, "Or you will have to choose a different role within our order. I will not have you be a liability to my other agents because you lack the social finesse to move through society without causing a ruckus."

I sank into my heels some, feeling the weight of those words settling around my neck like an iron collar.

No way around it. This was the new obstacle—the hoop she wanted me to jump through.

Ugh. Fine. So be it.

"When do I start?" I couldn't keep the groan of defeat out of my tone.

"First thing tomorrow, you'll find your way to a healer to have those fangs filed down. And every morning after, you'll report to Curator Vanora in her office for private instruction." Orvana flapped a hand at both of us, waving us out of her office as she went back to her papers. "I'll send word to you soon regarding the finer details of your mission as I receive them, Roxus. Until then, make the necessary preparations on your end. You are dismissed."

Gods curse it. No—gods curse *her!*

I managed to keep it together until Roxus and I had left her office. We were a few paces down the hall before all my frustration erupted.

"We're standing on the brink of another divine war, and she's worried about my *teeth?*" I fumed.

"She's worried about you keeping a low profile," Roxus corrected sharply.

I winced, feeling the sting of his disapproval like a smack to the face.

Did that mean he agreed with her?

"We lost a lot of good agents when they tried to crack the vault. Orvana hasn't forgotten that. She won't risk losing more. That means making compromises for the sake of safety," he muttered.

I traced the points of my incisors with my tongue. I knew they weren't exactly subtle. But would it truly make that much of a difference?

"The teeth aren't the primary issue," he said, like he was reading my mind again. Or maybe he just noticed my skewed, uncertain expression.

Yeah. Probably that.

"It's about beginning to see yourself as part of the whole," he clarified. "You're one of us now. Time to start acting and looking like it. You need to be able to move through social situations with as much finesse as you do combat maneuvers."

"I can be discreet," I grumbled.

A hint of a smirk tugged at the corners of his mouth, and I saw a bit of that mischievous glimmer return to his warm, cognac eyes.

"It's not about discretion, Vi," he chuckled. "You need to learn to be likable. Charming, even."

My lip curled. Seriously?

I was a Viperi. Nothing about me was charming.

"Delthene will be delighted," he mused as he shoved his hands into the pockets of his longcoat.

Great. Well, at least one of us would be.

Gods help me.

Maybe I ought to start praying, after all.

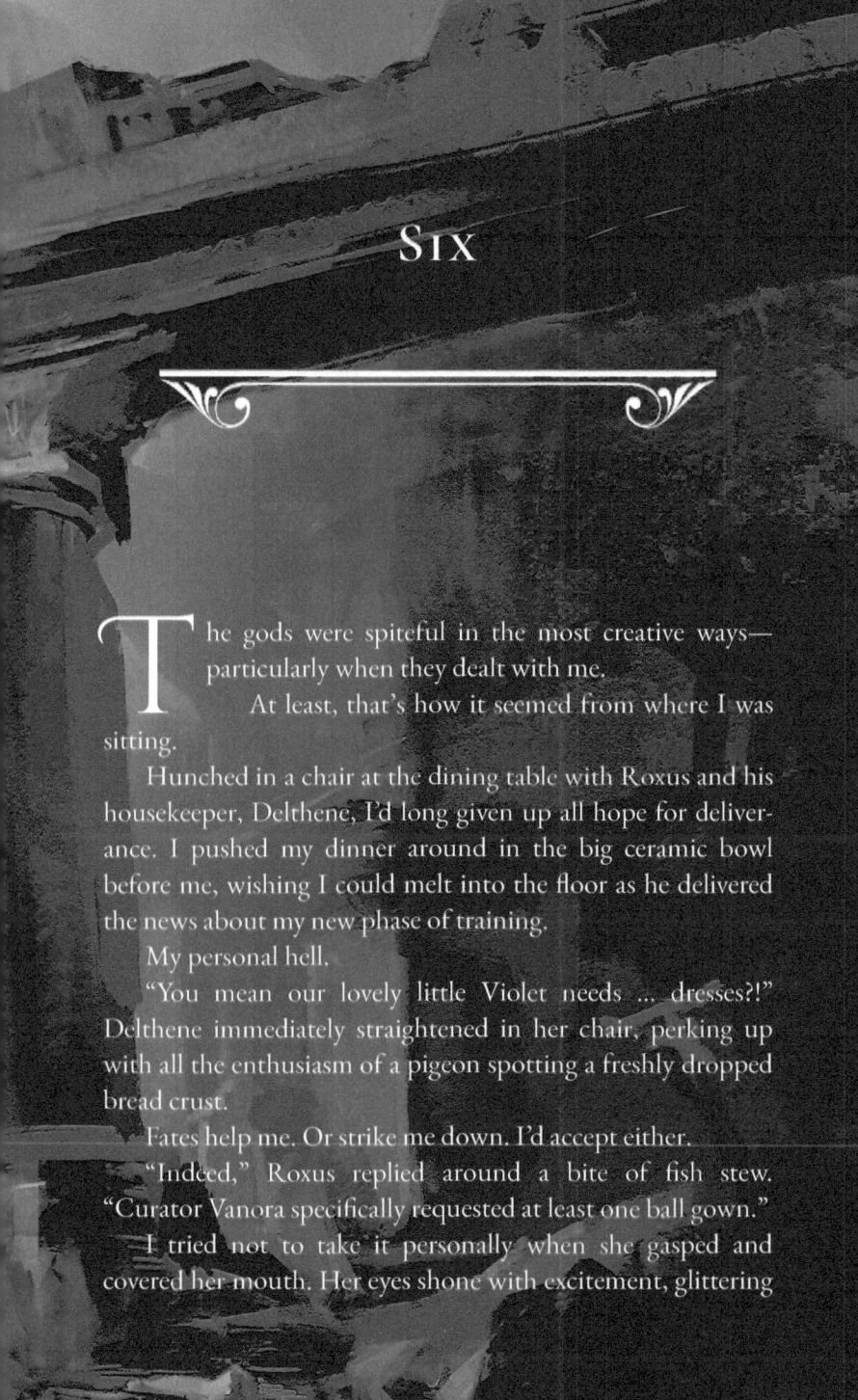

SIX

The gods were spiteful in the most creative ways—particularly when they dealt with me.

At least, that's how it seemed from where I was sitting.

Hunched in a chair at the dining table with Roxus and his housekeeper, Delthene, I'd long given up all hope for deliverance. I pushed my dinner around in the big ceramic bowl before me, wishing I could melt into the floor as he delivered the news about my new phase of training.

My personal hell.

"You mean our lovely little Violet needs ... dresses?!" Delthene immediately straightened in her chair, perking up with all the enthusiasm of a pigeon spotting a freshly dropped bread crust.

Fates help me. Or strike me down. I'd accept either.

"Indeed," Roxus replied around a bite of fish stew. "Curator Vanora specifically requested at least one ball gown."

I tried not to take it personally when she gasped and covered her mouth. Her eyes shone with excitement, glittering and misty as she looked at me. Like she was already plotting—already picturing what I'd look like draped in a lady's fashions.

Horrendous. Like a scraggly feral cat in lace.

"Red," she breathed shakily. "It *must* be red."

I sank lower in my chair.

Torture—long, brutal, and bloody—would have been *so* much better than this.

"Also, shoes, jewelry, and makeup. But keep it reasonable," Roxus said, his sideways glance apologetic.

I scrunched up my nose at him and glared back down into my bowl of fragrantly spiced stew.

He made a face around a cheek full of food as he leaned to one side while he fished something out of his pocket—a crumpled piece of paper.

A list.

I tried to read the fine, swirling script as he slid it across to Delthene, but it was too crinkled to make out anything.

She seized it immediately and began reading, her eyes widening and her face glowing with a wide grin. She pressed the note to her chest with a sigh of pure ecstasy and beamed at me again. "We'll have so much fun, darling!"

Right. *Fun.*

Roxus gave a bemused snort and shook his head. He didn't even acknowledge my glare as he shoveled the last of his dinner into his mouth and stood. "I'm sure it'll be an experience to remember. Just don't let her scowling and growling put you off. She's under orders to begin learning the fine art of social etiquette. And tomorrow, Mistress Orvana has insisted on having her teeth filed."

Gods, just strike me down and be done with it.

"I'm sure we'll be fine," Delthene promised. She was practically bouncing with joy in her seat as she went back to her own meal. "It's long past time she had something to wear besides grimy fighting leathers and rumpled undershirts. She's becoming such a beautiful young woman, after all."

My ears tingled, and my mouth pinched up, feeling embarrassment rise like a hot gust from a furnace over my cheeks. Was it really that bad? My clothes were usually clean, at least. Er, well, before I went to training.

Okay. Fine. They were clean first thing in the morning. Or if I had an audience with Mistress Orvana. But after that ...

"I'll leave some coin for you," Roxus said on his way out of the dining hall. "Try to enjoy yourselves."

The silence was crushing, filled only by the scrape of our spoons as we finished our food. Delthene and I always ate our evening meal together like this, like an odd little family, and it still felt about as comfortable as trying to shove my foot in a boot that was two sizes too small.

Not because I didn't like her, though. I did.

Delthene was lovely and sweet, always appropriate and stern when she needed to be. I knew she was responsible for every feminine detail of this place—the organized pantry and larder, the arrangement of the furniture in the sitting room, the spotless floors, and fresh flowers adorning the entryway table. Little hints of her were scattered through every room, as though she were the stitching that held this place together.

But I still didn't know all that much about her personally.

She was human, yes. Damarian, if her deep, brownish-gold-tinted eyes and tanned skin were any evidence. But where had she come from? How had she started working for Roxus? And why did she keep so many of his secrets?

The only other person who might know was her enormous old orange cat, but Gibb gave no hints. In fact, all he gave anyone were vacant stares through half-closed eyes as he sat on the beds or basked in the sun on the balconies.

"We'll set out right after the healer finishes with your teeth," Delthene promised, her brow crinkled with worry as she held my gaze. "We'll have Leruna do it. She'll make sure it looks lovely."

I nodded once, determined not to let her detect how my insides squirmed like I'd swallowed a live eel at the thought of having anyone mess with my fangs like that.

"I'm sorry if I seem ... it's just that this isn't really my thing," I muttered. "Shopping. Clothes. Wearing rouge and kohl and jewelry."

Her expression melted to something warm and earnestly hopeful, a soft smile playing at her lips. "I know. But you're worthy of it, Violet. You'll see. This isn't about pleasing anyone else. This is about honoring your own beauty. You need to take ownership of it."

"Everyone keeps comparing it to fighting," I murmured. "Like beauty is a weapon I can wield."

The light in her eyes dimmed a little. "For some, it can be. And a very dangerous one at that."

I frowned down into my bowl again.

Part of me knew she was right. I'd seen the female Viperi of our clan competing for the Brood Father's attention. Their beauty was a snare meant to catch his eye, then his favor, and finally his power. I had seen how that process played out in a pageantry of silks, flawless skin, ruby lips, and dazzling smiles.

But I'd also seen the brutal aftermath of failure.

Somehow, a blade felt like a far simpler, less risky tool of warfare—one I could understand without as much effort. Gods, I didn't even know if people outside of the subterranean realm of my kind would ever consider a Viperi beautiful. We were the monsters of their darkest nightmares.

How could anyone find that—find *me*—attractive?

That question kept spinning slowly through my thoughts as I lurched up the stairs to my room. Gibb let out a wide, yawning mewl from where he sat on my bed, and I ran a hand down his back on my way to my wardrobe.

Flinging open the doors, I stared into the shadowy depths of the big wooden armoire. Three white shirts, all of the same style, hung in a row. An assortment of fighting leathers and gear was arranged beside them, and a spare set of boots lay on the floor. I also had a few sashes, a decorative belt or two that had never been worn, and a headscarf.

But that was it.

No lace. No silk. Nothing that sparkled or shone. I'd even taken to just wearing undergarments and one of my tunics to bed.

I rubbed at the back of my neck.

Maybe Delthene was right. I was sixteen—or somewhere near it. It might be time to adjust. To learn a new skill. My mother had been taken before she could impart any of this knowledge to me. But if Delthene and Curator Vanora were willing to take up the task, who was I to refuse?

I dared a glance at my reflection in the dressing mirror pushed far against the corner wall like an afterthought. Until now, it had been.

My hair was long, as pale as sun-bleached bone, and wild. But I'd never done much with it except tie it away from my face. My lashes were long and dark, and my lips were full but a little pasty.

Frankly, most of me was pasty and pallid. Viperi didn't have the bronzed complexions of the surface-dwelling races, and I didn't tan, no matter how long I spent in the sun.

I did burn rather easily, though.

I leaned in closer, pulling my lip up to get a better look at my pointed incisors. They weren't drastically long, but definitely noticeable—especially when I smiled. All Viperi had them, though, and since I didn't spend a lot of time admiring myself in the mirror, I had never really given them much thought. I hadn't considered how different they made me look compared to humans and elves.

Hmm.

I poked at the sharp points with my tongue.

I could understand why Mistress Orvana wanted them filed down. But my toes curled in my boots at the thought. Would it hurt? What would it feel like after?

I winced and backed away from the mirror.

Stripping down to my undergarments and light, linen tunic, I left my boots in a heap by the bed and crawled into the sea of downy-stuffed pillows and satin sheets. Tomorrow, I'd try to do something with my hair before we left. I'd leave the leathers and blades behind. I'd sit still while Leruna filed my fangs away.

I'd learn something new—become something new—even if it hurt.

Even if it meant leaving this old version of myself behind, once and for all.

I had to. If I was going to make my way through this world, I had to adapt.

No matter what the cost.

SEVEN

I couldn't hide from her.

Not when she found me in the deepest depths of my dreams, slipping in like a soundless specter and catching me completely off guard.

Two years. It had been two long, insufferable years. But I could still hear her. I could still see her dangling from chains hammered into the cold, bare rock in the depths of that prison. A place so far from the sun, so filled with aimless screams of pain, it must have felt like a living hell.

Necrolis Prison was the nearest thing to it.

"Remember me."

Chrysa's voice twisted in my brain like a tri-tipped dagger, cutting so deep it made my chest seize in agony. I couldn't scream. Couldn't resist. The warmth of blood filled my mouth as I stared up at her. The rest of the world fell away to black—endless and empty.

"Remember this was a mercy."

No.

No, no—*NO!*

I bolted upright in bed, my body shuddering as the memories replayed. Cold sweat ran down my cheeks and neck. My stomach gave a spasming lurch.

This wasn't mercy.

It was a little death every day. A rot inside, eating me away slowly.

Every time I remembered her face. Every time I passed a place in Arx Eburna where we had sat together. Every time someone whispered at my back.

The dagger twisted. Deeper and deeper.

I'd never understand it. Why she hadn't just killed me quickly and been done with it. Why she wanted me to remember. Why her ghost still passed like a poisonous vapor through my head.

Why couldn't I let her go?

Why couldn't I hate her enough to forget?

Would the memories ever fade? Would her voice ever go away?

Questions without answers spun in my head, around and around. And when the morning sun finally broke over the far horizon, I lay there, tangled up in my sweat-dampened sheets, her voice hissing in my head.

Chrysa.

The first person I'd dared to call a friend and mean it.

So I turned my face into my pillow and cried until I had no strength left.

EIGHT

Roxus nearly dropped his teacup when he saw me. His mouth opened and closed a few times, like a fish gasping for air, before he finally managed to speak. "Well now, you look ..." He paused, as though he had to search for a word that wouldn't be insulting. "Awake."

Curse him.

Curse sleeping.

And especially curse dress shopping.

I didn't need to see my reflection again to know there were dark, heavy circles under my eyes. My back ached, and I could barely keep my head up as I sat across from him at the table again, picking at the sugar and cinnamon-dusted toast, poached eggs, and bacon Delthene had spread out for us. A feast probably meant to put me in a good mood before our errand today.

So much for that.

The rich flavors might as well have been ash on my tongue as I ate a few mouthfuls and avoided eye contact. Not even the crisp mint tea did anything to calm my flipping, clenching stomach.

Neither Delthene nor Roxus did a good job of masking their concern as they sipped at their own morning tea and watched me push the rest of my food around on my plate. They probably thought I didn't notice how they kept glancing sideways at one another, communicating shared concern with those subtle expressions.

Ugggh. I wasn't in the mood for pity. Or questions.

I managed a few bites before I retreated to my room, dodging more of their probing, concerned stares. Flinging myself down at my dressing table, I brushed my hair until it fell more smoothly down my back, then wove it into another long braid. I took a little more care to make sure it was neat, and then wound it into a large bun at the base of my neck.

It took a few tries to get the black wooden comb Delthene had given me for my birthday last year to hold in place properly. Today seemed as good an excuse as any to finally wear it.

I wondered if she'd notice.

My clothing options were limited, but I picked the least wrinkly of my three shirts, some black fitted leggings I normally wore under my leathers, and tied a long dark purple sash with golden little stars stitched on it around my waist.

That was it—the best I could do.

Delthene was already by the door when I came downstairs, chatting merrily in the sitting room with another woman in flowing sky-blue robes. Healer's robes.

I hadn't seen Leruna in months, which was mostly a good thing. It meant I hadn't needed any serious or life-saving medical treatment in a while. An improvement on my part.

She moved gracefully, robes rippling like a sweeping sea wind flowing through a ship's lofty sails, as she turned to smile broadly at me. Her long dark hair was braided down her back, and little crystals and pearls dangled from her pointed ears.

Her eyes shone like turquoise sea glass as she rushed over to embrace me. "Look how you've grown!"

I returned the gesture, even if hugging anyone still felt stiff and awkward. I wasn't used to people *wanting* to touch me like that. In friendly ways.

"I, um, I thought we'd be coming to meet you at the temple."

"Oh, well, when Roxus sent word last night, I had already planned to go out to the market for some tea today," she sang in her light, breathy voice. "I hear you're going on your own shopping trip, too."

A twitchy, painfully forced smile was the best I could muster. "Y-Yeah."

"We're to find her a whole new wardrobe," Delthene added. "Finally, she'll have something other than those fighting leathers!"

Leruna laughed and gave my shoulder a consoling pat. "I take it this all has something to do with Mistress Orvana, and she's the reason for wanting your teeth filed?"

I nodded. "She said I have to become more 'socially acceptable' so I don't draw unwanted attention during our missions."

Her brow tensed slightly, genuine sympathy shining in those sea-glass eyes. "I see. Perhaps that's understandable, but it's still your body, Violet. You shouldn't change it just because someone else wants you to."

I swallowed hard, my gaze dropping to the floor.

"Is this what you really want, Violet?" she pressed, fixing me with an earnest stare.

Delthene shifted beside me. The crushing weight of the silence, of expectation, settled over me like a noose tightening around my neck.

It was my choice. I knew that. Did I really want to get rid of my fangs?

I traced my tongue over them again. My stomach flipped

and fluttered, sending flashes of strange, panicked heat through my body.

Was this wrong? Should I let them ... change me?

I didn't know. Gods, I wasn't even sure if I liked who I was now.

Whatever I thought of Mistress Orvana, and whatever she thought of me, I knew she was right about me standing out. I didn't look like the general public in this region—or most parts of the Southern Kingdoms. Or anywhere, I guess. Viperi didn't come to the surface world frequently enough to be commonplace. But our reputations were nefarious enough to make us very recognizable here.

That alone would make me a danger to the order. To Roxus.

I couldn't allow that.

However I felt, I couldn't put him at risk.

Clothes, shawls, and cloaks could cover my fair skin. My near-white blonde hair could be dyed easily if I needed to be more inconspicuous. But my teeth and my eyes? Those would always stand out—always mark me as *other*.

And I could only do something about one of them.

"This is what I want," I said, meeting her gaze with resolve.

She breathed a small sigh, and I couldn't tell if it was sympathy or sorrow that made her smile droop a little. "Very well, then. Come and have a seat. We will do this quickly."

We moved into the sitting room, where she had already set out her tools on the low table. Leruna gave me a few sips of a strong herbal tea that immediately made my head spin and my arms and legs feel strange and heavy. I could hardly hold myself up straight as she helped me lie down on my back with my head on a cushion. Staring up at the bare wooden beams of the ceiling, the flavor of that strong tea still stinging my throat, I tried not to think. Not to care.

The room seemed to slip away, everything going foggy and distant while she worked.

It didn't hurt when she worked the file against my incisors, but the smell of it made my stomach wrench, and the grating sensation—gods, it made my toes and fingers want to curl. Too bad I couldn't move them much.

Fortunately, it didn't take all that long before Leruna was helping me sit up again and rinse my mouth. Everything still felt a little muddy and hazy as I blinked owlishly into a small hand mirror. I held my lips up, looking at both sides. Then I drew back and forced a smile that showed all my teeth.

Straight. All my teeth were perfectly flush now. No fangs or points. She'd done a good job of filing them to look similar to the rest of my teeth in size and shape. It looked natural.

Pretty, even.

"I have to admit, it does change your looks a bit," Leruna said as she packed up her tools. "But you've always had a lovely smile, regardless."

I snorted at the lie. I doubted Leruna had ever seen me *really* smile. The people she routinely saw as part of work—the wounded and sick—probably didn't smile at her much, either.

But it was nice that she tried to compliment me. From her, unlike Axien, I knew it wasn't a veiled insult.

"I was thinking we should have her hair trimmed a little, too," Delthene mused as she padded around the living room, collecting the bowls of water and teacups Leruna had used. "Just to get rid of some of these scraggly ends."

My mouth mashed closed. I set the mirror down, still tracing my tongue over the places where my fangs had been only minutes before.

No one spoke as Leruna finished gathering up her wares, and Delthene rushed to take the dishes back into the kitchen.

"Thank you," I remembered to murmur at last.

Leruna paused, and I could feel her gaze on me without having to look up.

A minute passed. Maybe longer. Finally, she whispered so quietly I barely heard her, "How long has it been since you saw Declan?"

My heartbeat stammered and I instantly met her worried stare.

"Weeks, I guess," I answered. "Why?"

She shook her head some. "I haven't heard from him either. Usually, he comes by the temple for clean bandages, more healing tonics or salves, or to have a bone set. But it's strange to see nothing of him for this long."

Dread sank into the pit of my stomach, sending chills of panic through my entire body.

"Maybe you could drop in on him? Just to make sure he's all right and give him a few supplies?" She fidgeted with the hem of her robes, her tone cautious. "I would go myself, but you know how he is about having visitors."

Right. I did know.

That idiot had ostracized himself from everyone out of fear that Sulam might use them as leverage, the same way he was already using his sister. Declan didn't like that I knew where he lived, either. But Sulam couldn't use me like that—not now that I was Zenith's Call.

That, and a healthy fear of Roxus's wrath, meant I was untouchable.

"I will," I promised.

She breathed a shaky word of thanks and dug through her bag, taking out a small parcel wrapped in clean white linen and placing it on the table. She let her hand rest atop it for a moment, murmuring words that might have been a prayer or blessing before she stood, shouldered her pack of tools, and started for the door.

I walked her out, my legs still a little wobbly from the tea, and let her hug me again before she slipped away into the warm morning sunlight.

Leaning in the doorway, I watched her slender form disappear down the sidewalk as the sea air filled my lungs. That, and the fresh pang of dread still souring in my stomach, sharpened all my senses.

I had to check on Declan. Soon. I'd do it this evening, after this ridiculous shopping trip. If I timed things right, I could get there after he finished his pit-fighting bouts at Sulam's little arena. Then he'd be too exhausted and sore to put up much resistance to my presence.

"Ready to go?" Delthene appeared beside me, bright and cheery.

"As I'll ever be," I groaned.

She just laughed and looped an arm through mine, practically hauling me out the front door and into the bustling morning streets.

Onward to shop. To try and bury all my Viperi viciousness beneath silks, lace, and rouge.

I just wondered if that sort of miracle was even possible ... or if today would be yet another disaster with my name written all over it.

NINE

People were staring.

No, men—*men* were staring.

Some were ladies, yes. But that didn't bother me nearly as much as all the burly dockhands, keen-eyed merchants, and scrawny fishermen looking me up and down like I was a puzzle they couldn't solve.

Or a prize they felt entitled to.

I edged closer to Delthene's side, mouth mashing up as I fought to keep a snarl from my lips. Every gaze lingered on my skin like the brush of a shadow, making heat tingle up my neck and across my cheeks as I walked next to her through the bustling market streets.

It'd taken hours at the tailor to get a complete wardrobe assembled for me—hours, and gods only knew how much of Roxus's coin.

Most of it would be delivered straight to his doorstep after the tailors and seamstresses made all the necessary adjustments. Silken pants that billowed down and gathered at my ankles, beaded tops in vivid colors, flowing blouses trimmed in shining embroidery, and a dozen different gowns and shawls. I was happy to see it all tossed in a large trunk to be dealt with later. Just the sight of all of it made my head swim.

But then Delthene had suggested that I wear one of the new outfits home. And, Fates preserve me, I couldn't say no. Not after she gave me that sad, motherly, pleading look like I was the most precious, lovely thing she'd ever seen. Like saying no would break her heart.

Not fair.

It wasn't the white satin pants that bothered me. They were slim-fitting and tucked nicely down into my black leather boots. Comfortable and easy to move in.

The top, however, was constructed for one purpose—to make all those grimy fishermen trip all over themselves when they saw us walk past.

And it was *working*.

The black bodice had boning like a corset and fit tight against my skin, pushing my figure into far more interesting shapes than the gods had given me to begin with. Deep red and purple sleeves slouched off my shoulders and billowed down, bell-shaped and so long, they nearly dragged the ground.

A strange, sweeping skirt-like garment of that same blood-red fabric was fitted to the back and open in the front, so that it flowed behind me when I walked. Almost like a skirt, I guess, except it did nothing to cover the front of my legs.

I'd put my old waist wrap back on, but Delthene had insisted I let my hair flow down my back rather than pinning it up. She'd led me off to a boutique to have it trimmed and styled. It had been a real test of skill not to look as miserable as I felt while the same finely dressed shop owner showed me how to paint dark kohl around my eyes and rouge on my lips.

By the end of it, I didn't recognize my own reflection anymore. New teeth. New hair. New clothes. Gold and red glass earrings that jingled musically whenever I moved.

My stomach swirled and bound up in knots. Something about the young woman staring back at me in the mirror looked dangerous in ways I didn't even understand. She was a stranger I didn't know.

"Stars, look how lovely you are. Just let Mistress Orvana try to complain about this!" Delthene praised as she practically skipped along beside me. She ran an adoring hand through my hair, brushing some of it away from my face.

I let out a shaky exhale. Or, I *tried* to. The corseted top made it difficult to do much breathing at all.

"I don't know how I'm supposed to do any fighting in clothes like these," I muttered, more to myself than her.

Her smile was vicious as she stared down a handsome young sailor who had let his path wander closer to ours when we passed on the sidewalk. I'd seen that look before. Her cat, Gibb, looked a bit like that whenever he cornered a sparrow in the garden.

"Oh, my dear. These clothes are for a different sort of warfare. You'll see soon enough," she said.

I swallowed hard. Maybe it was best not to ask any questions.

We made our way out of the harborside district along sloping sidewalks that led deeper in the island, going farther up the terraces that all clung to the steep landscape like barnacles. Some were residential. Others were expansive gardens, restaurants, or squares lined with shops and craftsmen. All were busy at this hour of the day, though.

Amidst the bustle of the island's routines, Roxus's house was unassuming, perched on a remote corner, away from all the markets and shops. All the homes in this area were built relatively the same—tall and narrow with three levels, lots of little balconies, and large open windows to let the sea air blow in.

He did a good job of keeping up appearances. I doubted

our neighbors thought he was anything more than an eccentric investor who'd made his living supporting the right merchants. An investor who'd recently acquired a troublesome young daughter.

I smirked at the thought.

Right up until we reached the front door and found two figures standing in front of it.

Gods, Fates, and all things divine.

I froze mid-stride halfway up the front steps, watching in mute horror as Sanja turned to face us. With her slender form draped in sleek, deep green satin that showed off quite a lot of her deep bronze skin, she practically glowed with effortless beauty. Like a wealthy noble's wife had come to call on us.

But she was no noble. And she certainly wasn't anyone's wife.

No, no, no, *NO!*

What was she doing here?!

Sanja and Delthene exchanged cries of surprised delight and immediately rushed to greet one another with laughter and light kisses on the cheeks.

"There you are! And here I was thinking you'd all gone out this evening!" Sanja held up a bag that clanked like she had several full bottles of wine inside, her sea-green eyes twinkling with mischief as she waggled her slender dark brows suggestively. "I hope you don't mind our dropping in unannounced."

"Of course not!" Delthene beamed as she opened the door to let us all inside. "Roxus isn't home just yet, but you're more than welcome to come in and make yourselves at home."

They went on chatting, Sanja tossing her curtain of smooth black hair over her shoulder and tucking a few locks of it behind one of her pointed ears. She let out an airy laugh as Delthene unlocked the door. I couldn't help but notice that I was now dressed more like *her*.

Granted, her figure was much more adult and luxurious when it came to her curves. She wore lots of golden bangle bracelets and even had a small ring through her nose—a Damarian fashion trend I had no interest in adopting for myself. But she wore similar satin harem-style pants and a fitted bodice.

I stared at her.

Then at him.

Axien.

And I couldn't move.

His gaze caught mine and tangled up every single one of my thoughts, just like always. It paralyzed me, mind and body, while quiet, seething rage filled me from head to toe.

I couldn't even think past his tall, wide-shouldered frame as he loomed before me, blocking my path up to the front door. What, by the cursed tongue of the Foul Father, was *he* doing at *my* house?

I would have asked, would have demanded an explanation from Sanja herself, but she and Delthene had already whisked merrily away inside.

I was alone, standing on the front steps in that ridiculous new outfit, all manner of makeup slathered on my face, the bodice of my new ensemble mashing my breasts up practically into my neck, staring at his oddly blank expression as he seemed to take it all in.

Axien's lips bowed smoothly into that wistful, knowing, razor-tipped smile that made his eyes gleam like aquamarines. As though he could sense how awkward and uncomfortable I was.

Gods, just strike me down.

"My, don't you look *extra* lovely today," he said, his tone careful and soft. Calculating. "That color matches your eyes perfectly, doesn't it?"

My hands curled into fists at my sides. Quiet rage simmered in my chest, like I'd swallowed hot coals.

It wasn't a question or a compliment. Not really. Not when he was pointing out the one aspect of myself I couldn't change to blend in with the rest of the surface races.

No, it was bait.

Control—I had to stay in control. Don't give him an inch. No weakness.

"It hides bloodstains rather well, too," I answered, making my tone match his own flavor of too-sweet venom.

His dark brows rose slightly. Seconds passed, and he just kept staring at me without a word. Like I was a two-headed sea monster someone had just fished out of the bay and dumped at his feet.

"Get out of my way." I bared my teeth and bit sharply at each word.

He blinked, drawing back some in surprise.

I took that opportunity—that tiny hitch in his guard—to step past him and make a speedy dash toward the open front door.

"You filed down your fangs, as well?" he asked suddenly.

My body jerked to a halt, my toes nearly at the threshold. Even with my back now to him, I could still feel the heat of his gaze on me. Watching me, like always. It made that strange tingling heat rise in my cheeks.

But something was different about it now. Like that eerie aura of his had shifted. The light in his eyes had changed, too. Somehow it felt ... worried.

Maybe even a little sad.

"I didn't have a choice," I snapped without looking back at him. "Mistress Orvana demanded it."

"I see." He *almost* sounded sorry about that, but I didn't dare glance at his face to make sure.

"Why are you here?" I demanded, still keeping myself angled away.

"It wasn't my idea to pay you a visit, if that's what you're wondering. I certainly didn't insist on coming here. But since we're going to be working together, Sanja thought it would be a good idea to ... get better acquainted," he replied, sliding back into that smooth, soothingly deep tone. I caught a hint of an accent, although I couldn't quite tell from where.

Then it hit me.

I whirled around. "What do you mean '*working together*?'"

Axien stood, his arms crossed over his broad chest, head tilted slightly to one side. All his handsome, half-elven features were still drawn into that stupid smirk that made me want to put my fist through his teeth.

Like I'd taken the bait and fallen right into his trap.

"I take it Roxus hasn't told you?" he baited, those wicked eyes glinting. Studying me. Evaluating every tiny move I made. "Interesting."

My mouth screwed up.

"Told. Me. What?!" I snarled through clenched teeth.

"That we're going on this mission together—Me, Sanja, and Roxus," he drawled lazily, counting on his fingers. "Oh, and you, of course. Can't forget you, can we? It is strange that he didn't let you know sooner. But perhaps he just wanted it to be a surprise, hm?"

All the air rushed out of me at once. I stared up at Axien, waiting for the other boot to drop. For him to laugh and say it was all a bad joke. Then I could punch him, break his too-straight nose, and lock him out here on the doorstep. Good riddance.

But he just kept smiling that stupid, know-it-all smile.

Heat sizzled in my veins, scorching down my throat, through my chest, and down to my toes. It made my hands shake and my vision swerve for a second or two.

Humiliation. Pure rage.

I ... I had to go on this mission with Axien and Sanja? And Roxus had known this the whole time and not said anything? Why? Why wouldn't he tell me?

I couldn't make sense of it. I could barely even breathe, thanks to my stupid outfit still squeezing the life out of me.

Why was Roxus hiding things from me? I was his *tandem*. We were supposed to be partners ...

I opened my mouth, ready to fire back. To curse Axien and slam the door in his disgusting, smug face. But a larger male form stepped between us suddenly.

"Shouldn't you both be inside?" Roxus asked as he breezed by, hands stuffed deep in the pockets of his favorite old coat.

I flinched at the hint of warning in his voice as he let his gaze catch on mine for the briefest instant. Like he knew I was seconds from losing it and doing something reckless.

"I'm sure Delthene could use help preparing dinner," Roxus said as he continued past us into the house. "Come inside."

It wasn't a request.

I stiffened, glaring at Roxus's back. Angry words filled my mouth like bitter poison. Things I desperately wanted to shout.

How dare he keep this from me. How dare he treat me like I was still just a bumbling prospect. Hadn't I earned more?

Axien shifted uncomfortably, brushing some of his shoulder-length dark hair behind a pointed ear. "I didn't mean to imply that—" he started to speak, but I threw a hand up in front of his face to stop him.

"I know exactly what you meant," I hissed. "Stay away from me."

I didn't give him a chance to reply. Whirling on a heel, I stormed into the house and up to my room.

Whether or not Roxus had special plans for his new favorite friends this evening, I had other matters to attend to —far more important things than sitting around like some plaything for Axien to toy with while Roxus and Sanja jabbered on.

And apparently, I wasn't privy to the finer details of the mission, anyway. So what did it matter if I was there or not?

Flinging off all my ridiculous fine clothes, I redressed in the same plain ensemble I'd put on this morning and rubbed the rouge off my lips. The kohl didn't surrender so easily, and I only managed to smudge it around before I finally gave up.

I belted on my favorite pair of daggers and swiped my haversack from its hook by my bedroom door. Seizing my boots off the floor and quickly lacing them up, I dashed back down the stairs.

Merry voices and the smells of roasting lamb drifted in from the dining room. Delthene must be making her specialty tonight. She knew I loved it when she made the little meat pies stuffed with lamb and potatoes, all drizzled in spicy red curry, and nestled into a bed of warm fluffy rice. But *I* wasn't the one she was cooking for tonight.

I scowled at the doorway and stormed past it without stopping.

Axien's laughter mingled with Roxus and Sanja's, making a new melody that struck me right to the core. My eyes welled, and I gripped the strap of my bag tighter. I kept quiet, picking my way carefully through the sitting room and swiping Leruna's parcel from the table. I tucked it securely in my haversack, then crept to the front foyer and snatched my cloak off the hook by the front door.

I gave one last look toward the glow of warm light ebbing in from the dining room. Somehow, I'd become *other* even in my own home.

No.

It was good they had come tonight. They'd be so busy carrying on that no one would notice me leaving. No one would wonder where I'd gone. And I had to do this as discreetly as possible.

I repeated that over and over in my mind as I slipped out the door and into the freshly fallen night. A prickle of unease swam in my gut as I started away from the house. I kept my head down and my cloak's hood pulled low as I let my senses stretch outward into the dark.

Sol'Karr had been my home for long enough now that I knew its rhythm like my own heartbeat. Every scrape of a footstep or distant yap of a dog, every faint glow of body heat from rats scurrying along the gutters, and the flavor of ocean brine in the air—all of it wrapped around me like a familiar embrace. Not all of it was lovely, but all of it was mine.

I moved like a flicker of shadow, taking back alleys and darkened side streets I knew would be abandoned after sunset, and made my way to the dockside avenue. All the shops and merchant stalls were closing up. All the sailors and fishermen had moved indoors to the taverns and bars to waste away the moonlight.

But I didn't stop there.

I slipped down another side street and hurried on, farther into the depths of the Backdock Slums. There, the buildings were tightly smashed together, some even leaning precariously against one another so that it seemed a stiff sea wind might just topple them all at once. The roofs were patched or falling in and the light within the windows made the cracks in the panes sparkle like dew-kissed spider webs.

I crossed a trash-strewn street and stopped before it. My throat went dry, hand clenching harder at the strap of my bag.

It was a miserable, rat-infested deathtrap more than a house, but Sulam didn't pay Declan for any of his fights and only provided him with the bare minimum to survive. This, I could only guess, was the *very* least Sulam could do to keep his prized pit fighter housed.

Honestly, the side of the street might have been better.

Each floor of the house was a different apartment—if they could even be called that—and Declan's was at the very top. From the sidewalk, I didn't see any lights burning in any of the windows.

Strange. Shouldn't there be other people milling around?

My nose wrinkled as I ascended the rickety wooden stairs that led from one floor to the next. They groaned under my weight and shifted when the wind blew in fiercely from the bay.

At the top, I stopped in my tracks. My gaze froze on the open doorway.

Open—like it had nearly been ripped right off the hinges.

There was nothing but darkness beyond it. No lanterns or firelight coming from within. No motion. No sound at all.

My heartbeat kicked fiercely as I took a step closer.

"Declan?"

No answer.

Chills prickled my skin, making every tiny hair on my arms stand on end.

I slowly let the haversack slip from my shoulder and reached for the hilts of my daggers. One hard blink shifted my vision into the heat spectrum.

Then I saw it—a dull yellow glow shone on the wooden surface of the door. A handprint?

My breath caught.

No.

It was a *bloody* handprint.

TEN

There was blood *everywhere*.

It glowed in spatters, swipes, and puddles all around Declan's cramped apartment. Fresh. The smell of it tinged the air and set all my nerves ablaze.

Calm—I had to stay calm.

Think. Read the signs and remember my training.

I bit down hard, hating the way my newly altered teeth gnashed together. My heartbeat thrashed wildly in my ears as I peered deeper into the gloom of the dingy apartment. The small table was toppled over, chairs flipped, and the rickety cot he used for a bed was tossed with bedding strewn everywhere. A few plates and bowls shattered on the floor.

Signs of a struggle.

No. A fight.

Deep, long gashes on some of the furniture and floor were likely from swords. They'd caught him by surprise, but I knew Declan. He wouldn't go down without a fight, even if his attackers were heavily armed.

"Declan?" I called out again, louder this time.

Still no answer.

My heart twisted, panic rising like a frigid tide in my veins as I stepped over the debris, always turning to keep one eye on the doorway. Just in case whoever had done this decided to return.

Then I saw it—the white glow of body heat crumpled in the far corner, mostly obscured by the toppled table.

Surrounded by a puddle of blood.

"DECLAN!" His name ripped from my throat in a feral shout.

I surged toward him, throwing the splintered chairs and overturned table aside. Hitting the ground on my knees, I gasped and sputtered as I slammed my daggers back into their sheaths.

Propped up in the corner, his back to the wall, I could see that his body heat color was warm. Still alive. But when I reverted to my normal vision, his face was far too pale. His clothes were soaked through with blood, and his head had lolled forward so his chin rested on his chest. His lips were dusky blue, and his face was bruised and bleeding so badly I barely recognized him.

Holy gods above. They ... they had tried to beat him to death.

"G-Gods. No. You will not die, not like this," I rasped as I pressed my fingers to his neck.

He still had a pulse, but it was weak. Slow. Fading. Gods, if I hadn't come to check on him, or if I had been even an hour later ...

I bit down hard.

Curse it. I wouldn't think about that right now.

I had to do something—anything.

Dashing back for my haversack, I dragged the door as far closed as it would go on busted hinges and crammed one of the chairs under the handle to reinforce it. Then I dashed back to his side, already pulling Leruna's medical kit out of my bag.

"Just hang on. Don't you dare die, you stubborn idiot," I muttered frantically as I spread out the tools.

It wasn't much—a few spools of clean bandaging, some healing tonics, and a tin of that powerful herbal salve from Luntharda. Gods, would it even be enough? Should I run to get Leruna right now? What if he died while I was gone?

Help—I needed help! I couldn't do this! I wasn't a healer!

My mind suddenly went still, silence slamming down over all my racing thoughts. I could practically hear Roxus's voice echoing in my ears.

"You're the only one who can, Violet."

He'd said that to me once before. And right now ... it was true again.

There was no one else. No one I could reach in time.

I had to help him. Right now.

The salve was the strongest remedy of them all. I'd use that first. I'd try to get him stabilized, and then I would go find Leruna.

Thanks to being half Holvradix elf, Declan was easily more than twice my size, so it took every ounce of my strength to get his big, brawny body laid out on the floor. With his head resting on some of his bedding, I started assessing each of his injuries, looking for the most serious.

He'd taken a horrible beating to his face. His eyes were swollen shut, and his lip had been split twice. His nose was a bloody mess, his cheeks were blue, and his neck had red marks like someone had tried to choke him by the throat. Gods, they'd bashed his face until he was barely recognizable. I could tell by the way one of his legs was turned that it had to be broken.

But none of that would cause all this bleeding on the floor.

I barely stifled a terrified scream as I lifted the arm Declan had draped around his middle, covering a deep slash across his abdomen. Blood. So much blood. The smell was so thick and coppery, so intense, I could taste it in the air.

I gagged.

Breathe. I had to breathe. Think. Stop the bleeding.

Tears welled in my eyes as I dug through the rubble of his ransacked apartment until I found a pair of washrags. I rinsed them in the sink basin and hurried back to his side. I used one of my daggers to cut what was left of his tunic open. My hands trembled as I began wiping away the blood, revealing a deep gash that went straight through flesh, muscle, all the way to his organs.

A sword wound. Someone had tried to gut him. They'd almost succeeded.

A sob broke past my lips as I immediately stuffed one of the rolls of gauze into it and began wrapping the rest around his middle, applying pressure. Then I pried open his mouth, taking a big glob of the foul, green healing salve and forcing it down his throat.

He let out a sudden weak groan. One of his big hands reached up, slapping uselessly against mine in protest.

"No! Swallow it, you idiot," I said, holding his mouth closed so he couldn't spit it out.

His expression skewed. He groaned again and struggled weakly.

I knew exactly how foul that healing salve tasted. I'd taken it before. Bitter and sour, and as putrid as pond sludge—of course he didn't want to swallow it. No one would, even at death's door.

But, Fates, it might be the only thing that saved him now.

"Do it! You're going to die if you don't," I begged, my voice breaking as I held him down with a hand still over his mouth. "Swallow it, Declan!"

One of his swollen eyes opened a crack. Enough that he must have been able to see me. His brows drew up and he made a choking, gagging sound as he swallowed hard.

"Yes! Good!" I swiped my fingers through the tin again, getting another sticky, slimy glob of it on my fingers and forcing them through his lips. "Do it again!"

He did.

I sank into my heels, staring down at him as tears rolled down my cheeks.

He coughed again and immediately let out a sharp, agonized cry. His hand went back to the deep gash on his abdomen.

"Vi-Violet," he moaned.

I reached for his hand, gripping it fiercely. "I'm here. It's okay. I'm right here, Declan."

His head rolled to the side, eyes shut tight as his strong jaw clenched so hard a vein stood out against his neck. "Y-You ... run ... p-please ..."

"No. I'm not going anywhere. Not until I know you're going to be okay." I sucked in a shaking breath, trying not to sniffle out loud. "Who did this to you?"

"R-Run ..." he pleaded, not seeming to hear me at all. "Please ... run ..."

The memories rushed through my mind so suddenly they throttled all the breath from my lungs. My mother's white bones half-buried in the golden sands. The creak and groan of the slaver's wagon as it rattled across the desert. Her last words still echoing on the dry, scorching wind that howled through the canyons.

"Run, Visha."

"Stop saying that!" I nearly screamed. "You don't get to say that to me! I'm not running. Never again!"

Declan fell silent, his expression going slack as his broad

chest took in slow breaths. Maybe he'd heard me. Or maybe he'd just gone unconscious again. I didn't know.

I'd lied to him, though. I did have to go. I had to find Leruna. I'd bought him time, sure, but she was the healer. And now he desperately needed her help.

I squeezed his big, rough-palmed hand one more time before I slowly stood.

This was it. I had to go right now. Before it was too late.

Leruna was probably at the temple at this hour, but if she wasn't, then I'd have to search the city. That could take a while.

I couldn't spare a single second.

So I turned on a heel, darting and leaping across the rubble of his apartment. I yanked the chair away from where I'd wedged it under the door and flung it open wide. The night air rushed in, salty and cool.

It made the tears on my cheeks turn cold.

And then I saw it.

A symbol painted onto the ruined door in blood, as though someone had come right behind me and done it while I struggled to save Declan's life inside.

An eye in the center of a sharply angled spiral.

The Eye of the Foul Father.

Right below it, a small knife pinned a lock of silvery-white hair to the door, as well.

My heart stopped. My mouth was open, but I couldn't breathe or make a sound. That was the symbol of the Viperi. My kin.

Had they done this?

No. It couldn't be.

The Viperi would never come here. Not for Declan, anyway. And even if they had, they would never leave him half-dead like this. They would have finished the job far more cleanly and efficiently. No mess in the apartment. No victim still clinging to life. No evidence left behind except a cooling corpse.

That symbol was meant for something else—to send a message. And that lock of hair, gleaming like platinum in the moonlight.

I'd seen it before.

My blood went cold, all but freezing in my veins as I panned my gaze back to where Declan still lay on the floor in a puddle of his own blood, fighting for his life.

Oh gods.

This wasn't about coin, or a lost fight, or thugs feuding over what happened in the fighting pit. This was about sending a message. A message meant for me.

That hair looked like Aeron's—the Gray elven boy I had liberated only a few nights ago. I didn't know anyone else with hair that color, let alone anyone who might be affiliated with the Viperi or Declan.

It was me. I was the point of connection between them all.

Someone had nearly killed Declan because *I* had been interfering with the slavers.

This was Sulam.

He knew what I'd been doing. That I'd attacked his thugs and murdered them like the animals they were. That I'd freed those would-be slaves and cost him a lot of coin.

And now he'd shown me exactly what would happen if I dared to do it again.

Fear rushed up my spine like the scrape of cold steel.

What would happen to Declan's little sister if he wasn't able to fight in the pit? Would Sulam torture her? Or do something worse? The whole reason he fought in that gods' forsaken place was to prevent that exact thing from happening. Sulam had only agreed to keep his filthy hands off Nora as long as Declan kept winning matches.

My stomach sank to the soles of my boots and my knees wobbled.

My fault—this was my fault.

Was Aeron still alive? Had Sulam's men found him? Killed him? What about all the other slaves I'd freed? And Nora?

Oh, Fates … what had I done?

ELEVEN

Declan might already be dead.

That thought pierced me like a rusty iron spike driving straight into my chest as I ran headlong through the darkened city streets. My eyes stung with fresh tears. My legs burned as I skidded around corners and through twisting avenues.

All I could hear was his gasping, desperate voice. All I could see was the blood on the floor. That symbol on the door. The small dagger with a lock of long silvery-white hair twisted around it.

A message for me.

I'd hastily wiped it away and ripped the little knife wrapped in a lock of long silver hair from the wood, tucking it away in the side of my boot. I didn't even know why. Leruna wouldn't care. She might not even notice it at all.

Gods, what had I done?

I'd left him—but I didn't have another choice. I couldn't help him. I didn't know much about healing beyond the basics. I couldn't just sit there and watch him suffer and die slowly.

Running was my only option.

But what if I'd just left him to die alone?

Faster—gods, I had to go faster.

We both did.

Leruna panted as she sprinted alongside me. Her cheeks were flushed, and her long, braided dark hair flew behind her as we raced for Declan's apartment.

It hadn't taken me long to find her, thank the Fates. Sure, I'd gotten a lot of strange looks from the other priestesses at the Temple of Undae when they'd found me banging on their door.

Thankfully, they hadn't questioned what a blood-spattered Viperi girl with blades belted to her hips was doing there, demanding to see one of their healers in the middle of the night. If that wasn't a testament to their truly being pacifists who rejected all forms of prejudice, nothing was.

"Was he conscious when you left him?" she gasped without ever looking my way, her sky-blue robes billowing around her and her gaze fixed straight ahead.

"Yes, barely," I wheezed.

She didn't answer.

Leruna followed me around another corner, staggering and almost losing her balance thanks to the big bag of supplies she carried.

I'd done my best to explain what I'd seen as fast as possible, but not knowing the full extent of Declan's injuries meant she brought literally everything she could cram into two large canvas bags.

We each lugged one over our shoulders, and the strap dug into my skin as I pumped my legs faster.

There.

Declan's apartment stood just as I'd left it, and I led the way up the rickety stairs to the barely standing door. My breath tangled up in my throat, caught around a hard knot of panic as I forced it open and let her go in first.

"In there," I urged. "He's in the back corner."

Leruna forged straight into the dark of the apartment without hesitation. Her long golden earrings jingled musically, filling the tense silence as we picked our way across the debris-strewn space.

Then she gasped.

"Oh, Declan ..." Her voice quavered as she rushed for him, dropping her bag and falling to her knees at his side.

Still lying on his back, he blinked at us groggily with his one usable eye.

Relief flooded my body like a rush of freezing water, leaving my teeth chattering and all my extremities trembling. My knees threatened to buckle. I barely felt the strap of Leruna's other bag sliding off my shoulder. It hit the floor beside me with a *thud*.

Alive. He was still alive.

"Bring clean water and see if you can get a fire going in the fire pit. We need to sterilize everything," Leruna ordered, already digging through her bags of materials. "Focus, Violet. I cannot do this without you."

I flinched, blinking hard, and suddenly everything around me seemed to snap into focus. Augh! I'd just been standing there, gaping like a beached fish.

I cursed under my breath as I scrambled to obey, clearing away the smashed furniture, glass shards, and bits of smashed plates until I'd made a path to the small firepit in the middle of the apartment. It wasn't much more than a sunken metal and tile square roughly two feet in diameter, but it would do.

I used hunks of wood from his smashed chairs to start a fire, and dug a large metal pot out from the wreckage in the kitchen. Filling it halfway with water, I set it on the flames to boil, and hurried to help her set out the rest of her tools.

"I gave him two big doses of the Lunthardan remedy," I explained as I spread out a stack of cut, clean bandages. "Will that help?"

"It's likely the only reason he is still breathing. It has bought him time. But this amount of trauma will require surgery. I have to close the wound on his abdomen. It will take a while, and he needs to stay unconscious for it," Leruna explained.

With her expression set in a grim, focused scowl, her sea-green eyes flashed in the dim light. Her slender hands moved quickly to unfurl a leather pouch with surgical tools, small blades, and spools of thread. She had bottles of strong-smelling tonics. Not the usual healing ones I'd been accustomed to. These were acrid and sharp, with an almost metallic scent.

Strange.

She chose one in a thin vial that was only as long as my finger and pulled out the silver stopper from the end. The aroma filled the air swiftly with something pungent and sickly sweet. The dark red liquid oozed slowly around in the glass vial, almost like old blood or red-stained honey. Maybe it was a mixture of both? I didn't know much about healing potions and remedies.

"Thornwine nectar," Leruna explained as she turned the vial in her fingers and held it up to the light, as though critiquing it. "More powerful than the Lunthardan remedy. It's extremely rare and difficult to get. A vial like this would cost a thousand gold. It will put him into a deep sleep and speed his recovery."

I swallowed all my questions as she opened the vial and poured the contents into Declan's mouth, then rubbed his throat to get him to swallow.

His expression twisted some, but he didn't wake up.

"That should give us the time we need. Bring hot water and wash your hands carefully. Then bring the same for me. I can't touch anything other than my tools once you do, so you'll need to hand things to me as I need them. Understand?" she asked.

I did.

My mind churned, twisting through every terrible scenario as I raced to follow her instructions. I washed my hands thoroughly in the first; the water turned a pale pink from the dried blood caked along my fingers and under my nails. Then, I cleaned out the bowl, refilled it, and placed it down so she could wash her hands carefully in it, too. No cross-contamination. Minimal chance of infection—especially once she had me douse both her hands in some of that sharp-smelling tonic. An antiseptic.

"You're going to rinse each tool in the tonic before you hand it to me," she instructed. "I'm going to give him a potion that will put him into a deep sleep. I need you to watch his chest and make sure he is still breathing while I work. The combination of it and the other tonics is ... risky. But there's no other choice. I'll start with the abdomen and then address the leg. This is going to take time, Violet, so make sure you don't lose focus."

It took *hours*.

First, she cleaned out the wound in his gut, and bile rose in my throat as she pulled out lengths of his intestines, felt around his organs, and looked them over carefully for punctures. Then, she cleaned everything and began stitching the wound closed.

Her hands were smeared red when she finished, sweat beading on her brow and running down the sides of her neck. But Leruna didn't stop. She rinsed her hands clean again, smeared more of the Lunthardan herbal remedy over the freshly stitched wound, and began wrapping it securely in layers of bandaging and cotton gauze.

His leg was so much worse.

The moment she began to touch it and assess the break, Declan groaned, and his eyelids fluttered. Even unconscious, the pain must have been awful. Seeing the white of the bone peeking through blood and torn flesh made my head spin and my stomach clench dangerously again.

It took almost as long for her to set his leg and bind it, using metal splints and strips of plaster-cloth dipped in water to mold around the injury so he wouldn't be able to move it. My back ached from sitting and squatting, bent over the basin of water to dip each length of the plaster-cloth in before handing it to her.

Leruna only stopped once to sit back, wipe her face clean of sweat, and get a sip of water. Then she went straight back to work.

The hours crawled by. Dawn stained the sky purple and pink beyond Declan's broken door and smashed-out windows. Soon, Roxus and Delthene would notice I had not come home last night. Would they start looking for me?

I didn't know. Regardless, they'd want to know where I had been all this time.

I shuddered at the thought.

"He can't stay here," Leruna murmured suddenly. "It isn't safe. He needs a proper bed to recover in, regular meals, and medicines."

I glanced up, not sure what to say.

Sitting at Declan's side, Leruna's face was set in a tense frown that creased her brow right between her eyebrows. Her mouth mashed into a rigid, uncomfortable line as she wiped a warm, wet cloth over his face, neck, and shoulders.

"When he wakes up, he'll be a lot better off. The thorn-wine nectar will speed up the healing process significantly, but it will take time for him to fully recover," she continued. "At least two weeks. Maybe longer."

My throat went dry. Would Sulam overlook his absence for that long? He was the one who had done this to Declan, after all. How could he not give him some time to heal before he forced him back into that fighting pit?

I clenched my teeth and looked down at all the blood-stained rags we'd used.

—Because Sulam was a ruthless, vindictive bastard, that's how.

"Where else can he go?" I asked, still keeping my head bowed.

Gods, I didn't even know how we could get Declan out of the apartment. And where would we take him? It was a long way back to her temple, and we couldn't possibly carry a man his size.

But Leruna was right; he couldn't stay here. It wasn't safe, even if the stupid door had still been in one piece. Sulam's thugs might come back. They were probably watching us right now.

"We need to move him with a stretcher," Leruna decided aloud. "He needs to be at the temple. I'll have to go get more help."

I sat up a little straighter. "Go, then. I'll stay with him."

Her gaze narrowed at me, as though trying to determine whether I was hiding something. Or maybe it just felt that way since ... I was.

"I'll be fine. I can handle myself." I glared back at her, doing my best to seem insulted. Maybe if I pretended to mistake her suspicion for concern, she wouldn't push the issue.

It worked.

Her expression broke into a look of apprehension. She put

a hand on my shoulder and assured me she would return as quickly as possible.

I just nodded and did my best to look appropriately stubborn as she dashed for the door and disappeared out into the early dawn light.

Alone again with Declan, I sat beside him with my legs crossed and my face in my hands. I just had to think. I could figure this out. I could stop Sulam from targeting him, couldn't I?

Of course, I could.

I just had to stop interfering with his slavers.

The thought turned my stomach sour, and I growled a Viperi curse through my teeth. Sulam had outmaneuvered me this time. He'd also revealed his hand a little.

I now knew he was watching Declan and me much more closely than I'd ever imagined. He knew Declan was important to me and would use him like a pressure point if I dared to overstep again. But, gods, what else would he do? This was only the beginning, wasn't it?

Who else would he hurt if he found out I could be so easily manipulated? Go after Delthene? Roxus? Leruna? I didn't have friends in the conventional sense. But they were the most important people in my life. The ones that mattered.

Knowing Sulam might do something like this to them to force my hand made me want to throw up.

Or scream.

Or both.

Trapped. I was trapped.

If I kept helping the slaves, Sulam would retaliate again. If I didn't, then he'd know he could extort me and might decide to try forcing me to do something awful for him—just like he was already doing to Declan in that fighting pit.

I screamed into my palms, trying to stifle the sound as I

squeezed every shred of frustrated energy into that sound I could.

I *hated* him.

Somehow, someway, I would kill him with my own hands.

For now, though, I had to play the game. I had to pick my next move carefully.

One false move ... and someone I cared for might pay the ultimate price.

TWELVE

I didn't even make it three feet through the front door. Smeared with blood and so exhausted I could barely see straight, I didn't notice Roxus sitting in the living room until he cleared his throat. "So. You're alive, after all."

Every muscle in my body locked up solid. I stood frozen, watching him like a doe caught in an open field as he casually put down the book he'd been thumbing through and fixed me with a hard stare.

The silence crushed down over me, tense and thick with expectation.

Roxus arched one of his eyebrows, tilting his head slightly, as though to tell me to get on with it—the blathering of pitiful excuses.

Only ... I didn't have any. Not for this.

So I just stood there, staring back at him with my mouth screwed up and my knees shaking until he let out a long, exasperated sigh and rubbed at the bridge of his nose.

"Go clean yourself up. You've got to report to Curator Vanora in an hour for etiquette instruction." His tone had a bitter edge.

"An hour?" I choked. "I'm exhausted! I can barely—"

"You should have thought about that before you disappeared to do gods-only-know-what all night," he snapped back suddenly.

I bristled, taking a small step back as my pulse thundered harder in my chest. A prickle of unease stirred in my gut. This was different. Wrong. Not the man I knew.

In two years, I'd done more than my fair share of stupid and ridiculous things. But Roxus had *never* raised his voice to me like that. Once, it might have terrified me enough to cower and submit.

Now, it pissed me off.

Angry words burned in my throat and hissed past my lips before I could stop them. "I'm surprised you even noticed. Seems like you have a hard time noticing anything past Sanja's cleavage. I guess you had to come up for air at some point, though."

Roxus's eyes went wide, and his scolding frown slipped to something that was either shock or horror. A bit of both, probably.

I didn't give him a chance to retort, though.

Storming up the stairs, I slammed my bedroom door and threw the lock.

Seriously—how *dare* he? He was the one who'd pushed me to the side first. Now, I suddenly owed him explanations for everything I did?

It's not like he felt it was necessary to keep me informed about our missions anyway, right? He hadn't considered it important for me to know we'd be working with Sanja and Axien. No, he'd let Axien—someone I absolutely despised— be the one to dangle that little fact in front of me like a taunt.

I seized one of my soft, cool satin pillows off my bed and pushed my face into it to muffle another furious scream of rage. It didn't help the second time either, though. And there wasn't time to try anything else.

I didn't want to go to etiquette instruction. I would have preferred being boiled alive. But staying here with Roxus lurking around downstairs, just waiting for our paths to cross so we could have another verbal showdown?

I hated that idea even more.

So, I locked myself in the washroom, angrily throwing perfumes and soaps around in the tub while I hastily scrubbed myself clean. The fragrant bathwater was stained pink from all the blood that was caked and dried onto my skin.

Declan's blood.

Right now, Leruna and a few of her fellow healers were carrying him to the temple on a gurney made of bamboo poles and canvas. They'd look after him. He would be okay.

But none of them knew what had really happened at his apartment. The reason he had been targeted so brutally and left to die. I'd erased all the evidence.

And now I was alone with that truth hanging like a mill-stone around my neck.

Too late, I realized I wasn't even all that angry at Roxus. *Of course* he wanted to know where I had been all night. *Of course* he'd be irritated I'd ducked out of dinner with no explanation. He wasn't my father, but he was the nearest thing to it. Attacking him about whatever weirdness was rekindling between him and Sanja wasn't fair.

Not when I was really only angry at myself.

I'd miscalculated everything. I'd underestimated Sulam. I couldn't afford to make that mistake again going forward.

I washed my hair and climbed out of the tub, combing and twisting it into another simple braid down my back. I eyed the pot of rouge and kohl on my dressing table as I threw on clean black leather pants and a simple, dark purple silken blouse.

No. Not today. I was in no mood to fool with all that ridiculous makeup, and it's not like I knew how to use it properly, anyway. I'd just look even more foolish.

"My, my, don't you look lovely."

Just the thought of Axien's smirking face made me want to punch my fist straight through my mirror.

It wouldn't have helped, though.

Gods, this was going to be a disaster. How could I go into any kind of training like this?

Somehow, I had to collect myself before I got to Arx Eburna. I had to be focused. Controlled. Composed. Disheveled, reckless, and angry was exactly what people like Mistress Orvana and Axien wanted from me. I would not give them that satisfaction.

My body ached with fatigue, my arms heavy and fingers clumsy as I threw on one of the corsets Delthene had picked out. This one was simpler, made of supple black leather to match my leggings, with only a little golden filigree embroidered around the sides. It only bound my middle to cinch my waist.

I left the front of my blouse unbuttoned far lower than I ever did normally. Low enough to see the muscles of my chest rippling as I sucked in fast, angry breaths. Enough to see plenty of cleavage. That's what they wanted, right? For me to look more appealing? To strut around with everything on display like Sanja did?

Fine.

Snatching a pair of black boots from my armoire, I laced them up quickly before fastening my belt with my daggers back around my hips. Good enough. I wasn't sure what the dress code expectation was for Curator Vanora's so-called instruction, but this would have to do.

I stormed downstairs and straight past the sitting room, not seeing Roxus anywhere as I flew out the front door and let it bang shut behind me. Good. I needed a few hours of space before I tried standing in the same room with him again, let alone having any kind of conversation. Sleep would have been nice, too, but I wasn't counting on that.

Tonight, maybe we could clear the air. Talk it out like we always had before.

Providing I survived etiquette training today, of course.

I snorted at the idea as I started for the temple, the glare of the morning sun warm on my chest and neck. It was bound to be a bunch of nonsense. Curtsying, dancing, and using the right forks and spoons, right?

Pfft. I'd survived a duel with an evil Rajinna sorcerer. I'd fought Tibran soldiers and out-maneuvered trained guards.

How difficult could a little curtsying possibly be?

Thirteen

L ate—I was so freaking *late*.

But, in my defense, I'd never been to this wing of Arx Eburna before. It was a long way from all my usual haunts, like the sparring rooms and archives. After stumbling around these halls, I'd finally been forced to stop and ask some of the Vindexori for directions.

Now I was over half an hour late, and I had no idea what sort of punishment would be waiting for me. I'd never met this woman before. Would she lecture me? Or just kick me out and refuse to see me at all?

My heeled boots clicked over the polished dark stone floor, filling the chilly silence as I passed door after door on the long corridor. Each one was labeled with the name of a scholar in swirling golden text—the private offices of the curators.

The spaces between each door were marked with old, crumbling busts of gods, heroes, and some figures I didn't even recognize. The empty eyes of each one seemed to follow me as I passed.

Creepy.

I stopped, finally staring up at the dark-stained wooden

door marked with her name: Curator Vanora. The candlelight from the chandeliers overhead flickered, making each of the golden letters seem to waver. My skin prickled and my stomach flipped as I raised a hand to knock once.

The silence seemed to crush in around me as the seconds ticked by.

Footsteps echoed from the other side of the door. The gilded knob rattled, and the door swung open to reveal the tall, buxom form of a woman. Her luxuriously curved body was draped in a slinky, dark red gown that plunged at the neckline, exposing a generous view of her throat and chest.

All I could do was stare—at her plump red lips that were painted to match her gown, at her hooded eyes adorned in shimmering black makeup that made them seem to shine like opals in the dim lamplight. She held a half-empty wineglass in one hand, swirling it a little as she seemed to give me a similar head-to-toe appraising glance.

Then her mouth bowed into a bemused little smirk. "You're late."

"I ... got lost," I stammered stupidly.

Her smile widened, and she tossed some of her silvery-white bangs away from her face as she stepped aside and motioned for me to come in.

The rest of her hair was draped in an impossibly thick and intricate braid over one of her shoulders. Long strings of little gold and black gems hung in long cords from her slender neck down her back. Matching earrings dangled from her pointed ears.

A knot clenched in my stomach as I studied her. Everything about Curator Vanora—the way she moved with a smooth, easy confidence to sit in a deep velvet chair in the middle of her office's lounge area—smacked of subtle power.

It made me want to shrink into myself like a clam into a shell.

Even the air in her office chambers smelled sweet and faintly spicy, a seductive mixture of clove and cinnamon edged with something sweetly floral like jasmine. The main room was open, with dark wood panels on all the walls and a plush, colorful wool rug on the floor. The hearth was more northern-styled, like the one in Roxus's office, and was built into the wall with marble busts of nude Avoran warriors on either side.

All her furniture was mismatched, but the deep colors and textures complemented one another. There were no paintings on the walls or ancient bits and baubles lying around, like in Roxus's study. Instead, there were a few modest bookcases with glass fronts that held neatly arranged books. No scrolls. No dusty relics. Even her desk, positioned on the farthest wall, was mostly empty. Just a small inkpot and quill, and a mostly empty wine bottle.

Strange. Maybe she didn't stay here often?

The wall windows were half-covered with heavy, dark purple drapes. The faint light from outside ebbed in through the beveled glass but never reached the seating area.

"Don't idle in the doorway, girl," she said as she crossed her legs, the split in her dress exposing even more of her bronze-hued skin all the way up her thigh. "Have a seat. Seems we have a lot of work to do."

"You're Lunthardan," I realized aloud as I shuffled over to sit in the chair across from her.

She took a sip from her glass. "I am. Or was. Like you, I came here as a child."

I fidgeted, unable to meet her gaze for more than a second or two. Gods, what was it about her that made me feel so ... small? Inadequate? Pathetic, even?

I'd seen beautiful women before. But something in her eyes hit me with a pressure that put every nerve on edge. As though she were reading every tiny expression, every minuscule movement.

"Mistress Orvana wants me to teach you to be civilized," she mused in a smooth, melodic voice. Like it was a bad joke.

I guess, for her, it probably seemed that way.

I bowed my head some. "I'm Viperi, so—"

"I know exactly what you are," she cut me off quickly. Her eyes smoldered in hues of yellow, green, and red, dancing with the reflections of the hearth's light.

I swallowed, not sure what to say. Should I apologize for being late? Somehow, I doubted she wanted to hear excuses.

"What is it that *you* want, girl?" One of her dark eyebrows arched upward, expectantly.

I hesitated. What did *I* want? Fates, what kind of question was that?

She laughed softly under her breath and drained her wineglass before placing it on the coffee table between us. "I have worked for Arx Eburna for twenty years, and in that time, Mistress Orvana has never sent me a pupil to learn social arts. My specialty is, of course, reading people. Knowing them before they know themselves."

My back straightened, a pang of fresh dread stabbing through my gut. No wonder it felt like she could see straight through me.

She could.

"I am usually employed as a spy in noble courts. I am the serpent that slithers into their henhouses and robs them of all their finest eggs, only to disappear before sunrise," she continued. "And the best part? They thank me for my time and beg me to visit again."

A chill swept through me, making every tiny hair on my body stand on end. That was it. Her true power. She might have been a curator of some knowledge and history here, but that wasn't Vanora's true value to the Zenith's Call.

She was an entirely different breed of predator.

And for the first time in my life ... I felt envy. It was raw and ragged, like a hunger deep in my soul. I wanted that power for myself. To be like her. Powerful and confident. Magnetic and dangerous.

But I was Viperi, not a beautiful Lunthardan elf. Was that even possible for someone like me?

"I can teach you," she said, like she was reading my mind. Or maybe just all my body language. "But only if you're willing to accept that you will never see the world or the people in it the same way again. To see as I do means every mask will be thrown off, and people's intentions—the good, the foul, and the vile—will all be laid bare. There's no going back from it. Once the blinders come off, they are off forever."

"But that ... isn't what Mistress Orvana sent me here for, is it?" I hedged, fighting every self-preservation instinct to hold her ever-shifting gaze. It only made my insides clench harder and my palms get sweaty.

Her smile was sweet and razor-sharp.

"No, my dear, it isn't. But Mistress Orvana is a fool to cast you aside. Such a thing would be a waste. Womanhood is upon you. You may either learn to wield it for the weapon it can be or accept things as they are. The choice is yours."

My mind whirled, picking apart every word. Either I could seize this chance and gain a power that might give me a new edge as an agent for the Zenith's Call, or I could learn only what I needed to in order to satisfy Mistress Orvana. Enough to keep myself alive. To have a life here, albeit a mediocre one.

Someone in my situation and standing should have been rejoicing every day for that good fortune. Roxus had found me in a dog kennel, for crying out loud. To even dream of wanting more might be reckless and selfish. I'd been given so much already.

But honestly, it wasn't much of a choice.

There was only one issue still nagging at the back of my mind.

"I'm Viperi," I repeated, putting more force into the words this time. "People don't look at me with anything except contempt and disgust."

Curator Vanora leaned forward in her seat, that sultry teasing smile slipping from her features. What lay beneath was cold. Vicious. Bloodthirsty. Unpredictable in a way that made my blood go cold.

She had a monster under her mask, as well—and it might be far more dangerous than mine.

"I know," she purred. "But when I am finished with you, they will be on their knees begging for your smiles ... even as your blade slips straight through their hearts."

My hands curled into fists. Wave after wave of chills fluttered over my body. Half terror. Half pure exhilaration.

My voice held a tremor, catching in my throat as I answered, "When can we begin?"

Fourteen

I might never be able to feel my toes again.

After meeting with Curator Vanora for over a week, my body was worse off than when I'd first trained with Declan.

She'd started with the basics, all the things Mistress Orvana had sent me to learn. How to speak. How to sit. How to hold forks, spoons, and knives properly while I ate. How to sip from cups and wine glasses. How to fold a napkin in my lap.

And yes, how to do a stupid curtsy.

I'd managed to pick all of that up in about two days. None of it was all that challenging, and I saw it as a way to prove myself to Vanora.

Gods strike me down. I'd proven nothing. Absolutely *nothing*—except that I wasn't a wild animal.

Because on day three, the *real* training started.

Every morning, I had to get up before sunrise to prepare, assembling an outfit and applying my makeup with painstaking precision while Delthene styled my hair. I'd jabbed myself in the eye with my new kohl brush more times than I could count while trying to paint it onto my eyelids and lashes.

Just as the sun began to rise each morning, I scarfed a quick breakfast before dashing out the door, covering as much of myself with my cloak as possible so no one else at Arx Eburna could see what I was wearing.

Of course, Varren was the first to notice my change in schedule.

I'd been forced to give up our usual morning training sessions for now, which probably triggered his suspicion. But the instant he saw me slinking into Krin'Moir, wearing a clingy satin top that showed my midriff and a flowing skirt with a split on each side that showed my thighs, his eyes bulged like they might roll right out of their sockets.

Varren's mouth fell open, his face blanching as pale as a corpse. I couldn't tell if it was disgust, concern, or pure horror that made his brow wrinkle like that.

Gods, just strike me down.

I spent all day at Curator Vanora's mercy. Endless hours of lessons and practice, until I was finally allowed to hobble out. Sometimes, there was a little time left in the day to do actual combat training, but I was far too sore by then to even try it.

I hadn't expected beauty to be so painful and exhausting.

So, I limped home and began the eternal process of going to bed.

I had to bathe with certain oils. Then, I had to massage scented balms into my hair and comb it out perfectly smooth before wrapping it up in a silken scarf. I pinned it in place and gave my face a similar treatment with coconut oil lotion, leaving it on for a few minutes before gently wiping it away.

Vanora supplied a special blade for me to shave all the tiny hairs off my arms, legs, and ... everywhere else. I was not good at it and managed to cut myself everywhere. It took nearly two weeks before I finally got the hang of it, and the itching as the hair grew back nearly drove me mad.

Vanora suggested I could use hot wax instead. Some court women preferred that, apparently. But I couldn't decide which sounded worse—nearly shaving layers of my skin off with that tiny blade, or ripping all the hair out in one tug like someone taking up a carpet.

I had to rub more balms into my skin every night, and sit still while Delthene groomed my nails and scrubbed my feet with a rough brush until my heels were smooth. I'm not sure which of us hated that more, since I was especially ticklish on my feet and couldn't hold still for any of it.

Not the good, silly kind of ticklish, either. The kind that makes you irrationally violent while you try to get away. I only kicked her once, on accident. But that was enough to get a scorching glare of warning. Delthene had never glared at me like that, and for a moment, I wondered if she might actually hit me back.

Horrifying.

Then came the high heels.

Not the normal ones I wore that had about an inch or two of lift. No, these must have been crafted somewhere in the abyss by the most vicious foul spirits ever to breathe in the immortal world. I wasn't even sure where Vanora got boots with heels like this. A torture chamber seemed most likely, though.

They were four or five inches tall, with a thin, spindly heel that was nearly impossible to walk in. My toes throbbed, then ached, and then went completely numb. The balls of my feet cramped when I tried to walk on flat ground again afterward.

Somehow, I doubted that was a good sign. But Curator Vanora wouldn't hear any complaining.

Every morning, she insisted I put them on and walk along

lines of wooden blocks to learn to control and contrive my stride.

"Head, neck, and shoulders remain level. Do not look down. Remember, eye contact is your most potent weapon. You cannot wield it if you're too busy staring at your toes," she scolded as she watched me stagger down the line again and again. If I knocked over one of the blocks, she made me stand before her so she could smack my open palms with a leather riding crop.

Then I had to start all over.

"I'm ... trying," I seethed through my teeth, pain stinging through my hands in waves that made my eyes well.

"And yet you still look like a warhorse thundering off to battle," she snapped. "Did you think this would be easy? Or that I would be gentle? Chin parallel to the floor. Shoulders back and dropped. Feel the arch of your neck and the extension of your throat."

I bit back a curse and staggered back to the starting line.

"The movement should come from your hips. Feel the curve of your spine as your hips shift from side to side. You're not swaying. It's more subtle. You're gliding," Vanora instructed as she paced, watching my every movement like a lioness observing a limping baby antelope.

She twirled the crop between her fingers like she couldn't wait to pop me with it again.

It didn't even hurt all that much when she did. I'd certainly suffered far worse in my life. It was more about the principle of the thing—the embarrassment of being swatted like a naughty goat.

I absolutely hated it.

After several hours of walking, we worked on other body language. I could sit and stand politely. Now, I had to learn to do it in ways that meant things. One turn of the head, shift of my hips, or angle of my shoulders all sent specific messages. It was an entire conversation of gestures and counter-gestures. A language that I hadn't even realized existed.

Then came eye contact.

Vanora showed me how to communicate things without even saying a word. Where I pointed my gaze mattered. How long I held it there mattered even more. According to her, I should be able to seduce a man from ten feet away before I ever said a word to him. One look—she was insistent that I could do it with just one look.

Gods help me.

"Remember, you're projecting from the moment you enter a room. Everything about you radiates an energy," she said as she circled the chair where I sat with my legs crossed. "That energy matters."

"And you really don't think people will find me disgusting when they realize what I am?" I dared to challenge.

Men weren't exactly lining up for Viperi lovers after all.

Vanora gave a sarcastic snort.

"You give people far too much credit. When something is beautiful and alluring, they don't care where it came from. Instinctual attraction is surface-level. That is where our game is played. To them, you will be exotic. Mysterious. And yes, some may realize what you truly are. And to them, you will offer the thrill of danger. A pretty poison they want to see if they can survive."

I curled my lip. "You say people—but you really mean only men, right?"

She laughed melodically and tapped the end of my nose with her crop. "My dear, sweet, innocent child ... men aren't the only ones who appreciate beauty."

I frowned. I'd never spent a lot of time thinking about ... you know, *romantic* things. It seemed pointless, considering Varren and Declan were the only guys willing to be seen with me in public. Varren was gross and loud and conveniently stupid. I'd never felt anything even remotely romantic for him.

Declan ... well, it didn't matter what I might have felt. Or started to feel. Or wanted to.

I couldn't feel anything for him now. Or ever.

It would destroy us both.

There was Roxus, too, of course, but he might as well have been my father. He wasn't, of course, and he had never tried to be. But he was the closest thing I had to family now.

Basically, I had never considered I'd have to deal with anyone's romantic advances—male or female. Everyone had their own preferences, and I wasn't about to start lobbing judgment at anyone. I was pretty confident my own tastes didn't include other women, though.

Vanora rolled her eyes, probably reading my thoughts through my expressions as clearly as if I'd just shouted them at her. "My dear, sweet, innocent girl. Have you ever seen a queen with ugly attendants? Or a nobleman's wife who only keeps homely-looking handmaids?"

I had to think about that.

She did have a point. I'd seen nobles and wealthy women at the market or around the temple traveling with their female companions, and they were always dressed in the same sparkling finery. All of them were beautifully painted creatures of silk and gemstones.

Hmm.

"It is a slightly different game, yes. But the rules still apply. Women appreciate beauty and are drawn to it, as well. There are a great many wealthy ladies who like to collect other beautiful females in their social circles like a vase of lovely flowers," Vanora said. "But you are no flower."

I made a scoffing sound. No one would ever accuse a Viperi of being flower-like.

Curator Vanora traced the tip of her riding crop along my

jaw to my chin, lifting my face so I was forced to meet her gaze. "You will be a tigrex—a masterful predator from my home-land known for its beauty and terrible strength. It is respected and feared. Its pelt is prized more highly than gold. When the tigrex crosses the jungle, every creature falls silent to watch. They both admire and fear it."

I swallowed hard.

"Think on this. Practice every moment you can. Soon, I'll be ready to test you." She turned away and snapped her fingers. "That reminds me, did you get the appropriate kohl brush from the list I sent?"

I nodded slowly. "It was expensive." Delthene had looked ready to faint when I told her how much gold I needed for it. I didn't understand how a small, pointed brush that looked so much like an ordinary paintbrush would cost that much.

"Good, then you got the right kind. The hairs are from the pelt of a faundra fawn—the softest and most precise." She strode behind her desk and sat down, still fiddling with her riding crop. "Practice with that, as well. And remember how I showed you to outline your eyes."

"My greatest weapons?" I said, teasing as I mimicked her tone.

Vanora cast me a knowing smile. "Joke as you like. Those lovely ruby-red eyes will crush the hearts of nobles and kings. The eyes of beautiful women have brought whole empires to their knees."

It took everything I had not to laugh out loud at that. She sounded so serious when she said things like that. But it couldn't possibly be true, right?

"We're finished for the day. You're dismissed. Tomorrow, we will continue this. You must learn as much as you can before your next mission." Vanora sighed and sank back into her chair.

"That could be pretty soon," I said as I bent over to start

prying my feet free of those gods-cursed heels. "Roxus and I are waiting for the final missive. It could come any day now. We're supposed to be working with Sanja and Axien."

Ugh. It was impossible to say their names without sounding like I was trying not to gag.

Mostly because I was.

"So I've heard." Vanora twirled a lock of her silvery-white hair around her finger thoughtfully. "I would advise you to handle them both with care, dear little Violet."

I looked up. "Really? Why?"

"Sanja and I made rounds at noble courts in our youth. We crossed paths a few times. She was a courtesan before she became Zenith's Call," she mused. "She's very well connected and plays the game with great skill. I certainly wouldn't suggest making her an enemy."

My pulse gave a little stammer of unease as I pretended to put all my focus back on my shoes and sore feet. "She comes around a lot to chat with Roxus. Apparently, they have a history, too."

Vanora looked away. Something changed in her eyes—a shift of the light that flickered like dark memory. "Oh, yes. She latched onto him when they were prospects. He was big and strong—an exiled Vordegan warrior and an Ursinaar. A fine shield for a delicate, beautiful little girl. I think he enjoyed feeling like he had something to protect again," she said. "It gave him purpose when he had lost everything."

My heart twisted at that thought. I didn't know much about Roxus's life or who he'd been before he came here to Rienka. I knew he was Vordegan, and I knew he was Ursinaar, so he could transform into the shape of an enormous bear. According to what little I'd been able to unearth about the Ursinaar, it was an incredibly rare and prized gift among his people. It should have marked him as someone of distinction and power in Vordega.

But he had been exiled.

Why? When? Was it because of something he'd done? And how did he get all the way here to Rienka?

Declan had mentioned once, years ago, that the Zenith's Call had bought Roxus out of slavery. Had his own people sold him off?

I knew better than to ask him any of those questions. I understood firsthand that old trauma like that wasn't the sort of thing people liked to rehash on a whim. If he wanted me to know, then he'd tell me when he was ready.

I just had to make peace with that and be patient.

"And what about her tandem?" I pressed, unable to disguise my interest now. "Axien?"

Curator Vanora's eerie, multicolored eyes rose to meet my stare. Her expression never changed, but I saw the way her energy shifted in that single look.

It was an unspoken warning.

"As I said, my dear, I would suggest you handle them *both* with care."

FIFTEEN

"We need to talk," Roxus said.

I froze on the bottom step on my way up to my room.

His voice was low, and his words clipped slightly. Tense, but not angry. Nervous? I'd have to see his face to be sure.

Curse it, Vanora was right. I couldn't help but read between the lines of everything everyone said to me now.

Turning around, I stared back at Roxus. We hadn't had a full conversation since the morning I'd come sneaking in spattered in blood. I'd said some pretty harsh things to him, and he'd gone to great lengths to make himself scarce since.

Not that I'd gone out of my way to talk to him, either.

We were both skulking around, avoiding each other, and trying to act like the entire house wasn't thrumming with tension. Like it might explode at any moment, and we'd be back in another yelling match. I wondered if that was why I hadn't seen Sanja or Axien come back around, either. Had he told them to stay away? Or had he just been insisting on meeting them elsewhere?

Awkward.

Roxus shifted his weight slightly, brows crinkling in a little scowl as his gaze darted over me. Taking note of my new ... look. New, pristinely smooth hair. New makeup. New clothes that hugged my body in strange ways.

I probably looked like a different creature to him now.

"Yes," I agreed at last. "We do."

His frown softened, his expression flickering with surprise. Maybe he'd expected me to shut him down or lash out again. "I thought we'd go out to dinner and give Delthene a break for tonight. Seems like you've been working her ragged lately."

"*Curator Vanora* has been working us *both* ragged, actually," I corrected with a proud little upward tilt of my chin. Just enough to remind him I wasn't the one who'd insisted on all this.

His mouth flattened into an exasperated line. "And costing me a lot of coin, too, apparently."

"She says beauty is expensive," I recited.

"She says a lot of things," he countered, his tone oddly stiff and clipped. "Not all of them should be taken to heart."

I shrugged and crossed my arms, holding my ground. "I don't have much of a choice, though, do I? I've been given orders. I'm following them."

He sighed and pinched the bridge of his nose, right between his eyes. Annoyed. "Do you want to talk about this over dinner? I thought we could go to Rook's Roost, if you wanted to see Declan. I know you haven't had time to spar with him lately."

Oh? Was that an olive branch?

Whatever it was, Roxus was right. I wanted to see Declan. I hadn't been able to check in on him. Leruna had assured me he would recover, and I didn't doubt her ability, but ... I needed to see for myself.

It felt wrong to visit him when I was the whole reason he'd nearly been killed.

I nodded and uncrossed my arms. "Do you want me to change?"

He cast a quick glance over me again. Today's outfit wasn't as outrageous as some of the ones Vanora had made me wear. Revealing, yes. Lots of cleavage, as usual. But the purple blouse was more understated with flowing, sheer sleeves, and my pants were tucked into the gods-awful heeled boots.

"You'll be fine in that, I think. So long as you don't intend on doing any pit fighting." One corner of his mouth tugged into a roguish, half-smirk.

I smirked back as I went striding past him, flipping some of my hair over my shoulder on my way to grab my cloak off the hook again. "We'll just have to see, won't we, old man?"

———+ ←)) * ((→ +———

Rook's Roost was a reeking cesspit.

Some things didn't change, no matter how many years went by.

All the seaside taverns and bars that haunted the corners of the docks were loud, smelly, and packed full of vagrants, sailors, and fishermen looking for a way to blow off steam after a long day's work. But Rook's Roost was, by far, the roughest. Everyone in Sol'Karr knew it.

It had a long reputation for debauchery, mostly thanks to the underground pit fighting arena. No surprise, Sulam owned it. He had an appetite for blood sport and had become the most prolific and influential crime lord in Rienka.

Maybe that's why the Zenith's Call handled him with velvet gloves. They didn't like the things he did, but they needed the information and resources he sometimes sold to them.

I'd been stupid to pick a fight with him.

Too late for that now, though.

My stomach flipped and fluttered as we entered the secret subterranean level hidden beneath the tavern upstairs. Only the big spenders got to come down and revel in the pit fighting. It was exclusive. A dirty little secret—which I guess was part of the appeal.

I wasn't sure how Roxus had gotten the privilege of being welcomed down here. If I had to guess, it was because Sulam had some fleeting hope that he might participate in one of the fights. The mob down here would have *loved* to watch a giant Vordegan war bear rip someone else apart, and it would have made Sulam a lot of coin off it.

Roxus never volunteered though. Sometimes, he got challenged by some random muscle head too deep in his cups, but Roxus never accepted.

I had to wonder if Declan was secretly relieved about that. A fight between them would have been awful, brutal, and deadly. Roxus would win, of course. But Declan was no pushover. He'd been the champion of this area for years, and he fought to defend that title nearly every night.

Or he had ... until recently.

A sharp pang of guilt shot through my chest as I stepped through the entrance and let my cloak slip from my shoulders. The smell of wine, ale, salt, and sweat hung like a sticky fog in the warm air. The roar of the crowd rumbled the floor beneath my heeled boots.

The cavernous room was round and lit with big iron torches hammered straight into the stone walls. It had been built like an amphitheater, with sloped seating in ten levels around a central deep pit right in the middle. The pit was sunken into the floor, lined with sand, and the focus of everyone's attention.

I couldn't bring myself to look at it as I followed Roxus up the steps to an empty table on the fifth level. I didn't know if Declan was in there, fighting for his life and his sister's safety again. But the thought of seeing him back in there after what had happened... gods.

I just couldn't. Not yet.

Roxus held the chair out for me, and I eased into it with all the grace and poise Curator Vanora had taught me. I sat straight, back arched so that my chest was pushed slightly forward. Shoulders back. Neck arched. Chin level with the floor. Channeling that inner power. My aura, Vanora had called it.

I swept a finger along the back of my neck, bringing all my silky-smooth hair to the front and giving a generous view of the side of my neck. This, she'd told me, was a subtle invitation. It would draw attention, especially if I were wearing long earrings that brushed my shoulders.

And tonight, I was.

Honestly, I did it all without thinking. I'd spent the last two weeks having all this nonsense drilled into my head. It was becoming reflexive. But when I glanced over at Roxus, I could see him staring with that uncomfortable little furrow in his brow again.

He definitely noticed.

"Seems like Curator Vanora has been very ... thorough," he said carefully and coughed a little.

That last word seemed to stick in his throat, like it wasn't the one he really wanted to say. There was no mistaking the disapproval in his earthy brown eyes as he settled into his own chair across from me.

I let my posture slump a little. "For the record, I'm not exactly comfortable with it, either. But this is what Mistress Orvana wanted, isn't it?"

He let out a barking sound halfway between a surprised cough and a laugh.

"I'm not sure," he admitted. "She probably assumed Vanora wouldn't take you on for further instruction beyond the absolute basics."

"You mean Mistress Orvana assumed Vanora would find me as disgusting as everyone else and want to get rid of me quickly?" I read between the lines easily.

"You know *I* don't find you disgusting," Roxus corrected sharply.

Ugh. Fine.

I pursed my lips and looked away, my eyes drawn to the pit as if pulled there by some invisible thread.

And there he was.

Declan stood over a fallen opponent, his bare torso flexing with every breath so that the tattoos across his chest and neck rippled. His darkly tanned skin shone with sweat. His hands were wrapped in bloodied strips of cloth to protect his knuckles, and his gaze was locked onto mine.

We stared at one another for what felt like an eternity—like the entire world had frozen around us. The noise of the raging crowd seemed to fade. Everything else was just a blur of color.

My heart seemed to stop altogether.

He was fighting again. He looked healthy. Completely healed. Leruna was right—a few weeks and he was back on his feet like nothing had happened. That thornwine potion really was a miracle.

So, why did my stomach keep clenching? Even the back of my throat burned. That weight on my chest crushed down harder.

Guilt and shame.

Fates, I'd nearly killed him. And he still didn't know.

I looked away quickly, focusing back on Roxus as a barmaid brought out his usual order—platters of food and ale with a tea for me. I didn't argue. Wine would have been better, and was perfectly acceptable in Rienka to have it at my age, but this seemed like his way of reminding me I wasn't *that* grown up yet.

Whatever.

"Now then, let's talk," Roxus said as he pulled out his long wooden pipe and began stuffing it with his favorite tobacco.

I sat back in my seat, draping one arm across the back of it while I watched him. Roxus wasn't an easy man to read, over-all, but there was no mistaking the way his mouth quirked slightly to the side. Thoughtfully. Choosing his words carefully.

He put his pipe between his teeth and lit it, taking his sweet time puffing a few smoke rings before he finally announced, "You don't like Sanja and Axien."

I frowned. Really? Baiting me? Not much of an opening move.

"I never said that."

"You didn't have to," he countered.

Fair enough.

"I want to know why." He settled deeper into his seat, taking longer, deeper puffs on his pipe as he watched me.

I blew out an exasperated sigh, weighing my options for a second. He wanted to know the truth? Fine.

"Axien is manipulative," I replied evenly, like I was reporting on the weather. "He taunts and teases me whenever I'm in the same room with him, which is often since he seems to follow me around Arx Eburna. He watches me as if I'm an insect he can torment just for fun. I don't like it. I don't like *him*."

"You could have told me that sooner," Roxus pointed out, his brow furrowing some. Not with anger, though. No, this looked more like frustration again.

"Oh, really?" I feigned shock and then rolled my eyes.

"Because you would have heard me past all of Sanja's ridiculous giggling?"

"Why don't you like her, then? Has she done something similar to you?"

"No. She does the opposite. She pretends I don't exist. Ignores me outright," I said. "You know she's never said hello to me even once? I don't need Curator Vanora's training to be able to see straight through that game. She wants me out of the way so she can get closer to you."

Roxus's mouth bent in a calm, easy smile around the pipe he now held between his teeth. Something about it felt ... demeaning. Patronizing, even.

"So, you're worried about losing my attention to Sanja?" he asked, like it was ridiculous.

Quiet rage smoldered in my chest. I took a few deep breaths, trying to tamp it down. Control it.

"We used to talk," I said, forcing my tone to stay low and calm—the opposite of what he was probably expecting. "We used to discuss missions, training, and everything. You're not my father, but you're the only person in the world I've always been able to trust. The one person who would believe me. Now, I have to throw a fit just to get you to stop me in the hall. And you think this is about jealousy?"

Roxus's smile vanished. His whole demeanor sobered, and he slowly took his pipe out of his mouth. "Vi, you're not losing me to Sanja."

"Aren't I?" I traced a finger around the rim of my teacup. "She and Axien knew about our joint mission long before I did. They probably already know a lot more about it than I do. I know I'm a new tandem. I'm still green and untried. But I can't work with people who don't include me, and I won't fight to get the same respect other tandems are given freely."

I paused, looking up at him and letting my energy carry

my point. This wasn't funny. This wasn't something I would tolerate being teased about.

"So, am I a part of this mission or not?" I asked.

He slowly licked the front of his teeth behind his lips, eyes moving but staying on me while he thought. "You are."

"Then I want to be treated that way," I said. "I don't think that's too much to ask. I don't want any sideways looks if I have to put Axien in his place. And I don't want you assuming I'm just being dramatic if I point out Sanja's attitude toward me. Fair?"

He nodded slightly. "Fair."

Wow. This was ... not how I'd imagined this conversation would go.

"Why didn't you tell me about this mission? Why didn't you warn me Sanja and Axien would be coming with us?" I pressed.

He ran a hand along his jaw, scrubbing at the scruff on his chin for a moment. "I honestly thought Axien had told you already. I was under the impression you two got along, at least enough to talk."

"We don't," I said darkly.

He made a thoughtful grunting noise, as though he were still processing that information. Or maybe he was just coming to terms with this ... *new* me.

I'd never been able to be so composed. So controlled and concise in explaining how I felt. It sent wave after wave of chills through my body, all the way to what must have been the tips of my toes. I couldn't be sure since I still couldn't feel them in these stupid shoes.

"Then I was in the wrong. I shouldn't have assumed. And for that, I apologize," Roxus admitted as he went back to puffing on his pipe. "For what it's worth, I think Curator Vanora has had a good influence with all her training."

My eyes welled and I almost laughed, caught between

shock and a wave of relief that nearly took me to my knees. "Why? Because she taught me how to sit up straight and put on makeup?"

He grinned around his pipe, waggling his dark brows as he reached for his tankard of ale. "Because even though Mistress Orvana took away your fangs, she's given you an entirely new set. And this pair suits you much better."

I couldn't hold back a sheepish little smile of my own. "I think so, too. I still hate these shoes, though. Gods and Fates, how does she wear these all the time?"

Roxus laughed.

I did, too. It felt good—I felt good—for the first time in years. Ever since Sanja and Axien showed up, I'd watched that rift between us grow wider. I hadn't known how to fix it.

Now, it felt like maybe I could. We could rebuild things between us. Be an atrociously mismatched little family again. Or, that's what I thought ...

... right up until I glanced up and saw Sanja and Axien striding toward us through the crowd.

Oh, gods, not again.

SIXTEEN

I could see it written all over his face.

This wasn't a surprise. Roxus had known they were coming. He might have even invited them here himself.

Instantly, all the wind rushed out of me. All the confidence and warm, fuzzy feelings of trust seeped out of my soul, and I was left sitting there, empty of everything except that smoldering rage.

He'd done it again—kept things from me. And why?

I didn't understand it. Was this some sort of game to him?

Sanja stopped at our table, noticing immediately that there weren't enough seats. She made a big fuss about having a barmaid drag over two more and claimed the one closest to Roxus right away. She was dressed as exotically as ever, her teal-colored silk robes trimmed in gold that matched her bracelets, dangling earrings, and the lotus-shaped comb in her hair.

It was strange to see her wear things that were Damarian, since she was clearly a Rienkan elf. But then again, the people of the southern kingdoms intermingled, intermarried, and shared cultures and practices freely. I didn't know where she'd come from—except that Vanora had told me she had once been a courtesan.

Now, I had to wonder where, exactly, she had lived before now.

Axien sat down next to me, but I didn't so much as glance his way. I didn't have to. Thanks to all of Vanora's training, I could feel the energy wafting off him like heat from an open forge. He stared and stared and *stared*.

I kept my face pointed straight ahead, gaze locked onto Roxus without even blinking.

He stared back, a hint of pressure in his gaze. A soft warning not to make a scene. Not to be my usual self.

Fine. He'd get the reformed Violet, then.

We'd see if he really preferred these new fangs after all.

"Oh! I'm sorry, did we interrupt something?" Sanja said suddenly, like she'd just noticed that neither Roxus nor I had said anything to them yet.

I shifted my gaze to her, batting my lashes slowly and doing a smooth turn of my head with my chin slightly raised. Projecting authority, dominance, and just a tiny hint of disapproval.

"Does it matter?" I asked.

Sanja blinked back. She did a great job of seeming confused and uncertain, but I saw it—exactly what Curator Vanora had warned me about. The thoughts turned behind her turquoise eyes like finely oiled gears. Her gaze cut to Roxus, as though assessing his response, too.

"What do you mean?" she asked in that sickly sweet voice.

"You'll insist on joining us either way," I pointed out. "So, does it matter that you've interrupted?"

"Violet," Roxus said my name low and firm, like a warning.

Sanja's mouth opened slightly. She didn't have to fake her surprise then.

"Not that we don't both adore your company, *Sanji*. Don't worry, I'll be gentle with her." I winked at Roxus and let one corner of my mouth turn in a small, bemused smirk. I eased forward in my seat, arching my back and letting my elbows rest on the table. Claiming that space. Seizing control.

Getting her name wrong, according to Vanora, was another expression of dominance.

"It's *Sanja*, actually," she corrected, all sweetness gone from her voice.

"Is it? My mistake then. Honestly, you've been coming around so often, but we've never been formally introduced, have we?" I said without even looking at her. "I'm Violet, by the way."

Silence hung over us, thick and foul. Roxus looked ready to crawl out of his own skin if it meant he could leave the table. He opted to hide behind his ale tankard instead. Coward.

Or masochist. I couldn't decide which.

"Oh, I've heard all about you," Sanja said, leaning into Roxus's side and patting his arm possessively. "I hear you've been training with Vanora. What excellent timing, too. You're budding into such a beautiful young woman; it would have been a shame to have you keep running around looking so haggard and neglected."

"Vanora has told me *so much* about you, as well," I said coolly as I slid my gaze over to meet hers for the briefest instant.

Her nostrils flared a little. Her pupils dilated. Her mouth pinched tight for half a second.

I'd struck a nerve.

Good.

"We can all swap stories another time," Roxus spoke up suddenly, clearing his throat. He couldn't have looked more uncomfortable if he'd been straddling a cactus. "Right now, we've got business to discuss."

Sanja was forced to sit up on her own again when he shifted in his seat, crossing one ankle over his knee. She hadn't taken her eyes off me yet and was now busy spooling some of her long, black hair around a finger. A nervous habit?

At least I knew I had her on edge now.

I'd count that as a victory.

"I got the missive from Orvana this afternoon. The arrangements have been finalized, and the path is as clear as they can get it. We're expected in Esfolar tomorrow night," Roxus announced. "This will be dangerous, so we've been encouraged to pack accordingly."

My pulse skipped, breath catching in my chest, as I stared at him. Adrenaline poured through my body like a rush of scalding water. Every nerve was set ablaze.

Was it finally time? Oh, gods. So soon?

"She's probably worried we'll run into Tibrans," Sanja guessed, still twisting at that lock of her hair. "I'll reach out to my connections in Esfolar once we arrive and make sure things remain calm going forward."

Roxus nodded in agreement. "The objective is simple. We reach Salnis and retrieve the Moonscape staff. The priests there are already expecting us. Once we have it, we go straight to deliver it to the hands of the godling in the Temple of Adiana. It'll put us crossing the Pitch Graves—which will be a feat unto itself, but we'll cross that bridge once we get to it."

"All this while dodging Tibran spies?" Sanja guessed.

Roxus's shoulders rose and fell with a heavy, resigned sigh. "So it would seem. With any luck, we can keep a low profile and slip in and out of the cities unnoticed. But with our enemies already on alert, watching for our movements and targeting our agents, I would assume we'll end up in a few skirmishes."

"And this staff? It is an artifact we can touch without risk?" Sanja asked.

"As far as I have been able to research, yes," Roxus replied. "It's a precious and powerful relic belonging to Adiana, the moon goddess. With it, the godling that has manifested her spirit will be able to do ... considerable feats."

I sank deeper into my chair, absorbing that. There were so many ancient divine artifacts scattered around the world, and only a fraction of them had been found and secured by the Zenith's Call. The Moonscape Staff was one of the more well-known, considering it had been passed down over and over to people who had been born possessing the moon goddess's spirit.

There could only be one of those people—*godlings*—born with that spirit at a time. But there were three individuals in all, each possessing the spirit of a different deity that had been cursed to dwell in our world after the War of the Stones. They were reborn into a mortal body over and over, and the Zenith's Call did everything in its power to make sure they were found and protected at all costs.

That was its own very long story, though.

"I suppose, dear Axien, we should also perform the rite. Make sure everything looks good on your end, hm?" She glanced at her tandem, giving a suggestive tilt of her brow. "Perhaps we can give ourselves the upper hand?"

For the first time, I dared to look his way.

Axien sat eerily still in the seat beside me, his eyes on her but his expression as cool and empty as the surface of a frozen lake. His strange, bright blue eyes never moved. His mouth stayed in a straight line. Nothing about him gave away even the slightest emotion.

Looking at him was like looking at an empty night sky. Nothing but a void of darkness. No hint at all at what he might be thinking.

It sent a little chill up my spine.

How could I read someone who gave absolutely nothing away?

"As you wish," he said, his tone equally flat and empty.

No emotion. Just hollow words.

"Let's plan to leave at noon," Roxus suggested. "I can get us passage at the docks. We'll go as normal travelers, so we don't draw any attention."

"We should stagger our arrival, then," Sanja agreed.

They went on talking about all the fine details of our departure. When to arrive. What to bring. How we would move from one city to the next so that we didn't attract attention.

I couldn't tear my gaze away from Axien, though. His sharp features were so still and unaffected that it almost seemed like he might be wearing a mask.

That thought made my mouth go dry. The last time I'd seen someone hide behind a mask like that, it had nearly cost me everything. Now she was rotting in the depths of a prison, probably cursing my name with every breath.

Axien finally lowered his gaze, studying the arena below where Declan was finishing up another fight. His brow furrowed slightly, nose wrinkling. Was that disgust?

I looked too.

Declan was in the throes of another fight. This one would be brief, though. The human man paired against him was easily half his size and not even close to his build. Fates, had someone sent that guy in there as a death sentence?

Knowing Sulam ... probably so.

Declan's punches were solid and fierce. It probably felt like getting smacked with an iron hammer each time his fist bashed across the man's face. But I'd sparred with Declan enough over the years to recognize all his weak points, too. And tonight, more than ever, he was moving far slower. Was he still stiff from his injuries? He kept his body angled to protect his recently broken leg—going easy on it.

My mouth pinched tight as I fought the urge to let all those feelings, all those worries, reach the surface. Too many people here would notice a response like that. It would put us both in an even worse position.

Gods, I hated this.

"I'm going for another drink," I muttered as I stood and swiftly stepped away from the table.

I could have flagged down a barmaid, sure. But I needed some room to breathe. To move. To shrug this off and pull myself together.

There were two small bar areas near the stairs where the barmaids picked up all the drinks they delivered to tables. I chose the one at the far end of the arena from where Roxus and the others were sitting and leaned on the bar top, asking for a glass of red wine.

It would be terrible and far too expensive—but hey, it was Roxus's money, and if I was going to make it through an evening with Sanja and Axien ... he owed me some liquid assistance.

Especially since punching them was frowned upon.

As soon as the bartender slid the glass to me, I felt *him* standing right behind me. His presence, his energy, invaded my space like an encroaching storm front. The weight and pressure of it made my stomach flip again, but I didn't dare look his way.

That's probably what he wanted. For me to make a big scene. Throw a fit.

Axien always seemed to like it when I put on a show and embarrassed myself.

"I see you still find me wholly disgusting," he murmured as he sidled up beside me and leaned casually against the bar top.

"Don't count yourself as special. I feel that way about most people. Seems only fair, since they usually hate me, too." I took my glass and sipped at the bitter dark port. It burned all the way down the back of my throat. Ugh. Terrible.

"Ah, yes, but you seem to have a *special* place in your heart for me," he chuckled.

Yep. I most certainly did. Right next to Sulam, Mistress Orvana, and people who kicked puppies.

He didn't need to know that, though.

"Why do you even care what I think?" I demanded as I finally turned to face him.

I'd almost forgotten how tall Axien was by comparison. Not as big as Declan, of course, but nearer to it than I'd ever be. I only barely came to his shoulder, even with my heeled boots on.

Glaring up at him, those ensnaring deep blue eyes still seemed to peer straight into my soul. His sharp features were staggeringly handsome in the warm torchlight. Typical Avoran beauty that bordered on divine.

That sort of thing didn't usually matter all that much to me, but with him peering down at me from so close, it was ... difficult to ignore.

And the longer I stared, the worse it got. Like how some of his shoulder-length black hair was pulled back in a half-pony-tail that made his pointed ears more obvious. Or how he was wide-shouldered and leanly muscular, filling out his dark fighting leathers in a way that made a few other women sitting at the nearby tables stare.

And I was no better.

All of it made my insides squirm strangely. I had to turn away and give him my shoulder.

"I thought I'd made my intentions clear," he said matter-of-factly. "I think you're interesting. I'd like to be friends."

I choked on another sip of my wine.

Interesting? Friends? Seriously? What sort of idiot did he take me for?

"I have all the friends I need, thank you," I muttered.

"Oh?" He gave that disarming, roguish smile that dimpled his cheeks. "Is that fellow down there one of your friends? Is that why he keeps looking up here at us?"

He tipped his chin toward the fighting pit. Toward Declan, who was absolutely staring straight at us. I could think of a few reasons why, and it had nothing to do with being friends.

First, I hadn't seen him since the night Sulam's men had almost beaten him to death. Second, he hadn't seen me dressed like this. Third, he'd never seen Sanja and Axien before, either. At least, not that I knew of. He was probably trying to figure out who they were, since Roxus and I normally came here alone.

"Perhaps he wishes to be more than just friends?" Axien asked, moving a step closer to me.

Close enough that I could feel the heat of his arm dangerously close to mine.

I shrugged and took a sip from my wine glass. "Perhaps he just wants to fight you," I suggested, privately enjoying the thought of Declan beating Axien's too-straight nose in.

What a sight that would be.

I could hear the smirk in Axien's voice as he leaned in a little more, using getting a better view of the fighting pit over the bar as an excuse to put his mouth right against my ear.

Every muscle in my body locked up tight. I squeezed the stem of my wineglass so tight my knuckles blanched.

"That would be a very bad idea, I think," he whispered.

I couldn't hold back a snort, but it came out more like a panicked wheeze. Close—why was he *so* close to me?

"Are you even watching? Declan doesn't lose fights in his arena. He's half Holvradix elf," I snapped.

"Is that so?" His warm breath tickled the side of my neck.

It made my aching toes curl inside my boots.

"Do you want to know what I think?" Axien asked.

I most certainly did not—especially when he was so close to me now that I caught a hint of his scent. Eucalyptus and cedar. Maybe a hint of something spiced, like anise. It filled my nose and sent warm shivers over my skin. My legs squeezed together involuntarily, and my throat went dry.

"I don't think he likes how close I am to you," he bent lower to whisper right into my ear.

"Well, that makes two of us," I fumed.

Axien laughed softly, a deep rumbling noise in his chest that made my pulse skip and stall.

And I saw it, too.

As Declan stood over his fallen opponent, powerful shoulders still heaving with every ragged breath, his head whipped around to stare at us again. His mouth drew into a snarl. His eyes narrowed. His entire body bristled, and his hands balled into fists, still drizzling blood from his freshly fallen victim.

I didn't need any special training to read that body language.

"I wonder what he'd do if I were to steal a kiss?" Axien baited, his voice quieter. It stoked something primal to life deep in my soul. Something I hadn't even known existed.

I clenched my teeth and willed it away.

Control—I had to get control of this. I couldn't let him win.

Without looking his way, I slowly drew my bottom lip into my mouth, letting it slide out through my teeth as my arm brushed his.

The contact set every nerve in my body on fire immediately. My legs went tingly. My head spun. I almost didn't notice him jerk away suddenly, like I'd burned him with that small touch.

"I think you should be a little more worried about what *I* would do," I warned, sliding a gaze up at him over my shoulder. "Maybe that works on the other girls around Arx Eburna, but I don't want *anything* from you."

"We'll see, won't we?" he whispered, his voice simmering with a tension I didn't understand. "Sounds like you and I will be spending a lot of time together."

I worked my jaw from one side to the other, taking in deep breaths to try to cool the strange heat that simmered in my chest.

No. Not here. This was what he wanted—for me to lose it. To cause a scene.

I wouldn't give him the satisfaction.

Turning my body slightly toward his, I focused on my posture. On the subtle language Vanora had taught me over the last two weeks. I let my eyes meet his, panning across his face, then dipping to his lips, then back up again with a slow blink.

His brow rose ever so slightly. His pupils dilated, and once again, I saw that strange shift of the light in his eyes. That tiny hint of a furrow in his brow. The way he slowly began to clench his teeth.

I smiled sweetly. "If you cross me, Axien dear, the only time we will be spending together will involve me gutting you very slowly. I am not some toy for you to bat around as you like."

His eyes darkened, that smile twisting faintly into something more sinister. "Prove it. Duel me down in that pit, and if I win, I get a kiss."

My heartbeat slammed against my ribs so hard it knocked me breathless. What the—? Was he serious? Or was this just another one of his games? A way to throw me off balance?

The rage took me, mind and body, so fast it made my

vision spot. My lip curled, and I downed the rest of my wine and set the empty glass on the bar top.

"Fine," I said. "And if I win, you have to bow out of the mission. Tell Sanja and Roxus you won't be going."

Axien's menacing smile faded and he drew back slightly, those eerie eyes narrowing as he studied me.

Seconds crawled by, filled by the roar of the crowd around us and the distant thuds from the fighting pit, as we stared one another down like lions in a cage.

Axien was bigger. Stronger, too. But I wouldn't back down.

I had my own arsenal of tricks, and this wasn't my first time spitting blood into the sand of that pit.

A muscle feathered in Axien's jaw, and he took a step back, fiery sapphire gaze flicking away to where our tandems sat at their table, chatting over their drinks, completely oblivious.

"Fine," he agreed through clenched teeth. "I'll have a word with the fight-caller. Next match is ours."

SEVENTEEN

I'd never seen Declan's face that shade of purple before.

I had seen the big pulsing vein that stood out against his forehead, though. Many times. It was practically an old friend by now.

"What, by all the gods, are you doing, Violet?" he demanded as I stopped at the edge of the pit. "And what the heck are you wearing?"

He towered over me, still spattered with blood and slick with sweat from his last match. Anyone else might have found his deep, guttural snarls terrifying.

I knew better.

Declan wouldn't hurt me.

"It's a long story," I muttered as I hurried to unbuckle the daggers from my hips and shove them into his hands, belt and all. "Hold on to these for me, okay? Hello again, by the way. Nice to see you're back on your feet."

He gaped, looking between Axien—who was doing the same thing with the cross-sheathed scimitars he wore belted across his back—and me. With his face turned so he could glare at Axien, I spotted a new white scar across his upper lip. He had a bigger, more obvious one on his abdomen.

I cringed and quickly looked away.

"Don't give me that crap. Who is that guy?" Declan growled again, lower this time. "At least tell me that much."

"A jerk I'm forced to work with." I sighed, rolling my eyes and quickly throwing my hair up into a tight, messy bun on the back of my head to get it out of my way.

His eyes narrowed. "And you're fighting him?" He didn't sound convinced.

"It's the only way to get rid of him," I answered sharply.

"That doesn't make any sense," Declan kept on protesting as he followed me to the edge of the pit.

"No," I agreed. "It doesn't. Just do me a favor, would you? Keep an eye on the dark-haired woman Roxus is sitting with. If she does anything that seems off ... go ahead and break her neck."

Declan raised an eyebrow. "All right." He cleared his throat. "Not that I don't have the utmost faith, but ... how do you plan to win this match, exactly?"

I scowled up at him as I took off my high-heeled boots. "What is that supposed to mean? You've sparred with me enough to know I'm not some rookie. I can hold my own."

He shook his head slowly, as though in disbelief. "Against most people, sure. But didn't you notice those weird, glowing gold eyes? He's half-Avoran, Violet. He doesn't *need* a blade to turn someone inside out."

All the warmth drained out of my body. My fingertips went numb as I stared across the pit, watching Axien leap down into it and land in a perfect crouch. He'd shed outer layers of his leathers, wearing only a sleeveless black linen shirt and his breeches.

"No ... no, that's not right. His eyes are blue," I said without looking away.

Declan snorted as he threw my belt over one of his thick shoulders and crossed his burly arms.

"Look again, girlie. They're as bright as setting suns," he scoffed. "I would have thought a well-read Zenith's Call agent would know that only Avorans have eyes that glow gold like that. Their veins run thick with magic given straight from the gods. Even their half-breeds are dangerous."

Oh.

Oh no.

All the wind rushed out of me in an instant as the truth crushed down like a wagonload of boulders.

Anything with a magical aura glowed blue to me, and I'd never met an Avoran elf or any of their descendants before now. Axien's eyes only looked blue because of the magic. Because of my runesight.

Oh, gods.

I hadn't told Axien no magic. Did the pit's rules allow for that kind of thing? Fates, I doubted they even cared. It would just make for a better show.

I had no choice. I couldn't back out now. If I lost ... if I surrendered ... then he would ...

My head spun, panic fresh and frigid in my veins as I dropped down into the pit. Flashes of Kalsin's sneer replayed in my head as my body went cold. My fingers twitched, and my pulse raced.

It had hurt so much before when that foul magic touched me, like burning from the inside out. Could Axien do that kind of thing, too?

The roar of the crowd intensified as the fight-caller raised his hands, shouting to the masses. "My lords, ladies, and insatiable guests—tonight, we are most fortunate! Tonight, we bear witness to an ancient rivalry. Thousands of years of hatred, of murder, of brutal vengeance will culminate before us!"

My chest shuddered with a desperate gasp as I stepped forward, not even feeling the sand beneath my bare feet as I moved toward Axien.

His eyes locked with mine, glowing so brightly—gods, how could I be so stupid? How could I not notice the color was the same?

"The blood of the Avorans, the great elves who walk with the gods, has sent this champion to defeat the foul spawn of the Dire King," the fight-caller bellowed and motioned in my direction.

That was me. The evil one.

The Pitathi Murderess.

My head bowed slightly, feeling the sting of curses spat in my direction. Of course, they hated me. Of course, they wanted to see me lose and get beaten within an inch of my life. My people had been the foul creation of the God of the Void. The devourer. We had been crafted to hunt, kill, and destroy —and we had for thousands of years.

We were murderers. We were thieves and liars. Assassins who lurked in the deepest shadows of the world. And even though I'd sworn myself to the service of the Zenith's Call, I still felt the pull of that dark appetite. That's why killing Sulam's slavers had felt so good.

I was still Viperi, even if I'd chosen to use my talents in the service of another master. My soul was still twisted and malformed.

And Axien's people were the opposite. The forefathers of all elves. The ones who still walked in the presence of the gods and shared in their great power. The first wielders of magic— and the source of it for all their descendants.

Gods, if I'd known what Axien really was, that he had magic, I never would have agreed to any of this.

The caller raised his hand, face beet-red as he shouted, "FIGHT!"

I held perfectly still, staring at where Axien stood only five or six feet away. His body tensed, veins standing out against his arms and the sides of his neck. His eyes shone like two blue stars, focused squarely on me. Waiting for me to make a sudden move.

I narrowed my eyes and angled my chin up. I wouldn't give him the satisfaction of swinging first. *He* was going to attack *me*.

Then I was going to defend myself.

Very thoroughly.

Axien flexed his hands, his jawline hardening. His chest heaved with one deep, steadying breath. Then he moved—as fast as a tongue of lightning.

Before I could blink, he was in my face, trying for a leg sweep and a palm strike to my chin.

I whirled out of reach, spinning to the side and ducking under his blow. I came up just as fast, landing a fast jab to the side of his ribs—hard enough I heard him sputter—before I dashed back and sank into a crouch. I raised my fists, glaring at him through a falling lock of my hair.

He turned slowly, shaking out both his arms and rolling his head from side to side to stretch his neck. Like this was all just a warmup.

"You're quick, I'll grant you that," he chuckled.

My lip curled back on instinct. Even if I didn't have fangs anymore, I couldn't hold back a snarl. "Not going to use your fancy Avoran magic to end this quickly?"

Axien paused. His expression sobered, and that eerie emptiness slowly crept over his handsome features. It was a mask. A void he hid in so I couldn't read his true feelings.

"What do you know of magic?" he spat as he prowled a wide circle around me.

I never let my guard down, turning to keep myself angled in that defensive pose.

"More than I ever wanted to," I muttered.

Axien practically materialized in my space again, moving so fast I didn't have time to react before he was in my face. He hooked an ankle around mine and seized my arm, trying to twist me into a wrestling maneuver that would take me to the ground.

I wrenched, trying to slip free, but his grip was like an iron vice. I waited for the burn of magic. But there wasn't any. No spell sizzling across my nerves, frying me alive. Nothing.

Was he hesitating? Holding back?

No time to question it.

BAM!

I threw my head against his in a headbutt, our skulls cracking off one another. It sent him reeling, but I didn't flee this time.

I landed a hit upside his jaw and a fierce kick against the side of his knee that had him staggering and leaning against the wall of the pit.

I sprang after him and snatched his neck in the crook of my elbow, then wrapped my legs around him, trying to pin his arms while I choked him out.

Sand flew. We scuffled like animals, grunting and cursing as he tried to sling me off. Axien threw himself backward so I hit the ground beneath his much bigger body.

Blood filled my mouth as I bit my tongue on impact. My grip on him slipped for a fraction of a second, and he was loose.

The crowd around us roared, stomped their feet, and slammed their tankards on the tabletops in a rhythm like war drums. Coins flew like glittering rain.

He whirled around and went for my throat with a hand, trying to pin me as he cocked a fist back like he meant to punch me right in the face.

I couldn't shake him. Not even enough to get a breath.

"Tap out!" he roared over me. "Don't make me have to—"

I spat a mouthful of blood into his face.

Coward. *He* was the one who wanted this. And now he was going to back down?

Axien let out a string of Damarian curses and drove a fist into my gut. I coughed another spray of blood, seeing stars. Gods, he hit hard.

He swung again, aiming for my cheek. I jerked my head to the side at the last second, his fist sailing so close I felt the wind as it slammed into the arena floor.

Before he could try again, I drove my knee into his groin with all my strength.

He reeled back, clutching himself, and I immediately sprang upright, grabbing his head and slamming my knee across his jaw.

Wheezing and still spitting blood, I staggered backward and tried to reevaluate. My ears rang and my vision swerved. My abdomen throbbed where he'd hit me, and each breath sent a sharp pang of pain through my chest.

Not good.

Axien hauled himself up and stumbled back a few steps with a hand to his face. Blood seeped between the cracks of his fingers, and when he looked up again, I saw it pouring from a fresh split across the bridge of his nose.

"All this rather than suffering one kiss?" he taunted as he spat blood onto the sand between us.

"All this rather than suffering a week with you following me around like a stalker," I fumed.

"You really do hate me, don't you?" He wiped his nose again. "Fine."

Fine? What did that—?

He was on me again like a springing wolf, feinting and dodging my punches as I struggled to match his speed. Curse it, he was a lot faster than Varren and Declan. But he hit just as hard.

I threw my weight back into a springing leap and landed in a squat, preparing to dash back out of his reach.

But as soon as I turned, he was already there. Waiting. Snarling. Eyes wide and crazed.

BAM!

His fist came out of nowhere, slamming into the pit of my stomach and knocking all the wind from my lungs at once. I sucked in a ragged breath.

He was too fast.

Axien moved like a mirage, sweeping my legs so I toppled forward. He seized a fistful of my hair and drove me face-first into the ground, using his other hand to drive his fingertips into a point on the back of my neck that made my entire body scream in agony.

I'd never seen that maneuver before. I struggled, pitching wildly to get free, but he held me down and locked his legs around me. Then he bore down harder, pinching a bundle of nerves that immediately made my extremities go numb.

Gods, fates, and all things divine—*what* was he?

My vision tunneled. Pain surged through me, down to the very marrow of my bones. But I couldn't draw a breath, let alone scream.

In a last-ditch, desperate attempt, I tried to slip my shoulders from their sockets so I could twist free of his hold.

But Axien just clamped down harder, leaning in so his mouth was against my ear.

"Maybe you should spar with someone other than that Vindexori fellow every day, hm?" he seethed, his tone so cold and bitter it slashed through my mind like the bite of a whip. "Now, be a good girl, and pass out."

Too much pain. He was cutting off the circulation. I-I couldn't do this. I could taste the copper of blood on my tongue, and smell it thick as fog in the air as I fought for the tiniest breath.

I was ... losing.

Curse it all, I was losing to *him!*

My ears rang louder. My arms and legs wouldn't respond. Even the chaos of the crowd faded to muffled silence.

But I heard Axien whisper again, his breath hot against my cheek. "I'll see you in the morning, lovely Violet. Bright and early."

EIGHTEEN

Pain ripped me from sleep with a frantic gasp.

My eyes flew open. Lying flat on my back, I stared up at the ceiling above a bed. *My* bed. My teeth chattered as I shivered. My clothes and sheets were soaked with sweat and stuck to my skin.

But I was ... home.

And judging by the darkness beyond the long drapes over my balcony's glass doors, it was either very late or very early.

I couldn't focus on anything except the pain, though. The back of my neck, where Axien had pinched that bundle of nerves, throbbed sharply. My eyes welled when I tried to turn my head, my neck throbbing so badly it made my hands shake.

Gods, what did Axien do to me? Had he used some sort of foul magic? Why did it still hurt so badly?

I didn't know. I didn't even know how I had gotten back to my room. Had Roxus carried me back here?

A whimper leaked past my lips as I forced myself to sit up. The room spun. I panted, trying to steady myself as I gently rubbed the back of my neck. Even the brush of my fingers against that spot made me whimper.

Fates, I probably had a horrible bruise.

My gaze drifted to the chair at my bedside. Once, I'd woken up like this to find Roxus sitting there, ready to talk. To hear me out. To make me feel better and get me back on my feet and fighting again.

But the chair was empty.

My heart sank slowly, seeming to shrink and freeze over as I sat there in the near dark.

I didn't remember seeing Roxus's face during the fight. I'd been so focused on Axien, on winning, I hadn't paid attention to anything or anyone else. He must have been furious, though.

Or ... otherwise occupied.

I set my jaw, steeling myself as I moved to the edge of the bed. I couldn't sleep. Not now. So, I might as well get up. I could get things packed and ready for the mission—or in case Roxus finally decided to kick me out.

I went to stand, but the floor yelped and moved under my feet.

"What the–?!" I cried out and toppled sideways—right onto a very warm, very large *someone*.

Axien.

Axien was lying on my floor, right next to my bed!

I screamed and kicked at him, flailing to get away as he groggily shambled to his knees.

"Easy! Calm down!" he said, raising his hands like he was trying to soothe a frantic horse.

"What are you doing in my room?! Get out! Get away from me!" My face burned with wrath as I sprang to my feet, immediately looking around for something to hit him with.

All I could reach was a pillow, so I snatched it off my bed and whacked him over the head hard enough to make him stumble.

"Roxus asked me to watch over you until he got back," he

shouted back, glaring at me through the gloom as he tried to shield himself from my wild swings. "I just needed to lie down for a bit—I didn't think you'd wake up!"

I whacked him upside the head again. "Get out!"

"I would if you'd stop hitting me!" On my next swing, he grabbed the pillow and yanked it out of my hands. "Gods, you are a spiteful one, aren't you? Is this bad temper something all Viperi suffer from? Or is this a unique trait of yours? Fates have mercy, what did I ever see in—"

He stopped short, mouth pressing into a tight, crooked line as he shook his head.

My thoughts scrambled, twisting with fury like branches whipping around in a tornado. I couldn't even put words together.

I'd show him a bad temper.

"It's a side effect of disgusting pigs making themselves at home in my room," I snapped.

Axien muttered something that might have been a curse in Avoran. I honestly couldn't tell. He kept his body angled toward me, as if he was bracing for another attack, as he slowly stood and backed up a few paces.

I took that opportunity to whirl around and turn up the flame on the little oil lamp I kept burning on my bedside table at night. Warm light bloomed through my bedroom, illuminating his tall frame and making him squint.

He raised a hand, blocking the light and wincing. With his sleeveless, unbuttoned tunic hanging loosely open, I got a good look at the bruises I'd left on him during our fight. Hmph. Good. At least I wasn't the only one walking away with some marks to show for it.

I glared down at the floor, where he'd taken one of my spare blankets and throw pillows and made himself a nice little nest right next to my bed. I bet it smelled of him now. Disgusting.

I'd have to burn it all.

"You do realize we're going to have to spend quite a lot of time with one another over the next few days?" he fumed as he combed his fingers through his hair, brushing dark locks away from his face ... and revealing a fresh black eye.

Well, it was mostly purple—not black yet—only because it was fresh. The big, swollen bruise went from his cheekbone, around the outside of his eye, to his brow. It must have been painful.

"Did ... did I do that to you?" I asked before I could stop myself.

Agh! What was I even saying? It didn't matter! He'd left plenty of bruises on me, hadn't he? I shouldn't feel guilty about a very swollen black eye.

Axien shook his head, his lips tugging at a weak smile as he cast me a cautious, sideways glance. The warm, wavering light from my oil lamp made the blue of his eyes shift and sparkle.

A shiver ran over my skin.

Magic.

Axien had ancient magic running through his veins. So much it made his eyes shine blue in my runesight.

"Hah," he snorted. "No. This was a parting gift from that big fellow at the fighting pit. You should have told me you two really were an item; I wouldn't have taunted him with you. He took it very personally."

"We aren't," I corrected. "An item, I mean. We're just ..."

I wasn't sure what.

"Friends?" Axien guessed.

I scowled down at the floor between us. The word felt wrong, considering that I'd almost gotten Declan killed. Friends didn't do things like that.

"Well, if that's the case, I suppose I still can't blame him for being protective. Even if you did hold your own fairly well." Axien waved a hand dismissively and turned to sit down on the edge of my bed.

I had to suck my teeth to keep from cursing at him. *Fairly well?* Gods, the nerve of this man.

"I'd have beaten you if you hadn't used magic," I spat.

He chuckled softly. "That wasn't magic. I was trained to use certain pressure points in order to gain control of opponents in close quarters—places on the body that are extra sensitive. You held out a lot longer than most do against that particular maneuver. Usually, people just throw up and pass out."

I frowned harder. "Who trains people to do things like that?"

Certainly not the Zenith's Call. That meant he'd been trained by someone else, someone before he'd been recruited to the order. Someone who taught a more brutal fighting style.

He made a strange face, gaze dropping along with those broad shoulders as he held his silence.

"Ulfrangar?" I guessed when he didn't answer.

Axien gave another derisive snort. "No. I'm not an assassin, Violet."

Hmm. Fighting techniques like that certainly smacked of assassinry. He might be lying.

Besides, I doubted anyone who had been a member of that brutal and secretive organization would openly admit to it. Supposedly, trying to flee the ranks of the Ulfrangar was as good as a death sentence. They didn't tolerate defectors.

"How's your neck?" He actually sounded concerned.

I angled myself away. The way he looked at me out of the corner of his eye, his steeply angled jawline tense and his brow slightly creased—it almost looked like remorse.

I hated it.

"It hurts," I said and crossed my arms. "A lot."

"Sorry," he murmured low, bowing his head some. "I

wasn't sure how else to stop the fight. You really are quite skilled, not that I'd expect anything less after watching you train every day. You're ruthless, even with yourself. I'll admit, I've asked myself many times, '*Does she enjoy pain? Or is she just trying to distract herself from something else that hurts more?*'"

I swallowed against the stiffness in my throat. It made my eyes sting and the dull ache in my neck throb. "Is that a compliment or a critique?"

His smile was thin and forced. It never reached his eerie, glowing eyes. "It's whatever you want it to be, dear Violet."

A strange, prickly silence closed in around us. He sat there on my bed, wearing only a long-sleeved black tunic and breeches. Not the same ones he'd worn in our match.

The front of the tunic was unbuttoned a bit, offering a view of something inked into his skin across his chest. A tattoo? Maybe his oathmark?

Every member of the Zenith's Call had one depicting the shape of the crescent moon and sword. I couldn't see enough of it to be sure, though. I couldn't tell much of anything about it, except that the dark hue of the ink stood out in sharp contrast against his deeply tanned skin. Something about it scrambled all my good sense. It was ... beautiful.

More than I'd ever dare to admit.

"You should rest while you can. I'll go back downstairs, since you find my presence so revolting," he offered quietly as he stared down at where his hands rested in his lap. No conniving, vulpine smiles. No teasing or taunting.

If anything, the shadows under his eyes seemed much deeper than I'd ever seen them before. There was a strange hollowness in his expression. Exhaustion, maybe? Or ... sorrow?

I didn't know him well enough to be able to tell for sure.

"When will Roxus be back?" I asked, my tone stiff. Awkward. I didn't know how to talk normally to him.

Axien shrugged, put his hands on his knees, and stood up with a groan. He faltered some, stumbling and almost falling over. I flinched toward him on pure instinct, but he caught the edge of the bed and steadied himself.

Fates, was he more hurt than he let on? Or was this from something else?

"Soon, probably," he replied quietly. "He and Sanja have been very busy preparing. Packing things, going back and forth to Arx Eburna, arranging transportation—the usual. You'll need to get your belongings together in the morning. They might choose to leave sooner than we had hoped."

I sank down slowly to sit on the edge of my bed. It seemed safe to do it now that he was heading for the door. His gait was all off, though. I'd seen him prowl around Arx Eburna, every movement calculated and effortlessly smooth.

Now, he was shuffling along strangely. Stiffly. Almost like he was in pain or having trouble getting his arms and legs to respond.

Something was definitely wrong.

Something prickled in the back of my mind—a suspicion that it wasn't from the fight or whatever beating Declan might have given him afterwards.

"Sanja said something about a rite you needed to do before we left," I remembered. "What was she talking about? Is that why you're ... not right?"

Axien froze mid-step, his back to me and his hand outstretched for the knob of my bedroom door. Something odd mottled his skin, peeking out from under the cuff of his shirt. Dark veins? Or a tattoo? I couldn't be sure from this distance.

His head bowed slightly, but he didn't look back as he

murmured, "It's nothing you need to worry about, sweet Violet."

Oh? Now he was going to be all evasive and vague? After insisting on following me, staring at me, and teasing me all these months?

"It is if it affects the mission somehow," I protested. "Does it have something to do with your magic?"

His other hand slowly drew into a trembling fist at his side as his shoulders tensed beneath his thin linen tunic.

A second ticked by, then another, and I realized I was holding my breath. Waiting for him to snap. To turn on me and start attacking.

He didn't.

I barely heard it when Axien whispered, "You know, I never told you or anyone else here that I had magic."

"You didn't have to," I said. "You're half Avoran, aren't you? You'd be born with their power, then."

I decided not to tell him I could see it—magic literally glowing in his eyes like two crystalline blue stars. He didn't need to know everything about me. Not when I knew basically nothing about him.

"I'm a lot of things. None of them you need to concern yourself with right now. Get some sleep. I'll stay far away from you, I promise." Something about those words, and the faint way his voice broke when he said them, squeezed at my heart. This wasn't his usual game of dangling information in front of my nose to taunt me.

He was hiding something. Something personal.

Something that hurt.

Axien didn't look back as he opened the door and strode out, letting it slowly shut behind him.

I sat on my bed, neck still aching, listening to his steps retreat down the hall while my heart kept on hammering, slowly and fiercely, in my chest.

Axien wasn't at all who I'd assumed. That, or he was an excellent actor. Everything about him seemed so contradictory.

He was fierce when backed into a corner, but never reckless. Careful, guarded, but quick to slip those cunning smiles my way. Something simmered beneath that veneer, like a slow-burning fuse. It sent waves of tingling chills across my skin.

I didn't know him. He might be far more dangerous than I ever imagined. And that emptiness that sometimes slammed over his features ...

It was like an all-consuming void. Bottomless. Slowly devouring him from the inside out.

Why? What else was he hiding?

I didn't know. I had no idea who or what Axien actually was. But I'd be spending the next several days forced into close company with him.

And like it or not, I'd lost the fight.

I still owed him a kiss.

NINETEEN

He was gone.

When I came downstairs at dawn, creeping as quietly as a cat down the stairs and peeking into the front sitting room, Axien was nowhere to be found.

Roxus was back, though, busy piling all his gear by the door. He flicked a cursory glance my way, then nodded to the haversack I wore slung across my shoulders.

"Got everything?"

"And then some," I said quietly.

He stood with a grunt and leaned from side to side to stretch his back. "Good. I've about got the rest of it together. We've got to be down at the docks in half an hour. You should grab something to eat first. It could be a while before we get to eat again."

"I'm not hungry." I moved slowly, picking my way across the floor one step at a time until I stood beside him. "Hey, um, Roxus?"

His mouth flattened into a tense line, as though he knew what was coming.

"Are you angry with me about last night?" The question crawled out of me like a beetle from a rotting log.

His chest rose and fell with a heavy sigh. "No, Vi. I won't pretend to understand the nuances of female relationships, but I realize you're not one to start a fight where there isn't one already brewing. Whatever issues you have with Sanja, I trust you can work them out on your own."

I pursed my lips, trying to recall everything I'd said to Sanja last night. It all felt like a blur now. But I didn't have much choice. If I was going to be forced into close proximity with her, I couldn't tolerate being treated like I was invisible.

"She wanted you to stay behind after the fight with Axien," Roxus said as he began buckling a longsword to his hip. "She was afraid you two might do something like that again on the mission and draw unnecessary attention to us."

I couldn't hold back a scoff. *Of course* she didn't want me to go.

"What did you say to her?" I dared to ask.

His smile was as warm and roguish as ever when he patted the top of my head roughly. "You're my tandem. I'm not leaving you behind unless you're physically not up to the task."

I had to blink hard to keep my eyes from welling up. "Thanks."

He just nodded and shuffled past me, grabbing his own bag and slinging it over one shoulder. "How's the neck? Axien was concerned he'd been too rough with you."

I decided to ignore the hint of a smirk on his lips and the daring little twinkle in his eyes.

"It's fine." I flexed my shoulders, still feeling the pinch of aching soreness on the back of my neck. It was a lot better now, though. I wouldn't let it get in the way.

His grin widened. "That was quite a fight."

I wrinkled my nose at him. "Did you make lots of coin betting against me?"

His laugh was deep and rough. "Not at all. Lost a hundred gold."

"You bet a *hundred* gold on me?" I gasped.

He laughed again. "What sort of partner would I be if I bet against my own tandem? Besides, I thought you stood a chance of winning. Axien is very skilled, and he's got a couple of years and quite a few inches on you, but I've never met anyone who can match your spite."

I rolled my eyes and followed him out the front door. "Right, well, I didn't realize I'd be going up against a half-Avoran sorcerer. Not enough spite in the world to offset that."

Roxus's face skewed strangely, like he didn't approve of my choice of words.

Before he could reply or correct me, Delthene suddenly burst out the front door. She ran after us with her airy white dress flying, waving her hands for us to wait. "Don't you dare leave me without saying goodbye!"

I froze when she caught me in her arms in a tight hug.

"Oh, my sweet, darling girl. I've been dreading this since the moment you came to us," she crooned over me, patting her hands gently on my cheeks before leaning in to kiss my forehead.

I did my best not to squirm away. Contact like that—affection—was still so bizarre. My mother had never done things like that. She'd slapped me plenty, though. Viperi weren't exactly huggers.

I tried to return the hug. Gods, it felt so stiff and strange. "I left a letter on my dressing table. It's for Leruna. Would you mind sending it for me?"

Roxus arched a brow. "Since when do you write letters to anyone?"

I forced a smile and lied. "I'm supposed to be practicing my handwriting. According to Vanora, it's very unrefined."

The slight squint of his eyes told me he wasn't buying that for a second. Great. How is it that he could always see right through me?

I quickly turned my face away, back to Delthene. While my handwriting was, in fact, still pretty terrible—that letter was more than just practice. I owed Leruna a lot already, but I still had to ask her for more. I needed her to keep an eye on Declan. I needed her to check in on him and make sure he was all right.

At least until I got back and could do it myself.

Now that she knew where he lived, she could use delivering medical supplies as an excuse. He would be irritated, of course. Stubborn idiot. But I doubted he'd refuse her help.

He wasn't exactly in a suitable position to be refusing anyone's kindness right now.

"Can you make sure she gets it?" I asked again, batting my eyes hopefully at Delthene.

It worked better than any kind of magic. "Of course, of course. You promise to be careful?" She sniffled and looked at Roxus. "Both of you?"

We nodded sheepishly.

She dabbed at her eyes and gave my hair another stroke before she started to shoo us off. "Go on, then. Before I cause a scene. Fates preserve me."

Too late for that. I bit back a smile as I followed Roxus into the street. My stomach flipped and spun with every step we took away from that house. Away from safety.

Away from home.

I didn't dare look back as we turned away from our street. It would hurt too much, seeing Delthene standing there. Wondering if I would ever see her again. This mission was supposed to be dangerous, after all.

Was she wondering the same thing?

I kept my head down and matched Roxus's brisk pace as we started the hike down to the port, sealing away all those thoughts and questions. I couldn't worry about any of it now. I had work to do.

The early morning sunlight warmed my back and shoulders as we made our way down the sloping avenues and into the bustling dockside markets. Gulls floated on the stiff, briny wind that blew in from the bay. Merchants called their wares from stalls divided by colorful woven tapestries.

"I didn't realize you and Leruna had gotten so close. You're really exchanging letters with her?" Roxus asked once we were in the thick of the morning crowds.

I shrugged. "It's not a big deal ... I just wanted to thank her. You know, for fixing my teeth."

Another lie. I'd thanked her for that, yes, but I also told her about seeing Declan back in the pit. He had seemed okay, but that was the whole reason I wanted her to look in on him. He was back to fighting, even after Sulam's men had nearly killed him. He still had no idea who was really to blame for that.

Gods and Fates, he was probably blaming himself for it.

My stomach turned at the thought. Curse it, I'd tried so hard to put some distance between us. To make it seem like he wasn't a big part of my life anymore—for his own sake.

Sulam hadn't bought it, though. He'd known exactly which pressure point to pinch to get me to leave his slavers alone. Fates, what was I going to do?

Roxus didn't reply, and I was happy to lose myself to the chaos of the markets.

The smell of street vendors selling skewers of fried fish, roasted potatoes rolled in curry spices, and candied fruits saturated every breath I took. My mouth watered, and my stomach gave a loud, angry grumble.

"Sounds like someone skipped breakfast," a familiar voice scolded from far too close behind me.

I shot Axien a scorching glare over my shoulder—until we passed a cart selling fresh pastries and my stomach growled loudly again. My face blazed with embarrassed heat. Gods, strike me down.

He laughed again, looking frustratingly perfect in the golden light of dawn. The sea wind blew through his shoulder-length hair and tugged little wispy locks of it free. They framed the sharp lines of his face and cheeks, making the smile on his lips seem softer. Gentler.

Sanja was barely a step behind him, carrying her own bag and dressed in no-nonsense travel leathers for once. Granted, she still had a little jeweled ring through her nose and dangling earrings from her pointed ears, but I almost didn't recognize her. She had all her dark hair braided and wound into a complex knot on the back of her head, and a belt studded with a dozen silver throwing darts strung low across her hips.

Every single one of them glowed faintly blue. Magic. But what did that mean? What could they do?

A jolt of alarm made my whole body tense when her vivid sea-green eyes darted up to meet mine. She didn't smile, though, just held my gaze for a few, long, uncomfortable seconds before glancing away again.

Awkward.

Well, this would be ... fun.

Roxus led the way to the waterfront avenue, passing by all the huge merchant ships that rocked at their moorings, their white sails bound up tight. Hundreds of sailors loaded cargo up the steep boarding planks. Barrels. Crates. Some even had cages of strange animals with airholes cut along the sides.

I passed by one that shuddered as the creature inside let out an ear-splitting shriek. Through the holes in the side, I could barely make out the flash of brilliant, mirror-like scales.

Strange ... what sort of creature had a hide like that?

Farther to the west, we came to the network of long, wide docks that jutted out into the bay. There, local ferrymen parked small, sleek barges pulled by teams of hippocampi and called their destinations. Groups of people stood in lines carrying crates and baskets from the market, waiting for their turn to take one of the little ferries to the different islands.

They didn't even glance our way as we passed, forging on to the very end of the docks where a pair of saddled hippocampi were tethered and waiting. The beautiful animals stirred in the crystal waters, their colorful scales and fins shining like gemstones as they nibbled at baskets packed with kelp. I squatted down to get a better look and bit my lip to suppress a smile.

I'd never ridden a hippocampus before, but I'd seen them streaking through the waters like flashes of lightning. They could outrun a dolphin ten times over, even carrying a rider. Each one was about the size of a horse—which made sense considering how they favored one in body shape. Well, apart from the tail. That end was distinctly fishlike.

"These ought to get us to Kua'Tar," Roxus said as he threw his bag down on the dock. "From there, we've got a spot on a ship that'll take us into Esfolar's port discreetly. We should arrive by nightfall. Then we can discuss the plan going forward."

"Excellent." Sanja strolled over to stare at the hippocampi with her hands on her hips. "Only two? Looks like we'll have to double up."

"Shouldn't be a problem." Roxus rubbed his stubbly chin. "It is a long ride, but we'll manage."

"Allow me to ride with Violet, then," Axien volunteered without even trying to hide his wolfish grin. "I promise not to let her fall off and drown in the abyss."

I glared at him. "Why would I want to ride with you?"

His grin widened, showing a flash of white teeth. "Because I'm *very* experienced."

"I'm sure you are ..." I muttered sourly as I stood and crossed my arms.

"Watch your mouth, boy," Roxus growled suddenly, making us both turn and stare as he began untying one of the hippocampi. "This one's smaller. It won't be able to keep up with a heavy load. Violet, you and Sanja weigh less together, so you'll carry the gear and ride on this one. Axien, you're with me."

I couldn't decide what I enjoyed more—the sour look of disappointment on Sanja's face as she took the saddle behind me, or the awkward way Axien had to put his arms around Roxus's waist while they steered their hippocampus out into the bay. Priceless.

I'd have to find a way to thank Roxus later.

Sanja flat-out refused to handle the reins, since apparently she hated riding, so I got a very brief lesson on how to ride a hippocampus. Overall, it didn't seem much different from riding a horse. There was a slim saddle, but no stirrups. The bit and bridle were similar, too, but the movement of the animal was bizarre between my legs.

Its spine rippled with each flick of its powerful tail, and I had to keep myself balanced as we picked up speed. I followed along behind Roxus and Axien, wobbling some as we made our way past the breaking surf and into the open ocean beyond the bay. Then we started to pick up speed.

I squeezed my thighs and gave a little pressure with my heels, urging my hippocampus to go faster. It gave a squeaking cry, blasting deep breaths through its nostrils and the gill openings along its jaw.

I couldn't stop smiling.

We skimmed the surface of the water with the sea wind snatching through my hair; the creature bounding over waves and darting through the currents. Water rushed past my legs, and Sanja had to grab onto the back of my belt.

We raced through the wide bay of Rienka, passing islands that dotted the water like towers of jade. It was a strange place that was more water than land. But every inch of it was breathtaking.

Rienka had once been a kingdom unto itself ruled by seafaring elves, the ancestors of Sanja and Leruna, but it had long been controlled by the larger human kingdom of Damaria. Rienka profited from the rich trade routes that streamed through its islands with a constant flow of merchant vessels from all around the world. But the vast granite palaces carved into the cliff sides that looked out over the ocean were older than the throne of Damaria.

They'd all originally come from the Avoran Empire.

The thought drew my gaze to Axien. I'd read quite a lot about the Avorans now. About their history and power. But seeing him sitting astride that hippocampus, clinging to Roxus's back like a scared baby squirrel? I couldn't help it.

I threw my head back and laughed out loud.

I spotted him staring back at me. He wasn't glaring, though. He didn't even look embarrassed. He was just ... looking at me, eyes wide, and expression eerily slack with something like awe.

I didn't understand it.

Adrenaline sang through my veins as the salty spray seeped through the seams of my lips, filling my mouth with that rich, briny flavor. The sun blazed down over us, sparkling through the rolling waves. I wanted to shove Sanja off the back of this marvelous beast and see just how fast we could go. How high we could leap. How deep we could dive.

But I doubted Roxus would like that.

We rode for hours, skirting lines of ships and zooming through the currents that twisted around all the islands like reeds in a basket. My legs grew tired, and my neck started to ache again.

At midday, we finally cruised into the massive harbor of Kua'Tar—another large island with a semicircular bay almost as big as Sol'Karr's. But where our home island was known for its temples and protective garrisons, Kua'Tar was the heart of trade. Here, enormous ships docked and unloaded their wares straight into the largest market in Rienka.

It was the sort of place you could feel even from a distance because of the energy that hummed in the air. The roar of crowds. The rumble of wagons and carts. The smell of spices, fruits, fish, breads, animals, all intermingled with a tinge of sweat and sea salt.

But that wasn't what turned my guts to mush as we handed off our mounts to the ferryman who had loaned them to us.

Kua'Tar was the trade capital, yes. But it was also where the Necrolis Prison had stood for a few thousand years. Where Chrysa was now, and would be for the rest of her life.

And now I was here, standing on the same patch of ground she was. Only, there were feet of stone, iron, and gods only knew what else between us. I couldn't have reached her even if I had wanted to.

And I didn't.

Thankfully, I couldn't see the prison from here. It was built on a smaller chunk of land that only connected to the main island by a retractable bridge. That, I'd heard, was to prevent inmates from escaping. The currents around the tiny spit of an island were extremely dangerous, so even if an inmate decided to make a swim for it ... they wouldn't survive. The ocean would devour them.

No one had ever escaped Necrolis. And if the stories about it were true, no one ever would.

My thoughts stirred around that notion as Roxus thanked

the ferryman, passing him a few gold coins before we all went on our way.

"I've got us set up in an inn just off the Kaltori Plaza," Sanja announced. "It's right next to a public bath, thank the gods. We can settle in and discuss our next moves over dinner. Sounds wonderful, doesn't it? I just love jobs like these."

I had to agree with her—especially about the food.

My stomach was now in full revolt, and my knees felt weak and wobbly. I really shouldn't have skipped breakfast.

My neck throbbed in protest as I lugged my haversack across the vast network of piers and boardwalks that stretched nearly half a mile out into the water. Everything was soggy. My hair, our bags, clothes—all of it was soaked with seawater.

My boots sloshed with every step as we walked into the sprawling market district right off the harbor. No wonder the Rienkan elves traditionally rode without shoes. I'd have blisters the size of dinner plates.

The plaza opened before us in a massive square surrounded by tall buildings that overlooked the patchwork of tents, booths, and stalls. People wandered through the maze of merchants, food-sellers, and artisans. Music floated over the rumble of conversation, and the air was thick with the fragrance of spices, exotic perfumes, and roasting meat.

My gaze caught on displays of brightly painted pottery, glass lamps, strings of pearls, and wide baskets filled with grains, dates, and nuts. Silks of every color and intricately embroidered linens flapped and fluttered in the breeze. Children ran and giggled, herding little goats with copper bells around their necks. Women balanced baskets on their heads as they milled about, doing their daily shopping.

The rhythm of the plaza thrummed under my feet like a heartbeat. It was chaotically beautiful. The noise. The smells.

I loved it instantly.

Following along behind Sanja, I bumped and jostled in the

crowds. My whole body went stiff and tingly when Axien suddenly put a hand on my shoulder and leaned down to speak right into my ear—which was quickly becoming an annoying habit of his.

"Mind your things," he warned. "Pickpockets thrive in the Kaltori Plaza."

My mouth pinched sourly, and I put a hand on my haversack, pulling it around to hold it tighter.

It only took twenty minutes to find the inn. It was small but very well kept and stood on a far corner of the sprawling plaza with four levels of rooms. Each had a private balcony set neatly with low tables, lanterns that dangled from long gilded chains, and fine velvet poufs to sit on.

The owner, a fidgety little man with thick spectacles, greeted us with wide, mystified eyes. Sanja flashed the Zenith's Call brand on her wrist, and we were immediately led up a narrow staircase to the top floor.

The long, narrow room was separated by ornately embroidered silk screens that partitioned the space into little sleeping areas. Four plush futon beds were spread out on the floor, and the innkeeper rushed around to light some of the lamps and stoke the coals in the small firepit.

Sanja asked him to bring up dinner and hot tea, then thanked him sweetly. I had to admit, her honey over vinegar approach worked like a charm. The innkeeper stumbled all over himself and flushed as bright as a cherry on his way out.

"I'm going for a bath," she announced with a noisy sigh.

"Vi, go with her," Roxus commanded suddenly.

I hesitated where I stood, about to throw my haversack down next to one of the beds. What? He wanted me to go with Sanja? Why? It was a public bath, so why couldn't Axien go? He was her tandem, after all.

I guess I didn't do a great job of masking my shock and

disgust because Sanja clicked her tongue disapprovingly and strolled over to loop an arm through mine.

"He's right," she said, her words clipped and sharp. "We shouldn't go anywhere alone until the mission is complete. Perhaps we can use this as an opportunity to get to know each other better, hm?"

Her turquoise eyes slid my way, and there was no mistaking the look of haughty superiority there. She wanted to get to know me, all right. She probably wanted to pick me apart like someone dissecting an animal to figure out where all my weak points were.

I cast Roxus a long-suffering glare as I gathered a fresh change of clothes and let Sanja haul me out the door. This would be terrible. But what choice did I have? Rejecting outright would only give her something to point to when she filled Roxus's ears with all the reasons I shouldn't be here later.

I didn't trust her. Zenith's Call or not, I could sense that she wanted to drive a wedge between Roxus and me. Why, I didn't really understand. It didn't matter, though. She wanted me gone. So, I had to play the game perfectly.

I had to suck it up and be nice.

For now.

TWENTY

There was no getting rid of her.

I had to resist the urge to groan as Sanja slid into the deep, misty green waters of the public bath right beside me. I settled for angling my body away, making sure to give her my shoulder.

"Let's clear the air, shall we?" she purred.

Ugggh. This would be a delight.

It was a quaint place with three large, two-foot deep tubs positioned in a dimly lit, windowless room. One was cold water, another warm saltwater, and the one where we sat was filled with mineral water treated with fragrant oils and bath salts.

We'd found a spot to relax away from most of the other customers—men and women who reclined in the pools and chatted casually. A bath attendant took our saltwater-soaked clothes to be cleaned and provided a tray of soaps, sponges, and towels. Nothing out of the ordinary.

Well, except that I was sitting next to Sanja.

"You are such a lovely young girl. No one would dispute

that, even if you do scowl at everyone like a cranky old cat," she said as she settled against the warm stone wall. "But your ... relationship with Roxus is—"

"—Strictly professional," I finished for her.

I didn't like the way she'd said that word—*relationship*—one bit. Like she was implying that he was keeping me around like some sort of mistress. Or grooming me to be his future bride.

Ew. Absolutely not.

Sanja's slender eyebrows rose, her gaze tracking over me as though searching for signs of deception.

"Oh." She sounded genuinely surprised. "So, you're ... what? More like a daughter to him? Clearly, he cares for you more than just a work associate."

I took in a slow, steadying breath, trying to collect myself before my temper caught fire.

"I suppose, in some ways. But I don't think of him as a parent, if that's what you're asking. He's more of a mentor. That's it," I said. "He might consider himself more of a guardian, though. I don't know. We've never really discussed that."

She pursed her lips, still seeming unconvinced. "You've some other romantic partner, then?"

I choked out loud. "N-No. Why does that matter?"

She shrugged her bare, slender shoulders and leaned her head back to let her long curtain of dark hair swirl in the water. "Forgive me, then. But after I heard Vanora was tutoring you, I just assumed. And to be honest, a girl your age is usually quite busy exploring herself."

I curled my lip and looked away. "A girl my age usually isn't a Viperi working for the Zenith's Call. I'm not interested in that, and even if I was, I doubt anyone else would ever see me that way."

"Not true. You're a lovely young woman, even despite

those eyes and scowls. If you're ever curious, I'm sure Axien would be more than happy to educate you on matters of physical pleasure. He has more than enough experience for both of you," she said, muttering the words coyly. Like it was a dirty little secret she didn't want anyone else to overhear.

Gods, this woman ...

"No, thank you," I grumbled and swallowed hard. For whatever reason, hearing that sort of thing about Axien left a nauseating pit in my stomach.

I had to wonder if she had some sort of relationship with him. She'd accused me of it with Roxus, after all. It wasn't much of a leap to think she might be messing around with Axien, even if he was considerably younger.

If she was close to Roxus's age, that would put her somewhere in her mid-thirties. And Axien looked like he might be nineteen? Twenty, at most? Elven blood made it hard to tell. Even halfbreeds aged more gracefully than humans.

Still, I shuddered at the thought.

"Well, perhaps we can start over, then. I realize I haven't been that friendly to you. I was very close with Roxus when we were about your age. He's always been such a pillar of dependability. So stoic, but so kind," she went on. "Truly a good man, through and through."

Well. I couldn't disagree with that.

"I was thrilled to be called back here to work with him again. It's been so many years, but he hasn't changed at all." She poured some of the soap into her hands and started working it through her hair while she talked.

I did the same, scrubbing the salt and grit from my skin, and kept my mouth shut.

"I heard a lot of stories about you, as well. Not many of them were flattering, I'll admit. Truly, I am sorry for not giving you a fair shake. I should have known better than to count gossip as fact," Sanja rambled as she washed and rinsed her hair, then offered to do the same for me.

I turned around and dunked my hair, getting it wet before I let her wash it.

She jabbered on and on, and I tried not to listen. To let my mind go somewhere else. It didn't work, though. She talked too loud and her hands were rough as she worked the soap through my hair with a stern, practiced efficiency.

"You were quite skilled in your bout with Axien in that fighting pit," she praised. "I don't think I've seen him that off balance in a fight in a long time. Very impressive!"

Without seeing her face, I couldn't tell if she meant it. I sat with my back to her while she washed my hair, trying to pick up the nuances in her tone. It was useless, though. She was skilled in the social arts, just like Vanora had said. I wouldn't be able to read her that easily.

"How is it you came to know him?" I finally asked. "Axien, I mean."

"Oh, now *that* is a tale for the ages." Her tone took a secretive, somber edge. "It must have been three years ago. To be honest, before I found him, I didn't realize Avorans even had children with others outside their own kin. But there he was, chained to the stocks in the pouring rain like an animal, awaiting a very public execution."

My heartbeat skipped. Axien had been in prison, too? Why?

I wanted to ask, but my voice hung in my throat.

"It was fate, I think, that I just happened to be on a sensitive and dangerous business errand in Lancea that day. I'd heard some mutterings about a manhunt in the area, but I had no idea it was him they were looking for. Poor boy. He was only fifteen and scared of his own shadow," she continued. "I'll admit, the more I learned about him, the more it broke my heart. We had a similar start in life. I decided the least I could do was grant him the same mercy I'd been given."

"Lancea?" I wasn't sure I'd heard that right. "That's the capital city of Tibrus, isn't it?"

She gave a weary sigh. "Yes, indeed. The order has been very invested in keeping an eye on things when it comes to the greedy expansion of the Tibran Empire. Being there, in its royal city, was dangerous enough. Conscripting from foreign lands isn't easy, even when the one you're working with isn't at war with the entire world. I had to pull *quite* a few strings to get that madwoman's family to loosen their grip on his leash."

"What do you mean?" I forced myself to ask.

Sanja clicked her tongue, her hands hesitating for a second as she worked on my hair.

"Well, I'm sure Vanora has told you we were courtesans, once upon a time. It's a difficult life, but in the southern kingdoms it is an art," she said quietly. "We were trained from an early age to dance, paint, perform tea and wine ceremonies, sing, play instruments, the art of conversation, ... and in Axien's case, to fight, as well."

I fidgeted with my hands, flexing and curling my fingers while I tried to picture that. It was unlike any life I'd ever imagined—to be made into a walking piece of art meant for someone else's entertainment.

"Our peers were also our competitors, and we were always vying for a place at the sides of the most powerful people. You never feel safe. You learn never to trust anyone, because you're all vying for the same customers and patrons—all with the ultimate goal of securing a place of power at a nobleman or woman's side," Sanja explained.

My heart wrenched ruthlessly in my chest. No wonder Vanora and Sanja had a history. They might have been raised together, but they were also forced to compete.

It reminded me a lot of how my own kin acted in our

clans. Always plotting paths to the Brood Father's side. Murdering and scheming to win his favor and become a part of his court.

A deadly game of daggers and smiles.

"Vanora and I were both employed by the royal palace of Damaria, so we moved through those circles from the age of thirteen," Sanja explained. "But neither of us could have held a candle to Axien. He was ... bred for that sort of life. His Avoran blood made him a rarity. He was a prized jewel that would fetch a staggeringly high price. He was trained by the Aurati from birth, and they only produce the best."

"I've never heard of them," I admitted.

I frowned down at the hot, cloudy green bathwater and took in a deep breath of the steam that rose from it. It filled my lungs with the strong scents of lavender and marjoram oils.

"The Aurati? Oh, that's not surprising, my dear. Theirs is a name only spoken in certain circles, and usually behind closed doors. They called themselves a guild that produces only the finest professional social artisans, but what they really do is facilitate high-profile individuals with ... pedigree pets."

I tensed. "O-Oh." I couldn't keep my voice steady.

"Peddling flesh is the least of their crimes." Her voice grew sharper, more bitter, as though the thought of them made her temper flare. "They arrange for children to be born with certain traits, like breeding horses or hunting dogs, and train them up to be sold. It's a nasty business hidden behind a gilded mask."

My stomach churned and rolled, and I couldn't tell if it was from hunger or feeling like I might puke. I couldn't fathom living in a world like that. Even I had a mother who had raised me. It sounded like Axien didn't even have that.

And then to be made into a pet and sold to some nobleman ... It made my skin crawl. But if Sanja was telling the truth, that was the world Axien had lived in up until four years ago.

Fates ... how in the world had she gotten him out of Tibrus? And who was the madwoman he'd been working for before?

I couldn't work up the nerve to ask before Sanja quickly changed the subject. Her voice was still tense, her words a bit too fast and clipped, as though she were eager to break away from that subject.

It must have brought up difficult memories for her.

She rambled on about missions they'd worked together, traveling across Damaria, and kept tugging on my hair. Before I knew it, she had combed it through with softening coconut oil and braided it into an intricate bun on the top of my head. She didn't even need pins or combs to hold it in place.

"Fates, I just hope this little errand goes smoothly. Normally, the mistress wouldn't bother sending so many of us on a simple delivery—even if it is for a highly valuable item. But enemies abound and these are proving to be interesting times. I've discovered more than one Tibran spy lurking in some of our usual haunts. That's partly why I chose this inn. It's far more public than we would prefer normally."

"Hoping to throw them off the scent?" I asked.

Sanja sighed and sat back against the wall, shrugging her slim shoulders. "That—and if it were up to Roxus, we'd be sleeping in someone's barn. That old bear might not mind roughing it, but so long as the Zenith's Call is paying, I'm going to have at least one night in a civilized bed with a fine glass of wine."

The image of Roxus as a big bear, making himself a nice little nest of hay in some random farmer's old barn, made a giggle burst past my lips.

Sanja's eyes went wide—then she burst out laughing, too.

It felt ... good. She wasn't exactly my choice of company,

but maybe she wasn't as bad as I'd first thought. We'd gotten off on the wrong foot, mostly thanks to our both jumping to conclusions. We could work together, though. And I might not mind having her around so much if she was what kept me from sleeping in barns.

It was sunset when we finally finished our bath and redressed, chatting on and on about my lessons with Vanora while we took our time. She offered to tutor me a little if I needed more practice, and I agreed. I could use all the help I could get.

"Vanora and I trained under an elder, more experienced courtesan in an apprenticeship," Sanja chatted as we made our way out of the bathhouse. "They call it a patronship, and our teachers are called sponsors. It takes years to learn everything, and you have to pay your sponsor a percentage of your earnings in exchange until you are old enough to debut to the court on your own, usually at about fifteen."

"So ... how old was Axien when he started his ... career?" I wasn't sure what else to call it.

She shrugged. "I'm not sure. He doesn't like talking about it. Typically, Aurati never make public debuts. They have already been sold before they ever appear at court. The rules are different for them, and they have far less say in what happens in their lives. Some go as young as ten, but I'm uncertain how old Axien was when the senator's wife bought him."

I stole a glance at her, my next question writhing on my tongue like a live eel. I wanted—no, *needed*—to know why he had been thrown into the stocks for execution. What had happened? She'd mentioned a manhunt for him, so it must have been something terrible. Something only conscription to the Zenith's Call could save him from.

It couldn't be worse than accidentally killing a blacksmith, right? Murder? Or had he tried to flee that life?

My chest prickled with unease, and I took a deep breath,

steadying myself to ask. Even if the answer was something awful. I had to do it now, before we went back into the inn. I seriously doubted Axien would love knowing he'd been a major topic of conversation for us.

Sanja stopped suddenly, right in front of the inn's door, and put a hand out in front of me. Her head moved slowly, turning until her gaze locked with mine.

My stomach dropped.

All the light seemed to drain from her expression. Her big, dark eyes darted to something behind me for the briefest instant. Her brow creased faintly, and her hand slowly moved back to brush against the place where she had a small knife tucked into her waist wrap.

We were being followed.

My pulse slammed against my ribs, hard and slow like a smith's hammer on an anvil. Each beat sent a surge of adrenaline sizzling through my body. I felt it all the way to my toes.

Was it Tibrans? Or someone else?

I couldn't tell. Turning to see would give away that we were onto them. We only had seconds.

Sanja threw her head back and let out a too-loud laugh. She clapped a hand onto my shoulder and leaned in like she was whispering a secret. "Alley in the back. You know what to do."

In an instant, all the training that had been hammered into my head for the last two years snapped into perfect focus. I clenched my fists. My shoulders tensed. Every flurry of panic and dread fell as silent and still as snowflakes in my mind.

My senses opened, feeling the pressure of her presence, the eyes of someone else watching us like a tickle on the back of my neck. The distant murmur of the crowds at the plaza seemed to fade to silence. My breathing slowed.

I didn't have my blades. Sanja hadn't brought any weapons either, apart from that little knife.

But I didn't need daggers to be deadly.

A little head start would suit just fine.

Sanja jostled me a little, putting on a show. Pretending this was all normal. She laughed again, and seized the doorknob with one hand, her other still close to her waist wrap.

Then, through a wide, toothy smile, she whispered, "Break away 5 ... 4 ... 3 ..."

On one, we both moved.

TWENTY-ONE

T his would be ugly.

There was no room for second-guessing or foul-ups.

We had to move as one.

Sanja ripped the small knife from her waist wrap and thrust it into my hand, then tore the door open and dove inside. At the same moment, I darted to the left, sprinting for the narrow alleyway that ran between the bathhouse and the inn.

She needed time—a diversion—to reach Axien and Roxus and let them know what was happening. I was smaller and faster. Probably better with a blade, too.

It had to be me.

I'd give her all the time I could.

Gripping the little blade in my hand, I raced the length of the alley. My feet flew over the cobblestones, and I whirled around the corner of the building to the back of the inn.

The scrape of footsteps behind me set my blood aflame. They were following.

Good.

I ducked into the gloom of a nook between two large crates and waited, holding my breath. Every nerve in my body sang with a rush of energy.

Footsteps approached, getting closer. Panting breaths. The rustle of fabric, probably a cloak. The faint straining whine of a crossbow string.

Curse it. I'd have to strike first—before they spotted me and tried to fire that crossbow.

I changed my hold on the knife, coiling my legs beneath me, as two men stepped into the narrow passage behind the inn. It wasn't eight feet across and crowded with barrels and crates. Close quarters for a fight.

"*Vedra'tavas!* Do you see her?" a male voice rasped, still heaving for breath as he walked closer to my hiding spot.

My heart hit the back of my throat as they stepped into view.

Two men, medium build, dressed in common clothes. No armor apart from some pauldrons, vambraces, and leather waistbelts with shortswords strung on them.

Mercenaries? Tibran spies? Why would they be after us already? We didn't even have the artifact yet.

I held perfectly still, not daring to breathe, as one of them passed within two feet of my hiding spot and turned his back.

"No," the other man growled. "She can't have gone that far."

"She's pitathi," the first argued. "You have no idea what they're capable of. And he warned us she would be dangerous, so what does that tell you? If he's worried about—"

"I don't care what he thinks," the second man interrupted. "I've never let a quarry escape. I don't intend to start today."

"She's not just any quarry, and he's not the one out here risking his neck." The first man, the one standing with his back to me, had that crossbow clutched in his hands like his life depended on it.

Because it did.

He had to go down first. Before he had time to fire a shot.

Then it would be close combat. Reloading a crossbow took time and no small amount of effort. I had to make sure he stayed down. No chance to fire again.

My lips curled back in a snarl. They'd come here for me, apparently. So I'd give them as much of me as they could stand.

Like the snap of a whip, I lunged for him. My arm snagged around his head, covering his eyes while I plunged that little knife into the side of his neck.

He let out a garbled cry and pitched wildly, trying to fling me off. The bowstring snapped, the arrow pinging off the stone side of the building. I twisted the small blade, digging it to the hilt.

His companion shouted in alarm, rushing for us with his shortsword drawn.

Blood soaked my hand, making my grip on the small knife slip. I couldn't get it free. With a hiss of frustration, I kicked away from the first man and sent him crumpling to the ground, clutching at his neck and gasping.

The second one lunged, and I dropped into a backbend as his sword sailed over me. The wind howled off the blade's edge. My legs burned as I kicked over and landed in a crouch, then sprang straight for him.

He was far bigger, but I was faster. Each swing of that blade was a commitment. A chance.

Or so I thought.

I whirled, dodging another strike of his sword, and cocked a fist back. One hit to the nose, at an angle, would break it and push the bone up into his brain. Instant death.

Black powder suddenly filled the air, burning my eyes and throat.

I staggered back, gasping and coughing. My lungs

spasmed, eyes immediately welling. Curse it! What in the abyss was this?

CRACK!

Something slammed against the side of my head, sending me reeling. My head spun, and I hit a stack of crates with a crash.

"You thought you'd get the upper hand on me? You disgusting beast," the man seethed, his voice coming from somewhere close by. "You should have stayed underground."

My vision swam as my eyes stung, still tearing, and my throat burned with every gasping breath. But my ears worked just fine.

His clothing rustled with a fast movement. I ducked to the side, and the wood of the crate crunched right next to my head. My attacker let out a howl of frustration and pain, and I launched myself at him full speed.

It wasn't enough to take him to the ground—not when I was scarcely half his size. It did throw him off balance, though, and I hooked a leg through his and twisted him into a wrestling throw. His sword clattered across the stone, and he barked another curse, already trying to throw me off.

I set my jaw, pain flaring through my body as he hit me in the side. But I refused to let go, wrapping my thighs around his neck and wrenching his arm into place so I could twist and pull it back—an arm bar I'd done to Varren countless times.

"Who sent you?" I snarled as I applied more pressure.

The man tried to flail, screaming and gasping.

I bore down a little more. "You shouldn't make a lady repeat herself," I scolded. "Talk. Or you can try fighting me with one arm and a broken collarbone. Your choice."

No answer.

The ligaments began to slip. I felt something in his arm snap. He screamed louder.

"I'm about to lose my patience," I warned.

"H-he ... didn't give us ... a name!" the man wailed. "Just coin! A lot of it!"

"For what? My head?" I demanded. "Or the others, too?"

"Just you!" he cried frantically.

I gave his arm a solid jerk. Cartilage cracked, and his screams reached a new octave.

"You should have known better than to fight a cornered Viperi," I hissed and flipped over to give his collarbone the same treatment with a sudden yank.

He wouldn't be swinging that sword again anytime soon.

I licked my lips, my eyes still stinging and streaming tears. But it was too delicious—the sound of his agony. He deserved it. He was an inferior predator, and he'd crossed into my territory and *dared* to hunt me.

He would pay dearly.

And I would relish every single second of it.

"Now, let's see how many fingers it takes for you to tell me your name and how long you've been following us." I seized his thumb and began bending it backward.

"VIOLET!" A deep, booming shout thundered over us.

I squinted up, trying to force my eyes to open. To see who it was. I couldn't.

"He's done. Let him go." I recognized Roxus's voice when he growled again.

Slowly, I let my victim go and scooted away across the ground.

"He attacked me *first*," I said, wiping at my eyes with my sleeves. "They were following us from the bathhouse."

"I know," Roxus muttered as he stomped over and seized the man by the collar. "Sanja warned us. She and Axien are doing a sweep of the area to see if there are any others."

"Maybe you can just ask him." I snorted and nodded to my would-be murderer dangling from his grip, sobbing like a child. "I've already softened him up for you."

"Perhaps," Roxus agreed, although I could hear the hesitation in his tone. "Go inside and wash your eyes out. Get your things packed up, too. We can't stay here tonight."

I wanted to argue. To curse at him. This was *my* kill—hadn't I earned it? They'd come after me, not him!

Unfortunately, I knew that edge in Roxus's tone. I didn't need to see his face to know he was giving me that smoldering, forbidding glare that made his eyes narrow and his nostrils flare a little. This wasn't up for debate. Whatever he had planned for that would-be murderer, it wouldn't be pleasant.

And he didn't want me to witness it—like I'd never seen violence or torture before. Ugh.

Fine. Stupid, overprotective, bear-man.

I shuffled to my feet, dusting myself off and wiping my eyes again. My vision was still foggy, but I could see well enough to limp back to the inn's front door and make my way upstairs.

Our room was dark and empty, with a tray of tea left out on the low table along with several covered metal dishes that undoubtedly held our dinner. My stomach gave a mournful growl as I limped past it. Gods, I needed to eat soon.

I used the basin of water on the shared washstand to rinse my face and eyes. Whatever powder that guy had thrown at me stung terribly and left my throat raw. A useful trick—I'd have to get some of it for myself.

I grabbed my haversack and my weapons, stole a swig of bitter, cold tea from one of the cups, and went back downstairs. Roxus was already waiting by the door, blood on his hands, a faraway expression on his stern, rugged face. He blinked when he saw me, his brow lifting as though to silently ask if I was okay.

I had a fresh bruise on my ribs, and my eyes were red and puffy. It hurt to swallow, too. I would survive, though.

"Come on, and keep your head down," Roxus murmured as he held the door open for me.

"It won't help if someone is already out there sending assassins after me," I grumbled. "They knew I was Viperi. They targeted me on purpose."

"Take it as a compliment," he chuckled softly as we set off across the lamplit plaza. "If they went after you first, they consider you the biggest threat."

Hmm. I hadn't considered that. It put a wry little grin on my lips, and I stole a glance up at him. "Jealous?"

"Offended, actually," he replied.

I laughed, and it made my bruised ribs flare with pain. Worth it, though. "Don't worry. We all know you're super dangerous and strong," I cooed in a patronizing tone as I petted his arm.

He chuckled again and nudged me away with his elbow. "Just keep your eyes open, kid. We're not even a day into this, and someone is already coming after us. Orvana warned this mission would be dangerous, but now I suspect she has severely underestimated our enemies."

Me—someone was coming after *me*.

It was sweet of him to make it collective. To subtly suggest that targeting one of our group meant targeting us all. But I was the one who really stood out. I was a liability now.

If this was indeed the Tibrans sending mercenaries or assassins to take me out, then going forward, I would have to double down on being more discreet. I'd have to find a way to make my Viperi traits less obvious.

Maybe Sanja would have some suggestions about that.

Until then, Roxus was right. I had to keep my head down. I had to work on keeping a low profile.

Otherwise, I would keep putting our entire mission in jeopardy.

TWENTY-TWO

Axien and Sanja were still missing.

My thoughts circled like vultures, wheeling slowly at the back of my mind in constant rotation. What if they had gotten attacked, too? Or worse ... what if they were both dead? How long were we supposed to wait for them? Would Roxus want to try tracking them down?

Or was it too dangerous now?

We had no idea what our enemies might be capable of. We didn't even know who they were, exactly. Tibrans of some variety seemed most likely, but even the pair of swordsmen who had come after me hadn't known the name of the people who hired them.

Whoever it was had enough sense to keep that a secret.

That knowledge sent a chill of unease up my spine as Roxus and I moved quickly through the darkened streets. Hoods up, heads down, fingers brushing the hilts of our weaponry. Every one of my senses drank in the stillness of the night, and my heartbeat thundered deep in my chest.

At this hour, the plaza was silent. All the shops, booths, and food stalls were closed, and the only figures staggering through the night were patrons who had overstayed their welcome at the local taverns.

And us, of course.

Roxus kept a brisk, anxious pace as he led us down side-streets without a single hitch or hesitation, as though he knew this city like the back of his hand. Maybe he did. I had no idea how far he'd traveled over the years or where he'd gone. He'd obviously been working with the Zenith's Call for a long time, so he had likely been all across the southern kingdoms.

I started to ask him if he'd been to Salnis recently—but we crossed onto a narrow road that led right along a steep cliff side, twisting around the very edge of the island. My steps dragged to a halt as my pulse skipped. Cold washed through me in a numbing flood.

I couldn't look away.

Bathed in the light of massive iron beacons, a dark stone structure stood atop a spire of exposed reef right offshore. It gripped the rock like a massive barnacle, less than five miles away. There were no visible windows. No signs of life anywhere, apart from the huge torches that flickered and danced in the night wind.

Necrolis Prison.

The name tolled like a doomsday bell in my head, so heavy and loud I felt it vibrating me to my marrow. It sent a jolt of panic through me from head to toe.

Chrysa ...

Her name scurried through my brain like the scrape of fingernails. There—she was right *there*. The Zenith's Call had locked Chrysa away in that place. She hadn't seen daylight in two years, and probably never would again.

My body refused to move, and my mouth went dry. I'd turned it over in my mind a thousand times—how close I had come to being where she was now. Or worse. Roxus had come to my rescue a lot over the years, and it was only because of him that I was standing on free ground right now.

But no one could save Chrysa from her fate. I tried to remind myself that she'd chosen this. She had gone through with her attack on Arx Eburna and the vault. She had murdered. She had lied right to my face.

And I hadn't been able to see through any of it.

Now she was there, locked away. Was she still seething with rage? Carving my name into those stone walls and dreaming of all the ways she would kill me if she ever got free?

Or was she wasting away in rusted iron chains, drowning in guilt and agony? Wishing none of it had happened? Praying to the heathen god of the void to set her free? Or to the god of mercy to end her?

Bile burned in my throat. My jaw clenched hard.

"It wasn't your fault," Roxus said, his voice nearly a whisper.

I flinched back, suddenly realizing how close he was standing. Fates, how long had I been staring at that place?

I shifted and looked away. "I know."

"Doesn't seem like it."

My mouth pinched up, and I flashed him a glare of warning, hoping he'd drop the subject.

He didn't.

"Chrysa made her choices. You're not responsible for any of that," he murmured without even looking my way. "Now she's alone with the consequences, and that isn't your burden to carry."

I swallowed hard. "I know that."

"Then what's got you so caught up?"

I had to think on that. On how to put it into words. The words were buried deep in the silt and mire of my wicked little heart.

"I should have been able to see what was happening. I

should have suspected something was wrong—or maybe she slipped up and I just missed the hint," I admitted, my tone sharp and bitter.

"That's the risk we all take when we begin trusting people, Vi. Sometimes you get hurt. But you get to decide if that experience defines you or refines you." He put a steady hand on my shoulder. "I know you'll make the right choice."

I made a scoffing sound—if only so he wouldn't notice how my eyes were welling again. It wasn't from the powder bomb this time, though. This man had so much faith in me for absolutely no reason. I'd never understand it.

I'd never deserve it, either.

Roxus didn't push the issue any further as we hurried along the narrow road that hugged the sheer cliff side. We didn't pass other travelers, and it would have been difficult for anyone to follow us without being spotted. That, I assumed, was why he'd chosen this path.

Still, he didn't slow his pace. His every movement was sharp and swift, eyes panning the area and checking behind us.

"See anything?" he murmured, and I knew what he meant.

I glanced back over my shoulder, blinking hard to switch to my heat vision. But there were no warm bodies lurking in the shadows. Nothing but a faint glow off the stones on the road that had spent the day baking in the sun.

"Clear," I replied.

He gave a grunt of approval and forged onward.

The road ahead was fully exposed to the ocean on one side, though, and the blast of the chilly wind off the water left my cheeks and nose numb. The ocean was nothing but a vast, dark void in the night, lit only by ambient starlight that occasionally caught on the white crests of waves. Far offshore, away from the dangerous reefs that lurked just beneath the water's surface, the lights on ships bobbed and winked.

Once we rounded a sharp curve, the lights of a port city

came into view close to the water's edge. It wasn't anything like the Kaltori Plaza, though. If anything, this looked like a shabby little fishing town.

Fantastic.

The streets weren't lit or paved, and I had to dodge where wagon wheels had worn deep ruts in the mud. Drunken sailors ambled along the roadsides or were passed out on the front steps of ratty, rundown taverns. Everything—the docks, the buildings, and even the ships in the small harbor—seemed to be worn, waterlogged, and crusted in barnacles and sea salt.

This place was nothing like the fine sprawling port off the plaza. It smacked of shady debauchery. The sort of place you went when you had nowhere else to go.

I loved it instantly.

Roxus brought us to what must have been the most dilapidated, sketchy-looking tavern right on the easternmost edge of the docks. The ragged little place looked like someone sneezing too hard inside of it might make the roof cave in. Er, well, it and every other structure on this street. They'd fall like a house of cards thanks to how they all seemed to lean against one another.

Off-tune music filled the air as thickly as the stench of sour ale as we walked inside. It was packed nearly wall-to-wall with sweaty sailors in threadbare, weather-beaten clothes. A few buxom barmaids wove through the tables, carrying platters of food and tankards overflowing with frothing ale.

In the far corner, a pair of minstrels plucked at lutes and sang merrily, obviously too deep in their cups to care that their song was horrible. Pipe smoke hung like a low cloud in the room, filling the space with the scent of strong tobacco. It almost covered up the stench of all the body odor.

Almost.

Not a soul looked up from their ale, food, or card games as we moved toward the bar.

I stole a glance up at Roxus from under my hood.

"Pirate town?" I whispered.

His broad, cunning smile was answer enough.

Right. Definitely a pirate town.

We settled at a table near the back of the room and waited. Roxus ordered drinks and meals—a platter of unidentifiable roasted meat, hard cheese, and stale bread. I didn't care how old any of it was or how bitter the ale tasted; I hadn't eaten a real meal all day. Food was food. So I wolfed my plate down and picked at his like a thieving crow until he finally surrendered it.

Normally, I wouldn't have given a meal like this a second thought, but the past two years of eating Delthene's fine cooking must have weakened my constitution. My stomach was already aching by the time the tavern door opened again, and two familiar figures stepped inside.

Immediately, my shoulders dropped, and a breath slipped past my lips.

Axien and Sanja made their way toward us, sliding into the chairs across from ours with their hoods still pulled down low to hide most of their faces in shadow. It did nothing to hide the way Axien's glowed like two blue stars, though.

I fought not to react when he gave me a quick wink.

Ugh. Curse him.

"All clear," Sanja said in a low, breathless whisper. "They were mercenaries—hired muscle. We found a few more, but were able to lead them off our trail. But this complicates things, I'm afraid. We can't wait for the ferry in the morning, so I've made arrangements for us to leave for Esfolar within the hour. Best not to tarry here any longer than necessary. It's much harder to hit a moving target, after all."

Roxus gave a slow nod of agreement. "And you're both all right?"

"Tired, but whole." Axien's gaze flickered in my direction,

those bright spots of his eyes doing a speedy pass over me as though assessing for signs of injury. "And you?"

"I had to pry her off one of them like a feral alley cat," Roxus chuckled.

Heat tingled across my cheeks. Why did he have to say it like that?

Sanja reached across the table to grasp my forearm, her expression drawn in earnest concern. "I'm so sorry you had to go through that alone. For a young tandem on her first mission to wind up fighting two mercenaries completely on her own ... Fates, I should have stayed with you."

I stiffened, not sure what to do. Or say. Or think. No one had ever apologized to me like that before. Not about fighting, anyway.

"I, uh, it's okay," I said stiffly. "It wasn't a big deal."

"You followed protocol," Roxus said. "And Vi can handle herself in a skirmish. Now, we need to look to our next steps. Everyone ready to move?"

We all bobbed our heads.

Standing as one, Sanja led the way out of the tavern. We traveled swiftly along the rickety, rotting docks to where a small sloop bobbed and dipped at its moorings. Nothing special about it. If anything, it looked as battered and ramshackle as the rest of this place.

Maybe that was the whole point, though. A clever ruse. A shabby vessel like this wouldn't draw any attention ... providing it didn't sink.

Then I'd be swimming for my life and praying those tales of ancient, ship-swallowing sea serpents weren't actually true.

TWENTY-THREE

We had to get off this island—*now*.

Every second set my nerves on edge. Made me wonder how many of those mercenaries might be watching us, just waiting for the right time to strike.

Sanja was right. The sooner we got aboard the ship and left, the better.

A portly older man emerged from below deck as soon as we approached it, waving us in with a broad smile. "Welcome, welcome! Yes, this way! We'll make sail straight away!"

He motioned us toward a precarious little gangplank, guiding our group across the deck to the entrance of the cabin below deck. Sanja and Roxus lingered above, talking to the captain in hushed voices, but with my stomach now aching and my side throbbing from the hit I'd taken, all I wanted was a place to sit down.

Below deck, the cabin wasn't much—a long room with porthole windows, stacked crates and barrels tied down to the floor, and walls with thick nets. Rusty iron lanterns hung from hooks along the ceiling down the middle of the cabin, swaying with the motion of the rolling waves.

I found a place near the door and dropped my bag before sinking down onto my rear. No soft bed or luxurious cushions. No tea or glittering view of the bustling plaza.

Not at all where I'd been expecting to sleep tonight. Er, well, today. It was nearly dawn now.

I puffed a sigh, crossed my arms around my middle, and leaned back onto my bag, using it as a lumpy pillow. Good enough. My ribs were still throbbing. My stomach had already started making ominous grinding sounds thanks to my food choices. The sloshing of the ship wouldn't help me in that department.

Uggh. This was going to be a long ride.

"Roxus will want us to set watches," Axien muttered as he stood over me. His tone was frostier than usual.

"Well, then feel free to wake me if you need me to kill any more mercenaries," I said and closed my eyes.

He made a scoffing sound. "Not worried about another attack?"

"No."

"Why not? You were the one they were targeting, correct?" he sounded genuinely puzzled.

I smirked. "People wanting to kill me isn't new. Besides, I imagine it'll take a while for them to find another batch of mercenaries willing to take up the job once they see what happened to the last ones."

Fabric rustled and the floor thumped as he dropped his bag next to me and sat down. "Very well, then. I guess I'll keep first watch."

I cracked an eye open to peek up at him. He'd brushed his hood back, revealing an expression I couldn't quite interpret. His brows were drawn together, and his mouth was set in a hard frown. Dark circles shadowed his eerie, glowing eyes. His cheek and eye were still swollen from where Declan had apparently given him a warning pop, and he had a hint of dark stubble on his tense jawline.

Interesting. He must have been mixed with human blood, then, since elves didn't grow body hair.

Hmmm.

"His Avoran blood made him a rarity ... he was a prized jewel."

I shuddered as Sanja's words replayed in my head—the tale of how his life had begun. Was his mother the human? Or his father? Had he known either of his parents? If not, who had named him?

The naming ceremony was one of the most important moments in a Viperi's life. We weren't given names until we survived our fourth year of life. Then our mothers brought us before the brood father to be inspected. Only then would he give us our name.

"I thought you were going to sleep?" he murmured suddenly.

I flinched. Fates, how long had I been lying there staring at him?

Axien leaned forward, resting his elbows on his knees. Some of his dark hair spilled forward over his shoulders as he bowed his head. "If you want to say something, then just say it."

I rolled onto my side, facing him, and crossed my arms under my makeshift pillow. "Do you enjoy working with Sanja?"

"It's better than the alternative," he replied quietly.

Right. No surprises there, I guess.

"I don't particularly like the fighting, though," he added. "I had hoped for a ... different role within the order. But it seems my particular skill set makes me best suited for this."

I blinked, unable to hold back a confused frown.

Huh? He didn't enjoy fighting?

"You could have asked for a different assignment here, though, right?" I asked. "Surely Mistress Orvana would—"

"Sanja needed my help, and I owe her," he interrupted sharply.

Oh. Right. Because she'd spared him from being executed. But he didn't know that she had told me about that. Somehow, I doubted that was information he would have wanted to share so freely.

"And what about you?" His head turned, and he stared at me over his broad shoulder. One corner of his mouth quirked upward slightly.

I pursed my lips. "What about me?"

"If we're going to be sharing personal feelings, then I have questions, too."

I snorted. "Haven't you heard? Viperi have no feelings. Only black knots of iron and poison where our hearts should be."

"Would a girl with no feelings really go to such lengths to help a friend? I have it on good authority you even broke into a patron's private quarters to save her," he countered. "Even if it all wound up being a conspiracy that nearly brought down Arx Eburna. Still, you clearly had strong feelings for that Chrysa girl. We can discuss it, if you like."

I had to suck my teeth to keep from snarling. "No, thank you."

As if I would ever want to talk about that with him.

"Oh, come now. That's not fair, is it?" he scolded. "Let's have a trade, then. A truth for a truth?"

My body tensed, hands drawing into fists under my bag. Roxus had said almost the exact same thing to me when we first met.

Truth for truth.

"Ugggh. Fine. Ask—since there's clearly something on your mind," I grumbled.

A second slipped by, and his mouth quirked from one side to the other, almost like he was trying to sort out what he wanted to ask. Or how he should ask it, rather.

"That fellow you train with at Arx Eburna, the Vindexori," he began. "What is he to you? Apart from a willing punching bag, of course."

"Not much other than that, honestly," I replied flatly.

"Really? Interesting." He didn't sound convinced *at all*.

I rolled my eyes. "It's really not. We train together. It's ... simple."

Axien tilted his head to the side, his expression puzzled. "Is it? I've overheard the things the other Vindexori say to him about you. He never protests. Never defends you to them."

A laugh burst past my lips. "Why would he?"

Axien's eyes widened, looking more confused than ever.

"Varren's a jerk and an idiot, but he can take a beating. So we spar together. That's it. We're not friends," I said. "I don't need him to defend my honor."

Somehow, it didn't come out as convincing as I'd hoped. More like I was desperately trying to explain myself.

I guess Axien wasn't buying it, either. His bewildered stare gradually drew into a thoughtful frown as he watched me. "I see."

I scowled indignantly. "You see what?"

"It's safe—having him be the one you train with. There's a boundary there neither of you will cross. An understanding. Unlike before ... with *her*."

My heartbeat skipped. I clenched my teeth.

He was talking about Chrysa again. Why did he have to keep bringing her up? Was it some sort of tactic to try and pry his way past all my mental fortifications?

I flicked him a scowl of warning.

Axien ignored it. "You let her become more. You let her get close. Too close. Right?"

An ember of rage sparked to life deep in my chest. "Screw you. I'm not answering that. Besides, it's supposed to be *my* turn to ask a question."

He chuckled softly, as if he found my angry hissing amusing. "Ask, then."

Fine. If he was going to go straight for the painful, personal stuff ...

"You won our match," I reminded him, trying to pour as much snark into my voice as possible. "So why haven't you claimed your *prize*? What? Did you realize too late how disgusting it would be to kiss a Viperi?"

His eyes widened before he blinked hard a few times, like I'd just slapped him or something. Then, that wolfish grin split his thin lips and stretched so wide it dimpled one of his cheeks.

Axien leaned a little closer. "Is that an invitation?"

"No!" I balked. Gods, that had backfired spectacularly.

He chuckled darkly and leaned away again. "Good. I'd have to refuse even if it was."

"What? Why? You were the one who wanted to wager on—"

"Because I'm saving it." He shrugged.

"Saving ... a kiss ... with me?" That made exactly *no* sense. Why save it?

Unless he was waiting for a moment when it would humiliate me the most.

His smug little chuckle was irritating. Something about it made me want to throat-punch him. Hard.

"You never know. It might come in handy later," he mused.

My lip curled, which only made him laugh again.

"Fine, then. Why didn't you use any of your fancy Avoran magic in our fight in the pit?" I demanded. "It's like you wanted a physical beating, too. Is that what gets you off?"

His smirk became dark and utterly vicious, like all that glee had suddenly been devoured in the flickering depths of those brilliant blue eyes.

It made my skin prickle wildly.

"You've been wondering what gets me off? Naughty girl. And here I thought we were going to keep things strictly professional."

Heat bloomed over my face, and I looked away. "N-no! I'm not—that isn't what I meant!"

His laughter was deep and rich. Sincere. And for an instant, his smile almost reached his eyes.

"Just ... just answer the question, idiot."

Axien tipped his head back, glancing up at the lantern that creaked and groaned overhead.

"First, you ought to know from your studies that magic of any kind is rare. It's a highly valuable skill to possess, and one that only races who can trace their lineage back to the foundlings first sired by the gods can possess. Flaunting it in a tavern full of criminals and influential people from Rienka's underbelly would be ill-advised. They'd absolutely remember me, and might even try coming after me. Not exactly an ideal outcome for an agent of the Zenith's Call."

Something in his tone, in the way he hesitated and dragged his bottom lip through his teeth, made it seem like that wasn't it. Whatever came next was the *real* reason.

"And?" I pressed.

Axien puffed a resigned sigh. "And second, I didn't need to use magic to win. It seemed like a waste."

I sat up a little. "Oh, but pinching nerves and bruising my pressure points? That's all fine?"

That devious smirk flickered across his lips again. "You never said it was off-limits."

I glared at him, letting the tense silence thicken between us before I finally rolled over and gave him my back.

"What about you? Is it true you fought that big fellow in

the pit before? The one who tried to put his fist through my face." I could still hear that irritating smirk in his voice.

I didn't move. "Yes. And I lost that fight, too."

Axien clicked his tongue. "Unsurprising. I imagine it was entertaining, though. He must have felt very guilty afterward."

I rolled back just enough to cast him another scorching glare. "What makes you say that? We've been sparring partners for years."

"Does this count as your question?" he asked, his tone still edged with smugness.

I blew an exasperated breath and went back to lying on my side, my back fully to him. "Sure. Fine. Whatever."

This little back-and-forth game was stupid, anyway.

"Well, he obviously cares about you a great deal," Axien said, like it should have been obvious.

My chest constricted, heart wrenching in a slow, painful twist at the thought. Thank the gods he couldn't see my face, because I couldn't hold back the way my mouth screwed up.

Yes, I knew Declan cared about me. He might have even thought we were friends. But friends didn't do the things I had done to him.

Gods, I'd nearly killed him.

"He doesn't," I fumed, knowing full well Axien would never buy that lie.

"He was very offended by my treatment of you. And while there's enough bad blood between our kin to make the ocean run red, his grudge against me seemed quite *personal*. You're special to him," his tone went sharp—almost accusatory.

"Why do *you* even care what Declan thinks about me?" I shut my eyes tightly, not expecting him to answer. Doing so would force him to show his hand, after all. His motives for all these stupid mind-games.

I doubted he'd want to risk that.

Axien's voice lowered, growing deeper and softer in a

way that sent chills scurrying over my skin. "Because if I'm going to pursue you, I need to figure out who my rivals really are."

My eyes flew open.

What?!

I started to sit up, to turn on him, but before I could even face him properly ... Axien burst out laughing.

"You take everything so literally," he snickered and dabbed at his eyes. "Rivals—honestly! As if I might just toss my hat into that arena. Someone in my position wouldn't dream of it."

Someone in *his* position? What did that mean? That he thought he was too good for someone like me?

A disgusting Viperi girl?

"And it would be a futile effort anyway, wouldn't it? With you spitting venom my way every chance you get. Why would anyone waste their time?" he continued. "But then again, they say love is a form of madness. For me, it most certainly would be."

Embarrassed heat flooded my face and crept up my collar. Even my ears were burning as I gaped at him, watching him double over and babble something else about teasing me. He flapped a hand at me and shook his head.

I ... *hated* it.

So, I stood, snatching my bag up, and stormed for the cabin door.

"Wait—where are you going?" He started to protest, doing an excellent job of looking genuinely confused.

I didn't answer. I didn't stop. I ripped the door open and left, letting it bang closed behind me. Even with that barrier between us, I could still hear him calling after me. Asking me to come back. To talk with him. I'd misunderstood. He'd only meant it as a joke.

Only, it wasn't a joke. Not to me.

I'd been teased in a lot of ways about a lot of things. But I did *not* like this. Not one bit.

He had no idea what it was like to be disgusting to everyone. To be seen as a vile little monster by any guy who might ever be interested in me. No amount of rouge, kohl, and social etiquette could compensate for what I was.

I knew I'd likely never know what it felt like to be loved like that. To be wanted. To be desired. I knew that I'd never be anyone's wife or lover.

I didn't have the blessing of alluring Avoran blood. Any love for me would be a waste.

And he didn't have the right to throw that in my face and call it a joke.

"Vi? Everything all right?" Roxus asked as I stormed past where he and Sanja were still out on the deck, watching the captain and his two-man crew ready our ship for sail.

I didn't answer and held my furious pace all the way to the bow of the ship. Sitting down with my back to the railing, I hugged my bag to my chest and glared at the toes of my boots.

Roxus didn't follow. Neither did Axien or Sanja. Good. What could I possibly say to any of them—especially Axien? I couldn't explain any of the thoughts that raced through my head. Not while all my words tangled like hot wire in my throat.

Stupid—how could I be so stupid? I'd let Sanja's tales of what Axien's life had been like before get under my skin. I had actually felt sorry for him.

That wouldn't happen again. Whatever else Axien was, he was not my ally. He certainly wasn't my friend.

I could be professional. I could work with him. But there would be no more personal discussions. No more questions.

No more trust.

TWENTY-FOUR

Axien was *still* sulking.

Sulking—like *I* was the one in the wrong for not laughing off his so-called "joke."

Whatever.

I'd lost all patience with it by the time we reached the eastern side of Esfolar. He still wouldn't so much as speak in my presence. He kept his gaze averted, his shoulders sagging, and his head down like a scolded puppy. Pathetic.

So much for professionalism.

I refused to acknowledge him and kept pace with Roxus and Sanja as we navigated what was, without a doubt, the biggest city I'd ever been in. The streets were wide—more than double the size of the ones in Kua'Tar—and paved with white stone that gleamed in the sunlight. Every road was packed with merchant caravans and wagons pulled by teams of horses and massive gray-skinned beasts I didn't recognize.

The sidewalks were just as packed, and I had to grab onto the back of Sanja's bag so we didn't get separated in the crowds of shoppers and civilians bustling through every square and avenue. The noise of thousands of voices, footsteps, and animals braying rumbled deep like the ocean. The smells of animals, spices, and sweat hung like a familiar balm in the salty sea air.

My still-sore neck throbbed as I stared up, mouth agape like a baby bird begging for food. Staggeringly huge buildings arched over roads and reached up to the sky with ten or even twenty levels crafted from more of that pearly white marble. Temples dwarfed the surroundings with golden-domed roofs, flanked on both sides by colossal sculptures of the gods.

I recognized one immediately as Undae, goddess of the sea. She was a favorite in Rienka, thanks to its coastal location.

But the other, Ishaleon, was new to me. I hadn't seen that many images of the god of mercy, his golden-leafed wings and arms outstretched as though he were embracing the population below. He was a younger member of the pantheon, according to the historical texts. He was also one of the so-called godlings who had chosen to remain in the mortal world, bound in flesh, to be reborn again and again after the Law of the Stones separated our realm from the divine.

Whatever or whoever he was, Ishaleon's face was youthfully handsome in this massive sculpture. His eyes were kind, and his mouth turned in a faint smile.

I couldn't help but smile back.

This whole place was odd—but not in a bad way. It made our home in Sol'Karr feel so ... insignificant. Just a distant speck of land.

I'd read that Esfolar was another major trade hub. This was the place where most of the goods brought in from the Rienkan islands were shipped by caravan to other cities around the southern kingdoms. Traders and merchants flocked here, doing business and managing their shipping routes in this dazzling urban splendor.

But to actually see it—to feel the rhythm of it under my

boots as we made our way through the tangled masses. Sweet Fates. I had no words. No thoughts except silent awe. I'd never felt so small in my entire life.

And that was saying something since I was barely five feet tall.

"We need to make contact with the caravan immediately," Sanja said, flicking a meaningful look at Roxus. "Let's not give our enemies a chance to realize we've arrived, hm?"

He nodded in agreement, then motioned to me. "We need to do a supply run, too. The caravan will provide a few things, but we need to bring our own water—enough to ration for at least five days."

"Does it take that long to get to Salnis?" I asked. After spending so much time studying maps of the various kingdoms, cities, and ruins throughout the world, I had guessed it might take two days, three at the most.

"That's if everything goes according to plan." Sanja puffed a weary sigh. "And, of course, it never does. So we need to be prepared in case there is a delay."

Ah. Right. Well, that made sense, I guess.

"Violet, Axien, both of you will see to collecting supplies before we embark," Roxus decided aloud. "Then meet Sanja and me at the caravan departure point on the eastern side of the city. Look for the lighthouse and then find the caravan with a black trio of diamonds painted on the sides of the wagons."

I couldn't keep my mouth from scrunching into a sour frown, my heart sinking straight to the soles of my boots. Great. I was stuck with him. *Again*.

Axien said nothing and accepted a few coins from Sanja to pay for the supplies, then took the lead as we parted ways. He made a point not to look my way as he wove through the crowds.

I moved swiftly, frantically trying to match the speed of his much longer strides. I ducked around the throngs of midday shoppers, merchant stands, and armored city guards patrolling in feathered gold helms. A lady balancing a basket on her head rushed between us, tugging along a string of four little children who were wailing in protest, sucking their thumbs, or squabbling with each other.

When she and her brood finally passed, I stared around for any sign of Axien's shoulder-length dark hair, pointed ears, or understated black leather armor.

Nothing. Just an ever-moving patchwork of fabric and people.

I turned in a circle, still searching as my pulse began to race. Where was he? What was I supposed to do if we got separated? I had no idea where I was in this gods-forsaken city. I might be able to find the eastern side, but that would mean walking all the way there on my own and hoping no one decided to attack me again once they noticed what I was.

A lump of panic lodged in the back of my throat a second before I felt a much larger, calloused hand close around mine firmly.

"Come along, little one," Axien muttered as he tugged me after him, still avoiding eye contact. "I'm surprised you, of all people, need to be led around like a lamb."

I wanted to snatch my hand away. His haughty tone immediately made me envision myself stuck at the end of that line of toddlers being towed around by their frazzled mother. Never mind that this was my first time being outside Sol'Karr since I was a child. And even then, where I'd been before didn't exactly count, did it?

The dark, subterranean halls of my father's kingdom?

Hardly.

Like it or not, I needed some guidance. To learn how to move in places like this.

That didn't mean I had to be nice about it, though. So I gave him a rude gesture with my other hand instead. Jerk.

Axien ignored it and pulled me after him until we crossed into another large square, moving to a portion of the market district that was thick with gridlocked wagons like a hopeless, eternal traffic jam. Each one was massive, grinding away on wheels of iron and wood, and pulled by teams of huge beasts I had no name for. They paid no attention to anyone walking past, swatting flies off their leathery gray hides with long, swishing tails with little tufts of coarse hair at the end.

Axien must have caught me marveling at them, because he muttered, "They're called olifants."

I mouthed the strange word, my thoughts whirling with a thousand new questions as I studied them—their milky brown eyes and long, almost pig-like snouts. Each one stood a good ten feet to the shoulder and had a ridge of thick, bony spines down its back that had been sawed down to accommodate the harnessing for the wagons.

Fates, they must have been fiercely strong to haul the lines of wagons loaded down with cargo.

"There. We need to hurry." Axien tugged on my hand again, urging me to walk faster as he led the way to the edge of the square, where large stalls were busy selling cargo directly to merchants.

Bags of rice and grain, dried meats and vegetables, large pots of oils, and large barrels of water were available to stock the caravans before they disembarked. Crews of sweat-soaked workers moved mountains of goods onto the waiting wagons, using lines of rolling poles to slide the heavier crates, barrels, and bags to their destinations.

All I could do was stare and try to absorb it all with my mouth hanging partway open in awe while Axien all but dragged me to a stall near the end of the square. It was smaller than the others, and the goods being passed along were also much more reasonably sized—not things sold in bulk, I guess.

Or, at least, not in the insane quantities the others were.

Axien wore one of his familiar, sickly sweet grins as he spoke to an elder merchant lady and placed our order. It must have worked, or he was using some of his magic, because she grinned back and flushed a little when she took his coin.

I curled my lip and jerked my hand away from his, opting to stand at his back with my arms crossed. I watched the constant movement of all the loading crews all around us until one individual caught my eye, standing head and shoulders over everyone else like a giant.

My breath caught.

The woman must have been nearly seven feet tall, her ruddy hair hanging down her back in thick woven locks adorned with golden rings and beads. Her deep bronze skin was covered in blue swirling tattoos, and her long pointed ears were pierced at least half a dozen times.

Her sleeveless tunic was short to expose her midriff, and her knee-length skirt was split up the sides all the way to her hips, exposing every inch of her brutally chiseled form. Fates, she was a tower of thick, hard muscle. Her wide jawline was clenched hard, expression fierce and focused, as she picked up two barrels and hefted them over her shoulders like they were nothing.

She was ... a Holvradix elf. And not just a half-blooded one like Declan.

I stared as she moved into the crowd, carrying the barrels and passing them to other workers inside the backs of the wagons. It took two or three men to manage the loads she handled like children's toys.

It was impossible to see her and not picture a massive claymore or greatsword in her hands, sneering down at an enemy that had dared to encroach upon her territory. A towering barbarian goddess, ruthless and mighty, suffering no fools.

Then I realized ... Holy Gods above, Declan's *mother* had probably looked like this. She had been a full-blooded Holvradix elf.

And his father ...?

His father had been a *very* brave human man.

"Why is your face so red?" Axien asked, appearing back at my side with two heavy canvas bags slung over his shoulder. He followed my gaze to the elven woman, his brows going up slowly.

"Oh," was all he said, and for an awkward moment, we both stood there gaping at the burly elf woman carrying around more barrels. I could have sworn his face paled a little, and he shrank back whenever she came close to where we stood.

But she never so much as glanced our way.

Thank the gods for that, I guess. Holvradix elves hated Avoran ones—a long-standing feud that practically went back to the dawn of creation. And, well, of course, no one was bound to be thrilled to see me, either.

Although, I had to wonder if maybe Holvradix elves didn't know about Viperi? They were from far off in the north, after all. Way beyond my kin's territory. As far as I had studied, there had never been any sort of battle or conflict between them.

But I didn't know for sure, and I was not about to ask.

I flinched some when Axien suddenly waved a slip of parchment under my nose. "Here, this is the receipt. Give it to Roxus later. They're bringing the water barrels to the wagons for us. We need to get going."

I crammed the paper into my pocket without replying and followed him again, keeping my hands to myself this time. My head throbbed with a dull ache right at the base of my skull.

Probably a side effect of being out in the sun too long. It was a common misconception that just because Viperi came from the desert; we were creatures of it.

No. Absolutely not.

Viperi lived *under* the desert, the cool reprieve of caverns and the forgotten ruins of Avoran cities. Not in the sun. Not even a little.

You didn't stay this pallidly porcelain otherwise. And you certainly didn't need pristine heat vision unless you lived in a place of perpetual cold darkness.

I would have welcomed some of that right about then. Or a little shade. Maybe a sip of water, too—but I was not about to be the one whining about being thirsty when we had work to do.

Gods, how long had we been out here? Hours?

The crowds thinned as we left the merchant and market district behind, keeping to a main road that ran straight through the city like a main artery. It funneled all that traffic and the long caravans to the east. Toward the yawning mouth of the desert that led into the kingdom of Nar'Haleen.

The sun sank at our backs, and my feet grew sore from hurrying over the hard stone. But I refused to slow down and matched Axien's gait so he wouldn't try leading me along like a child again.

The white marble of the sidewalks sparkled and shone faint orange under the evening glow. We passed block after block of towering buildings with fine balconies decorated with silks and plants, bustling restaurants and lounges where patrons sat at low tables under the glow of colored glass lamps, and beautiful homes like slim palaces with jade columns.

Small squares boasted gardens with more sculptures or fountains at the center, and for the first time in a long time, I didn't smell the sea. No brine on the wind or hint of salt on my tongue. We were moving too far inland.

And it set all my nerves on edge.

I studied every person we passed, noting their features and whether or not they glanced my way. Were they carrying weapons? Did they seem too interested in us?

Were they more mercenaries? Were they looking for me?

An individual on the far side of the road made me stop cold. He sat at a street corner, minding a modest little fruit stand made of a hodgepodge of wooden crates. His dark face sagged from protruding cheekbones, skin wrinkled by days spent in the blazing sun. He wore a faded purple cloak and a wide-brimmed straw hat—not exactly the garb of a trained killer.

But his entire body was wreathed in a faint halo of glowing blue.

Magic.

A disguise.

My stomach gave a violent twist. It couldn't be ... Domitri?!

No. *No*—that was impossible. That Rajinna man was dead. Roxus had told me he'd succumbed to his injuries after trying to break into the Vault of Whispers to steal the Black Ledger. And he'd never been Domitri. His name was Kalsin.

He was gone. Gone forever. Roxus would never lie about that.

I shut my eyes tightly, taking in a shaking breath before I dared to open them again.

I wanted to believe that Kalsin was really gone. That even if he hadn't died of his injuries after Roxus had literally bear-mauled him, the Zenith's Call had put an end to him for what he'd tried to do.

But I'd never seen the body. I didn't know for sure.

My heart pounded wildly, sending flashes of cold across my body in waves.

"Is there a problem? Are you hungry or something?" Axien had wandered back to my side.

I tried to speak, but my voice cracked and faltered. "That man ... he's ... something's not right," I barely managed to rasp.

His eyes narrowed as he followed my unblinking stare across the street to the old man sitting behind the fruit stand. Axien frowned thoughtfully, his mouth scrunching to one side.

"Ah, yes. The cloak. It's faint, but I can sense it. Old magic. Probably some sort of enchantment for luck or prosperity," he announced. "Completely harmless."

I gaped at him. What? The *cloak?*

"But the whole man seems ... off." I chose my words carefully.

Curator Faera had warned me about telling people about my so-called gift. My runesight. So far, only Roxus knew about it, and it had to stay that way.

"He's probably had it for a long time. After a while, artifacts like that have a way of bonding to people. Likely a family heirloom," he said.

I looked again, squinting harder at the man at the fruit stand. The glow definitely resonated from the cloak more strongly. Maybe he was right.

Hmm.

Axien flicked me a suspicious sideways glance. "How is it *you* can sense it at all? I did not think Viperi were born with any magic."

My pulse skipped.

Oh no. I couldn't let him catch on.

I scowled and turned to start walking briskly again. "I didn't *sense* anything. He just seemed strange." Not a complete lie.

Axien fell in step beside me quickly, still lugging the two

bags over his shoulder. He made a thoughtful humming sound, like he didn't quite believe me.

"I assume you sense it because you're Avoran?" I added, turning the subject back to him. A redirection, as Vanora called it. A subtle way of controlling the conversation, since most people enjoyed talking about themselves.

"Something like that," he replied, his tone ominous and tight. "Magic is a fickle thing. But the things it's touched tend to call to one another. Not loudly, mind you. It's more like a whisper on the wind. It's not always clear, but I can sense its presence like a scent lingering in a room."

I swallowed hard. Goosebumps rose on my arms. I'd never heard anyone talk about magic that way, and yet Axien must have known so much about it.

"Also ... I've bought figs from that man before and we chatted about it," Axien added suddenly, flashing me a wink and a wolfish grin. "There are Avoran runes stitched all over the inside of it. It's obvious. I'm surprised you didn't notice it. Tsk tsk. What a slacker you are."

Ugh. Of course. Back to teasing. Gods forbid we have any real conversations that didn't end with him taking a jab at me or treating me like an idiot.

I shot him a scathing glare. "I really can't stand you."

His smile dimmed a little. "I know."

We continued on, crossing streets and opting for quieter back roads as we drew closer to the far eastern side of the city. Minutes crawled by, and the sun sank lower and lower behind us. We passed fewer people and only the occasional wagon or two, and there was nothing to fill the tense silence apart from our footsteps.

Then, at last, Axien spoke up. "Am I allowed to know why?"

"Why what?"

"Why do you despise me so much?"

I stopped again, wheeling on a heel to face him with my hands on my hips. "You really want to know?"

He stopped, too. Facing me, his expression a strange mixture of uncomfortable concern and curiosity. Like he couldn't decide if he really wanted the answer or not.

His thin lips mashed into a crooked line as he nodded once. "I do."

Fine, then.

"Because I don't think you're trustworthy," I said flatly, pulling no punches for the sake of social grace. Vanora would have been horrified. "You talk constantly, but only in half-truths. To me, that's the same as lying. Then you walk around with this sense of assurance that everyone finds you *so* charming. You tease me, mock me, and treat me like a joke—then wonder why I don't adore you like everyone else at Arx Eburna. You even act shocked when I'm upset about it!"

Stop. I should stop.

But I couldn't. Not when my blood was roaring in my ears and every word felt like the twist of a dagger I'd been longing to plunge into his puffed-up chest.

"You think I'd ever put my trust in someone who can't wait to point out everything wrong with me? To do everything they can to make me feel small and worthless? Smirk and laugh all you want, but I know when I'm being mocked and patronized. It's not hilarious or endearing." I took a daring step closer and jabbed a finger at the center of his chest. "I'm fully aware nearly everyone considers me vile and the last person in the world they'd ever want to be with."

He cringed back, his eyes wide.

"But you just love reminding me of that, don't you? Does it make you feel superior?" I demanded. "Are you so desperate for an ego-boost that you feel the urge to constantly punch down?"

Axien winced, lips twitching in a snarl. His cheeks flushed in anger, and he leaned down closer like he might snap a reply.

But I wasn't finished yet.

"That is why I don't like you," I hissed, stepping forward to meet him nose-to-nose. "Because you've got everyone else fooled, but I see who you *really* are behind that stupid smile. Like knows like, right? And you're a twisted, insecure, sick monster, just like me. You just had the good fortune to be born with a prettier mask to hide it all behind."

His brows furrowed slightly, his mouth opening like he might protest. A second passed. Then another. His chest heaved in angry breaths, but he didn't say a word.

He didn't have to. There was nothing else he could say—not to me.

"But it doesn't matter how I feel about you. Like it or not, I have to work with you. So let's just be professional. Surely even you can manage that for a few days," I muttered.

I shut my eyes tightly and rubbed my throbbing temples. Just looking at him for too long gave me a headache. He made all my instincts rage against all my better sense like a beast against a cage. Hungry to break free—to break him.

But that wouldn't help.

I was already braced for another joke. One last taunt or a jab at me for having the typical sour Viperi temper. He always had to have the last word.

But Axien stayed quiet. Seconds passed, and the silence grew heavy. Stifling.

I forced myself to look up at him again.

Axien stood eerily still, staring down at me with no traces of that roguish, easy smirk or even a snarl of fury. His brow was slack and his lips slightly parted, like he'd started to speak but lost the words. His strange blue eyes barely had a hint of light in them as they searched mine with quiet desperation.

Then, slowly, his gaze lowered. His head bowed, and he blinked owlishly.

He looked ... utterly lost.

Our eyes met. Something tugged at the pit of my stomach. Dread? Or regret? I wasn't sure, but it stung.

"Very well, then," he answered quietly. "Professional it is."

A sinking ache burrowed through my chest. And in an instant, I felt something deep inside me crack.

Something buried so deep I hadn't even known it existed until it was far too late.

TWENTY-FIVE

Nothing felt the way it should.

I'd finally done it. I'd said everything I felt about Axien right to his face.

So why did my stomach keep spinning and swirling like I was about to puke? Gods, it was the same sensation when I tried to fib to Delthene or Roxus. Like all the earth beneath me was suddenly unsteady.

I twisted my mouth to the side so I could chew at the inside of my cheek.

Why should I feel bad about speaking my truth? Especially when he'd asked me for it outright?

I lagged behind, my thoughts and heart still racing like mad. My skin had gone clammy and strange, like a tingling cold I couldn't shake. My vision swam a little and my head still pounded.

Meanwhile, he walked ahead and never said another word. Even as we reached the eastern edge of the city, the tension still hung so thick in the air I could practically taste it.

And, gods, it was bitter.

Every part of me felt cold, numb, and far too heavy as we left the cobbled streets behind and turned our path slightly north, heading for Esfolar's grandest and oldest monument.

One I'd prayed I would never see again.

The huge white stone spire rose up from the craggy earth, its base crowded with hundreds of wagons all preparing to disembark. It loomed well over a hundred feet, topped with an immense brazier half encircled in a globe of glass and mirrors to make the firelight within shine like a small star.

The lighthouse.

I'd read about it while I studied ancient Avoran architecture, of course. Even before that, I had known it was here, so seeing it still standing wasn't a surprise. It had guided caravans across the vast desert for centuries, built right where it would shine through the stone gap between the mountains like a beacon of hope. I'd heard you could see it all the way from Dumathis.

But I had only glimpsed it once before, many years ago, from the back of one of Sulam's slave wagons.

Standing before it again like this brought every foul memory of Sulam slithering back into my mind. My hands drew into fists. I didn't even notice when Axien stopped a few paces ahead of me and greeted Sanja and Roxus. Their mouths moved as they chatted, and Axien handed off the bags he'd been carrying, but my ears rang too loud to discern any of it.

I could only hear the scrape and groan of the wagon wheels over the rocks still echoing through my mind. Could only smell the putrid reek of the corpses around me—other captives who had succumbed to heat and thirst days ago. Could still feel the pocked, rusted iron bars between my fingers as I peered out and saw that manmade star glittering in the distance.

"You must have no mercy, Visha, because this world will have none for you."

A cold sweat prickled over my skin as the evening wind seemed to carry my mother's voice straight to the core of my soul. It made every muscle draw tense. Ready to snap.

Ready to run.

Sulam had found me in that desert. In a wretched, disgusting, completely unfair way ... he had saved me. But only because he wanted to use me for his wicked schemes. Only because I might be worth a little coin.

He'd thrown me into that wagon, amidst the rotting, bloated bodies of the dead. He probably hadn't expected me to survive the rest of the journey to this place.

But I had.

And now I was back.

Again ... again.

Not again.

The smell of the olifants hit me like a punch to the face. The sound of the wagon wheels grinding over the gritty soil, the crack of whips, the creaking groan of axles, and the hiss of the dry wind. It brought it all back.

I couldn't breathe. I wasn't safe. Not here. I had to run, I had to—

My knees buckled.

The ground rushed up, and I couldn't stop it. I couldn't force my body to move. Or react.

Someone caught me, grabbing me out of the air before I hit the earth face-first. I gasped wildly, fighting for every breath as my lungs seemed to squeeze tighter and tighter.

"VIOLET!" A deep voice barked my name as a hand gripped my chin and jaw, forcing me to look up.

Roxus.

My head lolled forward against his shoulder. "I'm okay," I slurred.

"Curse it, no, you aren't. Have you had anything else to eat or drink since that slop at the bar?" he scolded, his voice rumbling deep against my ear. "You can't do that out here. We're not on the island anymore. You have to keep hydrated."

"What's wrong?" Sanja's voice sounded close, too. But I couldn't get my eyes to open to be sure.

"Fates, she's burning up. We've got to get her somewhere cool right now. Get her something to drink," Roxus ordered. "Idiot—weren't you paying any attention? I told you to look after her!"

"I-I—" Axien stammered. "She didn't complain! She never said she was thirsty!"

But Roxus cut him off. "Well, she wouldn't, would she? When she's used to everyone judging every move she makes? She never complains when she's in pain. She'll push herself until she's nearly dead. That's why I told you to pay attention, idiot!"

Stop. He needed to stop.

I didn't want this. It wasn't Axien's fault. It was mine.

I should have known better than to assume a little rotten food and some sour ale would be enough. I hadn't had anything else since. No wonder I'd felt sick all day. My headache. The cold sweats. It was heat exhaustion.

Idiot—*I* was the idiot!

"Calm down, Roxus. We'll get her seen. There's still plenty of time before the caravan departs," Sanja cooed softly. "Axien, dear, why don't you take her? That wagon there is for us to take breaks. Our stuff is already loaded, and there are a few waterskins by our bags. Roxus, take a second to cool your head, too, hm? We'll see if we can buy a few melons so she can eat something with a little sugar in it."

Roxus made a growly, huffing noise that must have been agreement, because he jostled me some, muttering angrily under his breath as he passed me over to Axien. The only words I caught were "... watching you, boy."

Great. He was fussing like a broody old hen.

And I couldn't do anything about it.

How utterly humiliating.

I managed a pathetic groan of protest, drifting in and out of consciousness as Axien carried me away, his arms sturdy but stiff. Almost like he was afraid I might suddenly sit up and punch his teeth in for holding me like this.

Sadly, that wasn't an option. Not with my head still spinning and throbbing. My pulse wouldn't slow, and my arms and legs flopped uselessly. My head came to rest against his chest, right at the crux of his throat, and I could hear the rapid thump of his pulse in my ear.

Fast with anger. Or panic. Or fear.

I wasn't sure, and I couldn't see his face to check. I couldn't see much of anything, really.

I caught only blurry glimpses of the caravan we were joining—a long line of wagons with a trio of black diamonds painted on the sides. All of them were tethered to teams of monstrous olifants, aimed for the gap between the distant mountains.

This barren, chalky-white valley was the only road out. The Deadlands, they called it. It was the biggest pass through the Dei'Lurn Mountains that made a sort of natural boundary line between Damaria and Nar'Haleen. There were a few other places you could cross, but they were hundreds of miles to the north.

No, the fastest path was straight ahead. Right into the teeth of the vast desert that waited beyond those mountains. The same desert that had claimed my mother's life.

Axien brought me to the back of one of the covered wagons, hefting me into the cool reprieve of the shaded interior where a few bedrolls had already been arranged for us amidst stacks of crates.

"You should have said something. Fates, why didn't you? No wonder you've been angrier than usual," Axien murmured as he laid me down, cradling my head so I didn't crack it off the floor. "Focus on breathing. In and out. You've got to slow your pulse."

I tried. But it was nearly impossible to concentrate when my brain felt like sloshing soup in my skull. Every thought was blurred. My body flashed between hot and cold, and my skin was slick and strangely chilled with sweat. I couldn't get my teeth to stop chattering.

My common sense was lost somewhere in that murky mess, and as soon as Axien sat down next to me, bending over to hold my head gently and press a waterskin to my lips, I gripped his arm like a lifeline.

I drank, and drank, and drank.

At first, he didn't say anything. Not even when he yanked a handkerchief from his pocket, poured more cool water over it, and pressed it against my forehead. His expression stayed focused, jaw tight, and sharp brow creased.

His eyes gleamed like two pale blue stars, flickering over me with intense appraisal. Or was that concern?

Nooo. Nope. Not possible, not from him.

He wiped the sweat from my neck with that handkerchief, and I could have sworn I felt his fingers comb through my hair, raking it away from my face gently.

Almost tenderly.

Or maybe I'd just imagined that.

Minutes passed, and Axien remained close, feeding me swallows of cool water and forcing me to stop now and again to catch my breath. With every gulp of water, my pulse began to slow. My thoughts slowly cleared, although my body still felt so weak I could hardly sit up without his help. There wasn't a single part of me that wasn't limp and trembling with exhaustion.

But the fog in my brain was fading. The ringing in my ears ebbed away, and I heard him muttering something under his breath. Something familiar I couldn't quite place.

Then, little by little, those whispered words began to make sense.

I-I knew that language. I'd studied it for two years.

It was Avoran.

Granted, reading a language on paper was a lot different than hearing it spoken. And this was the first time I had heard Avoran spoken by someone native to it. Someone who knew the right inflections and accent. Who understood the rhythm of the sentences.

It changed everything.

"She looks to the stars and laughs, for her beauty outshines them all. She dances through the halls of time, the winds of fate in her hair, and the light of a thousand ages in her eyes. She sings, and the mountains bend a knee. The seas roar in answer. She winds the threads of my soul as ribbons in her hair. She wears my heart as a jewel at her throat. And I am lost. Lost to her unto the end of days."

Was that a poem? Or a song? It had to be, for each word to match in rhythm and flow in the Avoran language. But it wasn't one I had ever read or heard before. It wasn't in any of the Zenith's Call books.

I stared at him, totally entangled in those words. A language as old as the foundations of the earth that flowed like music from his lips. My grip on his arm tightened, and I told myself it was so he wouldn't take the waterskin away.

Then his gaze shifted, fixing on me with sudden force.

My heartbeat skipped. I tensed, gasping in sharply through my nose.

Axien looked away just as quickly.

No smile. No hint of any emotion at all.

Why? Why say things like that? What did it mean? Was

this something he'd been taught before—when he was still with the Aurati?

Yes, that had to be it. It was meant to soothe, like a lullaby. Not something he'd expected me to actually understand. It didn't mean anything.

It couldn't.

"Axien?" I started to ask. Or maybe apologize. I honestly wasn't sure.

I'd been too harsh with him, hadn't I? I'd been irritated because of the dehydration. I'd thrown aside all Vanora's training and acted like a feral little monster again. I'd lashed out instead of staying in control.

He pulled away from my grasp and set the waterskin aside, his empty expression never changing as he started to get up.

"W-wait, I—" I reached for him again, but he swiftly angled himself to be just out of my reach.

"You should rest," he said, his tone a firm warning as he got to his feet. His long black cloak rippled in the dry wind, licking at his boot heels as he turned away. "Drink more, if you can. I'll be back in a few minutes to check on you."

"Where are you going?" I managed to wheeze.

His broad shoulders tensed, but he still didn't look back. "Not far. I just ... need some air. I'll be right outside."

I swallowed hard, unable to muster another sound before he hopped out of the back of the wagon and let the canvas flap shut behind him.

Right. Air.

Air was good.

Air was professional. Which is what I wanted—for him to be far away and not smirking at me or using those patronizing pet names.

I sagged back onto the bedroll, rubbing my forehead with the heel of my hand.

Ugh, gods, why was I such a moron? Where was Vanora when I needed her?

I had no idea what was happening anymore, or why it felt like I'd done something terrible. It would've been better if he yelled back, called me a few of those stupid names, or made a few jokes at my expense.

But this?

I didn't know what to do with this.

Vanora had only warned me to be careful around Axien and Sanja. So was I supposed to accept that every time he and I were forced to be in the same space, it would be extremely uncomfortable?

Gods, even fighting with Declan and Roxus had never been this complicated. It had never left me feeling so empty and confused.

Axien had started all this. He had treated me like a joke. Mocked me. I shouldn't feel bad. I should feel vindicated. Empowered. Proud. I'd set my boundary loud and clear.

But as I sat alone in the cool reprieve of the covered wagon, I wasn't proud of anything.

I listened to the sounds of the caravan beginning to prepare for departure outside, and I couldn't feel much at all except numb, exhausted, and embarrassed. I was already dreading the worried looks I'd get when I finally got back on my feet. Roxus would go on fussing over me like a child.

And he should. I'd been reckless. Having Axien and Sanja here threw my focus off. Made me question everything. Made me forget all my training.

I had to pull myself together. Get in control. Focus.

There was more to it, though. Something else still hung beneath the surface of my mind. A feeling that stretched and fought, writhing against my sanity to get free.

Axien was gone. I'd put up a boundary. He'd agreed to it and was abiding by it.

And now I had to deal with this.

With feeling ... lonely.

With not knowing if drawing that line between us was right.

With wondering if it could ever be undone.

TWENTY-SIX

S oft—I was getting *way* too soft.

All this time living with Roxus and Delthene, sleeping in soft beds, eating hot meals, taking fancy baths, and training with people like Varren and Declan who would never actually hurt me—all of it was making me lose my edge. The edge that had landed me this life to begin with. The edge that made me worth anything.

My Viperi edge.

I cursed under my breath as I laced up my boots. My stomach clenched and fluttered like I'd swallowed a live eel. Every time I closed my eyes, all I saw was Axien's stupid face. All I could hear in the back of my mind was Roxus yelling at him for not watching me, like I was a freaking little kid he had to babysit.

I had a *lot* to make up for.

Going on a mission with Roxus, finally proving myself to Mistress Orvana and the rest of the Zenith's Call—that was all I had wanted. It was everything I'd worked for over the last two years. The reason for my entire existence.

And so far, the only thing I'd proven was that I was a massive liability. A stupid rookie.

No more.

I hadn't come this far, worked this hard, just to buckle under the pressure. To be put on the sidelines because I'd done something exquisitely stupid, like *not drink enough water in the desert.*

I had to do better.

I *would* do better.

Downing the last of the waterskin Axien had left me, I tossed it onto the bedroll where I'd been writhing in guilt and embarrassment for the last several hours. Roxus and Sanja had taken the first shift of watch while the caravan slowly lurched across the gritty, salt-encrusted Deadlands. Now, it was time to switch.

And I'd be tap-dancing in the flames of the abyss with bells on my toes before I ever let a little thirstiness and heat exhaustion hold me back from my duty again.

Especially in front of Axien and Sanja.

Buckling my daggers back around my hips, I secured each sheath with the strapping around my thighs. I checked over each of the slender, arced silver blades one at a time, admiring the beautifully curved, fang-like shape of each one. The way the weak light danced off the engraving of feathers made each of the two daggers look like a bird's wing.

The perfect balance of efficiency, beauty, and lethality.

"Spelldrinkers," Axien spoke up from behind me suddenly.

I whirled to find him lurking just inside the wagon's canvas-flap entrance, arms crossed over his broad chest, and brow creased with a pensive frown. Somehow, with the starlight painting every plane of his features in sterling relief, he reminded me of the statues in Arx Eburna—the ones of ancient Avoran warriors.

Fates, how long had he been standing there watching me? And why did that make my face feel so hot?

Frowning, I slipped my favorite weapons back into their sheaths and snatched up my small crossbow, slinging the strap over my shoulder. Then I turned to approach him, willing my expression into focused neutrality. No anxiety. No awkwardness. Just calm, composed confidence—just like Vanora had taught me.

Ugh. Easier said than done.

"It's not like you haven't seen my weaponry before," I quipped on my way past, making sure no part of me brushed up against him in that narrow doorway.

Whatever happened before, whatever he had said while he was taking care of me, Axien didn't need to know I had understood or even remembered any of it. Maybe I owed him an apology for not phrasing things as ... *nicely* as I should. But it didn't make any of it less true, right?

Right.

I'd just figure out the whole apology thing later. Work had to come first from now on. I'd tolerate his teasing, if he started up with that nonsense again, and keep my emotions locked down.

"Yes, I noticed them. But I didn't get a good look, and I doubted you'd appreciate me rifling through your belongings," he replied as he followed me out of the back of the wagon into the clear night air. "They're an interesting paradox. That seems to be the going theme with you, though."

"Is that a compliment or an insult?" I asked as I tossed my hair over my shoulder, using that as an excuse to glance his way for a fleeting second.

"It's merely an observation," he said, his gaze trained forward with intense focus. "Even so, I find it hard to believe you brought along weapons like those purely by chance. Dwarven metals, but Vordegan in style, all crafted with the specific intent of butchering Avoran sorcerers. A gift from Roxus, I take it?"

I sighed so loudly it made my cheeks flap, just so he would know I wasn't going to take that bait. I hadn't picked these weapons just to send a message to him. I hadn't picked them at all. They were the ones I had the most training time invested in. The ones I felt most at ease using in a real fight.

"I wouldn't call them a gift," I said. "More like hand-me-downs. These didn't suit Roxus, so he gave them to me. I do better with light weapons. And when he gave them to me, I'd found myself on the wrong end of powerful magic. They'd been collecting dust on his wall before that."

"It does seem a bit providential that they wound up in your hands now, though, doesn't it?" he remarked. I could have sworn I heard that stupid, baiting smirk in his tone again, but another stolen glance proved otherwise.

Axien still focused ahead, his chin dipped slightly, and his gleaming gaze intent on our surroundings. No trace of teasing smiles.

"Why? Because now I'm in forced proximity with an Avoran sorcerer?" I shot back.

"Hah! Calling me a sorcerer... Have you not read anything about true Avorans?" His bark of a laugh was hollow and bitter.

I frowned. "Fair enough. What kinds of things can you do with your magic, then?" I dared to ask. Maybe a change of subject would clear the air a little?

His gaze panned to me, broken only when some of his dark hair blew over his brow. Something about the way he stared, like he was seeing through me once again, down to the very core of my being, made my steps drag and slow.

"I'm still puzzled as to how you even knew I had magic to begin with," he countered.

"I-I didn't. It was just a guess," I stammered, grasping at

the first excuse I could come up with. "Declan made a comment about it before our match in the pit—that you might try using magic against me, that is. I hadn't thought of it until then."

There. That wasn't *entirely* untrue, right? I hadn't suspected anything until Declan pointed out his eyes were a different color, so it was a half-lie at worst.

Axien was silent for a beat, and I was sure he could hear my heart pounding sloppily. A panicked, cold sweat prickled on my skin, and my hands squeezed involuntarily.

"I suppose that makes sense," he spoke up at last, his tone more hushed and guarded. "Why does it matter to you what I can do?"

"It doesn't. Forget I asked." I tried to sound as confidently defiant as before as I looked away. I didn't need him using this like some sort of leverage to twist my secrets out into the open as repayment, anyway.

More tense silence filled the night between us as we walked on, and I assumed the conversation was over.

Then Axien murmured low, "Rest assured, I am capable of great and terrible things, dear Violet. Just like all the old stories warn of."

I frowned and almost stopped to face him. Was he kidding? Was this a new way of baiting me?

Ugh. It had to be.

If Axien was *that* powerful, then what in the world was he doing on a low-threat delivery mission like this? Wouldn't Mistress Orvana have him running point on far more critical matters?

I pinned him with a sideways glare and opened my mouth to ask, but Axien quickly looked away, his expression closed and bitter.

"I suppose I ought to be more careful, hm? Especially with those blades you're carrying," he said, biting sharply at each word. "One more wrong step might put me at the wrong end of them."

Uneasiness swirled in the pit of my stomach as he quickened his steps and left me behind. The night wind stirred in his cloak and shoulder-length brown hair, and the radiant moonlight shone off the steel of his vambraces and pauldrons —the only bits of armor he wore.

My mind reeled as if the entire world was spinning off-kilter under my feet as I watched him march on ahead. Something really was off about him now. I couldn't put my finger on what, exactly, but there was a definite shift in the air.

Yes, I'd unleashed my temper on him. I'd drawn a line between us. But there was more to it than him just having his feelings hurt.

Something about the way he carried himself, with his head lower and his shoulders bunched tensely, hands fisted at his sides—it felt like he was bracing for impact. For something terrible to happen that no one else could see coming.

But what?

Yes, this mission was proving more dangerous than expected. We were getting a lot more interference than even Roxus had planned for. Even so, it wasn't like we weren't capable, right? We could still handle this. It was just a retrieval and delivery. Nothing cosmic.

I rubbed at the back of my neck, trying to smooth down the prickly anxiety that buzzed over my skin. Focus. I had to stay focused. Mission first.

Axien and all his weirdness would just have to wait.

I spotted Roxus and Sanja patrolling just ahead of our wagon. They sat astride a pair of horses right in front of the oliphant team that steadily dragged it along, chatting and laughing like they'd been friends for an eternity.

It made my mouth twist to one side, especially when Axien caught up to them and joined in. He flashed a wide, false smile that never reached his blue-flame eyes and took hold of the reins long enough for Sanja to dismount. He took her seat in the saddle with one fluid leap, then waved Sanja off.

I tensed when Roxus glanced back in my direction, an expectant arch to his brow. By the time I reached him, Roxus had already dismounted and stood waiting, watching me with an all-too-familiar probing stare as though silently asking if I was up to this.

I snatched the reins from his grip and met his concerned gaze with a stony one of my own.

I was fine. Couldn't he see that? I didn't need to be coddled or babysat.

"We'll change out again at dawn," Roxus said, almost like he was checking to make sure I would be okay with riding for that long.

"Fine," I replied and turned away toward the horse.

I had to get a little running leap to swing myself all the way up into the saddle. Chalk that up to being substantially shorter than, well, pretty much everyone else. It didn't help that Roxus's horse was a sizable stallion as black as obsidian. It blew and stamped as I slipped my feet into the stirrups and settled into the seat, finding my balance before urging the creature forward.

"Keep beside the olifants, but stay clear at least ten feet," Roxus ordered, his focus still on me like the glare of the midday sun. "Stay alert. The closer we get to dawn, the more likely predators are to make a move. If anything seems off, you need to remember to—"

"Now, now, let her be. You're only being fussy because you're hungry," Sanja scolded, looping her arm through his and tugging him away to the back of the wagon that was creaking closer and closer. "It's just night watch, and they're both more than capable."

I stared after them, my shoulders dropping a little when

Sanja slipped a little smile and wink back at me over her shoulder. I managed a weak smile in return, enough to let her know I appreciated her keeping Roxus off my case.

Nothing worse than making a mistake and having everyone rub your nose in it for days after.

Fates, I'd read Sanja all wrong from the beginning.

Settling into the rhythm of my stallion's gait, I took in a deep breath, and it stung at all the still-raw places in my throat and lungs. I tried to lose myself in the noise of the clattering wagons, the deep, breathy grumbling of the olifants, and crunch of horse hooves on the craggy earth. To send my thoughts far away from the half-elven man riding a slim, dapple-gray mare on my right.

He wouldn't even so much as glance my way, expression steeled like he was lost in his thoughts, too. Maybe that was for the best.

The hours dragged, and I let my gaze wander, panning out across the landscape awash with moonlight. The valley cut stark and deep through the lofty mountains on either side, the dark stone of them bare of any life. No grass. No trees.

Just emptiness and starlight. And somewhere far, far away in the distance ... a cave that delved deep into the dark heart of the world. Into the Viperi kingdom I'd crawled out of like—

I stiffened when Axien suddenly started coughing, almost like he was choking on his own spit. He cursed under his breath as he reached for the waterskin fastened to the back of his saddle.

"Are you about to throw up?" I frowned, watching his face pale and his hands shake as he gulped down water from the skin.

"No. Gods curse it, the air is so dry," Axien scowled down at the waterskin and took a few more long sips before he put it away. "The salt grit in the wind only makes it worse."

"You've been drinking enough water, too, right?" I asked, unable to keep a hint of smug satisfaction from my tone.

"You literally just witnessed me do it. And that sounds an awful lot like concern for my well-being," he retorted. "Careful with that. It's dangerously unprofessional."

Ugh. Fates. This guy.

It was like he had an anchor line straight to my last nerve.

"Look, I didn't mean we couldn't talk at all," I muttered. "It's weird to ride like this for so long and not say anything."

"Sounds like you're just afraid to be left alone with your thoughts," he said.

I made a scoffing sound and rolled my eyes, just to make extra sure he wouldn't realize he was right about that. Jerk.

A few awkward seconds passed, the wind whipping through my hair as I raked my gaze across the horizon again, looking for anything out of place against the barren landscape. Nothing. No movement. Just eerie shadows from the moonlight cast over the jagged rocks and boulders.

It kindled those flames of memory smoldering in my chest. Of how jagged rocks had cut my feet open after shredding my leather sandals. Of how my mother had tried carrying me on her back at first, until her strength gave out.

"We must keep going, Visha. We cannot stop. Not yet."

I shuddered, pushing that voice—her voice—back down. I couldn't do this. Not now. I had to focus, keep my eyes open, and my senses sharp.

Axien shifted in his saddle again, muttering another Avoran curse as he adjusted his sheath on his back. The night wind teased his dark hair over his sharp, knitted brow, and the wash of silver moonlight only seemed to make the blue shine of power in his eyes all the more intense.

It stirred up a thousand questions in my mind. What if he wasn't just being a sarcastic prick about his magic? What if he really was capable of powerful magic, and I—

Something moved in the darkness behind him, a flash of shadow against the wash of platinum moonlight.

I froze. Every muscle locked up solid. Every other sound instantly died to a muffled haze as all my senses focused there like a spearpoint.

I saw it. The shape of a lean and sinewy body. The reflective glint of two big eyes.

It only lasted half a second. One blink, and it was gone.

My blood rushed with a bloom of heat, pulse immediately dropping into a slow, hard, steady thunder in my veins.

I blinked hard, opening that secondary lens that allowed me to see body heat.

Nothing. It was too far away. I'd have to get closer to be able to discern traces of fresh body heat against the dull red glow of the boulders still radiating the lingering heat from the day's sunlight. Maybe that's all it had been to begin with.

My jaw locked, lips drawing back in a silent snarl on pure instinct.

No—I was sure. I had to trust those instincts. I *had* seen it.

"Violet?" Axien called out suddenly, his voice tight with concern. "What's wrong?"

My stallion stirred beneath me, suddenly sidestepping and tossing its head. Its nostrils flared wide, neck arching, and back tensing between my thighs. It stamped and pulled at the bit, wanting more rein.

It could smell the same flavor of danger that faintly brushed at my senses like a feather on a spider's web. It was all the confirmation I needed.

Beside me, Axien's horse let out a shrill, panicked whinny. "What is it?" he shouted again. "What do you see?!"

The olifant team trundling along not ten yards behind us made nervous, low bellows, shaking their heads against their heavy harnesses. Men farther up the caravan line shouted. The wagons slowed, massive wheels grinding to a halt.

A breathless silence took the air like a chokehold. It strangled all the air from my lungs as my pulse continued to boom in my ears.

I scanned the dark horizon, every rock, stone, and boulder, for signs of body heat or movement. From his own horse, Axien fixed me with a fierce scowl, one of his scimitars already drawn.

He was trusting me to see it first. To give him the cue.

I sank back in the saddle, using my bodyweight to maneuver my horse around so I could get another look. I needed to be sure before I—

A sudden chorus of piercing cries split the night, yowling like the screams of feral cats. It came from everywhere at once, echoing off the canyon walls and looming towers of dark rock.

A pang of fear ripped straight through me. My mouth clamped down, teeth still bared, as my palms immediately went slick with sweat.

Th-that sound. I knew it.

Gods help us ... those were switchbeasts.

TWENTY-SEVEN

The crackle of battle sizzled through me—but it was all wrong.

A symphony playing off-key.

My horse bucked again, and I had to lean down into the movement just to keep my seat. Its dark hide already shone with sweat and its muscles quivered. Not good.

When I tried to bring it back around closer to the wagon, the animal flailed and whinnied, desperate to be free of my weight so it could run.

Ugh. Fine.

I pulled my feet from the stirrups and slid off the beast's rump when it reared up again, hitting the ground in a crouch, and slowly stood, watching my coward of a stallion thunder off into the night.

So much for a mounted advantage.

"RALLY TO THE WAGON!" Roxus bellowed as he and Sanja suddenly burst from the canvas flap, weapons already in hand.

My body burned under the rush of adrenaline, every muscle taut, and every nerve on a razor's edge. Reaching back,

I found the grip of my crossbow and fitted a bolt to the thick resin string. I kept my head on a swivel, watching the shadows as I slowly backed toward the wagon.

Roxus stood waiting, his own much larger crossbow already in hand.

"How many?" he growled low.

"I don't know. I spotted movement to the right," I replied.

"A lot, by the sound of them," Sanja interjected, taking up a position on my left. She had one of those glowing blue throwing darts between her slender fingers, arms raised and poised to fling them at a second's notice.

Ahead, Axien had his mount under better control, trotting back and forth and finally falling back to stand before us with his scimitar still firmly in hand.

"They'll coordinate and wait for the right moment to strike. Once you see them, don't wait. Kill as many as you can from a distance," Roxus instructed as he took another protective step closer to my side. "When we have to switch to close-combat tactics, do *not* let them bite you. If you're bitten at all, call it out immediately and fall back. Find cover and stay still. Understood?"

I nodded—not that I needed the lecture. I knew more than I wanted about these creatures. Their bite was a fate far worse than death, and moving would only spread their venom faster.

Screams sounded from farther down the caravan line.

I squeezed the grip of my small crossbow tighter, my sweaty palm squeaking over the leather padding.

Curse it, where were they? I couldn't find any traces of movement amidst the rocks. But the screams grew louder. Closer. More frantic. Horses shrieked. The olifants pitched at their harnesses and bellowed anxiously, making the metalwork of the wagon groan and some of the strapping snap.

My adrenaline ran like molten metal, sending surge after

surge of energy to my extremities like an electrical shock. Men shouted as more hired guards joined us in taking up defensive positions around the caravan.

A flash of brilliant white-hot body heat suddenly sprang from behind a nearby boulder. Then two more. Then another.

They bounded and leapt, crossing the distance so fast I could hardly track it. All six of their powerful legs moved together, propelling them forward without a single sound. They moved fast, flickering like living tongues of flame.

"Three on the left! Closing fast!" I shouted and whirled, widening my stance and taking the first shot. My bowstring cracked, sending my bolt whirring into the night. It pinged off a boulder roughly eighty feet away, missing one of the switch-beasts by less than an inch.

Curse it, they moved so fast.

Too fast.

I nocked another arrow just as the three beasts sprang for us, finally moving into the light where the others could see. Their too-wide jaws bristled with hundreds of needle-thin, fishbone-like teeth. Their long, whip-like tails lashed.

More bowstrings snapped and cracked all around me. Men shouted orders. The olifants screeched—a horrible sound that left my ears ringing.

At my other side, Sanja hissed in defiance. "Axien, keep your eye on the left! There'll be more!"

Curse it, she was right.

These creatures hunted in large family groups of around ten or more. They used their numbers to overwhelm larger prey. If I could see three, then we could count on at least twice that many surrounding us from all sides.

My focus narrowed, senses slipping into that state of numb release. Of primal instinct that settled into my body and guided all my limbs into fluid, flawless motion. I lost myself in the burn of it, letting it incinerate me from the inside out.

For their sake, I became Viperi again. Ruthless. Decisive. Relentless.

I fired my crossbow over and over, hands moving in a blur, until one of the monsters dropped less than ten feet in front of me—half a dozen of my arrows protruding from its skull.

Another of the monsters sprang over the fallen corpse, all six legs outstretched with curled talons fully extended and ready to rip me open from throat to belly.

I dipped low, kicking into a forward roll so the monster sailed over me. I came up behind it, feet wide and legs bent in a predatory crouch. My hands immediately went to my daggers.

The scrape of the metal hummed in the night, and my arms flexed against the weight of each slender blade. I kicked off the ground, whipping into a spin and landing two deep slashes of my blades through the creature's thin hide.

It let out a howl of pain, one of its legs falling to the gritty earth with a *thud*.

They didn't have much in the way of armor. Their hides were as thin and delicate as a dried-out corpse's. No fat. No meat beyond taut, gaunt sinew.

They were all speed. All bone and ligaments. Made for quick, ruthless assaults using that venomous bite.

Being down one leg was a serious issue for them, and one I immediately took advantage of without hesitation.

The switchbeast snarled and recoiled, striking at me like a coiled serpent until I drove the point of my daggers through its neck and gave a violent twist and jerk. Its eyes still blinked and tongue still writhed as the monster's head hit the ground at my feet and rolled away.

The body dropped limp before me, and I stole a quick glance around. Where were the others? Was everyone okay?

Somewhere off to my right, Roxus was still firing that crossbow. He shouted at me and Sanja, barking orders I couldn't hear over the noise.

Ahead a few paces, Sanja whipped her darts through the air with impossible speed, flinging one handful after another until I had to wonder where she was getting so many.

One glimpse and I saw it—the way each of those magical darts streaked through the night like a shooting star and hit a target ... then instantly reappeared on her belt with another flash of radiant blue magic. Over and over, so that she never ran out.

Fates, I *needed* some of those for myself!

"VIOLET!" A voice shouted my name over the chaos.

I spun on a heel.

Axien rode toward me at full speed, leaning low in the saddle with a hand outstretched. Blood spattered his clothes, and his expression was locked into a fierce snarl.

Our gazes locked. It was only half a second, maybe less, and his eyes tracked forward—straight at where a switchbeast had another one of the caravan's hired guards pinned.

Seconds. We had seconds.

Axien's jaw clenched. He never looked my way again, but the pressure there was unmistakable. That sense of knowing, of what he needed me to do, washed over me. I slid one of my blades back into the sheath at my thigh.

As his mount thundered past, I seized his hand and swung myself onto the horse's rump, perching there on the balls of my feet with one of my blades still in hand. I kept a hand on Axien's shoulder for balance, leaning with him into his horse's speed.

One second.

The pinned swordsman—a young elven man—screamed in pain and horror as the switchbeast raked its claws down his chest. Its powerful neck arched, jaws open wide, with all those thin teeth dripping with venom.

Ready to make the kill.

Two seconds.

I sprang from the saddle as Axien steered the horse into a sharp turn, and hit the creature like a javelin—dagger first. The impact snatched the wind from my lungs, but it sent me and the switchbeast rolling. My dagger sank in deep.

BAM!

We hit the ground, limbs entangled, and rolled. Warm wetness coated my hand and oozed through my fingers. It splattered over my face and into my hair.

The switchbeast hissed. It pawed at me, ripping at my skin with talons like razors.

I gripped my dagger with both hands, forcing it deeper. All the way to the hilt. Twisting it. Wrenching it. Doing as much damage as possible until we tumbled to a stop. I ripped my blade free of its chest and scrambled back, springing to my feet.

My chest heaved in deep, steady breaths. My body burned as every muscle tensed, poised for the next strike. I sank into low, calculated strides as the switchbeast unfurled its many legs and whipped around to face me.

I bared my teeth, missing my fangs more than ever, but still feeling that roaring inferno in my blood that drowned out everything else. There was nothing but the flames. The chaos. The need for blood.

I drew my second dagger, spinning them both over my hands before gripping the hilts firmly.

The switchbeast prowled to the side, forgetting its former prey altogether, and focusing those eerie, bulging eyes only on me. I mirrored the movement, and we circled one another slowly like a lion and a viper in the night.

I drank it all in. Every tiny move and gesture. Every breath the creature took. I'd wounded it badly. Blood ran from the gaping hole in its chest and left a trail behind it on the dry, salty ground. Its gait was hitched. Faltering. Weakening with every step.

That would be my opening.

The noise of the battle raging around us faded to a dull, muffled roar. Somewhere in it, I could have sworn I heard the familiar bellow of a bear. Roxus.

I clenched my teeth.

With a screeching cry, the switchbeast lunged with its jaws open wide, moving so fast it might as well have been a tongue of lightning aimed straight for me.

I darted in, blades swung wide. My feet flew over the ground, but everything seemed to slow. My pulse. My breathing. The beast diving straight at me.

At the last instant, I feinted to the left and kicked into an arching leap, twisting my body in the air so I landed on the creature's back. I wrapped my thighs around its neck, hanging on for dear life as it pitched in wild alarm.

Raising my blades high, I drove them both downward into the creature's skull—one through each eye socket.

Then I drew back ... and stabbed it again. And again. And again.

I stabbed until the flailing of its long, spidery legs stopped, and I heard a gargling, wet breath slowly leave its open maw.

Dead.

I stood, stumbling a little as my head spun. Must've hit the ground harder than I thought earlier. One of my shoulders ached, but not badly enough for me to call it quits.

Not when there was still more fun to be had.

Shaking the stars from my vision, I looked back to where the other hired swordsman still lay on the ground, alive and mostly whole. His injuries were severe, but not deadly.

I'd count that as a win all around.

"P-Pitathi," he wheezed frantically as I stalked past him.

"And don't you *ever* forget it, elf," I spat.

I didn't spare him even a second glance as I spun my silver daggers over my blood-soaked hands again and made my way straight back into the fray.

TWENTY-EIGHT

"Six dead," Roxus announced grimly as he came to stand with us.

Sanja, Axien, and I hung back from the rest of the caravan's hired hands, watching from a distance as they took stock of their injured and burned the bodies of the switch-beasts. No one spoke for a long time, watching the flames dance and embers sail upward until they disappeared against the night sky, lost amidst the stars.

"What about the injured?" Sanja asked quietly. She kept her arms crossed over her midriff, her fair brow drawn in a look of worry as the firelight danced in her dark eyes.

"Plenty," Roxus huffed. "But considering the size of that pack, only six dead is a miracle. Well, I should say seven, I suppose. There's another guard with a bite. The venom's already set in. He won't see morning."

"Is there nothing to be done for him?" Axien shifted uncomfortably, rubbing at his jaw and the back of his neck. "No antidote?"

"Sometimes you can amputate to stop the spread of the venom, but you have to do it within minutes of the bite. And, of course, that only works if it's one of your arms or legs that gets bitten." Roxus sighed deeply and shook his head. "No such luck for this fellow. A few of the others are helping him write a letter to his family, then they'll end his suffering before the venom starts to break his bones."

I cringed at the thought, every muscle locking up tight, and my toes curling in my boots. I'd never seen it happen to anyone, but I knew the details of how switchbeast venom worked.

It wasn't just a means of hunting prey for them. It was also how they reproduced. If the creatures didn't eat you, then the venom would slowly and excruciatingly turn you into one of them.

Just one bite would turn your insides to jelly, break and rearrange your bones, tear your skin, and warp your body into another switchbeast with absolutely no memory of what or who you had been before. They weren't just the desert's most fearsome feline monstrosities; they were parasites.

And apart from my kin, they were the only other surviving remnants of the Dire King Zarexius left roaming the world.

"I heard once that the Lunostri had an antidote?" Sanja blinked up at him, turning her face so I could see a fresh slice across one of her cheeks. Probably from a close call with a switchbeast claw.

Roxus shrugged. "Could be, but I doubt they'd be too keen on sharing it with anyone else. They're not fond of relinquishing their ancestral secrets."

I swallowed against a burning lump that rose in my throat. Gods, that man ... I just prayed they ended his suffering before any of the worst of it started.

In all, we had killed more than a dozen of those vile monsters. Each one was roughly six hundred pounds and around twelve feet from snout to tail, but there was nothing useful on them. Not even the talons were good for much once rot set in.

Not to mention, nearly every culture in the Southern Kingdoms regarded them as cursed. No one would ever want a weapon made of their teeth or claws, or anything made from their bones and hide. To touch them at all was enough to make even a Viperi's hair stand on end.

"Once they've finished sorting things out, the caravan master wants us back underway. Lingering here with the smell of blood so thick in the air will only attract more unwanted attention," Roxus said, sliding me a sideways look with one of his dark brows raised. "You're hurt."

I scowled at him and tipped my chin to where he was bleeding from a very obvious puncture in his arm. "So are you."

"Some rookie idiot shot me with his bow," he grumbled and flexed his arm, moving each finger as though testing the strength there. "Not serious, though. Dumb kid wouldn't stop apologizing."

"You'll have to forgive him, dear," Sanja snickered. "I doubt anyone beyond our party was expecting to see a bear out here, let alone one fighting on their side."

A fair point. It'd certainly thrown me off the first time.

"Let's get both of you bandaged up before they're ready to get moving again," Sanja urged, nudging Roxus's arm. "Come along. I suppose I'll be playing healer tonight, hm?"

I hesitated, watching them saunter off to our wagon—one of many now gathered in closer to where the heap of switch-beast bodies burned like an unholy pyre. Part of me wanted to give them space, to roam the battlefield and see if any of my crossbow bolts could be salvaged.

Anything to work off the shaky, queasy aftershock left over from letting all that adrenaline run wild in my system.

"You look absolutely terrifying," Axien chuckled suddenly, breaking all my inward, broody focus.

I blinked up at him in shock, then slowly stared down at my blood-and-gore-spattered clothes.

Okay, fine. It wasn't just on my clothes.

I had dried switchbeast blood caked all over my arms and legs. It was crusted into my hair and dripping from the end of my chin and nose. I could feel it drying on my neck, too.

Ugh. Gross.

I wiped futilely at my face with my sleeve, but that just smeared it around more, which only made Axien laugh even harder.

"Y-You look ... like an absolute nightmare!" He bent over, howling until he was gasping for breath.

My lips mashed up sourly as I watched him cackle, waiting for him to come up for air. "Are you finished?"

"It's like you just finished bathing in the blood of your enemies. Gods, it's a wonder anyone in camp can walk past you without pissing themselves," he wheezed, still collecting himself as he fished through his pockets until he found a neatly folded handkerchief and held it out to me. "At least wipe your face, woman."

I snatched it out of his hand and tried. I really did. But once again, I only managed to smear it.

"Oh, for crying out loud—here, allow me," he sighed and took his handkerchief back.

I stood still, glaring at him in smoldering silence as he wet the handkerchief with his tongue and seized my chin in one of his large hands.

My back went stiff as he drew me closer and tilted my head back, still snickering under his breath as he leaned down and started trying to wipe my face off. Something about that closeness, with the puff of his breath on my cheeks and his palm firm against my throat, made my knees wobble strangely.

Heat crept from my belly all the way to my cheeks. No one —not even Declan—had ever touched me like this. Too bad he seemed wholly focused on mopping up the mess on my face. Then again, maybe it was a good thing he didn't notice my face burning and my pulse thudding hard and fast in my neck.

He would have definitely used that as more ammunition for teasing.

I had to pinch my eyes and mouth shut as he worked, twisting my face into strange positions as he dabbed around my nose. Gods, I'd never felt so childish. It made me want to gut-check him with one good punch, just to reassert dominance.

Buuut that was the sort of thing Vanora had told me wasn't socially appropriate if I was going to act like a civilized lady. Granted, in my opinion, we'd abandoned civilized the instant we drew blades.

Whatever.

"There," Axien declared when he finished. "Much less terrifying."

I took a big step back away from him, my face so hot I knew my ears were probably bright red. Hopefully, he wouldn't read too much into that.

"What a relief. Can't have the lessers pissing themselves." I let the sarcasm drip from my tone like honey off a comb.

"No, indeed," he agreed.

And I saw it—that smile that made his eyes crinkle and glow a little brighter. The way it made the corners of his mouth turn up in a crooked, roguish way made my heart skip a beat.

It was a real smile. No games. No teasing. No hauntingly perfect veneer.

Just ... him.

A staggeringly handsome half-elven man with a few

freckles on his nose, a small dimple in one cheek, and the faintest hint of a long-faded scar on his chin that I had never noticed before. There was intense warmth in the lines of his sharply angled features. A gentleness that seemed to resonate from within him like a melody.

It made my head swim.

No. I had to turn away. *Right now.*

Spinning toward the wagon, I took off at a determined march without another word.

"A thank-you wouldn't go amiss," he called after me, his tone still playful as he followed a few paces behind. "Now I've got switchbeast blood all over my favorite handkerchief."

"What self-respecting warrior has a favorite handkerchief?" I grumbled.

"I hear many of the dragonriders of Maldobar carry them into battle," he quipped. "Tokens from their lovely maidens."

"Well, you're not a dragonrider, and last I checked, I wasn't a lovely maiden."

He laughed again, the sound so carefree and merry I almost looked back at him one more time, just to see that smile.

Almost.

I bowed my head slightly and clenched my hands into fists.

No—no, no, no.

Not going there. Especially not with him. Whatever lay beneath that mask he usually wore, it didn't matter. It couldn't.

I wouldn't lose focus again. I wouldn't make the mistake of assuming I could trust him. Not with so much hanging in the balance and a track record a mile long telling me that he would absolutely take any chance he could to make me out to be a joke.

I'd drawn the line between us. Now, I would hold firm to it.

Axien didn't follow me up into the back of the wagon, thank the gods. Sanja met us on her way out and asked him to escort her to check in with the caravan master. Apparently, he wanted a head count of just how many guards he still had at his disposal for the rest of our journey.

Poking my head through the canvas flap, I spotted Roxus sitting on the floor, tying off a length of gauze wrapped around his bicep. His brow furrowed when he spotted me, and he gave a gesturing nod for me to come in. No words required.

"Seriously, it's not that bad," I grumbled sheepishly as I ambled over and sat down beside him.

"Still need to clean it and put some salve on it," he said and handed me the small porcelain pot of Leruna's stinkiest healing poultice.

I sighed, letting all the pent up frustration leave my body in one breath, as I reached for the water basin and rag he'd been using. I shrugged off as much of my leather armor as I dared and washed out the places where the switchbeasts' claws had gotten lucky hits. Fortunately, it was all superficial damage.

Maybe I'd get a good scar out of it, but nothing more.

The powerful odor of the herbs made my eyes water as I opened the lid and took a swipe of the green goo onto my finger. I dabbed it into the long slashes left on my shoulder and chest before tugging my tunic back into place and strapping myself into the leather corset again. Done.

"You handled yourself well tonight," Roxus said. He'd pulled out his pipe and was busy lighting it.

"Yeah, well, I learned from the best." I slipped him a devious little grin. "The Viperi, I mean. Not you."

He snorted and grinned around the long, curved wooden pipe he held between his teeth.

"Lost a stupid horse, though," I groaned.

He made a thoughtful, grunting noise. "Can't blame an animal for having survival instincts, Vi."

"Yeah? I seriously cannot wait to use that against you the next time I stab someone for trying to bully me in combat training." I nudged him with my elbow and handed back the pot of healing salve.

That's when I noticed ... he was already holding something else out to me.

With his face turned away and his mouth a tight, tense line around the pipe, Roxus gestured for me to take the flat, round metal tag that rested in his palm. It wasn't much bigger than a coin, maybe an inch across, and made of battered, scuffed bronze with a series of numbers engraved into it.

032.

Not a number that meant anything to me. The tag itself didn't look familiar either.

I turned it over, looking for any other markings or features. But there were none. Not even the faintest glow of magic.

"I found it in the ear of one of the switchbeasts," Roxus said suddenly, his voice so quiet I could hardly hear him. "Thing was tagged like a spring heifer."

My stomach dropped to the soles of my boots. My entire body went cold. I stared at the tag, unable to breathe, as my mind whipped wildly in a maelstrom of questions.

Someone had tagged a switchbeast like cattle? Why? Who? Did the number mean there were thirty-one others?

Or was this just one of hundreds?

"This doesn't make any sense. Switchbeasts aren't animals. They can't be trained or taught," I whispered, trying to make sense of it. "It would be a massive undertaking simply to try to contain them, let alone—"

"I know," Roxus interrupted. "That's why I haven't shown it to anyone else. Not yet. The implications are ...

substantial." He stayed eerily still as he took a deep breath in through that pipe, making the bits of tobacco crackle in the small bowl.

So he hadn't told Sanja? Or Axien?

I tried to wrap my mind around that, as well. To fathom why he wouldn't share this discovery with them, even if he didn't share it with anyone else in the caravan. Unless he didn't want to start a panic, or have them jumping to conclusions too soon.

Sanja certainly seemed like someone who might leap into action first, before she had all the facts. She might even insist we call off the mission altogether, if it seemed too dangerous for just our small band to handle.

But what did I know? She was still essentially a stranger to me.

And Axien ... well, he wasn't much different.

All I could do was stare at the tag, my throat jumping with the pounding of my pulse, as the smoke from Roxus's pipe curled around us in fragrant, ghostly tendrils.

At last, I slowly dragged my gaze up to meet his. Chills tingled over my skin, pouring from my head to my toes like a bucket of ice water, when I found the same uneasiness there in his gaze.

"What does this mean?" I dared to ask, my voice a breathless rasp.

"Nothing good," he replied, his voice still hushed.

My heart twisted painfully, already half-frozen in fear.

"Stay on your guard, Vi, and let's keep this between us until we know more." Roxus growled low as he plucked the tag from my hand and tucked it away in his pocket, safely out of sight. "Something isn't right. I just can't put my finger on it yet."

"We have to tell the others eventually," I said, watching his reaction carefully. I needed to know why he hadn't trusted Sanja with this information first.

Unfortunately, even with all Vanora's fine training, Roxus's expressions were so controlled and guarded, it would have been easier trying to read the minds of the ancient statues in Arx Eburna. The man gave nothing away unless he wanted to.

Ugggh. Frustrating.

"When we have more information, we will bring them up to speed," Roxus agreed and took another long drag from the pipe. He blew the smoke out through his nostrils like a dragon, filling the wagon with the familiar, fruity fragrance of his favorite tobacco.

The smell of home.

"For now, we watch each other's backs. Zenith's Call stand by our own—always. Understood?" he added sternly.

"Of course. To the death." I nodded.

Roxus barked a rough, rumbling laugh and flicked my ear punishingly. "Let's not let it come to that, eh? Just keep those magic eyes of yours open wide. Salnis is a dangerous enough place in its own right, but at the rate we're going, we may need every advantage we can get.

TWENTY-NINE

Something was wrong with Axien.

Sitting astride another borrowed horse, he stared vacantly ahead as we closed in on the city of Salnis. The wind tousled his dark hair, blowing it around his deeply furrowed brow and tight, frowning mouth. Every part of him seemed tense, hands gripping the reins so tight the tendons of his fingers stood out against his tanned skin.

He didn't even seem to notice when the rest of the caravan began stirring, calling out orders and rearranging personnel for our arrival.

No more laughing.

No more playful grins.

At least, not until another hired swordsman approached him to ask for his horse back.

Axien didn't say a word as he dismounted and handed the beast off to its owner, giving the man a quick, painfully forced smile.

I watched in silence as he walked alongside the wagon where I sat up on the driver's platform, legs dangling over the edge and hand resting on my crossbow—just in case. With his head hung low, he made a point to look in every direction except mine. Or maybe that was a coincidence?

I couldn't tell.

And then it didn't matter, because our long caravan finally ground to a halt outside the city gates, just as the first brushes of scarlet began to bloom on the horizon. Roxus whistled for me, and I sprang down to join him as we walked down the long line of wagons to the front.

"Stick close," he warned, his own expression grimly focused. "Remember, eyes open."

"Yeah, yeah," I huffed, and stole a quick look sideways as we passed Axien.

He didn't so much as glance our way—not when Sanja was sauntering up to him with her own features drawn into a look of impatient frustration. She barked his name sharply, and he faced her, muttering something back I couldn't make out from a distance.

It didn't take any special training from Vanora to tell that this was the preamble of an argument.

Hmm. Was that what had him in a foul mood? Had she scolded him for something? If so, what? I couldn't even begin to guess, but we were both still considered green and untried. Rookie tandems. He was just as likely to foul something up as I was.

"What's going on with them?" I dared to ask once I was sure Roxus and I were well out of earshot. "Did he do something wrong?"

"Sometimes it's better not to know," Roxus replied. "That boy is far too sure of himself. She's had trouble keeping him in check in the past. Best to let them sort it out."

I looked back again, just in time to see Axien flail his arms angrily and shout something at her. Sanja stood, glaring up at him with her hands on her hips. Not backing down. And if her scowl was any indication, not happy with him at all.

"Yeah ..." I murmured, peeling my eyes away. "Better not to know, I guess."

We reached the gate ahead of the caravan, passing a large checkpoint where soldiers were checking each arriving wagon and traveler. They'd divided the lines up, with one for normal folk coming and going, and several others for merchants with their many loaded down wagons. That line seemed to stretch on for a mile, and I suddenly understood why Roxus wasn't interested in waiting around with the rest of the caravan to get into the city.

After all, we'd held up our end as hired guards. We'd be parting ways regardless.

When we got to the front of the line, all Roxus had to do was flash a glimpse of his Zenith's Call brand and the soldiers let us through without a second glance.

I stuck close to his side, watching all the crowds move around and steadily disperse within the city's high walls. An odd, ominous pressure in the air hit my senses immediately, like I was being watched from all sides. Monitored. Assessed to determine all my weaknesses.

It set my teeth on edge. Salnis wasn't just dangerous—it was malice in a gilded mask.

I'd never traveled far from Rienka, but I couldn't have even dreamed of anything like this. The intricately carved arched bridges, oval terraces, and twisting avenues were all carved directly into the dark slate stone of a steep canyon cut through the arid landscape for over fifty miles. It shone like an obsidian reef in the early light of dawn, with countless levels stretching down into the canyon on either side.

None of the texts I'd studied did it justice.

The arid wind made strange, lonely howling sounds as it twisted through the deep canyon. The waking sunlight danced off the dark stone, revealing veins of deep green and cobalt hidden within it. The polished streets met at half-moon shaped squares, where gold-detailed fountains were fed by waterfalls that trickled down the canyon from top to bottom. I couldn't see where the water began or ended, but the noise of it was a constant rush that echoed everywhere.

Beautiful—but only on the surface.

Only if you ignored the occasional flash of deadly steel tucked into the robes of figures weaving through the crowds, or the cunning sideways glances slipped our way from faces mostly covered with shawls and scarves.

What lurked underneath the veneer of this glittering obsidian city, passing us left and right in the finely dressed crowds, made the tiny hairs on the back of my neck stand on end. I felt the weight of those unknown eyes watching me, inspecting me, and heard whispers amidst the wind and whoosh of the fountains.

Pitathi.

I tensed, fingers dancing to the hilts of my blades before I could stop myself.

Not that I expected much else, honestly. Especially here.

Salnis sat like a jewel on the boundary between Damaria and Nar'Haleen. Although technically still under the control of Damaria, it was perhaps the most highly disputed city in the southern kingdoms.

Well, other than Rienka, of course.

Both were major thoroughfares for the main trade routes that ran through the southern kingdoms, and were essential for any kingdom to keep its coffers full and its people flourishing. So naturally, both were chock full of spies, mercenaries, assassins, arms and slave traders, and smugglers all working for both sides—sometimes at the same time.

A reef indeed, and one packed full of sharks of all shapes, sizes, and creeds.

"Hood up," Roxus warned as he sauntered along at my side, the cowl of his own ragged old coat already pulled low.

"The city sleeps in the heat of the day, so we need to find a place to take shelter and rest. Sanja has made arrangements."

Of course she had. She seemed to have connections no matter where we went. Hopefully, this time they didn't come with mercenaries already waiting for us at the door.

"I thought Salnis never slept," I said as I adjusted my hood, cramming my long hair down into it to keep it hidden from view.

"Not truly," Roxus agreed with a sly smile. "But the heat is far more intense here in the day, so Salnis is forced to move all debaucherous transactions indoors until nightfall."

"Gods, there she is," Axien gasped, all but materializing on my other side so suddenly it made me flinch away.

He didn't seem to notice, though.

With his blue eyes wide and his mouth slightly agape, Axien stared ahead to the center of the canyon-city where a massive black stone spire rose above everything else. At its pinnacle, a colossal golden statue of a woman stood in battle armor buckled over a flowing robe. Her angelic wings were outstretched to the sky, and she held a large staff in one hand.

I recognized Adiana, goddess of the moon and patroness of this city, right away.

Maybe that was why I couldn't tear my eyes away from the staff she held.

At one end, the statue's staff depicted a strange, crystalline-shaped adornment. The other end swirled into a brutal, tri-tipped blade. A strange contradiction of raw, uncut beauty ... and deadly lethality.

But that, I'd read many times, was her essence overall. Adiana was fierce, but fair. She was compassionate, but protective. She was slow to anger, but also slow to forgive. She and Avgior had come together to form the Zenith's Call over six thousand years ago, after the War of Falling Stars. A war between humans and elves that had nearly torn the world apart and had birthed the notorious god of the void, Vescor. They saw a need to protect powerful divine objects and secrets from being abused in mortal hands.

And we were their solution. An elite society sworn to forsake all other creeds, crowns, and kingdoms to preserve those divine secrets.

Somehow, I'd always felt a sort of kinship with Adiana. Not that I thought I was anything like her, but more that I understood her motives over the rest of the gods. The thought made me smirk to myself, wondering who would be more horrified to hear that—my father or Mistress Orvana.

"It must be more than a hundred times that I've walked this city, but she never ceases to amaze," Sanja sighed dreamily as she joined us at last, handing over a purse full of coins to Roxus.

Most likely our payment from the caravan master.

"And that's it, is it?" Axien's eyes narrowed, head tilting as the awe on his face seemed to harden to cold indifference again. "The staff in her hand—that's the relic we've come to retrieve? I hope the real thing is easier to carry."

Sanja gave a bemused little snort. "The real thing is fairly normal-sized for a staff, but is far more precious than anything made of gold."

A little chill crept up my spine. Precious ... and powerful. It was supposedly the same staff the goddess herself had once carried into battle. It would be overflowing with raw divine power.

No wonder they'd hidden it away in a temple.

With all the greedy hands in the world now grasping for power, and a tyrant eagerly gobbling up neighboring king-doms left and right, I could appreciate why Mistress Orvana thought this was a priority. We couldn't foul this up, no matter what the risk. Losing a few secrets or relics from the Vault of Whispers would have been bad enough.

But losing an artifact given straight from the hands of a goddess? One said to contain her essence and power?

No—we had to make sure this went right from now on. We could not let the staff fall into the wrong hands. No matter the risk.

And whatever the sacrifice.

THIRTY

My feet were going to fall off.

Trekking through the early dawn, I tried not to think about how numb my toes were, or how my heels were rubbing raw thanks to my blood-soaked socks. I'd be worn down to nubs if we didn't stop soon.

Sanja beckoned us on, her smile still bright-eyed and lovely. "Come along, keep up the pace. I know of a good place for us to catch our breath and clean up before we meet with the priests tonight. I'll send word ahead so they're expecting us at moonrise."

"I really hope that includes a bath," I muttered as I trudged along after them deeper into the city.

Despite Axien having wiped most of my face clean, the rest of me was still thoroughly crusted in dried switchbeast blood. Er, well, some of my own, too. It itched something terrible, but scratching just got it under my nails.

Sanja led the way, navigating the strange, winding streets that snaked down the canyon's walls. They doubled back, careened up and down slopes and staircases, and wound through the natural movements of the dark stone walls.

But none of that is what kept me staring up, down, and all around like a tourist.

The buildings of Salnis were also carved straight into the rock. Houses, shops, apartments, taverns, inns, and even small courtyards were engraved with meticulous detail and beauty. The styles were a mixture of cultures from all across the southern kingdoms—swirling, elegant columns like the Avorans, hard lines and sharp angles like the Damarians, and pear-shaped passages covered in tiny carvings like the Nar'Haleenans.

The mixture made the walls of the huge, twisting canyon seem like one giant mosaic. A tapestry of life carved into the very bones of the earth—and it was all adorned in swirling details of golden paint, as though to pay homage back to the goddess standing watch over the city.

The inn Sanja brought us to had a great view of everything, and we hurried to settle into the spacious, one-room suite just as the first powerful rays of sunlight hit Adiana's statue.

Roxus closed all the heavy drapes over the balcony and windows that overlooked the cityscape, warning me to keep them drawn. At first, I thought it was to keep out prying eyes.

Then the heat wave hit like a punch to the throat, and it all made sense. Why we were hiding out the daylight hours, why everyone preferred living back in the cool reprieve of the rock, and why those thick drapes had tiny metal tiles sewn to the outside to reflect the heat away from the interior of our room.

"We should get something decent to eat," Roxus suggested, making a point not to look my way as he counted out a few coins from the purse and tossed them to Sanja.

Good. If he made this about me and that whole heat-stroke fiasco, I'd hit him.

"I'll go down and ask the innkeeper if she can have a meal

sent up," Sanja agreed. "She mentioned we could use the tub, but you'll have to draw up the bath yourselves."

"On it," Axien said, his wide shoulders sagging and expression slack with exhaustion. He'd just finished kicking off his boots and peeling off his socks. They hit the floor with a soggy slap.

Sweat-soaked. Ugh. Mine were probably no better.

"But I get the first dip for my work," he added on his way to the tub.

No one argued.

Overall, the room was a good size, and there were plenty of tall, grass-woven screens we could use to partition off sleeping quarters as we pleased. Soft, silken cushions sat on the floor, arranged around a few low tables with settings for tea already in place.

The smell of jasmine and frankincense oils filled the room as Axien took his turn in the bath first, drawing water from a spout in the wall into a deep, round copper basin. He pulled screens all the way around it like a barrier before he even started undressing, muttering a soft Avoran curse under his breath that we probably weren't supposed to hear.

I shot Roxus a look.

Everyone in the southern kingdoms used public baths. It had been the social norm for thousands of years. Or so I thought, anyway. I mean, even Viperi didn't bat a lash at nudity when it came to bathing. There was nothing sensual about it, and being overly modest was considered suspicious or downright rude. It was probably the only thing we had in common with people of the surface world.

Sooo ... were Avorans more modest or something? Like the Maldobarians and northern kingdoms? I didn't know.

Either way, Axien closing himself off like that was weird.

Come to think of it, I'd never seen Axien use the baths at Arx Eburna, either. Eh. It was probably just an Avoran quirk.

Or maybe he'd simply had enough of us for one day and wanted some perceived separation.

I could sympathize.

Roxus made an indifferent, half-frowning face and shrugged before he went back to work unpacking his gear and cleaning his weaponry.

I did the same.

The day wore on, and I took my turn in the bath last—since I was definitely going to leave the tub fouled with blood. It would have to be cleaned before anyone else used it.

I took my time rinsing my hair and scrubbing my skin, using handfuls of soaps and oils to get the grit out of my scalp and from between my toes. That many days of sweat, grime, and blood meant the water wasn't good for soaking after, so I climbed out and quickly dried off.

I ignored the pinch of despair in my chest as I put on my last clean change of clothes. A dark purple silken tunic and my only remaining pair of clean black linen pants were buried at the bottom of my haversack. They still smelled like the citrusy perfumes Delthene used to wash our laundry when I slipped them on and started winding my hair into my usual long, soggy braid.

Gods, I hoped everything was okay back home. Had she delivered my letters? Had Leruna checked in on Declan?

Before I could tie my braid off at the end, Sanja grabbed my shoulders and huffed, spinning me around and forcing me to sit in front of her.

"Fates help me, you always put it in those ratty peasant braids," she scolded. "A proper lady of the Zenith's Call should look refined, not like some ragged northern bride with all those bangs hanging loose and blowing around. I'm surprised Vanora hasn't taught you as much. Southern ladies are polished. Our hair is neatly bound, not a lock out of place.

We're not on the road anymore. In the city, you must present yourself well."

My face flushed hot, and I bowed my head so I wouldn't have to look at anyone while her fingers worked sternly through my hair.

"She probably would have, but Vanora's likely had to spend all their time together teaching her not to snarl at everyone like a feral dog," Axien scoffed from across the room.

My gaze snapped up to him, rage like cinders sparking in the pit of my stomach. What the—? Was he serious?

"You best watch yourself, boy," Roxus warned in a low growl. "Don't make me warn you again."

"Ignore him," Sanja muttered behind me. "He's a pain when he's hungry."

Axien flashed her a killing glare from where he sat at the low table, reclined against the large cushions. He licked his teeth behind his lips, almost like he could taste the words he wanted to lash back with.

Part of me hoped he would. It might be fun, watching Roxus give him one good punch over that too-perfect mouth.

But Axien just blew a breath out through his nose like an angry stallion and looked away without another word.

What, by all things divine, was his problem now?

First, he treated me like a joke, teasing me with pet names and making backhanded comments about the fact that I was Viperi. Not totally unexpected. Most people did, and the fact that he was half-Avoran certainly didn't help.

But when I dared to swing back, to demand he treat me at least as well as he would any other work partner, he sulked like a child. Then he said all those bizarre, poetry-like things in Avoran, and even went to the trouble of wiping my face with his own stupid handkerchief, as though he really did like me.

Now this?

Calling me a feral dog? He'd made snide comments before, but nothing this directly vicious.

No one else said a word to break the heavy, tense silence as Sanja finished my hair. She arched an eyebrow expectantly as she handed me the little silk pouch where I kept my little pot of rouge and kohl in a slender wooden vial.

Ugh. Right. We were in the city now. I had to keep my image up, if only so I didn't draw any more attention than I already did.

I couldn't hold back a heavy sigh as I sat down and worked with my little hand mirror balanced between my knees to apply the makeup just as Vanora had taught me. I frowned at my reflection, even with my eyes now outlined in dark black and my lips brushed with red. Yes, it made me look older. More mature.

Prettier, I guess. Or at the very least, civilized.

But would anyone who saw me, even like this, ever see more than just a feral dog in makeup?

I hissed a Viperi curse through my teeth and made a point not to look Axien's way as I packed up all my things, laced up my boots, and went for the door. No one questioned it when I volunteered to go downstairs to retrieve some honeyed wine for our meal. Even Roxus seemed too tired to care what I did as long as it wasn't life-threatening.

And it wasn't. Honeyed wine aside, I just wanted some of that personal space Axien had tried helping himself to behind that screen while he was in the bath.

Only, I wanted mine farther away.

Far enough I might sneak in a scream or, at the very least, a private drink of something stronger than wine before I had to face any of them again.

I just wanted a few moments to breathe. To think and just be in my own head. We'd be heading into the temple to fetch that staff soon. I needed to be clear and primed for a fight, just in case anything else went wrong.

I needed Axien's stupid face out of my head for five minutes.

The instant the door shut behind me, I felt the weight of his stare slide off my back like a yoke of solid lead. My chest felt lighter. I let out a deep breath like a kettle venting all its steam.

Finally.

Now for some of that wine. Or maybe something a little stronger.

The first level of the inn was a finely decorated lounge with many low tables crowded with finely dressed patrons all relaxing on velvet and silk cushions. Men and women laughed, spoke quietly, smoked long pipes, and drank strong liquor from small glasses and polished silver cups by the light of dim colored glass lanterns. A minstrel picked at a traditional Nar'Haleenan instrument in the corner, singing a soft, sweet tune.

A few of the men tracked me with their eyes as I strode through the lounge, remembering to carry myself the way Vanora had taught me. I hadn't bothered practicing it in a while, but now seemed like as good a time as any. Especially since I was supposed to be keeping up appearances.

With every step into the room, I honed my aura like a smith sharpening a blade. Head up, shoulders back, neck arched, spine serpentine with every step. Hips swaying just so. Long braid swishing at the base of my back. Powerful, controlled, confident energy.

It must have worked, because by the time I reached the main bar to order a drink, a young man in fine silken robes was already waiting there, grinning from ear to ear. His eyes roamed over me, taking in every curve of my body and finally settling on my face.

My vibrant red eyes.

I saw the shock bloom over his features, a ripple of confusion tinged with uncertainty—and the tiniest hint of fear.

So I gave him what Vanora called the "secret" smile. A smile with my eyes and only a slight bow of my lips, like I knew something he didn't. I tilted my chin up and gave him my shoulder, making a point of standing several paces away at the bar. Out of reach, but still close enough for him to feel my energy.

It only took a few seconds for him to close the gap. Like a moth to the flame.

I had just called a barmaid over to order the bottle of wine for upstairs, along with a drink for myself—a small glass of a strong lemon liquor flavored with rosemary—when he sat five gold coins on the bar top.

The thick coins glittered, each one stamped with the Nar'Haleenan royal crest.

"I'll be covering whatever the lady orders tonight," he said, his Nar'Haleenan accent every bit as strong as the sandalwood cologne he wore. "If she permits me."

My stomach fluttered.

Gods and Fates, Vanora ... she was right. He didn't care that I was Viperi. Or maybe he did. Maybe he was enticed by it. Curious. Excited to see what other surprises I had hidden under that *secret* smile.

I eyed the stack of coins, along with all the jeweled rings on his fingers. Flaunting his wares. His status. Probably the son of a wealthy merchant, since he looked to be in his *very* early twenties.

Young, rich, *and* stupid?

My, the gods were kind tonight.

The server brought my drink, and I brushed the rim with my fingertips, tracing it once—delicately—before picking it up and turning to face him. I met his gaze for only an instant, then glanced him over and turned my face away.

Subtle dismissal to counterplay the way my body now faced him.

An invitation to try harder.

Because ... I liked it. The attention. The glitter of that gold on the counter. The free drink in my hand, and the promise of more.

Being seen as something desirable.

There was power in it I'd never experienced before.

"Is it too bold of me to ask if you have company this evening?" he asked, leaning his weight on the bar and sidling in closer. "I have room at my table for one more extremely beautiful woman if she's so inclined."

"She isn't," a bitter voice snapped an instant before I felt a hand on the base of my back.

I didn't have to look to know the energy of his presence, his smell, and the touch of his large, firm hand that slid up my spine and settled on the back of my neck.

Axien's smile was poison as he stared the other man down, his strange eyes flickering like fire-lit sapphires in the gloom. Thanks to Vanora, I saw every detail. Every hint of subtext that twitched at the edges of his handsome features.

The wrath that made his smile a little too wide.

The promise of violence that made a vein in the side of his neck stand out slightly.

The unspoken dare for the other man to make a scene in how he angled himself into me, his body brushing mine.

A declaration of ownership.

Anger flared in my chest. It twisted through me like a vine of thorns, cracking through all the walls and fortifications I'd built to keep myself in check.

"I'd rather see you both rot in the abyss," I sighed, forcing myself to sound utterly bored before I downed my cup, grabbed the bottle of wine I'd bought, and turned away.

I snatched out of Axien's hold and stormed back for the

stairs. I had barely made it two steps before I felt him behind me again like an encroaching sandstorm, all crackling wrath and booming fury.

"What are you doing?" Axien snarled, seizing me by the wrist.

I stopped and whirled on him, my empty hand already drawn up to slap him.

But he didn't so much as flinch. Almost like he was expecting it.

Almost like he wanted it.

"What are *you* doing?" I fired his own question right back instead. "Why does anything a *feral dog* does matter to you?"

His jaw worked from one side to the other, but he never looked away. Never even blinked. Even as his chest heaved with deep, shuddering breaths and his hand squeezed my wrist harder.

"Leave," he demanded suddenly.

I scowled, totally confused. "What?"

"You don't belong here—not with us or with the Zenith's Call. You never will. No matter what you do. No matter how you dress or fix your hair. No matter how much you paint up your face. You're still a beast underneath. You'll never be one of us. Ever," he seethed. "No one wants you here. They only tolerate you so they'll have a scapegoat when it all goes wrong. So they'll have someone easy to blame. So just give up and leave."

"Sh-Shut up," I gasped and snatched my arm out of his grasp.

"You think they'll see you as anything more than what you are, pitathi?" he continued, taking a prowling step closer. "You think Roxus's patience and pity won't run out? You're wasting everyone's time. You're fooling yourself to ever believe you will earn your place. Leave, Violet. Get out. Never come back."

I slapped him.

I hit him so hard my palm stung and his head snapped to the side.

My heart pounded wildly, like it might punch straight out through my ribs. Everything around us seemed to fade away until we were alone, facing one another in the darkness of a void.

"I ... I *hate* you." I breathed the words like a vow in that stillness.

His mouth screwed up, eyes twitching at the corners as he slowly turned his head back to stare at me again. But he didn't speak.

And neither did I. Not again.

Not when there was nothing left to be said.

I turned and fled the rest of the way up the stairs to our room. My legs and throat burned with every step. My mouth wobbled. My teeth ground down, gritting hard. My vision swerved and swam with fury.

But when I reached the door to our room, my entire body froze up solid. My hand trembled, hovering above the polished copper knob. Every heartbeat sent a pang of pain through me like a strum of harp-strings.

"You're still a beast underneath."

No. That wasn't true.

Was it?

I-I didn't know. Maybe it was. Maybe nothing I'd done mattered. All the training. All the practicing with Vanora. Changing my hair, my clothes, my gods-damned teeth.

Maybe none of that made any difference at all.

Maybe all I'd done was let them break me down, bit by bit, so when they left me in the rubble I wouldn't have the strength to fight anymore.

I drew my hand back slowly, fingers trembling.

"Run, Visha."

My eyes welled up.

I couldn't run. Not now. Not when I'd come this far—worked this hard.

Not when I still trusted Roxus. He had never given me any reason not to. He had *always* shown up for me, even when I didn't deserve it.

Even when no one else would.

I wiped the tears from my cheeks and took a few deep breaths in and out. Cooling the heat of the flames in my chest. Finding that kernel of strength.

Of trust.

None of what Axien said was true. Deep down, I knew that. He was an asshole for even suggesting Roxus was using me as some kind of scapegoat. Roxus wasn't like that. He didn't use people.

But ... but a part of me still wondered. Still questioned why Roxus had ever wanted to pull me out of that prison in the first place. He could have had anyone as an apprentice. Why choose me? Why choose a Viperi?

He'd never told me why. Not really.

And even after all this time, all the years of work, I still felt the sting of whispers that haunted my steps, even at Arx Eburna. Reminding me of what I was.

Reminding me that I'd never belong.

Somehow, Axien had known that. And now he was trying to force me out?

I didn't understand it. But I wouldn't just leave.

I wouldn't let him win.

Swallowing hard, I shut my eyes tightly for a moment. I had to get control of my expressions, to school them back to indifference. It took a minute or two.

Then I opened the door and went back inside. Thankfully, Roxus and Sanja were eating at the big low table in the far corner. Neither of them even glanced my way as I came in, set the bottle of wine on the table, and retreated to the corner where I'd spread out one of the soft, downy-stuffed mattresses on the floor.

Slipping off my boots, I crawled into the blankets and pulled them up around my head. When Axien came back inside, I didn't want to see him.

I never wanted to look at him again.

It made no sense. Why had he said those things like that to me? Obviously, it was to get me to leave. But why? What did it matter to him if I was here or not? It wasn't like my performance had any bearing on how the order viewed him.

Why did he even care what I did?

Fates, I didn't know.

And as I surrendered to the bone-deep fatigue that turned all my thoughts to mush, I swore I'd never forgive him. Not again.

From now on, Axien would be my enemy, no matter what his true motive was.

I just had to hope he wouldn't try anything else to force me out of the mission. Gods only knew what he might try next.

I had to be ready. I had to keep one step ahead of him from now on.

Otherwise, he might get his wish ... and I might be thrown to the gutter with the rest of the feral dogs.

THIRTY-ONE

Someone was shouting.

I jolted awake, blinking groggily around the room as my body throbbed with the rush of adrenaline.

Nothing.

Roxus lay only a few feet away, sound asleep on his own pallet. His mound of blankets slowly rose and fell with each breath, and the familiar rumble of his snore filled the stillness. On the other side of the room, Axien and Sanja's beds were spread out on the floor, but too far away to see them clearly through the gloom.

The wind rustled the heavy drapes, making flickers of sunlight dance across the walls. The faint aroma of spiced tea still hung in the air, mingling with the lingering fragrance of the bath oils. All my gear was still neatly arranged next to my bed, ready for me to grab it at a moment's notice.

Nothing moving. Not a sock or sword out of place.

I frowned and rubbed at my eyes with the heel of my hand.

Had it been a dream? Or—?

My heartbeat skipped as a muffled thud pounded against

the wall nearby. I sucked in a sharp breath, my hand immediately darting for my blades.

Then I froze.

A wash of cold, tingling chills swept over my skin as I sat perfectly still, listening. Waiting. Every nerve taut.

A pair of muffled voices shouted back and forth somewhere on the other side of the wall. In the hall just outside? Yes. I could feel the faint vibrations through the floorboards as they scuffled around. I couldn't tell who, though.

Their tones were deep. Men, most likely. And their words seemed off somehow. A strange mixture of sounds. Were they even speaking the common tongue? It didn't sound like Sokraal or Rienkan.

It wasn't Avoran, either.

Moving slowly, I pulled back my blankets and crept out of bed, making sure not to disturb anything on my way to the wall. I pressed my ear to the warm wooden paneling, trying to listen.

THUD!

I jerked back as something smacked off the wall on the other side. The vibrations shuddered through the wooden boards and an angry male voice snarled something in a sharp, hard-edged language.

Definitely not one of the Southern Kingdom tongues.

"What difference does it make? Nothing about the situation has changed," a voice rasped in the common language, coming from so close to the wall that I could hear him frantically wheezing and gasping for breath.

My blood went cold.

My stomach dropped so suddenly I had to mash a hand over my mouth to stifle a gasp. That voice. I knew it.

Was that ... Axien?

No. It couldn't be.

Could it?

I looked over at his bed, but it was only a faint outline in the near dark. Even with my heat vision, I couldn't tell if he was lying in it or not. Everything had a dull glow thanks to the ambient heat from outside, and I had fallen asleep before I'd seen him return to the room. To be sure, I'd have to get closer.

BAM!

Another crash made the wall shudder.

Someone gasped sharply. A pained sound.

"F-Fine. You've m-made your point," the voice against the wall said, words hitching. Almost like he was in pain.

The other voice answered, but it was still too far away. Too muffled. I couldn't tell who it was apart from a *very* unhappy man, but I did recognize one word. One, solitary, brutal word that didn't require any translation for me to understand.

"... pitathi!"

My pulse skipped, twisting to an agonized halt for an instant. Icy chills trickled down my spine.

They were talking about ... me.

Footsteps thumped beyond the wall. There was another grunt of pain. Another shudder against the panels. Then more heavy footsteps that gradually faded away.

And silence.

Awful, heavy silence.

I sat perfectly still, straining to hear something over the way my heart pounded in my ears, while my brain frantically tried to rationalize what I'd heard. I could be wrong. It could have been another word that sounded similar. It could just be two men from down in the lounge who'd had far too much of that pricy liquor.

There was only one way to be sure.

I had to check Axien's bed.

Pushing away from the wall, I started picking my way across the floor. Two steps. Three.

Then I heard the doorknob rattle behind me.

Oh no.

Hide—I had to find a way to hide! I only had seconds.

I ran for the door and flattened myself against the wall beside it. When it swung slowly open, I was hidden behind it as a tall figure lurched into the room. My hands knotted into fists as I held my breath.

Axien staggered forward, holding his face with one hand and keeping an arm wrapped around his middle with the other. Blood seeped through his fingers, running from his nose. He made it a few steps in, then nudged the door shut with his foot without ever turning around.

I didn't dare to even blink. He might see. Or hear. And what then?

Still—I just had to stay still. I was hidden in the shadows. He wouldn't turn back.

As long as I didn't move or make a sound.

My pulse was thunder in my chest as Axien made his way to his pallet and sat down, still holding his nose. I could barely see him pull out his handkerchief and hold it to his face as he let his forehead rest in his other hand. His broad shoulders shook some, almost like he was laughing.

But there was no sound. Nothing but a deep, ragged intake of breath.

Was he ...?

No. Absolutely not.

I wouldn't assume anything about Axien. Never again. Especially not when I couldn't even see his face clearly.

Confusion whirled through my brain, tearing at my thoughts and clawing through my sanity. What was happening? Had he been fighting someone out there? Why?

Gods, what was going on?

I waited, still not daring to move, as Axien unlaced his boots and threw them aside one at a time. When he finally lay back on his bed, pinching his bleeding nose shut with that handkerchief, I finally dared to let my shoulders slowly relax.

I chanced the tiniest breath.

He didn't react.

Minutes passed, and his arm, pinching off his bleeding nose, finally dropped back to his side. His breathing slowed and deepened.

He might be faking. Or he might be dead. I couldn't tell.

But I also couldn't stand by the door all night.

Curse it all, I'd have to risk it.

My pulse skipped and stalled, my gaze fixed on where he still lay, as I finally stole a step toward my bed. Then another. I hesitated, watching him for any sign of movement.

Not so much as a twitch.

My whole body shook when I finally slipped back into my bed. Across the room, Axien hadn't made another sound or stirred at all. He was just a mound amidst the shadows and blankets, like he'd been there all night.

Only … I knew different.

My mind whirled, heart still pounding like mad as I drew my knees in close to my chest. Had he gotten drunk? Fought with that young man from downstairs? That could explain why they'd said pitathi, wouldn't it?

I didn't know. And as the hours slipped by, I couldn't come up with an answer.

Asking him about it was out of the question, of course. Doing nothing felt wrong, too. The idea of saying something to Roxus or Sanja about it felt even worse.

It was none of my business what he did with his own time —even if that included getting a little drunk and disorderly with some idiot downstairs.

Axien issues were not my problem. And … if it was something worse. If it was something nefarious, then I couldn't just go off pointing fingers with no evidence other than what I'd heard through a wall in the middle of the night. Roxus and Sanja would never accept that.

"Zenith's Call stand by our own—always." That's what Roxus had told me.

So I had to be careful about this. I had to watch him closely and bide my time.

For now.

THIRTY-TWO

S omething was touching me.

A hand. A hand was on my shoulder, gripping tight, and—

I jolted awake to Roxus shaking my shoulder and leaning over me with that wry, crooked grin.

"So, she lives after all," he chuckled.

I bolted upright in bed, blinking blearily around the room. Sanja glanced up from where she was fixing her hair, bright-eyed and smiling. Axien sat at the low table, his back to the rest of us.

Gods, curse it all, I fell asleep!

So much for pulling myself together.

"Get something to eat," Roxus scolded gently as I scrambled out of bed and frantically threw on my boots and leathers. "You skipped dinner. Don't think I didn't notice."

"It was too hot to eat," I muttered, hoping he wouldn't detect the lie hidden in my embarrassment.

"It's much nicer out now," Sanja said as she pinned all her dark hair up into a large, ornate bun. "The moon will be up very soon, so be quick. Actually, I had a thought about our travel, if you'll entertain it, Roxus."

He made a grunting noise of interest.

"In the spirit of moving things along, and since time is always against us, I thought I might see to arranging for us to ride to Dumathis from here? Rather than waiting for the caravan to be ready. The less time we waste here, the better. I can easily get one of my friends to loan us some dunestriders. We'll be on our own, but we'll go much faster that way. What do you think?"

My heart leapt at the idea. I'd read about dunestriders, but never seen one in person. Their speed was legendary. Faster on the ground than a dragon in the air, some said.

Now, I might get to find out for myself.

Roxus made another grumbling sound and rubbed at his stubbled chin before looking at me. Almost like he was trying to decide if he thought I could handle something like that.

I scoffed and stalked off to the low table, giving him my back. I had handled riding a hippocampus, hadn't I? And then a horse, too. Riding a dunestrider couldn't be all that different.

Okay, fine. So maybe my performance with the caravan's stallion had been less than ideal. But dunestriders were supposedly far smarter and faster. Even switchbeasts couldn't catch them. What was there to worry about?

"Fine," he agreed at last. "We'll see to getting the staff and meet you by the western gate."

Sanja beamed. "Excellent! I'll head off, then. Best of luck, you three. Axien, at least try to behave yourself."

He didn't reply.

In fact, Axien didn't move at all—not even when I sat down across the table and began raking food from the break-fast dishes onto my plate. By the look of it, everyone else had already eaten. Fantastic.

That meant I could gorge myself without worrying about sharing.

I heaped candied fruit and roasted eggplant pastes onto thin, crispy squares of sesame bread before wolfing down three eggs poached in chili paste. I piled another few pieces of bread with slices of smoked fish and a strong cheese with dill sprinkled on top. All of it fresh, delicious, and completely mine.

The rich flavors hit my furiously empty stomach and made me bounce in my seat as I poured a glass of mango juice and downed it in one gulp. Sure, it wasn't Delthene's homemade fare, but it was better than anything else I'd eaten in days.

"You ought to eat something more, as well. Bread and tea won't last long once we start to ride," Sanja murmured as she stepped past Axien to fetch her bag.

I caught the tail end of her concerned sideways glance in his direction.

He didn't reply or even move from where he sat, leaning against the table, his head down and his expression sealed under that mask of cold thought.

As though mentally he was somewhere else completely.

I tried not to stare at where his nose and jaw were mottled with faint, fresh bruises, and his bottom lip looked a little swollen. He had taken a beating, after all.

But from whom?

I didn't dare ask or even look his way for more than a few seconds. No need to poke the ... er, well, not a bear. Roxus was the bear, obviously. Axien was more sleek, athletically lean, and poised most of the time. A lion might have suited him better.

If he weren't a massive, sow-faced jerkoff.

Sanja didn't press him again, either. She sighed deeply, swapping a concerned look with Roxus before she swept out of the room. The door clicked shut behind her, and suddenly, the pressure seemed to ease a bit.

Axien let out a quiet breath. His eyes closed and his head dipped lower, brow finally going slack in what might have been relief.

Or fatigue.

Both, perhaps.

"Moon'll be up in less than an hour," Roxus warned as he shouldered his bag. "We need to get moving."

I scraped what was left in the little bowl of eggplant paste into my mouth with a finger, crammed down a few more of the sesame bread wafers, and snatched an orange from the bowl of fruit in the middle of the table before I went to retrieve my bag, too.

Axien followed, shuffling stiffly and still saying nothing.

In less than five minutes, we were all armed to the teeth and stepping out of the inn's front door. The shining, dark stone streets of Salnis welcomed us with gusts of cool night wind howling through the canyon. Lights gleamed from hanging lanterns up and down the countless levels of the city that hugged either side of the steep rock faces. People moved in groups, chattering and laughing.

Under the glitter of a million stars, the city came alive. Or so I thought, until the first sliver of the moon began to rise above the horizon.

And suddenly, I understood why this was Adiana's city. Why her colossal statue stood watch over its polished shale and obsidian streets. Why her temple had been positioned here for thousands of years.

As the moon floated higher, so big it felt close enough to touch, its sterling light fell like streams of silver and hit the crystal at the top of the golden statue's staff. The massive crystal glowed to life, faintly at first, but then as bright as a small sun. It shed ethereal silver light over all the city that sparkled and wavered like sunlight through water.

Or at least, I thought it was from the crystal.

One glance beneath my feet revealed the truth—that the veins of blue in the rock were glowing—radiating magic that set the entire city alight. To everyone else, it must have looked silver. Or perhaps even gold. But to my eyes, it all shone pale blue.

Magic, raw and unfettered, was infused into the veins that ran through the city's stonework.

My steps dragged to a halt at the edge of one of the gilded railings, watching in awe as the night wind teased over my skin. My lips parted as chills tingled all through my body. I couldn't hold in a smile. Fates, I'd never seen anything so beautiful.

And then I spotted him.

Off to my left, Axien had stopped a dozen paces ahead and turned back. He stared straight at me, his eyes wide and shining the same sort of blue as the light from the crystal and the veins in the stone. Alive with magic.

But his gaze stayed fixed only on me.

His expression—I didn't understand it at all. The way his brows drew up, skewed with anguish. The way his mouth opened slightly, as though he were desperate to say something that never left his lips. It was something like grief, and a little like torment.

All I could do was stare back, my smile fading.

He'd looked at me like this before. When we'd ridden the hippocampi out of Kua'Tar, I'd caught him staring at me with that same awed, almost haunted expression.

It made no sense, especially given all the nasty things he'd said yesterday.

Why make a face like that at someone he compared to a feral dog? At someone he only wanted to get rid of?

My mouth pinched into a hard frown before I could stop it and I quickly looked ahead. Pushing away from the railing, I walked faster to catch up with Roxus, making sure I stayed in stride with him as we wound our way through the city.

"Hood up," he reminded me.

I quickly obeyed, tucking my long braid into my cloak to hide it from view. "How far is it to the temple?"

"Not far, but we need to be careful. Keep an eye out in case we're being followed," Roxus warned. "Axien mentioned there were some shady sorts milling around in the inn's lounge yesterday evening."

It wasn't a question, but I could feel the hint of curiosity in his tone. Probably wondering if I'd noticed that as well when I went down to get wine.

My stomach fluttered nervously. No point in trying to lie this time.

"I know. By the sound of it, he had a close encounter with them while the rest of you were asleep. I heard them fighting outside. It woke me up," I confessed.

Roxus flicked me a suspicious frown. "Why didn't you wake me up?"

"Because I wasn't sure it was him, at first," I admitted, keeping my voice down. "And when he came inside, I guess I thought it didn't matter then. He's been more intolerable than usual lately. Not surprising he'd start a bar fight."

"What did you hear?" he pressed.

"Nothing I understood ... apart from a few slurs thrown my way," I said flatly. "He tried to start something with a man at the bar who was being a little too friendly while I was buying wine. It was probably the same guy."

Roxus made a dissatisfied grunting noise, scowling ahead as he walked faster. "Let's hope that's all it was."

Only ... I knew it wasn't.

I just didn't know how, by all the gods, I could ever tell him the truth.

THIRTY-THREE

I should tell him.

I should tell Roxus what else Axien had said. That he'd tried to run me off. That he'd been the one to sling slurs first. That I suspected that encounter last night was more than just a drunken disagreement with some idiot down in the lounge.

But I couldn't.

The words hung in my throat, and I couldn't help stealing a glance at Axien over my shoulder. Thankfully, he had a fierce, stony frown aimed at the ground between us, as though he were still adrift in a sea of thought somewhere far away.

Or like he might be sick at any moment.

Whatever was going on with him, tattling to Roxus wouldn't fix anything—it would make it worse. Roxus would get angry. He'd go after Axien, either verbally or physically. Or both. Then Sanja would get involved. Our group would fall apart and our entire mission would be in jeopardy. Mistress Orvana would blame me, like always.

I couldn't allow that. The last thing in the world I needed

was to hand Mistress Orvana a golden excuse to never let me go on a mission again.

I took in a deep, centering breath, pushing air all the way into my belly before releasing it.

No, I wouldn't say anything to Roxus. I wouldn't risk jeopardizing everything I'd worked for over a waste of breath like Axien.

Besides, it wasn't like I'd never been insulted by people I was meant to be working with before. Varren called me names all the time. Granted, he wasn't trying to run me out of the Zenith's Call when he did it.

Er, well, not anymore, at least.

And I was allowed to punch him in the face as many times as I wanted in the name of training, which was a very satisfying trade-off. Just the thought of it made me smile.

I never got tired of feeling his bones crack under my knuckles.

Therapy in its purest form.

I was overdue for some of that when we finally got home. Punching Varren in the face a few times might be just what I needed to clear my head.

I kept my mouth shut as we pressed on, winding a path through the city farther and farther to the north. We doubled back a few times, crossing our own path and taking more obscure streets as we went. With every turn, we passed fewer and fewer people. The lights of the city seemed to fade, leaving only that ghostly blue-silver glow from the stones to light our path.

Roxus moved like a beast on the hunt, silent and swift. Every step calculated. His eyes never stopped moving, panning ahead and flicking back to make sure Axien and I still followed closely.

I prowled forward right behind him, brushing my finger-tips along the hilts of my daggers as I watched the shadows with my heat-vision. My every nerve attuned to the night, every sense wide open for anything that seemed off. Any faint sound or scuff of a footstep. A distant cough or rustle of fabric.

But as we pushed to the northern perimeter of the city, the twisting terraced roads grew thinner and I didn't see another soul anywhere. Here, the stone-hewn streets weren't as pristinely carved and seemed to slope upward to the rim of the canyon. Everything about it felt older. Archaic and nearly forgotten, but still quietly powerful.

Like the gods themselves.

We rounded a sharp turn, and my body jerked to a halt when I saw it. Our destination—Levanurith. The final resting place of one of the most powerful divine artifacts still in existence.

My breath caught, and I stared, drinking in every detail of the elegant structure that gleamed like sun-bleached bone in the moonlight.

The temple sat on the very edge of a steep cliff drop that plummeted straight down into the darkest depths of the canyon below. Flanked on both sides by arched bridges that connected it to either side of the canyon, it seemed to hang in the air like a pearl on a string.

Or, perhaps it had once.

"It used to be a waterfall," Roxus explained when he noticed my pause. "It made the temple seem to be floating as the water spilled around it, and the bridges were the only way to reach it. But the waters dried to a trickle after the War of the Stones. There's still a river far below, but the falls are all but gone now."

"Incredible," I managed to whisper.

"Another masterful piece done by the Avorans before the war. Most of their architecture is now buried, as you well know. Sand and time have done their work well. But a few places remain visible—like this. Testaments to the might and reach of their empire," he said, and gave me a nudge with his elbow. "We need to hurry."

"No wonder Sanja was looking for any excuse to avoid coming here." My stomach squirmed as Axien paused beside us, his expression cool and empty of all emotion as he considered the temple, too. "She hates heights."

Roxus's mouth split with a smirk that showed a flash of white teeth. "Heights *and* swimming," he corrected.

Ah. No wonder she hadn't enjoyed riding the hippocampus. Oops.

Axien didn't reply as we pressed on, closing the distance along the left canyon wall. The closer we drew, the more the winds seemed to howl in from the desert beyond. The moonlight poured from above, so clear and bright I could almost feel the heat of it like the sun on my skin. It made my heat-vision useless and blotted out the stars.

Two large statues of seated winged cats cut from pure white marble guarded the entrance to where the bridge began its sloping descent to the temple doors. They seemed to stare down at us disapprovingly with eyes of sparkling peridot as we passed.

Chills tingled along my arms and up the back of my skull as we crossed. I told myself it was just the height, since I couldn't even see the bottom of the steep drop mere feet away on my right.

Far on the other end of the bridge, the temple doors were open and half a dozen figures already stood outside waiting when we finally reached them.

Motionless and silent, the priests of Adiana stood draped in long black and silver robes with their hands clasped in front. All but one wore feline masks made of polished silver—a tall, thin elven man with many platinum beads woven into his long black hair. He had silver runes tattooed into his deep ebony skin with a small circle that swept over the middle of his fore-head. A moon-mark, reserved only for the highest of Adiana's holy order.

He was a Lunostri elf. The first I had seen since Curator Faera had ...

The memory snagged at my brain like a hook in a fish's mouth, jerking me out of my good sense. The memories of her, of her still-warm blood between my fingers as the light in her eyes faded, swelled in my brain like a tidal wave. The force of it hit, crashing through my soul and dragging me down.

"Follow the magic. Follow the light."

I shuddered.

And the Lunostri priest *noticed*. His eyes became steel. His lips thinned.

Oh no.

I swallowed hard, fighting to keep my expression schooled to indifference when his vivid yellow-green eyes fell squarely on me. My palms went clammy and cold, and my toes curled in my boots as I braced for it.

The disgust. The hatred.

The priest's brow furrowed, putting creases in his fore-head that rumpled those sterling marks. He stared me down for a beat, then cut an accusing glare to Roxus. "How is it that the Zenith's Call walks with the spawn of Vescor?"

"Well, personally, I find it easiest to just put one foot in front of the other, High Priest. The rest sort of takes care of itself," Roxus drawled as he pulled a folded piece of parchment from his pocket and handed it to the priest. "Varri'dasha. The Mistress sends her greetings."

I recognized Mistress Orvana's wax seal pressed into it as the priest snatched it away and opened it. His gaze darted over the missive, reading fast before folding it sharply and tucking it into his own robes.

He didn't even look at me as he bit out, "Fine. You may

come and take what you require. But *it* will remain here under watch. No fouled blood may pass onto this holy ground."

Ahh. By *"it,"*... he meant me.

I could feel the sting of Axien's stare suddenly on me again. Out of the corner of my eye, I saw him shift his stance and cross his arms.

As usual, Roxus was less subtle.

"She is oathmarked. She goes where we go," Roxus growled, bristling. "Do you think the order would mark someone it did not think was worthy?"

The Lunostri high priest bristled. His mouth screwed up bitterly as he finally looked down at me again. Angry veins stood out against his forehead and neck and his nostrils flared.

"I think the order has become very lax in its views on many things," he hissed. "Including the *worthiness* of its members."

"Then rest assured, she is under careful watch already," Axien spoke up suddenly. His smile was a charming balm as he stepped forward, offering a small bow to the priest before he motioned to me. "Why else would they send someone like me along, as well? I will keep an eye on her, so there's nothing to worry over. If you like, we can even wait far outside the sanctum while you retrieve the artifact."

I hated him.

I hated his stupid, beautiful smile that worked like a magic charm on the priest. I hated the way his eyes shone like sapphire candles, glittering with ancient magic that guaranteed him instant trust from anyone who knew a kernel of divine history.

Of course the high priest's expression smoothed. *Of course* he smiled tentatively back and began ushering us swiftly inside.

Gods, I wanted to puke at it all.

Only a few hours ago, Axien had been spitting all manner

of hatred at me. Now he was acting like some benevolent babysitter charged with keeping me on a leash.

I couldn't suppress it—the urge to snarl at him. My lips drew back slightly, but my fangs weren't there. I'd been leashed after all. In one aspect, anyway.

Roxus didn't look happy either as he kept close to my side, following along deeper and deeper into the temple. He glowered at the high priest's back and licked his teeth behind his lips, working his jaw from one side to the other.

Oh boy. I knew that look.

I had to talk him back from the ledge before the bear came out to play.

"I'm fine," I whispered as we made our way down what felt like an eternity of stairs into a long chamber lit by smoldering braziers filled with incense.

Roxus blew a furious snort through his nose.

"You can't fight everyone who doesn't like me, you know," I scolded him gently.

He rolled his eyes and shoved his hands deep into the pockets of his ragged traveling coat.

"It's bad enough to watch for outside attackers interfering with the mission without needing to explain ourselves to those who are meant to be on our side, as well," he fumed quietly. "The mark used to mean something. It used to negate all other opinions and prejudices."

"It probably still does, for most people." I shrugged, looking ahead to where Axien now strolled alongside the high priest, chatting merrily. "But I'm not most people, am I? You warned me yourself getting them to accept me would be an uphill battle. We both knew I'd face a lifetime of discrimination if I chose this path."

Roxus puffed a deep sigh of surrender. "That doesn't mean it won't piss me off when it happens."

"Obviously." I made a good show of grinning at him. Of

making it seem like none of this bothered me. But dread burrowed deep into my gut like an icy blade, twisting and wrenching until I could hardly breathe.

Should I have told him what Axien said? What if I had? He'd be furious, sure, but then he might also—

My thoughts went blank as we descended another flight of stairs and arrived in another chamber, this one even grander and more majestic than anywhere I'd ever been. My gaze roamed up to the cavernous ceiling, adorned in paintings of the night sky with all its constellations. The light of countless candles flickered, casting eerie, moving shadows along the carved walls that depicted scenes from the creation of the Reatia and the wars that had threatened to tear it all apart.

But none of that was what made my steps slow until I was the very last in line moving through the room, my neck aching as I stared up and struggled to take it all in.

Dozens of empty frames, like large dressing mirrors, stood along the walls of the candlelit chamber. They towered around us at over twelve feet tall, just like the ones in Arx Eburna. Each one stood on a small stone dais and was made from thick golden filigree that formed a pointed arch at the top. Every inch of that swirling, tarnished gold was covered in tiny runes.

Avoran runes.

I'd read about these gates more times than I could count. This was how the ancient Avorans moved throughout their vast empire, crossing thousands of miles in an instant whenever they wished.

Now, they were all empty. Dormant and useless without a source of immense divine power to activate them.

I'd seen Avoran gates like these nearly every day of my life since I'd first come to Arx Eburna. But no one, not even Mistress Orvana, could use them. Not when the divine magic that could power them had vanished in the north hundreds of years ago, along with the Avorans themselves.

I slipped a glance at Axien.

He was only half-Avoran, but he did have some of that divine magic in his blood...?

Hmmm.

The high priest and his acolytes began to chant softly as we made our way to the far end of the room, beyond the rows of golden gateways. There, a huge statue of Adiana stood like she'd been frozen in time. Her long robes flowed over her body, somehow engraved to look as thin and sheer as real silk. The circlet on her head showed all the phases of the moon, and her golden wings were outstretched and curved in, as though to embrace us all as we approached.

Just the sight of her seemed to fill the room with a reverent silence—one broken only by the song the acolytes murmured. Something about it made me want to hold my breath and step softly. As though the smallest interfering noise were a grave offense to the tranquility of her night.

Best not to anger the goddess of the moon in her own temple. Especially for someone created by her archenemy purely to spite her.

I was too busy gawking to see how he did it, but the head Lunostri high priest pulled a hidden lever somewhere, and the base of the statue opened. A fold in her robes became a pair of open stone doors that revealed a passage down deeper into the temple.

Standing on my toes, I could just see it: the narrow set of black stone steps that led down into a small room. There, a single altar cut from a solid hunk of obsidian stood in the center, bathed in the gentle light of flickering candles on golden stands.

I didn't dare take another step closer—not when the other acolytes wearing those strange masks stared me down. Like they were all waiting for me to make one wrong move and give them an excuse to attack. Ugh.

Axien had positioned himself right beside me, seeming just as transfixed by the sight of that altar. Or rather, what lay on it.

Not that I blamed him.

There, resting on an embroidered drape of black velvet, the Moonscape staff gleamed with an aura of radiant blue light around it like a halo.

Magical blue light.

Something stirred in the back of my mind like a shiver that splashed all over my body. Every tiny hair on my arms and neck prickled. Gooseflesh rose on my skin.

Gods and Fates, it really did look like the one from her colossal monument in the city—only much smaller, of course. The size of a common shepherd's crook, maybe seven feet to the tip.

It had the same strange crystal at one end, and that wicked tri-tipped blade at the other. Beauty and ferocity fused into one, breathtaking weapon.

The Lunostri high priest stepped down and gently lifted it from the altar. As he turned back to face us, Axien moved in front of me, his tall form all but eclipsing my view. Idiot. What was he doing? Making sure I didn't get anywhere near their holy chambers?

No—no way was I missing this. No way was I letting him edge me out.

I had to lean sideways to peer around him as the priest ascended the steps again, now holding the staff out as though he were about to pass it over to Roxus.

Then the high priest stopped with a strange, jerking lurch.

His expression went eerily slack. His eyes widened, staring past everyone else straight at me.

My pulse skipped as our gazes locked. And yet, it felt like he couldn't actually see me. Or anything at all. Wrong—something was wrong.

I didn't dare look away as I reached for my daggers.

In front of me, Axien bristled. He threw a hand out to block my path forward.

"S-Sir?" One of the other attending acolytes asked hesitantly.

The high priest's mouth opened, letting out a frantic, rattling breath right before he fell forward onto the stone ... with two crossbow bolts sticking out of his back.

Another acolyte screamed. The rest gasped back.

The staff clattered to the stone floor and rolled, stopping at Roxus's feet.

And in an instant, the quiet of the holy chamber shattered into utter chaos.

THIRTY-FOUR

The high priest was dead.

Or near enough to it that no one dared to rush toward him as his blood coated the marble.

For the flash of a single second, no one moved. No one breathed.

The staff rolled to a halt, the crystal tip shimmering with a faint blue glow only I could see. Then Roxus started to move, to bend down and reach for it.

TWANG!

I knew the crack of a crossbow string as it rang out through the chamber, the arrow glancing off the stone right next to Roxus's hand. A warning shot.

He froze.

"Not another inch, Roxus, darling. Let's not spill any more blood than necessary, hm?" a sickly saccharine voice called out.

Sanja.

My stomach turned. Bile burned in my throat, fists clenched on the hilt of my daggers as she prowled up from the altar chamber, stepping daintily over the fallen priest.

Of *freaking* course. Because why would it be anyone else —someone other than yet another person I'd begun to trust?

I bared my teeth, but she didn't even glance my way as she glided past.

Behind her, three male figures dressed in sleek black leather armor followed like a pack of sharks cruising by with heavy crossbows at the ready. They wore the same symbol emblazoned on their breastplates in gold: an open hand with an eye in the center of the palm. Not a symbol I recognized.

Curse it, what was happening? Who were they?

And why the hell was Sanja helping them?! She was Zenith's Call! She'd worked with Roxus for years! Even Vanora knew her!

I couldn't stop myself from looking to him for some kind of clue—any indication that he'd seen this coming.

All the color drained from Roxus's face as he watched Sanja, his brown eyes tracking her every move as she strolled over to snatch the staff up with a flippant, gleeful smile.

"I'll be taking this, thank you," she said sweetly.

Roxus growled—a deep, thunderous sound—as he slowly stood straight and glowered down at her. An ominous tower of wrath even in that ragged coat. His broad chest heaved in deep, furious breaths, and a muscle feathered in his jaw.

I tensed. Now that was a look I knew all too well.

He was thinking, weighing his options, and plotting his next move carefully as he studied her. Trying to stay calm through the fury.

Trying to hold back the beast beneath. One false move would get more innocents killed. Blood he'd have on his hands forever.

"Don't try to get clever with me now," Sanja crooned, as if this was all one big joke. She motioned to her men, and a pair of them stepped forward with a familiar set of shackles and collar.

My pulse skipped, and my blood rushed.

The same set that Mistress Orvana had bound me in years ago. How had she gotten them? Had she stolen them from Arx Eburna? Or had Mistress Orvana simply handed them over?

"Sanja, what is this?" he demanded, his tone rough with anger as he snarled at the armored men. "What the hell have you done?"

Her mask of sugary pleasure cracked, her lovely features twisting with something like manic determination as she snapped, "Don't you dare judge me, Roxus. You have *no idea* what the years have done."

He didn't blink, keeping a steady glare on her as his lip curled in disgust. "I might have. Might have tried to save you from it. You only needed to ask."

Her chin trembled, beautiful doe eyes welling even as they smoldered upon him. "I will *die* before I beg another man for his mercy," she seethed, voice trembling with soul-shattering fury, and snapped her fingers to her warriors. "Chain him and summon the others."

I surged forward, ducking under Axien's arm with my blades at the ready.

TWANG—TWANG!

The warriors fired, their bolts ripping through the air toward me.

I felt them, the hum of their speed in the air, and dipped under the first shot. It sailed past my cheek, barely grazing the skin.

Pain surged through my arm as the second caught me in the meat of my shoulder with such force I staggered.

"STOP IT!" Roxus roared suddenly, his booming voice echoing through the cavernous room.

His agonized glare was fixed on me.

Me—he was yelling at *me*. Telling *me* to stop.

Not them.

I froze.

Sanja's smirk oozed with wicked delight as she held up a hand, gesturing for her men to hold their fire.

"Oh, Roxus. You always did have a soft spot for the hopeless," she scolded.

His jaw clenched. "Clearly."

She shot him a venomous glare of reproach, her entire demeanor seeming to cool as all those emotions curled back behind that beautiful, contrived mask of calm.

"I'll show you hopeless. Be a good boy and cooperate," Sanja hissed, squaring herself toward him with her chin tilted up indignantly. "Perhaps then I'll give your vile little pet a quick death. Axien?"

She snapped her fingers at him with the same flippant superiority she had the other warriors.

Wet, sticky warmth soaked my shirt beneath my armor. Pain throbbed through my arm. But I didn't move an inch, didn't let her see a single flicker of it touch my features as I snarled back at her.

"Violet, don't," Roxus ordered again.

Don't? DON'T? Why the hell not?!

I flashed him a crazed glance, and I saw it.

The hurt that rimmed his eyes with tears. The betrayal that made his mouth set into a hard, thin line. It cut so deep, burned like hellfire, and I knew exactly what had to come next.

The burn of anger. Of rage. Of vengeance.

Sanja wouldn't leave here with that staff. We had to make sure of it. One way or another, we would stop her. Even if it cost us everything.

A glorious death.

I nodded once, understanding passing through me like a cool wind. It soothed the inferno in my chest. Honed it into a focused fury that awakened that monster deep within. My wicked beast. Gods, it had been a while since I'd let it off the chain.

I just had to choose the right moment.

I didn't look away as Axien moved, forceful and swift. He grabbed me, holding me against his chest with my uninjured arm twisted behind me until I was forced to drop my dagger ... right into his waiting hand.

I swallowed the hellfire in my throat as he pressed it—my own weapon—to the hollow of my throat.

I didn't resist. Didn't fight back. Not yet.

Not until Roxus gave the word.

We would do this together, even to the bitter end.

Then Axien leaned down, his head so close I could feel the heat of his breath tickling my cheek.

My entire body went stiff. Everything went numb as my heart pounded like a war hammer. Each pulse louder than the last as his lips brushed against the shell of my ear.

"There are twenty more of her soldiers waiting in the next room. We move on my count, little serpent," he whispered in Avoran.

Nothing made sense.

Why was Sanja doing this? How long had she been plotting against us? Was she behind the mercenaries who had tried to kill me before? Had Axien been helping her the whole time?

And why, by all the gods, was he saying these things now? Was he really about to betray her? Why?

Gods, curse it, could I even trust him? Maybe he was just taunting me, trying to tempt me into a reaction so he had an excuse to kill me outright. To make Roxus watch me bleed out and die right here on the floor in front of him like an animal.

Like a *feral dog*.

I didn't know.

My whole body trembled, half with rage and half with

terror, as the lethal edge of my dagger grazed the skin of my throat.

"Trust for trust."

The words tore through my brain with savage efficiency.

"One," he whispered, his words sending shivers up my spine that coursed out through every part of me in a rush of pure adrenaline.

Choose. I had to choose. Right now.

"... two."

Sanja's soldiers were moving forward, ready to put the shackles on Roxus.

"... three."

I made my choice.

THIRTY-FIVE

I was death.

I was hatred embodied. Vengeance personified.

And I did not hesitate.

The instant he counted to three, Axien dropped my dagger.

I snatched it out of the air as he released me, rolling me down the length of his arm like a dancer toward the nearest of Sanja's soldiers. One flick of my wrist sent my blade flying free, sailing end over end and lodging into his forehead.

His body jerked, reeling and releasing the bolt loaded in his crossbow.

TWANG!

It flew, sailing off randomly and clattering off one of the portal frames.

The rest of the soldiers didn't hesitate ... or miss their marks.

Roxus let out a booming roar as his beastly form burst free. He hit the ground on all fours, now a shaggy-furred bear over eight feet tall, and immediately took a crossbow bolt to the chest. He bellowed again and dove into the fray. One sweep of a mighty paw sent another of Sanja's men flying.

But Axien had told the truth. Their reinforcements were already on the way.

Ten more of those soldiers, all wearing the same breast-plate marked with the eye and hand, rushed the room with a chorus of shouts. They spread out, concentrating most of their efforts on Roxus—he was the biggest and most obvious threat.

"I need him alive!" Sanja screamed as she gripped the staff tight and backed away, watching it all unfold with her expression twisted somewhere between shock, rage, and panic.

The soldiers advanced. Some drew swords. Others fired more crossbows.

The acolytes screamed and fled like panicked chickens. Some fell immediately to the hailstorm of arrows that zipped through the air in every direction. Others dove for cover or huddled together and wailed.

They couldn't fight, even to defend themselves—because we, the Zenith's Call, were meant to be that protection.

I ducked and wove, dodging the incoming fire while keeping an eye trained on Sanja. She was the primary target. Their leader.

The head of the snake.

I would end her and feel her lifeblood ooze through my fingers while I watched the life leave her eyes.

And I would cherish every second of it.

Everything else fell away, eclipsed by the fury that ruled my body as I tore through another of her guards, carving a path for her.

WHOOM!

A column of blue fire roared past me suddenly, engulfing another soldier who had been rushing for me with a spearpoint aimed right at my head. Fates, I hadn't even seen him. Not with all my focus on *her*.

The soldier fell with an agonized scream, dropping his weapon and rolling to put out the magical fire that roasted him alive.

I looked back, risking an instant to see where that fireball had come from.

Axien stared back at me, pasty and wide-eyed, his outstretched hand shaking and glowing with that same eerie bluish light.

Fates, he looked as stunned as I did. Almost as if he hadn't even known he could do that.

Fantastic.

I was now in the middle of the battle for my life alongside a sorcerer who apparently had *NO IDEA* what he was doing.

This was fine. Totally fine.

The ground shook as Roxus barreled by, his back bristling with more crossbow bolts than I could count. He left a trail of blood in his wake, and fear ripped all the breath from my lungs when I saw him dive headlong into another cluster of soldiers like a battering ram.

Bodies flew. Blood spattered over the stone floor. Sanja screeched orders that none of the soldiers seemed to hear. Arrows sliced through the air.

One zipped past me, headed for Axien, and I whirled around to see just as he flung a hand out to catch it in mid-air. He immediately strung it on his own bowstring and fired it back without hesitation.

Impressive. I'd never seen anyone move that fast.

But the soldiers were getting too close. Ranged weapons took too long to reload.

Axien drew one of his scimitars and met an oncoming soldier with a parry, nearly knocking the man backward with the force. His face twisted, as though it hurt to grip that weapon, as his muscular form moved effortlessly through blocks and strikes. Not a hitch or hesitation. Just graceful lethality paired with deadly strength.

Fates, Axien may not have enjoyed combat, but he composed it beautifully.

Until another arrow caught me in the leg, right through the meat of my calf. I couldn't hold it in. A scream of rage and pain left my lips before I could stop it.

Axien's head snapped in my direction, his focus jarred. The soldier he'd been dueling struck, ramming his sword through Axien's lower abdomen and immediately ripping it out again. He drew back, ready to swing again. To make the killing blow. Axien wouldn't be able to block it. Not in time.

I screamed. All the fury blazing through my body turned my blood to pure flame as I launched myself at them, daggers swung wide. I closed the distance in an instant and leapt the final few feet, landing on the soldier and plunging both my daggers into his neck. With a brutal twist and spray of arterial blood, I wrenched both my blades to the side and slit his neck from front to back.

His head rolled off his shoulders like a cabbage and hit the ground as his body slumped beneath me.

I landed in a crouch and spun, ready to defend again. The soldiers just kept coming. Axien had said there were twenty, but it felt like more. Like an unending flood.

Like there was no possible way we would walk away from this.

"V-Violet," Axien rasped my name.

I ignored him, spinning my daggers over my hand and ignoring the flare of pain up my arm from the crossbow bolt still sticking out of my shoulder. No time for that. I narrowed my eyes on my next target and bared my teeth.

Two more soldiers were advancing from the side. Three more behind them. I'd have to move fast. I'd have to—

A strong hand seized me around the waist suddenly, hoisting me off my feet like a petulant child. I kicked and struggled, but the arm was strong. Relentless. Unfaltering as I drove an elbow back into whoever had picked me up.

Axien let out a bark of pain and an Avoran curse.

What? What was he doing?!

"Put me down!" I screamed.

He hauled me backward, struggling to keep a grip on me. His glowing blue gaze was fixed on something—one of the ancient Avoran gateway frames. It was only a short distance away.

His jaw set. Sweat beaded on his brow and drizzled down the sides of his face. His brow twitched as he fought to keep his grip on me and shamble toward that massive golden arch.

Too late, I understood.

Oh no.

Power, as ancient as the blood of the gods, flared in Axien's eyes. I felt it tingle through me, too, as it seemed to radiate off his entire body.

He dove the last few feet, hand glowing again as he stretched out to reach it. His fingers brushed it, and immediately the old, tarnished metal responded. It glowed to life like a blade fresh from the forge, bursting forth with power that filled the empty space within the frame with a rippling blue pool of magical energy.

The gate—Gods and Fates, Axien had opened the gate!

I looked back, barely glimpsing Roxus's monstrous form as he fell under the assault of half a dozen soldiers. They pinned him to the ground, already clapping shackles onto his paws.

He let out a mournful sound. A cry of anguish, like a dying animal rather than the man who had been everything but my father ... and maybe that, too.

I cried out again. Screamed his name.

In a flash of radiant white light, everything was gone.

THIRTY-SIX

My scream echoed in the dark.

It bounced off barren stone walls, seeming to go on forever.

Gone.

The temple of Adiana. The attacking soldiers in those strangely marked breastplates. The acolytes, screaming and trying to hide. The staff. The light within the gateway that Axien had just hauled me through.

... Roxus.

It was all gone.

Only *he* was left.

Lying underneath me, Axien's chest shuddered as he fought for rapid, shallow breaths. His face blanched as pale as death and he was rigid, as though he were being forced to endure burning torture. The dark circles under his eyes were new, and he stared, pupils wide and fixed, at the ceiling overhead. Strange purple veins mottled his neck, forehead, and hands, seeming to spread as his whole body trembled.

And I didn't care. Not one freaking bit.

I kicked away from him.

It must have jarred him from that catatonic state some-what, because he blinked and coughed, staring around owlishly until he found me in the gloom. His expression twitched, shakily becoming a thin, fractured smile. Almost as though he were relieved.

Gods, curse him straight to the abyss. I'd wipe that stupid smile off his face once and for all.

"YOU!" I sprang forward, snatching up one of my daggers from where I'd dropped them after we'd tumbled out of the gate. Landing right on Axien's chest, I pinned him down with my knees on his shoulders and my blade against his throat.

"You knew! You knew what was going to happen, and you said nothing! That's why you were trying to run me off! You wanted me to abandon Roxus before she betrayed him, too!" I seethed through clenched teeth. "I should let you suffer! I should let you die slowly, you traitor!"

"Y-Yes ... you sh-should," he stammered, staring up at me foggily with that infuriating, nearly blissful smile still on his lips.

"No! Not yet! Not until you open the gate again!" I leaned in to the blade, pushing it harder against his neck so he'd feel the lethal edge. It drew a line of blood that drizzled down the length of the blade.

Axien didn't respond. He just blinked slowly as he went on fighting for breath and stared up at me. His lips—gods, they were turning blue. Those dark veins were spreading down to his eyes and up his throat to his jaw.

Not a good sign.

"Do it!" I yelled down into his face. "You did it once! You can do it again! Open the damned gate! Send us back!"

"I-I ... c-can't," he managed brokenly. His smile faltered. His eyes went distant again.

The glowing blue rings of them flickered, dimming until they looked ... golden brown. Like sunlit amber.

Oh. Oh no.

I looked down, realizing too late how much blood was on the ground beneath him.

No, no, NO!

He'd been stabbed by that soldier. Run through the gut with a sword. Yes, he had on a wide leather belt meant to protect those vital areas. It might have made the blow less lethal. But it hadn't spared him completely. Not from a sword. Not from that close up.

"Don't you dare die now, you bastard!" I panicked as I crawled off him, immediately throwing my dagger aside and beginning to unfasten his belt.

"Y-Yes ... ma'am," he rasped. "I'll t-try."

Ugh. Idiot.

I hated him. But unfortunately, I also needed him. Or, his magic, anyway. The rest of him could rot for all I cared.

My hands shook and my pulse raced as I unfastened his thick leather broadbelt. I yanked it away and pulled up his blood-soaked tunic, revealing a wound that wasn't nearly as horrific as I'd been expecting. The sword had pierced him, yes, but it was a clean wound. Only about two inches deep at most.

Not that I was any sort of medical expert.

He tensed, hands clenching into fists and jaw tight, when I stuck a finger in to test the depth and whether I could feel anything lethally punctured. But there was nothing. A lot of blood, yes. But he'd been *extremely* lucky.

So why did he still look like he was a breath away from dying? And those dark veins ... they just kept spreading.

"Wh-What's the v-verdict?" he asked, his tone slurring as his body gradually relaxed against the stone ground.

I didn't know. My gaze fell on his hands, on the dark veins that went all the way to his fingertips.

My pulse skipped erratically as a memory rekindled in the depths of my mind. Fates, I'd seen them before, after our fight in the pit. After Sanja had made him perform some sort of magical ritual.

Was this because he'd used his magic?

"It's deep, but it's not lethal," I said and sank back onto my rear.

He didn't reply.

Staring down at him, a twinge of pain in my leg made me shiver. I'd have to tend to my own injuries, too. Soon. Before the shock set in.

I had a small medical kit in my haversack, which thankfully I'd had the good sense not to drop when the fight broke out. It was small and sleek, so I could manage it in combat. That was half the reason Roxus had insisted on picking this one instead of—

My breath seized in my lungs. My eyes welled up, tears streaming down my face and dripping off my chin.

Roxus.

We'd left him behind. Left him to die.

Oh, gods. I'd betrayed him.

I had betrayed the only person in the world who had ever cared what happened to me. Who had taken me in and treated me like family. Who had defended me at every turn.

A sob ripped out of my throat. I buried my face in my blood-soaked hands.

"Vi ... Violet," Axien's weak, shaking voice murmured as one of his hands fell onto my knee.

I flinched away. "Why? Why do this? Why save me after you went to so much trouble to deceive us? Will you tell me that, at least?"

"I-I didn't ... tell you to l-leave ... t-to hurt you or h-him," he answered, fighting for every strangled word.

"You were trying to save me?" I guessed, and I couldn't hide the dry disgust in my tone. "You thought if you scared me off, I'd be spared?"

"I-I couldn't ... save y-you ... both," Axien confirmed.

I shut my eyes tightly, hot tears still running down my face.

It wasn't a lie. Gods knew I wanted it to be. For him to be laying it on thick just to save his own skin. But that look on his face. The way his lips had gone ghostly blue. The way his breaths were shallower than ever.

He'd nearly killed himself doing this. Maybe he would die, regardless of any other injury he had. I didn't know what happened when people used too much magic.

And I didn't know if there was anything I could do to help him.

I could stitch up a wound, though. It might not make a spit's worth of difference, but I could try.

"You used magic in that fight. First to send that blast of fire, and then again to open the gate," I whispered bitterly as I began rummaging through my bag for my medical supplies.

My hands felt strangely numb. Like I could barely get them to move how I wanted.

Axien didn't reply. He'd gone eerily still, his eyes half-shut and his breathing now just short, gasping puffs.

"I've read a lot about the Avorans. About the ruins and monuments from their empire that still stand. It's supposed to take large amounts of divine power to open the gates—more than any person living in the Southern Kingdoms would ever have. More than someone who's only half Avoran should possess," I rambled, not expecting him to hear or care.

I just needed to think out loud. To make sense of this while I unfolded my little kit.

But the pain was getting worse. I still had two crossbow

bolts sticking out of me, and I'd have to figure out how I was going to extract them without ripping myself open even more.

Reaching up, I tried grabbing hold of the one lodged deep in my shoulder. My vision tunneled suddenly, and a fresh wave of agony tore through me. A whimper leaked through my clenched teeth.

No good.

My head lolled to my chest as a sudden wave of vertigo hit me like a runaway turnip wagon. I spat a curse, fighting to right myself. Trying to breathe. To keep my head clear.

I could not pass out. Not now.

Oh, gods, how was I going to do this?

Axien. I'd stitch him closed first, and then ...

Everything began to turn shades of gray around the edges of my sight. I could hear my heartbeat like thunder in my ears. The scrape of my uneven breathing. Tingling cold prickled up my arms and legs.

Shock. I was going into shock.

No—focus. I had to focus. Stay conscious. We couldn't both go down. Not when I didn't even know where we were. We might not be safe here, wherever that stupid gate had brought us.

I flicked my gaze up, barely feeling myself weaving from one side to the other. Was the whole world tilting? Or was I?

I got my answer when my cheek met the cold stone of the floor.

I lay, ears ringing with a high-pitched screech, my head next to his. Axien's eyes were closed now, his expression oddly serene. Like he was sleeping. Maybe he was.

Or maybe he'd already died.

I should try to wake him up. I should make sure he was still alive.

I reached for him, my hand shaking as my vision swerved in and out of focus in rhythm with my heartbeat.

I-I couldn't do it. I couldn't force my hand steady. I couldn't reach Axien. My arm and leg—it hurt so much.

My body went slack. A pathetic, choking sob broke past my lips as the world faded to darkness all around me, dragging me under into a toiling eternity.

A punishment I so richly deserved.

THIRTY-SEVEN

I'd never seen this street before.

Lost—oh, gods, I was lost.

The city was so dark and so much bigger than I'd ever imagined. The rain fell, stinging at my skin like a thousand icy pinpricks. It froze me to the marrow.

But I would not stop. Not for anyone. Not for anything.

I would keep running, just like my mother told me.

I could hear their heavy footsteps and shouts somewhere behind us in the dark and rain. Their sneers and mocking. Their promises of what would happen when they found us.

Terrible things I only barely understood.

But I didn't dare stop or even spare a second to look back and see how close they were. The other girl and I—we were no match for them. Not when we were both so weak from hunger. Hunger and running.

Terror made my scrawny legs pump harder. My filthy bare feet flew over the slippery, rain-slicked cobblestones. I bounded over puddles and darted around corners, running through a rat's nest of narrow, trash-strewn streets that all looked the same. Nowhere to hide. Nowhere to climb.

And she was so much slower—even if she was almost twice my size.

The other girl sobbed and sniffled, wobbling every time we took a sharp turn or raced down steps.

Thunder snarled over us. Webs of lightning spread from cloud to cloud, rippling the air with energy that glowed blue in my sight.

She whimpered and shrieked, tripping and nearly falling.

I didn't dare to hesitate, though. I was Viperi. I was fast. I was made of darkness and deceit.

Wicked to my very core.

If she fell behind, she stayed behind. That was the Viperi way. I didn't have to be the fastest to survive.

I just had to be faster than *her*.

THUD!

She made a sound like a wounded animal when she hit the ground.

Then she started to scream.

I didn't stop. Fear hit my body like a tongue of that lightning that sizzled and popped overhead. I scrambled on, spotting a stack of wooden crates leaning precariously against the side of a nearby building.

Good enough.

I climbed it as fast as a spider, cramming myself into a small wooden box at the very top. The sides were warped and split, offering a view of the alley below.

A view of where she lay.

Safe. I was safe here. They wouldn't see me. Wouldn't guess that I could climb so high so fast. Wouldn't search every crate.

"Get up," I whispered, my voice a hoarse gasp as I fought to slow my breathing. To stay still—too still for them to notice.

She still had time. She could make it. She just had to stand.

She tried, but something was wrong. She couldn't seem to put weight on one of her ankles. It bent oddly, and she screamed again. She was screaming *so loud*.

Too loud.

Through the pouring rain, I saw them. Three huge men crowded around her, armed with clubs and ropes like wrathful titans. Or maybe it only seemed that way because we were so much smaller.

They snatched her up and tied her like an animal, binding her legs and feet and throwing her back to the soggy earth.

She wailed, crying out in a language I still didn't understand. Her ragged clothes and drenched red hair stuck to her face and neck. Her face was pale in terror, eyes wide and frantic.

The men shouted, calling for me. I didn't understand most of what they said, but I knew their word for me.

Pitathi.

They called it over and over.

And when I did not come, they began to beat her. To make her cry out. To lure me back.

I put both hands over my mouth so I wouldn't reply. So I wouldn't breathe too loudly. I squeezed my eyes shut so I wouldn't see when they used the clubs.

But I could still hear everything, even with rain and thunder booming all around as though the entire world were being torn apart. Even with my heart thrashing in my ears and my teeth chattering.

I heard it when they broke her bones.

I heard it when they laughed.

I heard it when her screaming went silent.

And I swore that would never be me. No matter how far and fast I had to run, no matter what I had to do, I would never go back.

I would never belong to Sulam ever again.

"This is why you deserved it."

Chrysa's voice shattered over me suddenly, piercing through my mind like a barbed spearpoint. It twisted and ripped through the tapestry of the nightmare, shredding it apart until every other sound vanished.

No more rushing of bitter rain. No more agonized screams or wicked laughter. Nothing apart from my own ragged breathing and the pounding thump of my heartbeat.

"Do you really think you deserve any better than me?"

I stumbled and spun, looking for her. For a point of light. For any reference at all. But there was nothing, as though her presence were spreading through my soul, my heart, and even my memories like a plague. It infected the threads of my thoughts, twisting and warping them until I was drowning internally, consumed by her darkness.

"Remember this was a mercy," her voice crashed over me again. *"Remember what you really deserved instead."*

"NO!" I tried to scream louder, to drown her out as I covered my ears and collapsed onto my knees.

But there was no corner of my mind she couldn't reach. Nowhere she wouldn't be able to find me. No escape.

"I see what you really are, Visha," she hissed. *"And soon, they'll all see it, too."*

———+·⊰⊱·✳·⊰⊱·+———

Fire—I was on fire!

Pain tore all the breath from my lungs, ripping me from the grasp of the nightmare as my eyes flew open. My body jerked out of control, seizing upward as I cried out.

I started to pitch. To fight and writhe as the agony scorched through every nerve. Oh, gods, why did it hurt so much? What was happening? Why couldn't I—

A large, firm hand suddenly pressed against the center of

my chest, right over my heart. It pinned me down with a gentle strength, forcing me to lie on my back and remain still. Something about it, about that steady, warm pressure, made my body go still.

It felt ... safe.

"Breathe, Violet. Deep breaths. I know it hurts. Just bear with me," Axien's deep voice spoke over me.

I blinked hard, forcing my scattered vision to focus. But I couldn't remember. Where were we? What was happening?

None of it made sense.

"The arrow is in too deep to widen the wound and remove it. I have to push it the rest of the way through. It's going to be painful, but I have to get it out," Axien warned. "I'll try to make it fast."

Wh-What?

I stared up at him, then glanced at the blood-spattered arrow fletching sticking out of me. A cold shiver of panic surged out through all my extremities.

Oh gods.

He sat close at my side, leaning over me, one hand on my chest and the other gripping the shaft of the arrow still lodged in my shoulder.

He held my gaze like both our lives depended on it, his blue eyes glowing and intense. "Ready?"

I nodded.

"Keep your eyes on me," he said as he adjusted his hold on the arrow shaft. "We'll get through this."

Biting down hard, I sucked in a breath and held it. Steeling myself for what came next.

Axien drove the crossbow bolt deeper into my flesh, punching it through my shoulder until the head came out the back. And I felt every excruciating inch of it.

My vision went white. I whimpered through my teeth. My

eyes welled and my body shook out of control. But I held steady and kept my gaze locked onto his.

"Good girl," he murmured soothingly as he pulled the arrow free and immediately followed up with that stupid handkerchief, pressing it to the fresh gaping hole in the back of my shoulder.

"M-My leg," I managed to groan. "There's another—"

"I know. I already removed that one," he interrupted. "You were still unconscious, and it wasn't nearly as deep. With a little fancy dagger work, it came out nice and easy. I'm sure you'll be back to making my life a frustrating mess again in no time."

I blinked at him, probably looking a lot like a gaping caught fish while I tried to process all that.

I must have been out for a while. Hours, even.

Not that I had any way of knowing for sure. There certainly wasn't a view of the sky down in the depths of whatever wretched ruin this was. But there was light.

Strange, faint, ghostly light trickled down from a spot in the ceiling right overhead. There, etched into the stone just above the dormant gate, a series of interlocked runic rings glowed faintly blue, acting like a spotlight over the gate's empty frame below.

It was barely enough to see by, and rather than waiting for my eyes to adjust, I gave a hard blink to open my heat-vision lenses. Much better.

At least, it was, until I focused back on Axien.

"Your marks are gone," I realized aloud as I watched his handsome features go steely with focus, all his attention on preparing to treat my wound.

Axien hesitated. It was only for an instant, but I saw it. The shock. The shame. The way his mouth pressed down into a stiff frown.

He couldn't hide that from me anymore. I'd seen something he hadn't intended, and there was no lying his way out of it.

"They're from your—*agh*—your magic, aren't they?" I guessed, voice hitching as he held me under my good shoulder and helped me to sit up in front of him.

"Something like that," he dodged, now avoiding eye contact altogether. His jaw had gone rigid, and while the veins on his neck and face were gone, there were still heavy circles under his eyes. His complexion still seemed a little ashen, too.

Hmm.

"You were hurt, too," I pointed out, noting that he'd already fixed his own tunic and belt back into place.

"Like you said, it wasn't that serious," he said a little too quickly. There was no mistaking the defensiveness in his tone or the way he was now angling his face away, as though he were desperately trying to throw up any wall between us he could fabricate.

I frowned. We were way past that nonsense now.

Seizing the front of his leather breastplate, I jerked him closer suddenly and held him there. Our noses nearly touched, and I could see myself in the reflection of his wide, glowing blue eyes. He sucked in a sharp breath through his nose, but didn't resist.

I could have sworn a little rosy color bloomed in his cheeks.

"You owe me an explanation," I growled.

His throat bobbed. "Violet, I—"

"Tell me what is going on with you, or I'll finish what that fanatic started with a blade in your gut," I promised.

His expression fell, shoulders drooping some as he licked his lips and nodded slowly. "Very well. Ask. I'll answer truthfully."

I slowly released my grip on him, letting the oiled leather slide off my fingertips as I chose my words carefully. He might still try evading or playing games, talking me in circles rather than telling me what I needed to know.

"You knew what was going to happen? That we were going to get ambushed in the temple? That Sanja was going to betray us?" I just had to be sure. He'd said yes before, but we were both delirious. Maybe I'd imagined it.

I hoped I had.

Sadness flooded his features. It made every hint of lively color seem to drain away from him. His head hung slightly, and he turned away again, pawing through the contents of my little medical kit like he was looking for something.

"Yes," he answered quietly.

It hit me like another arrow to the chest.

For a moment, all I could do was stare at him in breathless horror. He'd known the whole time. And he'd let it happen anyway.

"You were working with her," I said, not really meaning it as a question.

He took it as one, though.

"*For* her would be more appropriate," Axien snapped bitterly.

I scowled, leaning away slightly when he moved back in to clean the wound with some of the healing salve. "What's the difference?"

He met my gaze then, glare-for-glare, and there was a bite of defiance in his words when he answered. "One implies I had a choice."

I stiffened—and not just because he'd begun pulling my blood-soaked tunic off my shoulder so he could clean out the wound. Something about his fingers on my bare skin seemed to make every other part of my body extra sensitive.

Suddenly, I couldn't look him in the eye, either. My heart was pounding, and not from the pain.

"So what? She's had you hostage all this time?" I seethed.

"I'm not stupid. That's completely ridiculous. You're her tandem. She doesn't have control over you. You can refuse orders if—"

"If I were actually a member of the Zenith's Call." His whole body had gone tense, his brow furrowed with smoldering intensity, and his gaze practically molten.

I froze. "You're not?"

It made no sense. How could he *not* be oathed in? Everyone had vouched for him. They'd fawned over him from the moment he'd hit the door. Even Mistress Orvana had allowed him into Arx Eburna with open arms.

Unless ... none of them actually knew the truth.

And I'd never seen his tattoo. Not all of it anyway. I'd glimpsed a hint of a tattoo on his chest, but not enough to be certain. I'd just assumed that's what it was. After all, every member of the Zenith's Call had an oathmark somewhere. It was what signified our bond to the order. What made us legitimate.

Too late, I realized why he had been so secretive about the bath. He had been hiding it the entire time. Playing us all for fools.

"Sanja is not my *tandem*, Violet," Axien gritted out as though each word were poison on his tongue. "She is my *master*."

THIRTY-EIGHT

Axien was lying.

He had to be, because none of this made any sense.

My heart sat cold and heavy in my chest as I watched the shadows dance over his sharp features as he went on cleaning my wound and stitching it closed. Watched how locks of his dark brown hair slipped from the disheveled little bun he'd pulled half of it into. Locks that brushed the side of his neck and prominent collarbone.

Everything about him had gone tense. His scowl was too deep, putting a crease right between his eyes, and a vein pulsed in the side of his neck. He practically radiated a shuddering, crackling energy—tension, like the fear of a cornered animal.

A thousand scattered words replayed in my head. Conversations I'd had. Things I'd all but dismissed and forgotten. Vanora's warning about both of them. Sanja's story about Axien, about how they'd first met when she recruited him.

Was it all fabricated, like his identity as one of the Zenith's Call?

Gods, how could Sanja hide something like that even from

Mistress Orvana? Or Roxus? Not a single person had even thought to suspect he wasn't one of us. Sanja had made absolutely sure of that.

Fool. I'd been an absolute fool!

"You're her slave?" I just had to be sure I'd heard that right.

He gave a derisive snort. "She considers me more of an object. A tool she can use to get what she really wants."

"But she said she found you in Lancea. That you were chained up in the stocks, marked for execution," I countered. "She said that she saved you."

"She *BOUGHT* me, Violet!" Axien yelled suddenly.

I cringed back, my heart pounding in my throat at the twisted look of rage that made his whole demeanor change. Like he'd briefly become something far more monstrous than I'd ever imagined he could.

Axien held perfectly still. We stared at each other, and I didn't dare to move, either. Not when he looked ready to snap.

Then, in an instant, it was gone. All that rage simmered away, and Axien's broad form sagged, leaning away from me. He ground his jaw so hard I wondered if he might crack a tooth. Fighting to push it all back down?

"I was marked for death, that much was true," he admitted, his tone hushed and his brow twisted in anguish. "But no one saved me. I was simply passed from one hand to another like a piece of currency. The Aurati sold me to a Tibran senator's wife. She had a special affinity for collecting rare things, slaves included. Something happened. I did something terrible ... and I-I ... I was deemed unfit for their use."

Something happened?

I frowned, trying to read between the lines of what that really meant. He was still being vague, still hiding something in those gaps in his story. Now didn't seem like the right time to press the issue, though. The fine details could wait.

For now.

"The Aurati took me back, promising they could fix me, but it was decided that I had to be exterminated. That's when Sanja found me. She bought me from the senator's wife, since I was still contracted to her. The Aurati didn't object. They were all too glad to be rid of me," he continued. "Make no mistake, I am not free to do as I please. One word, one misstep, and Sanja could have me back in those stocks in less than a day. The Aurati are all but invisible to everyone except the most elite of society, and so their reach is inescapable."

"Will she do that now that you've defied her?" I shifted uncomfortably.

It made a little more sense now—why he hadn't just come forward outright and told Roxus and I what was happening. He'd been afraid of what Sanja might do. Of the Aurati coming for him again. Of being executed.

That was a fear I could absolutely understand.

"Probably. But not right away," Axien replied. "Not that she'll forget about me, of course. But I'm not her priority. She knows I can't outrun her. I cannot hide. She's got more important things to do now that she has the staff and Roxus in hand."

"You're saying Roxus is still alive." I had to be sure I'd heard that right before I dared to get my hopes up.

"Undoubtedly." He sounded certain. "He's worth far more to her employer alive."

Her *employer?* The word stuck like a thorn in my mind, sharp and painful. And what it meant, the implications—I couldn't breathe. My throat closed and stars danced in my vision as I sat on the cold stone floor.

Sanja was working for someone else, someone who wasn't

Zenith's Call. Someone who wanted that staff and was willing to kill anyone necessary to get it.

A horrible sinking ache settled into the pit of my stomach. Suddenly, all those soldiers in matching insignia made sense.

"Tibrans." The word slipped past my lips like a whispered curse.

Axien went still beside me.

For a few agonizing seconds, neither of us spoke. As though the mere mention of them demanded a horrible reverence. Really, though, it was just the truth settling over me like a hard winter's frost.

"One, in particular," Axien clarified at last. "The senator, whose wife I once belonged to, struck a deal with her. When Tibrus fell to Argonox and the senate was overthrown, he tossed his lot in with their new little dictator. He was immediately promoted to High General—one of three directly under Argonox's command. His charge is to track down and collect as many powerful divine artifacts as possible from the realms they invade."

I couldn't hide my shock. It took everything I had to just sit there, trying to hold still while I watched Axien work. I did my best not to cringe or flinch at the little pinches from the needle.

"He was elated to be able to buy the cooperation of a member of the very guardians charged by the gods to protect such things. And Sanja? Well, she's got her reasons," Axien said dryly. He tucked some of his lengthy dark hair behind one of his pointed ears as he put the last few stitches on my wounds. "The former senator, now High General Crassus, sent her back to the Zenith's Call with a shopping list. First, the staff. Then ... gods only know."

"And she bought you from him?" I asked. "Why didn't he just give you to her?"

He nodded, avoiding eye contact again as he measured out

the small lengths of bandaging in my kit. There wasn't much left. He must have used a good portion for his own injury.

"Because Tibrans and the Aurati have a shared love for clear lines of power and authority. It is a significant act to transfer ownership of a phialim from one owner to another. There's a great deal of ceremony tied up in it. Ancient magic that binds me to my owner."

"Phialim?" I'd never heard of such a thing, not in any of my studies with the Zenith's Call.

His mouth twisted to the side, as though he were trying to decide how to explain it. "In simplest terms, a magical vial that contains my blood. Whoever owns it owns me. They can use it to track me, and in the right circumstances, even control me to a degree. Er, well, maybe strongly compel me is a better word for it. In ancient times, the Nar'Haleenans used such things to contain criminals who had magical power. The Aurati adopted its use for tracking their products."

My stomach turned. He meant *people*. Slaves. Children.

Not products.

But those were harder things to say out loud.

"So long as my phialim is intact, I am not to question the one who gives me orders. Sanja has it. Sanja paid six silver for it. For me. Or so I was told." He shook his head and gave a hollow, humorless laugh. "The shoes on your feet cost more than that. But I'd warrant she still considered that overpriced for a half-Avoran who can barely use magic without nearly killing himself."

Sitting before him, his hands working gently to wrap up my shoulder so that it covered both wounds left by the arrow, I tumbled helplessly through the storm in my head. I couldn't reply, not even to ask another question. So much of it made perfect sense, and I could feel the pieces slipping into place. Of lines connecting. Of lies and truths finally laid bare. Of things in plain sight that I should have noticed.

Of a feeling in my gut I should have trusted.

I'd felt something off about Sanja right away, but I'd let Roxus and others convince me otherwise. Her honeyed words and lovely smiles had fooled him, and now he was her prisoner. Sure, she'd probably used whatever history they had from before to pave the way to his heart. But in the end, she'd used Roxus. Manipulated and betrayed him.

And by all the gods, I would make her suffer for it.

"How do you feel?" Axien asked, his tone oddly stiff and reluctant as he tied off the bandaging and scooted away. Almost as though being that close to me was uncomfortable for him.

Or difficult.

"Like I want to put my fist through someone's skull," I muttered.

"Ah, good. Back to normal, then."

I rolled my eyes and pulled my sleeve back up over my shoulder. "There's something I still don't understand about all this."

"Oh?" He sounded genuinely curious, and maybe even a little concerned.

"If you were meant to be doing her evil bidding, making sure things all went to plan with my demise, why challenge me to that fight in the pit?" I questioned and pinned him with a meaningful sideways glare. "And why ask for a kiss as your prize? What part did that play in the grand scheme?"

Axien stared at me like I'd struck him square in the face. His eyes went as wide as saucers, and his mouth opened, but no sound came out. Not at first, anyway.

Then, little by little, his expression closed up. That mask of indifference crystallized, dousing the light of emotion in every corner of his face. All that remained was unreadable indifference.

It made my fists clench and my heartbeat skip with a rush of shuddering panic.

Gods, I was starting to despise that expression. It reminded me of watching a clam close up in fear of an invading predator.

"I needed you to trust me," Axien murmured, turning away to pack up what little remained of my travel-sized medical kit. "Most women find me appealing. I thought I might win you over that way."

I couldn't fathom why hearing that made my heart slowly sink down to the soles of my boots. I'd always been small, but suddenly, I felt that way, too. Insignificant. Like I was just a minor obstacle in the way.

A problem he'd needed to solve, nothing more.

"If you wanted me to trust you, then you should have just told me the truth from the start," I whispered, not really intending for him to hear, let alone respond.

But he did.

"I wanted to," he said softly. Pleadingly. Like he really meant it. "Every day, every second, I wanted to tell you everything. But you hated me so much. And part of me knew it would be better if you did. It would make it easier in the end for both of us."

My pulse skipped and stalled again, seeming to stumble all the way down to my toes before I remembered how to breathe.

Slowly, I turned to face him and found him already looking at me with a desperate agony that bled through the cracks in that well-constructed mask.

I didn't understand at all. The way he stared, as though he were mentally pleading with me to believe him, or to remember something I'd forgotten. The way his chest rose and fell with deeper, heavier breaths, like he was holding himself at bay.

It made no sense.

And it filled my lungs with a fluttering, tingling heat when he moved in closer.

He was so much bigger. More muscular. Intimidatingly perfect.

It made me feel small all over again, but not like before. Not in a bad way. His closeness made my toes squirm inside my boots and my thighs squeeze together. It made me want to close that distance just to see what he might do next.

Like take what he was owed.

"Don't do that," Axien warned, his voice deepening.

"Do what?"

"Don't look at me like that." He worked his jaw from one side to the other, eyes darkening with ominous ferocity.

"Or what?" I challenged.

He licked his teeth behind his lips like a wolf considering a wounded fawn. My thoughts tangled as his eyes moved over me like the glare of the sterling moon. His broad chest rose and fell with a deep, slow, weighted breath—as though he were fighting against his own right mind to stay calm.

His voice was rumbling thunder, low and purring like a jungle cat as he murmured, "Or I'll do something we'll both regret."

Thirty-Nine

This was all wrong.

I'd danced with death more times than I could count, stared into the eyes of people who wanted to gut me like an animal. People who eyed me with all sorts of dark and menacing ideas.

But sitting this close to Axien, watching the deliciously wicked thoughts flicker like flames in his eyes, was dangerous in a way I'd never experienced before. Not hatred. Not violence.

Desire.

A second passed, and I didn't dare look away. Or move. Or think too loudly. Or notice the pleasing way his Adam's apple moved against his warm bronze skin when he swallowed. He had a few days of dark stubble there and all along his hard, squared jaw.

No—no, I wouldn't. I would *not* sit there daydreaming about that like all the ridiculous babbling girls that followed him around Arx Eburna.

Even if it was a nice thought. Even if I could still smell a hint of the bath oils he'd used clinging to him. Eucalyptus and clary sage. Cedar, and that always-present aroma of oiled leather.

It saturated my senses and made my palms sweat and my fingers tingle.

At last, Axien shut his eyes tightly, muttering something I couldn't make out as he leaned forward to rub his forehead with his hand. He sat that way for a moment longer, staring down at the ground between us, before his hand slid into his hairline to rake his bangs away from his face.

I took that opportunity to wheeze and reassemble all the scattered shards of my sanity. I couldn't afford to lose my head now, no matter what he smelled like.

Ugh. Gods strike me down. Since when did I even care about things like that?

"We need to discuss what comes next, Violet," Axien sighed. "I can't open that gate again, even if I were ready to die trying—I don't have enough magic to manage it a second time. Not this soon."

"How long would it take for you to be able to try again?" I almost didn't want to know. By his tone, I doubted I'd like the answer.

"Days, if I'm ready to die in the attempt," he said. "Weeks, if I'd like to survive it."

Nope. I didn't like that at all.

Gods, what could we even do, then? Not just sit here, obviously. But where was *here*?

There were thousands of miles of ruins spanning the width and breadth of the Southern Kingdoms, most of them completely uncharted. We might as well have been on the surface of the moon.

"You can't do anything? No magic at all?" I pressed. "How long for a simpler spell?"

He rubbed the back of his neck with a groan. "Even if I knew how to do proper spells, a day at least."

Gods. A whole day? Sanja and Roxus would be long gone by then.

"I'm only half-blooded Avoran," he said apologetically. "What I get from my elven lineage is a drop in the bucket to what my father and his ancestors possessed. It takes time for it to accumulate in my blood, and even then, using it is always a risk. My human half is far too fragile to handle much of it, so I haven't exactly stood around practicing. It's too dangerous."

And yet he'd done it to save me—not once, but twice. In rapid succession, too.

That realization made my face burn like I'd lit my hair on fire. Now I was the one turning my face away so hopefully he wouldn't see it.

"We ought to look around. Maybe we aren't as far away from the temple as we assume," he suggested. "Sanja and her gaggle of soldiers will waste no time leaving the city. They'll be heading straight for Dumathis as soon as possible. With Roxus and the staff in tow, they'll be forced to use a caravan. It'll slow their progress. We might be able to catch them if we can find a way to the surface."

"Roxus told me once these gates connected Avoran cities across all of Reatia," I grumbled, my ears still burning as I scowled down at the toes of my boots. "We could literally be anywhere."

"Then I suggest we start walking." Axien stood with a grunt and a hiss, faltering and putting a hand to his stomach where his wound was. His expression seized a little, like he was in pain.

"You sure you're up to it?" I arched a brow. "I should take a look at that wound again."

He smirked and held a hand down, offering to help me up. "Don't fret. I'm no worse off than you, lovely Violet."

"Don't call me that," I huffed and seized his palm, using it to shamble to my feet.

Axien did an obnoxiously good job of looking genuinely confused. "Why not? Are we back to being professional?"

"No. Because pitathi aren't *lovely*." I turned to hobble away a few paces, using testing the strength of my injured calf as an excuse not to look at him. I hated how saying that made my mouth wobble.

When I turned to stagger back, gritting my teeth against the pain flaring up through my leg, I found Axien watching me with a face like he'd bitten into something bitter. His thin mouth mashed up and his brow was creased in a grimace.

"Violet, I ... you have to know I didn't mean any of what I said before. About you, I mean," he started to prattle nervously. "I know I crossed a line, calling you that, but I only wanted—"

"It's fine," I cut him off.

His mouth snapped shut.

"I've been called worse," I reminded him, the words oddly bitter on my tongue. For whatever reason, admitting that made my chest feel heavy. Like someone had a boot planted there and was grinding me into the ground.

"You shouldn't be, though," he said quietly. Grit crunched under his boots as he strode toward me, stopping when we were barely a foot apart. "And you should never have heard it come from me."

I had to tilt my head way back to meet his gaze. Ignoring the twinge of injustice that he and everyone else in the world was so much taller than I'd ever be, I willed my expression to stay cool and collected.

It worked, right until he reached out to brush some of my hair away from my face. His callused fingertips grazed my cheek.

Blushing—I was blushing again. He was too close. This was all wrong. I-I didn't even really know him. The man I'd been traveling with, the one I'd passed in the halls of Arx Eburna for two years, had been a fraud. A fabrication.

I didn't know this person. Not really. Could I really trust him now? Was this Axien the real one?

My cheeks burned, and I couldn't help shrinking back away from that contact. Away from him.

Axien's hand slowly drifted back to his side and he stood, staring down at me with a somber understanding that made the light that glowed from his ethereal eyes seem to dim. The smile that bent his mouth was all wrong as he bowed his head slightly.

"We, uh, we should get moving," I muttered. "You really think we can find them before they leave for Dumathis?"

Hope was dangerous. I'd put my faith in it before, and wound up nearly losing everything I held dear. Once again, I saw that choice rising before me like an encroaching storm front.

And I couldn't shake the fear that turned all my insides to quivering mush.

"It's worth a shot, but we have to hurry. Sanja will be keen to get there as soon as possible, and she's not one to take half-measures when it comes to planning ahead. You can bet she had resources already aligned to move them across the desert, maybe even tonight. It just depends."

I frowned, almost too afraid to ask. "On what?"

"How injured Roxus was in the fight. He's worth nothing to her dead," Axien replied, rubbing at the back of his neck and shifting his weight nervously.

Visions of Roxus being borne down by those soldiers, his back a pincushion of arrows, flashed through my mind. It made my chest burn and my throat tighten. My eyes stung. But I would not cry. Not now.

Not in front of Axien.

"Then we move. Now," I decided, my hands already in

shaking fists at my sides. "We do whatever it takes and find them—here, in the desert, in Dumathis, it doesn't matter. I will hunt them to the gods' doorstep if that's what it takes."

Everything went red. That fire in my chest smoldered and popped, ready to burst to the surface and explode. Ready to incinerate Sanja and anyone who dared to get between us. I would be her undoing.

I would become the thing she feared in the dark.

And then I'd make all her nightmares come true, one at a time. Slowly. Painfully.

"Violet?" Axien was standing close to me again, his face the picture of concern.

I shook my head. "Let's just go," I rasped.

"You ought to take the lead, Miss Violet," he said. "Of the two of us, you are the only one with any training in places like this. If anyone can get us out of here and back into daylight, it's you."

I frowned, wondering if he even realized that everything I knew was only what I'd learned from studying books. This was my first official mission. My first time in a ruin beyond what my Viperi clan had lived in as a young child, which was a place I barely remembered at all now.

Hmm.

"I think we should try it together," I quipped as I snatched up my haversack and began hobbling away into the ruins. Every step made my head cool a little more. Made the fire calm bit by bit.

But I wouldn't let it go out. Not fully. Not until I found her.

I only made it a few paces before I heard a crash and thud from behind me. Axien cursed and hissed, hauling himself up from where he'd apparently tripped over a pile of old rubble nearby. He went on staggering around with his arms out and his nose scrunched angrily. Almost ... blindly.

I stopped mid-stride and whirled to face him. Holy freaking gods.

"*That's* why you want me to lead! You can't see!" I smirked, watching him shuffle awkwardly to a halt.

"Good of you to notice," he fumed and made a rude gesture in the direction of my voice before he began awkwardly inching my way. "It's pitch black apart from that lovely little glyph on the ceiling. I don't suppose we can expect to find more of those?"

"That still work? No. I seriously doubt it. In fact, this one's probably only working now because you activated the gate." I crossed my arms, enjoying the show for a moment as he went groping through the dark like an idiot, still trying to find his way to me.

"Well, that is ... unfortunate," he muttered, stopping short when his hand slapped against the wall nearby.

"For you, maybe," I snickered. What an idiot.

He stopped, letting his hands fall back to his sides in defeat. "Is this how it's going to be, then?" he sulked. "You baiting me from the shadows? We won't make very good time this way."

"Poor almighty Avoran sorcerer, lost in his own great-grandparent's sitting room," I taunted as I limped back over and seized him by the arm, dragging him along.

"Brat," he muttered, jerking his arm away defiantly and seizing my hand instead.

My heartbeat skipped and faltered, pounding like mad as he wove his fingers through mine. Strong, warm, thick fingers that were twice the length of mine. There were hard places on his palms worn by years of handling the hilt of a blade. A subtle hint at the life he'd led before this.

And something we actually had in common.

My stomach twisted and ached, making the rest of me go achy and cold as I forced my throbbing calf to cooperate. I was injured, sure, but not out of the fight. We just had to keep pressing forward. We had to find a way back to the surface as quickly as possible.

Then I would deal with Sanja. I'd rescue Roxus, take the staff back, and fix everything.

But for now, we had to step carefully. We had to keep moving, as fast and as quietly as we could manage. There were creatures hidden away in these ruins that didn't remember the sky.

And to them, we would make the easiest of meals.

Forty

This place was where all nightmares were born.

Where *I* had been born.

All around us, the eternally sleeping remnants of a broken empire stood silent and still—a place my kin called the Pal Vassil. The Fallen Kingdom.

It had been thousands of years since the War of Falling Stars had buried what remained of the shattered Avoran Empire in this region, and every day since saw another layer of sand and stone pushing it down farther into distant memory. Their manicured streets were buckled. Their glittering castles were abandoned. Their libraries, archives, and temples were left to rot.

Now, only my kin, the Viperi, took refuge here after the death of the god and wicked sorcerer-king who had created us.

After all, this was a world no one had wanted anymore, even if it still hid countless secrets.

And now it held Axien and me like two rats in a maze.

Striding through the eerie endless dark of the ruins, my gaze tracked every cavernous chamber and crooked, crumbling hallway. The deep silence seeped into my bones, sending waves

of soothing cold through my body with every step. The smell
of rotting parchment in the archives and the occasional gleam
of gold filigree peeking out through centuries of tarnish on the
walls and archways sang in my blood like the sweetest dark
lullaby.

My pulse slowed and my senses cleared, my heat vision
revealing the slumbering ancient world that lay in ruin all
around us.

All while Axien blindly staggered along at my side like a
drunken goat. Gods. He might as well have had a bell around
his neck, too, for all the noise he made.

His breaths came in labored, rough gasps, and his steps
were hitched and jerking. He probably thought he was doing a
good job hiding how his arm moved protectively over the place
hidden under his broadbelt where he'd been stabbed.

Was it worse than I thought?

Sure, I'd checked the wound myself already, but maybe I'd
missed something. I wasn't a healer, after all. And I'd been
frantic in that moment.

He had said he treated it himself. He'd even used some of
the medical tools in my kit. Should I stop and force him to let
me look at it again?

I frowned and stole a glance up at Axien's face, keeping a
firm grip on his hand so he didn't go wandering off into the
pitch-black labyrinth. His skin looked more ashen than before,
and beads of sweat rolled down his brow and the sides of his
neck. Even his palm was clammy against mine.

Not good.

We'd been wandering from chamber to chamber, through
vestibules and the broken remains of bedchambers, libraries,
streets, and the occasional crypt. Searching for some way out.
We'd managed a good pace, but Axien's steps had begun to
drag.

And there was still no sign of a way to the surface.

Slinking through a cracked-open set of double doors, I peered around a massive dining room with arched engravings along the ceiling, and fine china on the nearly thirty-foot-long table. Portraits hung in gilded frames as big as windows along the walls on either side. I let my fingertips graze the table as I walked past it, leaving little trails in the thick dust.

It was as though this whole place was frozen in time, all its grandeur left to rot exactly where it had been the day the war ended. No wonder treasure hunters died down here so often. It must have been hard to pass up all the golden candelabras and silver place settings.

Even if it meant risking getting lost and dying slowly of starvation to find them.

Then there was the ever-present risk of getting eaten by something else.

I shuddered at the thought, ignoring the howling pain in my calf and feet as we forged on. We'd been going for, well, I wasn't sure how long. Hours? Or had it been days?

I didn't know.

There was a lot I didn't know—where we were, how far we'd gone, if we were headed into danger, or on track to find a way back to the surface. I didn't even know if Roxus was still alive. We might be running ourselves to exhaustion when he was already dead.

The thought put a stab of pain through my chest. My eyes stung, and my mouth screwed up.

I couldn't fail him. Not now.

"Let's take a break," Axien suggested, his breathing now so labored he could hardly speak.

I nodded—not that he could see it.

Ugh. Frustrating. Those pretty glowing eyes didn't do him much good.

"Wait here. I have an idea," I said and let go of his hand.

He sucked in a sharp breath, body stiffening at the break in contact, but didn't protest.

Stepping around the table, I swiped one candelabra that still had a nub of wax candle left in one of the arms and brought it back. Rummaging through my haversack, I pulled out my flint and lit the wick.

Er, well, on the third try, anyway. The old wick didn't want to catch, at first.

As soon as the small, dancing flame lit up the darkness around us, Axien's broad shoulders dropped. He let out a heavy sigh and bowed his head, relief plain on his features.

I dragged over one of the chairs from the table and he immediately sank down into it like all his bones had turned to goo.

"Thank the gods for that," he murmured.

"The gods had nothing to do with it," I snorted and brought a chair over for myself.

"Are there any more? Candles, I mean?" he asked.

I glanced back along the table. A few more candelabras had nubs of wax left in them, some longer than others. We could swipe them for us to use later, but for right now …

"It's risky to burn anything down here," I reminded him. "Things will be drawn to the light. I can gather more, but we have to be careful."

"Viperi?" he guessed.

"Goblins," I corrected.

He frowned and tilted his head to the side slightly, almost like he couldn't decide if I was joking or not.

If only.

"There's colonies of them down here all over the place," I explained. "They're a bit like rats. They build nests and roam for miles, looking for easy prey to drag back to their colonies. They're intelligent enough to make simple tools—weapons, mostly—but they know to stay away from Viperi settlements. We would look like a promising meal, though."

He made a face, scrunching his mouth up sourly. "And here I thought they were just a myth."

I shrugged. "Some people think Viperi are a myth, too."

Axien fell silent again as I settled into my chair and sat my haversack on the floor. I rummaged through my belongings until I found my waterskin and swished it. Gods, it was only half-full.

And it was all we had.

"Do you have any idea where we are?" Axien asked suddenly, his tone quiet and grave.

I glanced up, catching his gaze in the dancing candlelight. "No. But the Viperi have their own ways of navigating down here. I remember some of that from when I was little, and I studied more after I joined the Zenith's Call. Ironically, they both use the same methods."

His eyes squinted slightly, brow creasing as his lips pressed into a puzzled frown. He didn't have to ask. I knew what he was wondering.

"No, it's nothing magical. It's common sense," I said. "My kin have spent all this time down here, far away from the surface. For them, the war never really ended. All their training about how to navigate Avoran cities is still passed down because it's still relevant here."

"What kind of training?" He scooted a little to lean over and rested his elbows on his knees while he studied me.

Great. Now it felt like I was giving a lecture.

"Well, for instance, that way is north." I nodded ahead to the far end of the dining room, uncorking my waterskin to take a sip. "I'm sure you already know that Avorans are obsessed with the positions of the stars and moon. They think certain alignments draw invisible lines across the world that flow like streams of divine magic. They call them leylines and believe they mimic the same paths as the streets in the city of the gods. They built all their structures to face in certain directions, respective to those leylines, or to the stars and whatnot."

His frown had become thoughtful. "I ... I've never heard of that," he admitted.

I had to chew my lip to hide my surprise. "You said your father was Avoran, right?"

Axien nodded once and looked away. "We weren't close."

Oh. Right. Because of the Aurati thing.

He probably hadn't even known his father.

"Sorry," I muttered and held the waterskin out for him to take a drink.

"Don't be," he said around a mouthful of water. "I doubt he would have wanted to claim me anyway, being that I'm half-blooded."

Well, he wasn't wrong about that. Based on everything I'd read, the only thing Avorans loved more than their beloved divine leylines was their own bloodlines, which were obsessively curated and documented. Or at least, they had been centuries ago.

Now that their vast empire was long fallen, and what remained of the Avorans had been sequestered far to the north, no one really knew what they did or believed these days. No one from the outside world was allowed into their realm, and very few ever left it.

It made me wonder who, exactly, Axien's father had been. Why would an Avoran man leave their kingdom? Why would he sire a child with a human woman and then abandon them?

It didn't seem like the time to ask. Maybe there never was a good time to ask about things like that, though.

So, I scowled down at the toes of my boots instead.

"When it comes to navigation, if you know which structures are meant to face which leylines or constellations, it's pretty easy to tell which direction you're going," I said, my tone stiff and strange as I tried to change the subject without being too obvious.

Axien must have noticed my pathetic attempt, because when I glanced up again, he gave that easy, charming smile that enraged and bewildered me all at the same time. My face went hot. I quickly looked away again, snatching my waterskin back when he handed it over.

"What about getting to the surface, then?" He rubbed the back of his neck, breath hitching when he sighed again. His arm drifted back down to cover his midriff, where his wound was.

"That's harder. Viperi are wary of the surface. They keep careful watch on all exit points, always anticipating an attack. But the Avorans didn't build their cities with the idea that they'd someday be buried, so ..." I stuffed my waterskin back into my haversack and stared around the room again. "If I see stairs going up, we take them. If I sense a passage is ascending, we go that way. It's the only thing I know to do at this point."

A hand fell on my knee, and I looked back to see Axien staring at me earnestly. "I know you're doing your best."

I swallowed hard, trying not to read too deeply into what looked suspiciously like tenderness in his eyes. Like he well and truly believed in me.

Talk about misplaced faith.

And Roxus—gods, help me—he was counting on me. No one else even knew what was happening. We were his only chance now.

We had to get moving again. We were wasting valuable time.

"I'm trying to keep us at least moving north-eastward," I announced. Shouldering my haversack, I stood and picked up the candelabra. I took Axien's hand before I blew out the candle and handed it to him to carry.

Then I swapped back over to my heat-vision.

"Toward Dumathis?" he guessed, voice catching again as he slowly pushed himself to his feet. He used my hand for balance as his expression skewed in pain for an instant. Before I could ask or push the issue, he shook it off.

"Yes. If you're right, and they have to move Roxus by caravan, we might stand a chance of matching their pace. Caravan wagons have to move slowly over the dunes," I replied at last and hesitated, watching him take a few shuffling steps closer to me.

He still had dark circles under his eyes, and there were still trails of sweat on the sides of his face.

Something was wrong. Something he was trying to hide.

But maybe he knew as well as I did that if that wound was worse than I originally thought, or if something else was wrong with him, there was nothing either of us could do about it down here. Getting out was the only option. For him. For Roxus.

For a lot of people, if Sanja delivered that staff into Tibran hands.

I shuddered at the thought—at the memory of how that crystal had glowed so brightly. It was brimming with divine magical power.

What more could a tyrant hellbent on conquering the world ask for?

Axien's hand closed around mine again, still clammy and now trembling slightly.

I shut my eyes tightly for a moment, sealing myself within my own personal darkness and taking in one deep, slow breath. Then I started forward, towing him behind me just like before.

Onward into the deep dark of that sleeping empire.

We left the dining hall behind, grabbing a few more half-burned candles on the way out. On impulse, I swiped a few of the fine silver spoons, knives, and forks and stuffed them into my bag, as well. It went against Zenith's Call code to steal from the ruins, but these were desperate times. If we somehow made it to Dumathis, I had no money to buy medicines for Axien. I would need to barter something.

Roxus would just have to forgive me, just this once.

Beyond the dining hall, more twisting passages wound through the interior of what must have been a vast manor. There were parlors, ballrooms, studies, and a large gallery filled with armor displays and odd sculptures of the gods.

Our steps slowed as we passed through it—mostly because I couldn't stop staring at all the impossibly beautiful suits of Avoran armor. The swirling lines of tiny runes etched along the breastplates, pauldrons, gauntlets, and gorgets still glowed blue. I had no idea what they were for, of course. Some sort of enchantment, most likely.

Fates, a single suit of this armor would have sold for a merchant's fortune. Mountains of gold. Platinum. Jewels.

And the blades ...

I had to wipe a little drool off my chin when we passed a display of immaculately crafted scimitars, each one more lethal and beautiful than the last. Their runes still hummed with power that made my skin prickle, shining like they'd been dipped in pure magic that made them glow.

I couldn't resist. I had to touch one.

"Incredible," I breathed as I ran a hand along the padded leather hilt of one, ignoring the layers of dust.

"What is it?" Axien asked, still blundering along behind me.

"Weaponry. It looks like we're in an armory." I slowly drew my hand back, looking up and down the rows of blades. "That, or someone's private collection."

Each slot was labeled in Avoran, giving the names and owners of each weapon. Of course, they were all stunning. Shortswords with images of dragons engraved into the cross-guards. Longswords with gleaming inlaid silver along the grip. Rapiers as pristine and elegant as silver needles. And then there was—

I froze.

My heart hit the back of my throat, and I slowly approached a lone weapon display set at the very end of the room. Two slots were obviously meant to hold smaller swords or scimitars, but both were empty. The many fine layers of dust that had gathered over everything in this chamber were disturbed on the stand, marking the outline of the two missing weapons.

And both were labeled with only three words: *Viperi General, defeated.*

A rattling exhale left my lips as I stared at that empty display, then slowly panned my gaze to the floor just before it.

Two sets of footprints had smeared the dust on the marble floors just in front of it, pacing around this display and then leading out through an arched doorway to the left.

The ones that disappeared out the door still glowed the faintest hue of red.

They were fresh. Only minutes old.

Someone had taken some of these weapons mere moments before we set foot in this room. It was difficult to say how long, exactly, but they'd left all these other exquisite blades behind, and taken only the ones forged for and by my kin.

Dread twisted my stomach into cold, cramping knots.

Who would walk through all this splendor and want *only* something made by the Viperi? Who would loot those two blades, leave the rest of the room wholly untouched, and never even bother to return?

I knew.

Gods and Fates, I *knew.*

Looters and treasure hunters would take everything that wasn't nailed down if they found a place like this. Avorans would take their prized relics and give them back to whatever posterity from the item's lineage still lived. Vordegans wouldn't touch any of it, considering everything in this room unfit, flawed, and far below their standard. Zenith's Call didn't disturb anything unless it was absolutely necessary.

The only person who would specifically want a Viperi blade ...

... was another Viperi.

Oh, gods. We had to get far, *far* away from here.

Right. Now.

FORTY-ONE

"**W**hat do you mean we're in *Viperi territory?*"
Axien hissed.

He hobbled along, fighting for every breath, and staggering like a wounded stag as I dragged him behind me. We whipped around corners and back down flights of stairs we'd only just climbed minutes before.

Farther, faster—we had to keep moving.

We might already be too late.

My ears rang as the adrenaline roared through my veins, all my focus on going back the way we'd come and finding some-where—anywhere—safe.

Then we'd stop. We'd plan. We'd find some way out of this.

We had to.

Hiding spots were plentiful, but finding one that would be defensible was its own challenge. The best I could come up with was a servant's alcove off the dining room we'd rested in previously. At least I knew I had seen no traces of other traffic through that room. No footprints other than our own had disrupted the dust on the floor. I also knew the exit points and the terrain beyond all of them.

Good enough.

Shoving Axien into the cramped alcove ahead of me, I pulled him down into a crouch and fought to steady myself. My heart pounded so loudly I was sure he'd hear it. He'd at least feel it in my fingers as I gripped his hand fiercely.

I shut my eyes tightly and focused on deep, even breaths. Calm. I had to calm down. Think.

Think, curse it!

"Violet? Talk to me. Please. I can't do anything to help if you don't tell me what's going on. How bad is this?" Axien whispered, so close his breath stirred in my hair. Something about it calmed me. Made my thoughts clear.

Made everything snap into focus.

"I-I don't know," I answered.

"Do they know we're here?"

I opened my eyes, looking into his face and knowing full well he couldn't see me even if we were only inches apart. Otherwise, he wouldn't have been staring past my head like that. But still ... there was no mistaking that crinkle of concern in his brow. That look of somber determination.

A brave face.

But I saw his Adam's apple jump as he swallowed hard.

"It depends on how deep into their territory we are. The footprints I saw still had faint traces of body heat, and it appeared that the swords had just been removed."

"Maybe that's it—maybe they only came for the swords and left," he suggested.

Fates, I hoped so. But my gut twisted and cramped like I was falling from a height over and over. It left me shaking, my skin damp with a cold sweat.

I knew better.

Viperi didn't loot at random. They wouldn't take something from an unknown area.

And they had only taken, or reclaimed, what was their own. Why they'd decided to do it now, I wasn't sure, but I knew the protocol. They'd scout an area. Watch it. Monitor to make sure there were no movements from surface-dwellers in the vicinity before they disturbed anything in these ruins.

And, gods, we'd been so careless. We'd left tracks. Made noise. Plenty of evidence for them to follow right back to this spot.

"It's possible. But there's no way to know for sure they aren't still patrolling the area, unless ..." I ran my hands through my hair, raking it away from my face as I struggled to think.

"Unless what?" he urged.

I winced. He wasn't going to like this. I didn't like it, either. But there might be a way to use this to our advantage. It was insane, of course. Right on par with my usual antics.

"Unless I go back and scout it out for myself," I replied at last. "I need to know who they are, where they're going, and how many there are. I need to know the paths they're taking so we don't stumble across one another again. If we're heading into territory they've claimed, they'll have guards and scouts on rotation, watching the borders at all times. We need a path around them."

His silence was deafening. The look on his face said plenty, though. That tenderness faded from his features as his eyes went steely. His jawline hardened, a muscle twitching just below his ear as his nostrils flared a little.

Seething disapproval at its very finest.

"I'll go faster on my own. I know how to move through their territory. Moreover, if they do find me, they're far less likely to kill me if I'm not dragging a blind, wounded Avoran sorcerer," I argued.

"*Half*-Avoran," he corrected bitterly.

"Might as well be whole, as far as they're concerned," I growled back.

"And I'm not a sorcerer."

I rolled my eyes. "But you *are* wounded. And you're blind. You have to stay here. Wait for me to come back. I'll scout ahead and find a safe route—or better yet, a way to the surface. I told you, Viperi watch those areas closely. If I can find a way to one, we just might make it out of here, after all."

"All that, providing you don't get caught and slaughtered," Axien fumed, gripping my hand harder. "And I'm no worse off than you, injury-wise."

Ugh. Liar.

"Is that why you're gasping for air? Hobbling around? Covering your stomach like you're afraid your insides are going to come spilling out?" I snapped. "I know something's wrong. You don't have to tell me, but I can see it all over your stupid, sweaty face. You can barely keep your beady, blue-glowing eyes open."

His brows crumpled together, head angling down some, eyes moving like he was trying to at least focus on the sound of my voice to find which direction to glare in. "Blue-glowing? What is that supposed to mean?"

Augh! No!

I spat a Viperi curse and backed away, pulling my hand out of his. I wasn't supposed to tell anyone.

"It doesn't mean anything," I deflected. "Look, we don't have a choice. We can't keep this up for days on end. We only have maybe one day's worth of water left. We have no food. You can't even see down here. It's only a matter of time before we run into a goblin nest or worse. I'm doing this, Axien. I have to, or we're both dead."

He sat eerily still, blinking slowly and still glaring in my direction. Little by little, that frosty look of rage faded. The defiant fire in his eyes dimmed. His body bowed inward, and his lips pressed into a thin, defeated line.

"I-I ... I think the blade they stuck me with was poisoned," he confessed, his voice hushed and broken.

My mouth opened, but no sound would come out. No words. Just a swell of emotion that made my vision swerve and my hand instinctively reach out for his again.

No wonder he looked so awful. No wonder he seemed to be getting worse. He was already sweating with fever, and at this rate, he might not last much longer. The healing salve from my medical kit had likely bought him time, but if we didn't get him to a healer soon ...

He'd get worse.

He'd die.

And I would be forced to leave someone else behind in this gods-forsaken wasteland.

That realization kindled the embers smoldering deep in my chest. All of the fear seeped away. My pulse steadied. Suddenly, the path ahead was in clear focus.

I knew what I had to do.

"I have to go. I have to do this right now," I said. "And you have to stay here. Be quiet. No light. No noise. Even if you think it's me, there are things down here that will play tricks on your mind. Stay in this spot. Understand?"

"Violet, I—" he began, but hesitated. His expression grew tense as his eyes searched the darkness, still looking for me.

Maybe it was a good thing he couldn't see me staring straight back at him, at the way the glow of his eyes shone in my sight like rings of blue lightning. Beautiful. Strange. A secret only I could see.

Then his mouth closed. "I understand," he murmured quietly.

"I will come back, Axien," I promised.

"I know," he said, like he really, truly meant it. Like he had no doubts whatsoever.

I couldn't decide if that was flattering ... or completely weird.

Standing, I slipped my haversack from my shoulder and put it on the ground next to him. Then I slid one of the silver cutlery knives I'd taken into the side of my boot.

Yes, I had my own spelldrinker daggers. I had a small crossbow, too. But it was always a good idea to have something in reserve.

I couldn't think of a way to say goodbye that didn't sound like I'd be gone forever. So instead, I just whispered, "Remember, no light. No sound."

He didn't reply.

And I had no choice but to turn away, picking my way carefully out of the room.

I retraced our footprints, silently cursing myself for the trail we'd already left behind. Any scout worth a rat's turd would be able to hunt us down. They could follow our steps straight back to Axien's hiding place.

And he'd be defenseless. Weak from the poison, blind, and cornered—Axien would never stand a chance against well-trained Viperi scouts.

But they'd have to get through *me* first.

The realization set my teeth on edge, flames of quiet rage already scorching the back of my throat as I began to draw a plan together in my mind. I'd follow the trail left by whoever had taken those swords from the armory.

I'd hunt them down, kill them fast and quiet, and take what I needed from their corpses—weapons, supplies, clothing, even food rations if they had any.

Then I'd seek out where they'd come from.

Past the armory where I'd spotted the missing Viperi weapons, I picked up the trail and followed the footprints deeper into the ruins. Their path took me out of the estate, into halls lined with massive sculptures of draconic creatures, their horned heads and folded wings draped in cobwebs and the rotting remains of tapestries that had once hung above them.

That was where I found the first of the markings.

Sharp, twisting letters had been freshly etched into the stone at the base of one of the statues. Nothing about them was discreet. They were meant to be seen, to be noticed.

Dropping into a squat, I scowled at the markings for a few seconds.

I couldn't read much of the Viperi language anymore. It had been far too long, and I had no way of practicing even at Arx Eburna. They weren't full words, though. I could tell that much. Abbreviations, more like it. And paired with the arrows slashed into the stone alongside them, well, it was easy enough to tell what they meant.

Directions.

Memory flickered in the back of my mind. My mother's hand gripping mine so hard her knuckles were white. The stone walls blurring by as we ran. The voices echoing in the dark behind us.

My father's maniacal, booming laugh of sick delight.

I shut my eyes tightly for a moment, willing my mind to clear. I couldn't chase those demons. Not right now.

I had to focus.

I slowly rose to my feet again, my gaze drawn off to the left where a broad, open archway led out of the hall. A grand doorway if I'd ever seen one. What sort of place had this been all those centuries ago?

And why did it seem like light still ebbed from it, faint as a star's whisper?

Not just any light. Blue light.

Magic.

I held my breath, keeping along the wall as I moved from shadow to shadow of the huge stone dragons until I reached the edge of that archway.

Before me, the landscape spread out like a sea of a million tiny, shimmering blue stars caged beneath a gargantuan dome of solid stone. Gods and Fates, it was a city. A whole Avoran city, still teeming with magical power, was nestled in the very center. With towering spires, grand stone arches, and half-toppled columns looming over steeply pitched rooftops—I'd never seen one so large.

It dwarfed the little kingdom I had been born in.

And it was far better preserved.

That, I could only guess, was why it still glowed with life. There were thousands of them—specks of body heat that moved in the streets and along the towers.

People. *My* people.

This place ... it might have been built by the Avorans.

But the Viperi ruled it now.

And somehow, I had to find a way through it.

FORTY-TWO

N o one talks about how difficult undressing a corpse is.

It's not easy. Not even a little. Especially when you're smaller than the corpse and everything's tight-fitted and made of leather.

Gods, just strike me down already.

It would have been easier to hold them both hostage and have them undress themselves. But Viperi would never be so compliant, so I'd been forced to kill them both outright. Fortunately, murder had never bothered me all that much—especially when it was justified. Stealing suitable armor and clothes from a couple of Viperi scouts that had gotten far too complacent while making their patrol rounds was a good enough excuse by my standards.

Laziness in this eternally dark world was enough to get anyone killed, honestly.

I just so happened to be the one dishing out the conse-quences today.

The first one fell easily as I dropped from a rocky over-hang, sinking my blades into the side of his neck and giving them a brutal twist. I rode his writhing corpse all the way to the ground before I sprang after the other scout.

She hissed curses, floundering with a crossbow as I rushed her. I was within five feet of her, though. Too close for that ranged weapon to do her much good. Not when caught by surprise.

I slit her neck from ear to ear, deep enough that her head nearly rolled back off her shoulders as her body dropped to the stone.

They didn't even get a chance to scream or call for reinforcements.

Perfect.

I wiped my blades clean on the sides of my leggings before I slid them back into their sheaths and got to work. Unfastening belts, wrestling socks and leathers off ankles, and working myself into a sweaty, angry mess before I had them both stripped of what I needed.

Which was nearly everything—except their shoes and smallclothes. They could keep those. Gross.

I could only imagine redressing corpses would be even more challenging, but I wasn't in the business of preserving anyone's modesty today.

I just needed their scouting leathers, weapons, and whatever else they had in those lovely packs they'd both been carrying.

Of course, even the female scout's attire was too big for me. But I could roll the leggings up inside my boots and hide the way the leather jerkin gaped open with my belts, cinching it up tighter. Same with the undershirt, which wound up showing a lot more cleavage than I'd ever wanted put on display, thanks to the way the neckline swept far too low over my shoulders.

Ridiculous, all of it. But it didn't have to be perfect. It just had to be passable. Enough that other scouts or guards wouldn't give me a second glance. So long as I looked like I belonged from a distance, it would suffice.

Hopefully, anyway.

Refastening my weaponry to my hips and thighs, I hauled both of the bodies into the rubble and out of sight, making sure their body heat would be hidden from Viperi sight until their corpses cooled.

The blood was easily obscured with a splash from my waterskin, and the rest? Well, I'd been trained to be resourceful. Both the Viperi and the Zenith's Call had seen to that.

I snatched up their two small bags, the male scout's clothes, and stole away into the dark to go through them. Their wares were meager—not that I expected much, to be honest. But there was a small medical kit in each one, little vials of poison for coating weapons, small knives, a few caltrops, and some food rations.

My stomach gave a violent twist at the sight of food, and I didn't hesitate to rip open one of the packets of rations and start cramming the dry, hard pieces of bread into my mouth. The flavor of the crumbly, almost chalky little squares thrust me headlong back into that storm of memory. Of the last time I'd eaten Viperi food.

My face still throbbing from the last fight I'd weathered. My mother's soft, hissing words of praise in my ear as I sat, my gaze fixed on the fallen body of a boy only a few years older than I was, while his own mother tried to coax him back to consciousness.

Because I'd beaten him to within an inch of his life.

Not different from the Zenith's Call, honestly—although I'd never breathed a word of that thought to Roxus or anyone else. It was all fighting. Suffering. Training. Bleeding. Dying.

Just for a different cause.

For Viperi, it was for dominance. For survival. For the glory of service to the Brood Father.

To the Zenith's Call, it was to protect the divine secrets and artifacts hidden, slumbering, tucked away all across the world. To keep them out of the hands of tyrants and crowns who would use them to destroy. To protect the common folk from becoming fodder for the machines of divine war once again.

But in the end, blood was blood.

I took another bite, thinking on that while I chewed through what was left of the bread. I moved all the materials into my haversack, along with the clothing I'd swiped off the male scout.

It would be far too small for Axien. He was easily twice the size of the average Viperi male. But these were desperate times, and he'd have to make it work.

Saving the other pack of rations for him, I swung my haversack over my shoulder and stood, still gnawing on the dry bread and stealing a long, final swig from my waterskin before I threw it aside. I had two new full ones now, after all.

Emerging from my hiding spot, I stopped and listened, making sure there was no other sound or disturbance nearby before I slipped free of the shadows. By my best guess, I had about an hour—maybe two—before someone noticed that this pair of scouts had not checked in, making their usual rounds.

Time to move.

I followed along the scout's trail, backtracking their steps and keeping out of the open as much as possible. Their path was well-marked, probably one of the outlying perimeters by the distance and the way it zig-zagged through the rough terrain beyond the city. Fallen boulders, shaken loose from the cavern's lofty ceiling, lay in heaps as big as rolling hills. Stalactites hung as big as lighthouses far overhead. Some of them dripped into pools of cavern water as big as lakes and ponds on the ground, all of an eerie shade of mineral green.

None of it was drinkable unless you took the time to purify it. Naturally, it was far too acidic and would give you the runs something fierce. Some of it was even downright poisonous, though, if the toxic tar pits on the surface had fouled it.

Mother had told me stories of Viperi scouts stumbling across whole camps of surface looters who had died from drinking fouled cave water, their campfires still alight and their bedrolls spread out and waiting.

It was an eerie thought that had haunted my childhood dreams and made me leery of ever tasting it myself, no matter how crystalline and clean that water might have seemed.

I shook the thoughts away, minding my steps and moving faster. Every step brought me closer to the lofty walls, where the old ramparts were still mostly intact. Well, maybe calling them walls was generous.

The Avorans prized nothing more than aesthetics, so the walls themselves were more of an artistic choice than something actually crafted for repelling enemies. And the beauty of every sweeping archway, flanked with more colossal angelic statues with wings outstretched and swords drawn, wasn't completely lost on me—even if it was hilariously impractical.

The area between them was open, save for the remnants of what had been a huge ironwork fence. That could only mean this city had never even entertained the idea of coming under siege, or perhaps had relied more heavily on magical means of defense rather than physical ones. Based on what I'd studied about ancient Avoran sorcerers, I'd bet good coin on the latter.

Regardless, getting past those intricately woven iron fence bars would be a breeze—as long as I didn't do anything stupid to alert the guardsmen keeping watch up top. Now that I looked like I belonged, hopefully that wouldn't be an issue.

Another Viperi scout returning from patrol? That shouldn't raise any eyebrows.

Ugh, gods, show me a little grace, just this once.

My chest grew tight, lungs squeezing at every fitful breath as I approached the gates, finally leaving the scout's trail and daring to set foot on a clearly marked main road leading into the glittering metropolis.

This was it.

No turning back now.

I had to find a way to the surface, first and foremost. Medicines for Axien, if I had time and could swipe something easily. But getting out of here, getting to Dumathis—that had to stay top priority.

I bit down hard and straightened my spine, widening my steps to make my hips sway with confidence, as I drew upon all the training Curator Vanora had poured into me. How to walk. How to be composed, confident, and let my body language do all the talking.

Tugging my hair free of Sanja's stupid braid, I shook the lengths of my silvery, white-blonde hair down my back and smudged the kohl on my eyes to make it less pristine.

Viperi did wear it—or at least, my mother had. But a scout wouldn't be so composed. So I raked my hair into a ponytail, not caring if it was smooth or that locks of it fell around my face and neck. I held my head high. I threw my shoulders back and let my hands rest idly on my daggers.

And I walked straight into a hive of the people who had exiled me ... and prayed they wouldn't notice.

FORTY-THREE

I'd forgotten the energy of Viperi cities.

But the instant I set foot beyond the gates, it swallowed me whole.

My body shuddered involuntarily as the chill climbed my spine, one vertebra at a time. That frigid, invigorating cold rushed through my veins, opening my senses and singing to all the darkest parts of my brain. My soul came alive, blooming like a blood-red orchid.

Fates, how could I forget? How the atmosphere seemed to pulse with secrets? How the shadows crackled and licked like dark flame? How the air hung thick with the curling fog of sharp incense and figures moved along the sidewalks like specters in sweeping robes of black and silver, hoods pulled so low that they hid all but their vibrant ruby-red eyes.

Nobles—members of the Brood Father's private court. They would give nothing away about their identities out in the open streets, not when there was always a risk of being targeted.

Murder had always been their preferred method of social

advancement, and something most Brood Fathers ruling cities like this found amusing.

Common folk moved around their shops, taverns, and scurried through the streets in less elaborate clothing. Black-smiths worked at their forges, wearing goggles meant to shield their sensitive eyes from the heat-light. Butchers cut up animals harvested from the cave systems—things I doubted surface-dwellers could even name, let alone would dare to eat.

The smell of the slowly roasting meats, strange as they were, made my stomach writhe angrily again. A few bites of hard bread weren't enough.

But I couldn't risk talking to anyone, not when I knew my handle on the Viperi language would be *extremely* rusty. Only if I had to. Only if it was to buy medicines for Axien, or—

I paused on a street corner, glancing up and down a broad avenue that seemed to divide the city lengthwise. Lights hung along it, and not of the magical blue sort.

No—these were actual Avoran street lamps that had been lit with *flame*.

I stared, unable to mask my bewilderment at how each of the glass orbs atop the lampposts glowed, marking the street corners where smaller roads intersected. Flame. In a Viperi city.

Why? We rarely used lights like this except in ceremonies. Viperi didn't need them to see. Our vision in the dark was better than most in the daylight, and our ability to see body heat was always preferred to the glare of firelight.

Hmm.

Guards walked in twos and threes, patrolling the avenue down both sides of the main avenue. Their war-painted faces and fine leather armor were on full display, but behind them, there were more scouts. Their ensembles were more subtle, more like what I wore. Only glints of dark steel against polished black leather. Sleek and efficient.

But this was more than a mere security routine.

This was a show of force.

It was all fangs. All fierceness.

And with the lights burning?

Suspicion turned my insides to prickly, cold slurry. No. It couldn't be—I had to be wrong.

I frowned, searching along the sidewalks for more clues as I continued. A few streets up, the answer cruised by like a school of sharks passing a reef.

Men in full-body bronze armor.

Not Viperi. *Surface*-dwelling men. There might even have been elves mixed in, but I couldn't tell exactly. Not when their features were covered with helmets.

They walked by in a formation of six, striding shoulder-to-shoulder, complete with round shields in one arm and spears in the other. My heartbeat skipped and stalled, watching them pass and picking out the insignia emblazoned on their breast-plates and shields. The letter T with a serpent entwined around it.

The emblem of the Tibran Empire.

Inch by inch, my entire body went numb. My knees shook. My stomach clenched into a thousand, wrenching knots.

Why, by all the gods were there *Tibran soldiers* in a Viperi city?

But it wasn't just their soldiers.

Two more streets up, there were huge iron cages stacked four and five tall, each one holding beasts from the surface world I knew all too well. Their feral, ear-splitting screams made my blood freeze and my pulse kick wildly long before I glimpsed their six, sinewy legs and big, milky eyes.

Switchbeasts—dozens of them. They were all caged individually, their crates staged as though they were being moved between locations.

And their ears were tagged.

I stopped before one stack of cages, staring at the nearest switchbeast as the creature roiled and hissed, snapping its jaws hungrily. The round, bronze, coin-like tag punched through one of its tall, pointed ears had the number 126 engraved on it.

Just like the tag Roxus had found.

Every muscle drew tense under my stolen, ill-fitting scout leathers. Gods, Fates, and all things holy. This is where those switchbeasts had come from?

"Careful, *dikafta*. You stand that close, you're liable to catch a claw. Just one nip on that lovely skin would end your journey," a deep, masculine voice purred at my back.

A voice speaking the Viperi language.

A surge of adrenaline raced up my spine and out through all my extremities—hot and furious. Immediately defensive.

I hadn't even heard him approach. But I couldn't afford to look startled or anything less than annoyed as I turned and slid a slicing glare back over my shoulder to the man who lurked right behind me.

He was tall for one of my kin, and handsome by our standards, albeit quite a bit older than me. Mid-twenties, at least. He wore a circlet on the back of his head made of twisted whorls of black glass. Definitely a noble headdress. His flowing dark robes were also trimmed in silver, and his broadbelt was studded with obsidian and onyx stones. Even the hood was embroidered in tiny runes stitched in silver thread, and a fat coin purse hung against one of his hips.

He didn't seem to be carrying any weaponry, though. Interesting.

He must have felt very safe, then, to strut through the street all adorned in that noble finery with no means of defense. That, or he was a complete idiot.

Yeah. Probably that. He'd all but waddled up to me like a fattened suckling pig.

As my gaze met his, watching his mouth curl into a delighted smirk as he took in my features, I felt it—a sudden rush of realization that hit me square in the chest.

This ... this was it. All the time I'd spent with Curator Vanora, all her ruthless training in body language and the art of social manipulation—it was for *this* moment. One wrong word would decide my fate.

And Axien's, too.

But one right one could solve every single one of our problems.

My thoughts cleared. My pulse slowed and calmed and drank in the aura of the older man's presence. His energy. The glint of curious desire in his eyes as he watched me.

I only had seconds to respond. And he'd used that word; *dikafta*. It was a familiar term of endearment, similar to "sweetie" or "darling." He was Viperi, yes.

But he was still a man.

And I needed his cooperation.

I let one corner of my mouth curve in a quick hint of a smile before I slowly turned my back to him again, letting my spine arch just so and my shoulders flex in a rolling, feline way.

"I do not fear them," I said simply, measuring every word before I dared to let them leave my lips. Was my accent all wrong? Could he tell I hadn't used my kin's tongue in years?

"Confidence, girl," Vanora's voice hissed in my mind. *"Mind your own energy."*

Right. Focus. I had to focus.

"Oh?" The man took a step closer, moving beside me, his tone genuinely surprised. "You've not seen someone turned by switchbeast venom then, hm?"

"I have," I said. Safer to keep my responses short. Not rude, but to leave him wanting more.

"And yet you don't fear them?" He faced me, eyes roaming

over my body with a leering, hungry delight that made my skin crawl like I'd lain down in a vat of live spiders.

"They are beasts. Their motives are simple. They feed and reproduce. Better to fear those who think they can control them. That is a symptom of madness, some would say," I said slowly and carefully, while I let my stance shift, cocking my hips to one side and aiming my gaze defiantly away from his.

A dismissal.

One he didn't take well.

"Bold of a mere scout to say such things about her superiors," he said, biting each word through bared white teeth. "Perhaps those who caged them don't desire to control them, but to unleash them. To use them for a greater purpose. To use their power for greater things."

My mind spun, frantically trying to unravel the truth behind those words. The secrets he was dangling right in front of me in a pathetic attempt to prove himself superior. Somewhere in the depths of my mind, I could almost hear Curator Vanora's voice urging me on.

"Keep him talking. Find out all that you can. You have him caught in your grasp now. Dig your claws in, girl."

"What purpose could ever be greater than the dominance of the Brood Father?" I mused, tilting my chin up, letting one of my hands brush my hair away from my face so that my fingers grazed the hollow of my throat. Just above my chest, which was on far better display in this too-big jerkin.

He swallowed loudly.

"Oh, *dikafta,* whoever said that wasn't their purpose? You must know as well as I do that our Brood Father requires only the finest of weapons to ensure his sovereignty." His tone was velvet again. Soft and inviting, just a brush against the shell of my ear as he leaned in closer.

I finally rewarded him, giving him a quick sideways glance through my lashes.

His pupils dilated. His grin widened, taking that victory greedily, like a fish swallowing a worm on a hook.

"And while these beasts are decent weapons already, we have come to realize that they can be refined. They can be reimagined to fill an even greater purpose that will bring glory to all our kin." He spread an arm out in a sweeping gesture, motioning to the other cages all around us.

"Reimagined? Were they not made as we were, by the hand of the Foul Father? How can they possibly be refined further?" I dared to press him.

Just a little more.

Just enough to give me some idea what they were really up to. What all this—the switchbeasts and the Tibrans walking our streets like equals—really meant.

"Careful. Let him enjoy it. Let him think he's in control," Vanora's voice warned.

"Because the hand that will mold them now will rule over gods *and* men," the nobleman snapped as though he were relishing every sharp, jagged word. "His dominion will be absolute. He will restore us where the Foul Father failed. His empire will know no borders. No dissenters. No rivals."

Fear quivered in my chest like the vibration of a harp string. A single, frantic, reverberating note that sang his name over and over again.

"Argonox," the word, his name, slipped out of me before I could stop it.

The nobleman must have mistaken my breathless sound for a gasp of awe, because his smile stretched wider and his eyes flashed with crazed delight.

"Lord Argonox will rule the north and our Brood Father the south," he confirmed eagerly. "All those who dwell above will bow before our might. Those who spat upon us will bleed as they beg for our mercy. The vengeance of the Foul Father's children will be swift, and brutal, and everlasting."

Everything inside me went cold with a wash of horror. My lips parted, but I couldn't do anything except hold my gaze ahead again, staring into the cage where the switchbeast still twisted and writhed, clawing for any way out.

My kin were no different. Clawing at the surface world. Hungry for it. Wanting equally to shred and devour it, but so mad with reckless hate that they couldn't even see beyond the bars of their own cage.

But it sounded like Argonox had promised to give them a taste of that outside world ... in exchange for helping him turn switchbeasts into weapons.

Gods.

My body stilled, caught in a tangled trance of shock, horror, and sheer disbelief. How could they have agreed to something like this? What Brood Father in his right mind would make deals with kings of the surface? I couldn't fathom it.

And right then, I didn't dare to try.

When I didn't react, the nobleman's ruby eyes narrowed. He took a step closer, now fully in my space, looming over me as he drew in a deep breath of my scent. My stomach curdled, but I forced the disgust down.

No feeling. No emotion. I would not let him see anything but that mask of smoky-eyed mystery as I slid him another coy, sideways glance.

"What are you called?" he demanded.

I blinked slowly, then let the name roll off my lips like the sweetest poison. "Visha."

He licked his teeth. "Of what clan?"

"I am an unclaimed female scout. I have no clan name," I retorted, as though that were a sick joke and he should have known better.

The nobleman hesitated, seeming to ponder that for a moment. "Your mother does not claim you?"

"My mother is dead," I said simply, with all the dismissive complacency he would likely expect.

Another, much longer pause.

Oh no.

Had ... had I messed it all up? Said too much? Not enough?

Was he onto me?

My heart thudded hard and slow, each pulse like a punch to the center of my chest as I stood frozen. I had to get away from him. I had to find an excuse to leave. I had to—

"She died in shame, then. Why else would they disfigure you, her surviving daughter, by taking your fangs?" he concluded, his tone thick with smugness, like he'd just unveiled a nasty little secret I'd been trying to hide. A weakness he might be able to exploit.

He wasn't exactly wrong.

But, curse it, I couldn't afford to lose my grip on this situation now.

"Dig those claws in, girl," Vanora hissed in my mind. *"You must be ruthless. Strike. Now. Do not hold back."*

"Does it matter to one of the Brood Father's court? If she died in shame, then I am no prize," I dared to counter, angling my body toward him as I glanced him up and down. I let my gaze linger on his crotch area before giving a small, derisive snort and an unimpressed arch of my brow. "I must return to work."

His eyes widened ever so slightly.

Just enough.

I began to step away, to turn for the nearest side street, but he caught my chin in his fingers and snatched my head back so I was forced to look up at him. His eyes roamed my face, darting fast and glittering with all the falling shards of his fractured pride.

"I enjoy your boldness, *dikafta.* If you were mine, I would have the fangs of those who disfigured you ripped from their mouths. You would wear them as a fine necklace," he promised. "Would that please you?"

"This is your chance. Do not waste it," Vanora's voice warned. *"Use it. Now."*

"If I were to become yours, I would need permission to miss my assigned duties for the rest of the day," I murmured, letting my expression soften, eyes half-lidded, as I stared defiantly at his mouth as though I wanted it and hated myself for it.

His grin was maniacal. "Oh?"

I gave him a lazy, desire-drunken smile. "My commanding superior watches the nearest route to the surface. I am not permitted there, so I cannot seek him out."

His tongue traced his incisors slowly before he replied, "Shall I escort you, then? Shall I make him kneel as I order him to relinquish you for the evening?"

I dragged my bottom lip slowly through my own blunted teeth and loosed a slow, steady breath as though the idea had excited me *thoroughly*.

"Would you have him grovel? Crawl to you?" I baited.

"I would," he growled, squeezing my chin tighter. "If it would please you, fangless one."

"It would." I stood on my toes so I could purr right against the side of his cheek, my lips brushing his earlobe. "And I would wish to show you *all* my gratitude."

The hook set. His body went rigid, spine stiffening as he sucked in a sharp breath through his nose. His energy crackled like electricity in the air, reckless and dangerous and mine to direct.

His hand slid along my jaw, combing through one of my stray locks of hair before he snatched it back and motioned for me to follow. "Walk with me, *dikafta*. I will show you what a powerful male can do for those who please him."

FORTY-FOUR

None of this was going as planned.

Absolutely none of it.

And I couldn't tell if it was worse or better, even as I followed along after the finely dressed nobleman deeper and deeper into the Viperi city. With him before me, I didn't have to guard my expressions as much. Good thing, too.

Because the sights we passed—Gods and Fates.

I couldn't school my face to complete indifference. Not when I was staring at what must have been entire legions of Tibran soldiers camping in the side streets and alleys around every corner we passed. They had large canvas tents erected like checkpoints on every corner, moving lines of bronze-armored men through to be issued weaponry, armor, basic gear, and food rations. They moved crates of supplies from the backs of wagons, led lines of tethered war mounts, and dragged more crates of writhing switchbeasts with lengths of thick chain.

The only safe way to move them, most likely.

I hesitated, stopping for a beat as a team of ragged-looking men with their heads shaved bald and the Tibran emblem branded into the sides of their necks crossed our path. Standing alongside the nobleman, I barely kept my mouth shut as I watched them roll a huge contraption of wood and metal into an expansive open courtyard to the left.

A war machine—but not like any I'd ever seen, heard, or read about in all my studies at Arx Eburna.

And the poor souls hauling it by? Definitely slave soldiers. Argonox had all his new recruits shaved and branded like that. Even *she* had one of those marks on her neck when we—

My stomach clenched, and I bit down hard as Chrysa's face flashed through my mind.

No. I wouldn't think about her. Not here.

Not now, when the smallest mistake might give me away.

I had to play along just a little longer.

Every step, every second, was agony as we passed through the Tibran ranks and made our way out the other side to the northern edge of the city. The crowds seemed to part for my dark-robed companion fairly quickly, though. His status must have been just enough to spook even the Tibran soldiers into staying out of his way.

Perfect.

It was the last missing piece that might just give Axien and me the edge we needed.

A fool's hope.

The nobleman continued on, his shoulders thrown back, pride in every commanding stride, as he guided me through one of the city's broad, open gates. This one was nearly entirely blocked off with more Tibran soldiers and slaves moving a dozen more massive war machines through it.

Gods, just how many soldiers had Argonox stashed down here? And how many more were on the surface?

I rubbed at my throat, gulping against the bile that rose in my throat at the thought.

Patience. I wasn't here to fight Tibrans—I just had to find a way to the surface. A way out.

And as soon as we set foot beyond the city gate, past all the chaos of the Tibrans and their shambling legions, I knew we were getting close. The smell of fresh, free, crisp air stirred in my hair, filling my nose as it flowed in a subtle breeze from one of the two tunnels before us.

But which one?

The main road where we walked split, and the path to the left followed the cut of the landscape and twisted into a smaller, more crudely cut tunnel in the cavern wall to the northwest. The other careened uphill, feeding through a much larger tunnel that had been carved to be open and tall enough for the Tibrans to keep rolling those massive war machines through it.

Down from wherever they were probably camped up on the surface.

My hands curled into clammy, shaking fists at my sides.

That was the answer, then: we had to follow the Tibrans like a trail of bronze-armored ants if we wanted to get out of here. Back to the source, where there were undoubtedly even more camped and waiting.

Easy.

I cut a glare up to my would-be guide. He was useless now. I had everything I needed.

Well, except for one minor thing.

I waited, biding my time, until we had just entered that bigger tunnel and the shadows hung thicker. The echoes of armor clinking, thudding footsteps, and clamoring voices of Tibrans choked the air. Wagons heaped with teetering stacks of crates were lined end-to-end, ready to be taken through the city gate ahead.

It was a matted rat's nest of chaos, with hundreds of moving bodies packed into a dark tunnel lit by the constantly flickering glare of torchlight—better cover than I could have ever dreamed of.

As we moved around a bend in the tunnel, passing through a line of loaded-down wagons, I swept in close to the nobleman's side. He stiffened when I ducked under his arm, but as soon as I flashed him a devious, alluring smile, his body relaxed. He looped an arm around my waist to draw me in closer.

I giggled.

His ruby gaze flickered to my mouth, like he might try to steal a quick sample of what the rest of the night had in store for him.

I licked my lips, baiting him in. Closer. Barely a hair's width away.

His eyes rolled closed.

And I slid my long silver dagger through his false ribs. Fast. Hard. Deep. Angling upward, straight into his heart through his descending aorta.

His eyes went wide when I gave a twist and ripped it free.

His mouth dropped open. He staggered, brow twisting in a look of confusion and agony.

But he didn't even make a gurgle as his knees buckled.

He caved in against me, and I giggled again as I rolled him into the heavy dark behind a stack of crates and barrels, up against the tunnel wall.

Out of sight.

It wasn't a great hiding spot, but it would do.

The nobleman was dead before I laid his carcass on the ground and began the sweaty work of ripping off those robes. They'd work far better than the scout's gear I'd lifted for Axien before. They were also much lighter and easier to pack into my bag.

I didn't bother trying to redress him. Not fully, anyway. I pulled the male scout's jerkin and cloak over his head and left him sitting upright, leaning against the stack of wares like he'd nodded off at his guard post. It might take a while for someone to notice—especially since the incoming caravan of Tibran soldiers and supplies was moving at a snail's pace.

I had no time to waste, though.

Shouldering my bag, I seized his purse of coins and took off back into the dragging traffic that clogged the tunnel. I wove in and out of lines of wagons, formations of soldiers, and lumbering war beasts. There were several groups of Tibrans managing long strings of fine-looking war horses and muscular dunestriders, and I took note of how the animals were held together from nose to tail with ropes through simple rings on their bridles. One swift cut would let the entire string loose.

I only needed two, though.

And not quite yet.

I didn't stop or slow down until I'd left the northern end of the city and all the Tibrans behind, keeping my head down and my steps precise on the path we'd taken until I reached the quieter, unlit avenues where only Viperi prowled the dark.

I couldn't blame them for wanting to stay away from their bronze-armored visitors, but it did make me wonder just how much of the Brood Father's court here actually approved of the agreement he'd made. To ally with a surface-dwelling empire? To offer their own city as a place to harbor troops and weapons? That was a bold move, even for a Brood Father. Whatever bargain this Lord Argonox had offered him must have truly been too good to resist ...

Or too good to even be true.

Either way, clearly, the Brood Father's loyalty had been bought.

I smirked, wondering just how many plots there were against his life already.

Ducking into an alchemist's shop, I exchanged a handful of the nobleman's coins for a few bottles of antitoxin, healing tonics, and clean bandaging. None of it would be as good as what the healers of Undae had, the things Leruna used, but I couldn't afford to be picky.

Not with time already against me.

This had taken a lot longer than I'd anticipated. Hours. I had no idea if Axien would even be alive when I reached him.

Or if the scouts I had murdered had been discovered missing from their rounds.

Those worries looped in my brain, replaying and keeping my nerves on edge as I hurried back out into the streets. I retraced my steps, following the same path back out of the city the way I'd come in, keeping my composure until I reached the scouts' trail on the fringes of the cavern chamber.

Then I ran.

Pumping my legs as fast as they would go, I darted through the mountainous boulders, farther and farther from the glowing metropolis. I didn't dare look back and kept my jaw set tight as I sprinted back into the crumbling halls lined with those colossal dragon statues. Back through the ruins and rubble. Back to that fine, forgotten armory.

Almost there. A bit further.

I could make it.

He would be okay.

He had to be.

My body burned. My lungs ached. Sweat ran down every part of me, making my feet slide inside my boots and my eyes sting as it drizzled down my brow.

BOOM!

A bone-rattling explosion shook the labyrinth of dark stone around me. I staggered, my footing faltering. I bumped off the wall of the narrow corridor leading from the armory, barely keeping my balance as dirt and grit fell in a shower over my head.

Fates, what was that?!

I coughed and wiped my eyes, choking on the dust that hung thick in the air as I kept going. Onward. Closer.

Eerie blue light bloomed around the next turn—the one leading into the dining room.

An instant later, another low, concussive burst shook the world around me again.

My heartbeat came to a wrenching, twisting halt. Cold, crippling fear rushed in. My body went numb, ears ringing with the clatter and clang of combat.

Oh no.

That explosion ... that was a spell.

Axien was fighting. And he was using his magic!

FORTY-FIVE

They had him cornered like a mob of foaming, baying hounds around a treed jaguar.

With his back to the wall, Axien's face twisted in a desperate snarl at the six Viperi scouts before him. The area around him still glowed, smoldering where he'd cast some sort of fire-magic.

His chest heaved in manic, desperate pants as he drew his hands wide, palms glowing white-hot with fiery magic. Blood ran from his nose, ears, and eyes as he began mouthing words, speaking another spell in the ancient tongue of his ancestors.

Gods—NO!

He was pushing himself too far. Using that power had almost killed him before, after he'd carried us through that ancient portal. I couldn't let him do it again. I would not let him kill himself.

Something in my soul fractured—a tether that must have anchored me to reality somehow. Maybe being here among them, bathed in the light of their cities, speaking their language, and spilling their blood, had awakened something foul in me.

But in an instant, it was gone ... and a part of my soul I'd tamped down and tried to snuff out so I could survive on the surface came roaring to life.

I lost all control.

Flinging aside my heavy haversack, I skidded into the room and slid my daggers from their sheaths at my thighs, picking the closest of the scouts and springing for him without a second's hesitation.

I hit him full-force, wrapping my legs around his neck and wrenching him to the ground with my body weight while I flung one of my blades at the next scout. It hit the unsuspecting male in the back of the skull, dropping him instantly while I worked on choking the first out with a perfectly positioned squeeze of my legs over his jugular—just the way Declan had taught me.

Two down.

"NO MORE MAGIC!" I screeched at Axien as I bared my teeth at the remaining four scouts.

He just stared at me with slack-jawed horror.

The scouts did, too. All four of them remaining whirled on me at once, expressions blank in confused shock. Then they brandished their crossbows and scimitars. They barked orders, demanding that I drop my weapon and surrender. They ordered me to stand down. To reconsider my treason.

Good holy gods, had that ship ever sailed.

I grinned and sprang forward, dipping and whirling around crossbow bolts that hummed through the air and pinged off the surrounding stone. I was a blur in the shadows, moving with a speed no mere human could ever counter. I was ethereal. Untouchable.

Unstoppable.

My remaining blade hummed as I whipped it over my hand, ducking out of the way of enemy swings as two of the scouts pressed in with their blades.

The closest was still confused, still trying to work out why one of their own was attacking them. I seized his scimitar by the hilt and wrenched his hand backward, snapping his wrist, and stealing his weapon.

Then I drove it through his neck.

Another dying gasp.

More blood, thick as ocean fog in the air. It saturated my breath, rich and coppery on my tongue as I dove for my next enemy. And I was absolutely drunk on it.

"*Violet ...* " A deep voice murmured somewhere deep in my mind.

I pounced on the next scout, using her as a shield for the three crossbow bolts that ripped through the air, aimed right for my chest. She lurched and screamed as they hit, body arching against my grip.

I slit her throat with my dagger and kicked her floundering body into the two remaining enemies still rushing for me.

"*Violet ... you need to stop,*" the voice spoke again, low and deep like the distant rumble of thunder.

No. There was no stopping. No hesitating.

Not until they were all dead.

Another crossbow bolt zipped for me, and I coiled, feeling the graze of it pass my cheek as I arched into an aerial leap and twist. My hand shot out, quick as a viper's strike, and closed around the shaft of the bolt.

I snatched it out of the air and landed feet first on the next scout. I bore her to the ground like a wolf and rammed her own arrow down into her chest all the way to the fletching.

"*Stay with me, girl. You keep looking at me, you understand?*" the voice broke louder over my brain, demanding attention in a tone that made my spine stiffen.

I faltered, nearly dropping my dagger.

I-I knew that voice. Didn't I?

Pain split my lips with a primal scream as something

pierced my body right at my knee. The slice of a blade. My leg buckled, but I didn't fall. Not right away.

The fire roared higher, consuming my mind again. Blotting out everything—the voice, the pain, the sting of tears in my eyes.

It all died to the inferno.

The rage.

The hatred that poured like black ichor from the depths of my brutal, wicked heart.

I saw him—the last scout—drawing his blade back again for the final strike. To stab me through with that curved, silver scimitar. My features twisted. My body moved.

I dropped onto my wounded leg, whipping my body into a side-spin and hurling my last dagger straight for his head. It sailed like a sliver of moonlight. End over end. Silent and utterly perfect.

The scout's head snapped back as it caught him right between the eyes, the point of his scimitar barely pricking at the hollow of my throat. Just enough to draw one, tiny, pink line of my blood.

We both stood frozen for an instant. A second, or a lifetime—it felt the same. Then we both crumpled to the cold, blood-soaked stone floor.

I lay, my leg nothing but a dead weight of throbbing, splitting pain. My body shook, and tears filled my eyes. I didn't recognize the strangled cry that left my lips like a sob.

"*It's gonna be okay, Violet ...*" the voice—*his* voice—cooed over me.

Gentle. Strong. A fortress of calm and safety when I'd needed it the most.

Roxus.

But it wasn't his face that appeared over me, frantic and wild-eyed as he gripped my cheeks in his hands. Axien gripped me to his chest, lips moving frantically as he spoke. Or panicked, more like it.

I couldn't hear a single word of it, though. I could barely feel it as he cradled me against him, holding me as though I were something precious.

Something he couldn't bear to lose.

"Just keep breathing, girl," Roxus's voice rushed through me again, bringing peace like a spring rainstorm to the crackle and smolder of the flames in my heart.

"Help is coming, you just gotta hang on."

FORTY-SIX

I didn't know how to face him now.

Sitting across from Axien, I couldn't bring myself to look him in the eye as he wrapped my injured leg in layers of new gauze—gauze I'd bought for *him*, not me.

Neither of us had said a word yet. Or at least, I hadn't. He'd given up talking when I didn't reply, still reeling from the shock of what I'd just done.

Both of us were, though, I guess.

Gazing around at all my fallen victims, I didn't understand the strange, squeezing sense of pressure in my chest at the sight of their bloodied, twisted bodies. Was it shame? Guilt?

No, it couldn't be that. I didn't have any other choice. It had all happened far too fast, yes, but that didn't change anything. It didn't mean that going any slower or trying to reason with them would have made the outcome any different.

They were going to kill Axien.

So, they all had to die.

It was that simple.

He'd seen the ugliest side of me now, yes. But I'd done it with good reason, hadn't I?

Fates, I wasn't sure.

And if that voice—Roxus's voice—hadn't been whispering in my head, I wasn't sure I would have stopped at all. I might have turned on Axien next. I could never admit that to him now, though.

"That cut was deep. It probably severed some tendons," Axien murmured, his face drawn and haunted in the light of our single, flickering candle. "Can you stand on it?"

I grimaced and nodded. It didn't matter if it hurt, or if I had to limp. I *would* stand on it. There was no other choice.

"I've never seen anyone fight like that," he said quietly, his tone very careful.

Like he was afraid one wrong word might set me off again.

"I try not to make a habit of it." My shoulders curled in, and I angled my face away. "It took a long time, you know, to ... not fight that way every time. Until Roxus took me in and I started training with the Zenith's Call, I didn't even realize there were other ways to fight. Ways that weren't ..."

My voice trailed off as I struggled to come up with the right word.

"Intensely brutal?" he finished for me.

I shrugged. Close enough.

He gently put a hand on my freshly bandaged knee. "You learned to fight to survive. That's different from fighting for a cause. I understand."

My pulse skipped. I looked back up at him, and for whatever reason, the strange, knowing smile on his face made my body slowly relax. Somehow, it felt like he really did understand it.

"I'm grateful, Violet. I know you did it for me," he added quickly. "And ... I am very thankful."

My mouth mashed up bitterly. All I could do was nod a little as my face grew hot.

A tense, painfully awkward silence settled between us as he

went through the rest of the belongings I'd swiped during my little venture. The healing tonics and the antitoxins must have been things he recognized, because he immediately uncorked two of those vials and downed them, then took a few hearty swings from one of our newly acquired waterskins.

Thanks to my efforts, we now had plenty to go around.

"We can't stay here," I whispered as I took one of the healing tonics for myself and poured the thick, bitter liquid down my throat. It made my face contort as I forced myself to swallow.

Ugh. Disgusting.

"I know," he replied and dragged a hand through his sweaty hair.

His wide shoulders rose and fell with a deep, resigned breath. Then he leveled a grave, no-nonsense stare right at me.

"Tell me everything, Violet. Whatever happened, I need to know," he urged.

And I knew he was right. None of this would work if I didn't come completely clean about everything I'd just witnessed and done in the last several hours.

Fates, I just hoped he would actually believe me.

It only took a few minutes. I decided not to bore him with the details of how I'd killed two other scouts already, or how I'd slowly seduced the nobleman with Curator Vanora's mind games before I butchered him, too. Semantics like that didn't matter.

Not when I needed him to believe me about the thousands of Tibran soldiers camped not five miles from where we sat, arming themselves for what certainly seemed like a holy war.

I'd expected him to look more shocked about that. But as I spilled the details of everything I'd seen, Axien just sat eerily still and stared into the dancing flame of our one little candle.

I'd almost forgotten how involved he had been with Sanja and her schemes. She'd been working with a Tibran High General, after all.

Had he known this was coming all along? Or was this well above his pay grade?

I couldn't think of a way to ask without sounding accusatory.

"How are we going to get past them?" he asked, his tone somber.

I winced a little. "Well, that's where the nobleman comes in. Or, came in, I guess. I took his robes. Traditionally, Viperi nobles hide their faces except for their eyes. You can wear them, keep your head down, and follow me to the tunnel that leads to the surface. With any luck, we can take a couple of war mounts and make a break for it before anyone can stop us."

"And what about what awaits us on the surface?" he pressed, brow slowly creasing with a thoughtful frown. "If there are that many Tibran soldiers down below ..."

I nodded, agreeing. "There will certainly be more above— but if they're going to the trouble of moving their forces underground, I'm willing to bet they want to keep a low profile. Chasing down two Viperi deserters in the open would be ill-advised. Unless you think they've already laid siege to Dumathis. If that's the case, it's all for naught anyway, right?"

His mouth mashed to the side, and he gave a small, side-ways cringe that wasn't quite agreement. "I suppose."

I folded my arms and scowled challengingly down my nose at him. "You have any better ideas, sorcerer?"

He barked a dry, humourless laugh. "Not in the slightest. And even if I did, it's far too late to consider another course. You've set the board, lovely Violet. Now we must play the game, like it or not."

Well, he wasn't wrong.

Sooner rather than later, someone was going to notice the dead noble I'd left in the tunnel. Better to be miles from here, storming for Dumathis on the back of a warhorse, when that happened. Otherwise, the whole city might go on alert. The Tibrans and the Viperi might start fighting. They might close the tunnel down altogether.

We had to get moving—now.

I growled Viperi curses under my breath as I stood, my injured leg shaking and threatening to buckle the instant I dared to put any weight on it. Gods, Fates, and all things holy. How was I going to walk like this without drawing any attention?

I wasn't. I'd be limping along the entire time. Curse it all.

If Axien noticed the way my face screwed up in agony as I wobbled a few shaky, miserable steps, he had the good sense not to say anything about it while he redressed in the noble-man's robes.

He was far too tall to ever pass as Viperi, but bending over with the hood drawn low made him resemble an elder, some-what. It also hid the fact that his glowing eyes were definitely Avoran, not those of my kin.

It wasn't perfect, but it would have to do.

We picked weapons from the fallen scouts, arming ourselves for the worst with crossbows, bolts, and a pair of scimitars for Axien. Then we packed up the rest of the useful wares we could scavenge, just in case, and left.

Axien held my hand with a new ferocity as I led him back into the dark. Once we reached the city, he wouldn't need my guidance. The streetlamps they'd lit for the Tibrans would be more than sufficient.

But passing ourselves off as Viperi city folk would be more involved. We could try to disguise my limp as his, if we moved as one, and play off my need for his balance as him being a feeble elder being led along by a faithful scout. Hopefully, no one would care enough to stop and consider us too closely.

Or so I prayed, over and over, to whatever gods might be listening as we steadily made our way toward the Viperi city.

"You know, you might be the first Avoran ancestor ever to set foot in a Viperi city," I mused as we shambled along.

He snorted, as if he found that funny. "You may be right."

"What do you think they'd say if they could see us now?" I smirked. "Our ancestors, I mean."

"I can't really speak for mine," he said. "I've never met another Avoran, half-blooded or otherwise."

I couldn't mask my surprise. "Not even your father?"

He shook his head slightly, eyes glowing like two pale, aquamarine stars under the shadow of his hood.

My insides squirmed uncomfortably as I realized too late that I'd ripped open that sore subject yet again. Gods, I really was horrible at this whole small talk thing.

"Be honest," he spoke up suddenly, his tone quiet and cautious again. "Do you ever miss it?"

I frowned. "Miss what?"

He motioned to the endless, shadowed ruins and caverns all around us. "Being here. Being Viperi, instead of ... Zenith's Call."

He seemed to hesitate on that last bit, as though unsure if that was actually what I'd call myself now or not.

I hesitated, too. Not because I didn't know if I was Zenith's Call or not—that was about the only thing I was certain of, actually. But the rest?

Hmm.

Did I miss it here?

"Sometimes," I confessed, thankful for this one instance when Roxus wouldn't have to hear me say that out loud. "This can be a terrible world, and any Viperi city is the same— a horrible place filled with horrible people doing horrible things for the worst reasons you can imagine. But at least here, in their world, I understand the rules. I know what's expected of someone like me."

His eyes narrowed a bit, lips thinning. Not judgmentally or harshly, though. More like he was trying to understand.

"On the surface, it's always felt like the rules constantly change. As soon as I think I understand what's expected of me and what I'm supposed to do, suddenly I'm taking lessons on how to smile, what stupid fork to use, or trying to read languages that have been dead for a thousand years," I explained. "Like I said, until I took those first steps into Arx Eburna to become Zenith's Call, I'd never considered there was more than one way to fight. I'd never had to fight for anything other than keeping myself alive, in some way or another."

His hand squeezed mine a little tighter. But he didn't reply.

He didn't have to. The warmth of his rough palm and strong fingers woven through mine—it was enough.

It kept me grounded as the Viperi city slipped back into view before me, appearing in the dark like a mirage of twinkling lights. Axien must have been able to see it, or at least glimpse the parts that were illuminated by the flickering ancient street lamps, because he sucked in a gasp.

We both staggered to a halt and stared for a moment, and I realized now I could barely make out the movement of the Tibran forces bleeding into the city far on the other side, like a line of tiny golden flecks flowing in from the northern tunnel. Now and then, I could pick out the shapes of those massive war machines, too.

But from here, it all felt so far away.

"Are we really about to do this?" Axien asked, his tone a bit shaky.

Not that I blamed him. He'd probably meant for that to

be some sort of rhetorical, soul-searching question. I had to answer, though.

The words were too sharp to swallow down.

"We don't have a choice."

Gods, what were we doing? Had we completely lost our minds? This ... this would never work. We'd be caught. Killed. Butchered like sacrificial animals and fed to the switchbeasts, probably.

Or worse.

"Stay close to me," Axien said, his voice a deep, pleasing hum right next to my ear.

"Whatever happens, whatever we face, do not go far from me."

I slipped him a quick glance, my heart fluttering like mad in my chest to see how close he was. And that look on his face ... it wasn't fear. His brow was set as though it had been chiseled from stone, focused and relentless. Conviction flickered in the depths of his eyes.

It turned all my thoughts to complete mush and made my mouth go dry. My pulse raced, and my gaze dragged down to his mouth.

A kiss—I still owed him a kiss.

Should I remind him of that? Now wasn't really the time or place, but if we were about to die in the next few minutes, I'd rather not greet the gods with unpaid debts.

I'd also, you know, never done that before. Kissed someone. Or even wanted to.

"Violet?"

I flinched back slightly, my face burning as I frantically whipped my head back around to stare ahead, toward the city. Not at him.

Or his mouth.

"I-I'm ready," I gritted out. "Let's go."

But I wasn't. Not even a little. My thoughts churned and

spun like typhoon winds, even as we took our first step onward toward the waiting Viperi city.

Toward doom, or what might be the fight for our lives.

All I could do was trust that he meant what he said—that we were in this together, to whatever end awaited in the depths of that dark, wicked city.

FORTY-SEVEN

The city was already on full alert.

By the time we reached the gates, my leg throb-bing and shaking with every hitching step, the energy had completely shifted from when I'd left. More guards walked the lofty ramparts. More scouts prowled the streets, their hands on their weapons and their glittering red eyes keen on anyone who looked the least bit out of place.

So far, none of them had paid us any attention, though.

I couldn't tell if that was a testament to our *brilliant* plan, or just sheer dumb luck.

I'd take either, at this point. Whatever got us to that exit tunnel—I didn't care.

The streets had all but emptied, and a tense, heavy silence hung as thick as fog as we shambled along. All the shops that I'd passed were now closed up tight. The groups of nobles strolling together were gone. No voices.

None that were speaking the Viperi language, anyway.

Looking ahead, I winced at the fluttering, twisting in my gut as I saw the light of the fire-lit lamps glowing in the distance. Eight blocks ahead. Then we would be neck-deep in enemies who might not be so dismissive of our attire. I had no idea.

And it was far too late to stop now.

Two blocks away, my heart pounded so hard it felt like being punched right in the sternum with every frantic beat. My throat squeezed so tight I could hardly draw a breath. I gripped Axien's hand as tight as I could.

No. I had to stay focused. No limping. Control my expressions. Keep my countenance calm and composed. Body language.

Curse it all, where was Vanora's voice in my head when I needed it?

Where was Roxus's?

Gods, I'd have settled for my mother's, if it helped give me some sense of focus.

But in that moment, as we passed the first formation of Tibran soldiers, I'd never felt more alone in my own head.

Or so small in comparison to all those big, burly, armor-clad men.

"There must be an entire legion." Axien's voice was hardly even a whisper as he leaned down closer.

There were more than that, probably. Thousands more. But I didn't dare reply.

Axien played his part well, keeping his head down and his eyes obscured beneath his hood. With his mouth covered, he could mutter or whisper, and no one would suspect.

My face was bare, though. I had to look forward and keep us on the right path, moving through all these troops and avoiding any confrontation. We couldn't get in the way. We couldn't attract any attention.

Willing every shred of control and strength to my injured leg, I managed a walk with only a small limp that he could easily play off as his own, with me acting like I was the one supporting him, instead. We passed all the cages of switchbeasts, which had been shifted to the sidestreets so they would be out of the way of the incoming war machines that were now being rolled in one right after another into a line down that bigger, central avenue.

"Trebuchets and ballistas," Axien dared to whisper again. "But ... the designs are strange. I've never seen any like these before."

Frankly, I was shocked he'd ever seen any at all. Just what all had he done with Sanja before they came to us at Arx Eburna, exactly? Or were these things he'd seen when he was enslaved in the Tibran Empire?

Not knowing gnawed at my brain, but that conversation would have to wait for later.

Survival was all that mattered. Making it to the tunnel. Getting out.

Axien froze beside me suddenly, all but jerking me to a halt as his hold on my hand went rigid. His palm went clammy. What showed of his face from under that hood—his mouth, jaw, and tip of his nose—had turned a ghostly shade of white.

Without a word, he hauled me into the nearest alcove, where a door led into the interior of a building. The door itself was closed and most likely locked, but he pinned me there in the dark with his much larger form leaning over me, hiding me in the flowing lengths and long sleeves of his robes.

Then I heard her, too.

Sanja's melodic laugh rang out over the clatter and clink of armor, the shuffle of footsteps and ambient rumble of the legion swiftly filling the city around us.

I froze, staring up into the gloom of Axien's hood and seeing his face clearly as all his handsome features twisted with dread and terror.

She was here, somewhere close by.

How? When? Was she alone?

Had she brought Roxus here?

My body went numb, as though I were slowly being dipped in an ice bath. The pain in my leg faded to a distant ache as I focused every one of my senses on where her voice was coming from. We had to know. We had to get past her before she recognized either of us.

Thanks to his hood, Axien might be able to stride right past her without raising any alarm.

But I doubted she'd forget my face anytime soon, even in a city of my own kin where my features didn't exactly stand out.

"I have to look," I breathed shakily, the words so faint I wasn't sure he'd even hear me.

Axien's throat jumped as he swallowed hard. He nodded once, slowly.

I parted his voluminous black robes a little, pulling one sleeve back like a curtain to peer around it. Crowds of soldiers were still passing, marching along the sidewalks in rows of two and three with their shields firmly in hand. They didn't seem to notice us in the shadows. That, or they just didn't care.

But she stood out like an extra toe.

Strutting down the middle of the avenue, running her fingers adoringly along the huge wheels of the war machines, Sanja still wore her Zenith's Call attire with her long dark hair in a long, complex plait down her back. A smug, cattish grin curled her painted lips as she glanced back at the man following not even two steps behind her.

He was older and fairly tall, with a husky frame mashed beneath fine bronze and black armor. His pristinely polished helmet bore a mane of red-dyed horsehair, but he carried no shield. The jeweled, ivory hilt of a longsword stuck out of a fine scabbard strung on his belt, and his long crimson cloak fastened to the oversized, ornamental pauldrons on his shoulders fluttered along behind him as he passed.

The man scowled at Sanja as she spoke to him, not

seeming as amused as she was by this display. His movements were stiff, abrupt, and practiced. Like he'd spent a great many years behind one of those round Tibran shields, but had not progressed beyond that.

"There's some sort of officer walking with her," I whispered. "Big. Stocky and a little pudgy in the middle. Short, dark hair. Round face. Sparse beard. He's got a big ring on his right middle finger. Looks like it has the Tibran crest on it. His armor is very—"

"It's High General Crassus," Axien growled so low, the sound vibrated over my skin and made every tiny hair on the back of my neck prickle.

I pulled back slightly, my mouth snapping shut at that realization. There was a *Tibran High General* here? In a Viperi city? And he was moving what appeared to be one of his entire legions, maybe more, right into the streets.

Why?

Schemes and machinations danced through my brain as I tried to shift my perspective, to view it as though I were one of them. A tyrant on conquest. Not a hobbled Zenith's Call tandem.

Why would I want to move my soldiers below ground? Why would I bother striking deals with Viperi to use their cities and tunnels instead of marching above?

The answer hit me like a blade to the throat. I sucked in a sharp breath, flinching back and fixing Axien with a panicked, wide-eyed stare.

Because down here, there were no opposing enemy forces to attack my legion and thin my ranks—especially if I was allied with the Viperi, who already knew these caverns and the fastest ways to reach key cities above through them. There would be no way for the enemy to track our movements. No way for them to anticipate where we would strike next.

We would be able to hit city after city by surprise.

I'd already heard mention of the Tibrans attacking Nar'Haleen. At the time, it hadn't seemed like a problem I'd ever have to worry about. Nar'Haleen was vast, and most of its major cities were far on the eastern coast.

But if one of Argonox's High Generals was already here, then ... we must be a lot closer to Dumathis than I realized. And the Tibrans must be well on their way to taking all of Nar'Haleen.

"Sanja must have delivered Roxus to the High General already," I realized aloud, my voice shaking some. "He's here somewhere."

Axien's eyes darkened with what I could only guess was agreement ... and resolve.

He must have known I would not head for the exit tunnel now. No way. Not without looking for Roxus. I would die before I left him down in this hellhole to suffer at Sanja and High General Crassus's hands.

But how, by all the gods, could we ever find him in this tangled mess of soldiers, cages, war machines, and supplies? Hours. It would take *hours* to search every cage and wagon.

Hours we didn't have.

And if we found him ... what if he was still gravely injured? What if he couldn't even walk on his own? Or was still in his bear-shaped form? I could do a lot of things, but I couldn't drag a grizzly bear around by his ankle like a stuffed toy.

And then there was the staff. The whole reason we were even here to begin with. If Sanja was here, then she'd certainly have handed it over to the Tibrans. It might still be somewhere nearby, too, and I had oathed myself to protecting it because, for better or worse, I was Zenith's Call now.

I just didn't know what to do. Where to start. How to start.

And time was running out.

"I have to find him," I whispered, still paralyzed before all the things I needed to do. Or try to do, at least.

In truth, only one really mattered to me. The one person I would rather die than forsake in all this.

"I won't leave Roxus here," I swore.

Axien didn't respond. He held perfectly still, his gaze fixed on mine with unfaltering intensity. His chest rose and fell with deep, almost strained breaths. As though he were battling to keep his emotions at bay.

I couldn't look away.

My pulse skipped as the world around us seemed to glide to a halt, all the noise fading to that stillness between us. It was an unspoken understanding that I could never hope to put into words. A sense of knowing. And something else.

Something that cut so deep, it felt like staring into the last light of a dying star.

One corner of his mouth quirked into a weak, mirthless grin as he leaned down, his body invading the small space between us, one of his hands sliding up my back to grasp the back of my neck.

He bent down, breath warm on my face, his lips brushing lightly against mine as he murmured quietly, "Forgive me."

And he seized me by the hair, whirled around, and threw me to the ground in the middle of the street.

FORTY-EIGHT

My world of secrets, lies, and shadowed glass shattered.

This couldn't be happening. Not again.

I hit the ground and rolled like a ragdoll, my wounded leg collapsing under me so I couldn't even catch myself on the way down. Landing on my side, I wheezed and gasped, immediately trying to crawl away.

No, no, no—NO—Gods, just end me. *NO!*

It wasn't ... it couldn't ... I-I had trusted him. Just like Chrysa.

And it was the *same*.

The same agony. The same feeling as if my entire world had been turned upside down and dumped right in my lap. The same ugly truth that still haunted my nightmares: I was unworthy of real friendship.

And trying for it, believing I could ever find it, made me the biggest fool of all.

"You could have waited for me, you know," Axien shouted as he stalked from the shadows of the alcove after me. "Do you have any idea how hard it is for someone with Avoran blood to get into a place like this?"

"Is that you, Axien?" Sanja said sweetly, whirling around at the sudden commotion. Beside her, the High General already had a hand on that fine sword dangling from his belt, his dark eyes glittering with suspicion.

"Indeed. And I come bearing gifts," Axien snorted, throwing back the hood of his robes as he stalked forward.

Sanja's eyes narrowed. "My, my. And how is it you accomplished this grand feat, hm? Coming so far in such a miserable place? What these red-eyed beasties call a home is practically a warren of death."

Up. I had to get up. Now. I had to draw my blades and—

All the wind slammed out of my chest as Axien stomped a foot down onto my back and pinned me there, mashing me down into the street so I couldn't even crawl away.

"I had a very useful little guide," he said. "More useful than any of us suspected, it would seem. She's resourceful, I'll grant her that, but her true worth is something I doubt even Roxus knew about."

Sanja's brows rose slowly, her mouth making a little O-shape. "Is that so?"

Axien crossed his arms, curling his lip as he glowered down at where I still squirmed under his boot. "You wondered how she was able to work out who your last agents really were so easily? It's because she can *see* magic. The ancients called it runesight. I doubt if there's anyone else alive with her gift— otherwise the Aurati would have found them long ago. It's a trait they've desired to breed into their stock for a long time, but never found anyone with the ability."

She and her general exchanged meaningful sideways glances, almost like they'd discussed this several times over already and she had just been proven right.

"That's why I decided that bringing her here, to you, was

more prudent. It would have been a waste when she could fetch a mighty price from the Aurati ... or become a prized jewel for Argonox," Axien said with a shrug.

"So the pup has become a hunting hound—and a good one, at that. See? He *can* be useful, when held on the right leash." Sanja laughed and gave another gleeful, triumphant grin that curled her red-painted lips up at the corners. "Your wife had no patience for it, but *I* know his type. Conniving, but oh so eager to please."

Sick. I was going to be sick.

How did Axien know about my runesight? Had I done something to give it away? Was it because I slipped up about how his eyes glowed blue to me?

My face twitched, contorting with rage and grief as I set my teeth against the scorching heat of shame that flamed through my body.

Pay—Gods witness me, Axien would pay for this.

I'd carve my vengeance out of his flesh if it was the very last thing I did on this earth.

"Box her up, then," High General Crassus ordered, his voice deep and rough as he prowled toward me and drew his longsword with a flourish. He pressed the tip of it to my chin, forcing me to lift my face so he could look at me.

I glared at him, his face hardly more than a smeared blur through the tears in my eyes.

"If it is true she can see magic, then she will make a fine prize for Lord Argonox. She will hunt down more artifacts for him. The flesh-sculptors will have a fine time engineering her to suit his cause." He held my gaze, never smiling or gloating as he spoke even, calculated words. There was no hint of laughter or taunting in his hard-set features, just a cold resolve.

I fought.

When the High General snapped his fingers, summoning his bronze-armored soldiers to put me in iron shackles and bind my eyes behind a black metal mask that covered the top half of my face—I screamed. I kicked. Scratched. Bit. Anything I could to get away.

But I couldn't fight off so many of them. Not when they wore armor like that. Not when they were all twice my size and my leg was crippled so that I couldn't even stand without help.

I floundered in the dirt like a wounded fox until the world suddenly went dark behind that mask. Then I screamed again.

I cursed Axien and Sanja in every language I knew while they stripped me of my fighting leathers and weapons, leaving me in my under-blouse, leggings, and boots. I swore their deaths before the feet of the death goddess, and someone hit me hard across the back of the head with what felt distinctly like a gauntleted fist.

Stars danced in the darkness before my eyes. Everything seemed to spin, but I refused to go down. I wouldn't pass out. I would be hauled away like a corpse.

So I spat at them—or at least, at anyone who happened to be in front of me, and snarled, "My own mother hit me harder than that, you cowards."

Someone gave a bemused grunt, and then another powerful fist seized me by the hair and dragged me to my feet. My leg howled in agony as they forced me to walk. I only made it a few steps before my injured knee buckled and I hit the ground again.

"Pathetic," someone grumbled over me.

I snarled as they took me by the arms and started dragging me over the ground like a dead doe. Away into a hell I couldn't even see now.

Somewhere behind me, Sanja started laughing again. Like she was loving every second of the show. Like she couldn't wait to see what these Tibrans would do with me next.

But Axien didn't make a single sound.

And somehow I just knew, as though I could feel it like the glare of dawn sunlight on my skin, that he was staring right at me.

So just for good measure, I gave him a parting gesture with my finger.

He'd pay for this. Either in this life or the next, he would suffer.

I'd make sure of it.

FORTY-NINE

My face hit the cold metal bars of a cage.

A second later, the door banged shut behind me, and something clicked. A lock?

I couldn't see anything around me, but since my hands were shackled in front of me, I could feel around the interior of the cage. It was small, narrow, and rectangular. Probably the same as the cages of the switchbeasts I'd seen before. My fingertips traced the rough, pocked iron bars until I found the door at one end. There was a big padlock holding it closed.

Curse it all.

I clawed at the mask on my face next, trying to pry it off. But the device had been crafted so that it clamped down onto my head and was held with an inset lock. With nothing but a tiny keyhole to work with, I couldn't get it off.

Blind. I was blind. Trapped. Caged.

Again.

Panic swirled through my body like a cold shudder, sending shooting pangs of adrenaline out through my extremities. No—this wasn't happening. Out. I had to get out.

The cage was too small for me to sit up in, and it was

barely long enough for me to lie on my side. But I squirmed around inside it, angling my body just so with my feet down toward the cage door.

Then I kicked at the bars with all my strength. I flailed, slamming my feet against the door again and again, as hard as I could.

Each hit sent a wave of agony up my injured leg, but I didn't stop. My skin grew slick with sweat. My chest heaved as I panted. But I didn't stop. I couldn't.

I could *not* give up.

They'd taken everything—my gear, my daggers, but I wasn't helpless. I still had a trick stuffed down in the side of my boot, and enough venom in my blood to butcher them all just like I had those scouts.

I just had to get out. Get free.

The minutes dragged. Or maybe it was hours? I didn't know. I just kicked at the bars over and over, getting nowhere, until I had no strength left.

Lying on my side, I wheezed for breath and kept my eyes shut tightly under the mask. I didn't want to see it. That wall of darkness that now held me captive.

I just had to rest. Think. There had to be a way out. An option I hadn't considered before.

My other senses opened to the surrounding area, soaking in the sounds of growling, hissing, and screeching from other caged animals probably stacked all around me. The stench of manure, blood, and rotted meat stung at my nose.

I could still detect the voices of men and the clattering of armor somewhere in the distance. It was muffled, though, like it was beyond a door or a wall.

Had they set me aside somewhere special, then? Some-where away from the other mundane beasts they'd caught?

I cringed at the sudden, familiar groan of a door on rusty hinges being swung open, and immediately drew my legs in to my chest. Ready to start kicking and fighting if whoever had come inside even dreamed of opening my cage door.

Footsteps approached. Fabric rustled. The scent of eucalyptus, cedar, and blood tinged with Viperi incense wafted past my cage.

I froze. My pulse surged, and I bit down hard to keep my words bottled in.

Axien.

"I didn't want it to happen this way," his deep voice carried through the dark, coming from much closer than I anticipated. Almost as though he were standing right next to my cage.

I bared my teeth. "You think I care what you want? Why are you here? What do you want from me now, hm? To hear me beg you? I'd rather die."

He didn't reply.

His footsteps scraped over the stone, and the fabric of those stolen robes rustled as though he were dropping them onto the floor. Something else, something heavier, clattered with them.

I dared to lift my head, staring at the direction of the noise, but seeing nothing.

"I want what I'm owed," he growled low.

Wh ... what? What was he talking about—?

A strong hand seized my chin suddenly. I sucked in a sharp breath of alarm as Axien grabbed my face and yanked me closer to the bars, his mouth mashing hard against mine between them.

Before I could react, before I could jerk away, his tongue pressed through my lips. No. Not just his tongue. He was forcing something small into my mouth.

G-Gods, was that ... was that a *key?!*

I held it between my teeth, resisting the urge to spit it right back into his face. What, by all the gods, was he doing? Why was he giving me this? What was it for?

"We're even now," he said quietly, his breath puffing across my mouth as he let me go.

"Axien?" Sanja barked angrily from somewhere farther away, her tone laced with all the piss and vinegar of a grouchy little lapdog. "We need to go. Quit playing with your food."

He laughed—but it was hollow. Empty. Wrong.

Fake.

My stomach swirled and fluttered as all the thoughts in my head tangled back on themselves. What was happening? Was he helping me? Whose side was he on?

Could I even trust that he wasn't trying to set me up for a second time?

My head spun, and I couldn't move or make a sound as they left and the door slammed again. The noises of the animals in the cages around me stirred, growling louder at the disruption.

I spat the key into my hand, feeling around the edges of it. It was small—too small to match the padlock of my cage. It might even be too big for my shackles.

But my mask ...

It took a bit to find the keyhole again and work the tiny key into it, all while lying on my back. Sweat drizzled down the sides of my face, and my teeth chattered as the rush of adrenaline left me cold and my fingertips tingly and numb. My stupid hands wouldn't stop shaking.

What if I couldn't do it? What if it was the wrong key, or I dropped it by accident, or—

Clink!

The mask slid off the side of my face and landed at the bottom of the cage with a clatter. I squinted up into the gloom above me. The beams of a ceiling in what must have been a storage room were draped thick in shadow, and the ironwork chandeliers hanging from them had no candles even if they'd wanted it.

I slowly lowered my arms, looking at the tiny silver key in my fingers. Something hot and sizzling slowly rose up within me, like molten steel being poured into a blacksmith's form. Not rage. Not fury or wrath.

Understanding.

Axien was right. Our debt was repaid. He'd given me an inch of leverage—but it was the only inch that mattered. It was all I needed.

Sliding the key into the pocket of my leggings, I reached down into the side of my boot and slowly drew the only weapon I had left: the stolen Avoran knife I'd swiped off the dinner table. It was long and slender, more like a filet knife in shape because of the exaggerated, tapered point. It gleamed beautifully, even in the dimness of the room. It was definitely not meant for murdering people.

But that's exactly what it would do today.

That and so much more.

FIFTY

I'd gotten *really* good at picking locks.

Nearly starving to death as a street urchin had given me a lot of those kinds of skills, and I could do it in seconds with hairpins. That was child's play.

Knives were harder to work with, but the shape of this one made it far simpler, especially with the key to assist. It was small enough to help me work the shackles off my wrists in a matter of minutes.

Then I set to work on the cage door.

Padlocks were, by design, the easiest for me. And now that I could see to angle my tools just so, feeling for the slightest shift of the mechanisms within it, I popped the lock off even faster than the shackles.

In less than five minutes, my feet hit the ground outside the cage. Free.

My pulse thundered in my chest as I crouched low, examining where Axien had shed his robes—the same one's I'd swiped off the nobleman. Sanja apparently hadn't even noticed he'd left them there. Or maybe she had assumed it was a taunt of some kind.

Either way, he'd used them to cover up the other items he'd left for me: my daggers, still in their sheaths.

My eyes welled, half in frustrated confusion and half in anger, as I buckled them back onto my legs and pulled the robes over my body. They were far too big, but some cover was better than none.

And I had absolutely no idea what might be waiting for me outside that door.

Pulling the hood down low, I slipped my Avoran kitchen knife back into the side of my boot and drew my daggers instead. With my heart lodged somewhere in my throat, I cracked the door open an inch, just enough to peer out into the corridor outside.

I held my breath and waited. Listening. Stretched my senses out into the darkness beyond as far as they would go.

Just outside seemed to be a hallway in some sort of house or manor, with a huge vaulted ceiling and airy archways lined on both sides with stacks of more animal crates. The style was Avoran, but the furnishings ... this place had been redecorated by Viperi hands. The portraits and sconces had all been ripped down and replaced with sharp, angular accents made from obsidian, silver, and all featuring the design of an all-too-familiar eye in the center of spiraling runes.

The Eye of the Foul Father.

Braziers on elegant silver stands stood along the far wall, smoldering with bundles of sharp incense that sent up little wisps of smoke into the air.

Holding my breath, I dared to open the door wider and step beyond it, between the lines of cages stacked in towers of three and four. They all held switchbeasts, hissing and coiling like tangled masses of sinewy limbs, curled talons, and bristled fishbone teeth. I made sure to stay out of swiping range as I maneuvered between them and crept to the end of the hallway where it intersected another, much grander corridor.

Crouching low, I scanned the way forward. To the left, there was a dead end at a wall adorned with a defaced tapestry of Clysiros, the death goddess. To the right, the passage fed into a vestibule glowing with lamplight. There, the sounds and vibrations of Tibran soldiers seemed far louder.

I licked my teeth behind my lips as I considered my next move. Right now, I had the edge of obscurity. But I needed to know three things as soon as possible.

Where Roxus was.

Where the Moonscape staff was.

How to get out of this hellhole as quickly as possible.

My thoughts twisted, contorting back into that wicked state that had served me fairly well so far today. Clearly, I was sitting in someone's dwelling. Someone powerful, if the furnishings were any indication. Someone housing a lot of Tibrans.

Smart bets went to the Brood Father.

If I were correct, there were a lot more people in this place. People the Brood Father cared for, as much as a Viperi could care for anyone or anything. His court. His offspring. They were valuable to him, along with his trove of treasures, armories, and stolen Avoran relics.

More than that, though, this place was likely packed with everything High General Crassus valued most. Or at least, the things he'd deemed most valuable to his cause and his master.

Roxus and the staff had to be here close by.

And what did people rush to first in a fire?

The things they valued most, then the nearest exit.

Everything I needed.

I glanced back at the cages behind me, all those switchbeasts.

This would be risky. Dangerous. Reckless in ways that might put Roxus in his grave, regardless. I'd have to do it carefully, because outrunning anyone on my bad leg was completely out of the question. I'd do good at a speedy hobble.

But if this is what it took to get us out, then I'd start a fire unlike any other. One Sanja and High General Crassus would never forget.

Pulling one of the fancy, jeweled pins out of the waistbelt of the noble robes I wore, I prowled toward the nearest cage and stared into the milky, huge eyes of the beast within. It hissed and slammed against the bars, raking them with its talons while all six of its powerful legs flexed and coiled like a serpent preparing for another strike.

"You won't attack me," I whispered to the monster, baring my teeth back at it and returning the hiss. "You'll hunt and feast on them."

The creature bucked against the cage, screeching furiously.

I smirked and glanced over my shoulder to the nearest of those braziers again, then to the tapestry. Good enough. Time to work.

I cut down the tapestry first, dragging it to the back of the hallway behind all the cages. I used the thick length of rope that it had been strung on to tie down the cage doors, weaving it just so they would be tethered closed until I untied the knot that held them.

Even without their locks.

Then I got busy lock-picking again.

My fingers flew, popping the first three locks in under a minute. My body trembled, pulsing with flurries of anxious energy as I moved to the next stack. The rope stretched and strained with every door I opened, the force of the switch-beasts straining to force their cage doors ajar threatening to snap it.

Just a few more.

Two locks later, I heard the rope give an awful, creaking groan.

Time was up.

I tore off a length of my robes as I limped to the nearest brazier, setting the scrap of fabric ablaze, and moved to the back of the hallway behind the remaining cages. I set the heap of tapestry aflame and waited, crouching behind the wall of flickering, licking flames that hopefully would be enough to discourage my agents of chaos from attacking me instead of, well, everyone else in their path.

CRACK!

The rope snapped, and immediately all the unlocked cage doors burst open at once. Five angry switchbeasts barreled out into the hallway, took one look at the growing wall of fire behind them, and loped away into the manor. They never considered me, never even looked back, as they rounded the corner on those six, powerful legs and disappeared.

Seconds later, the screaming started.

I ran forward as fast as my leg would allow, past the remaining cages with the creatures still trapped inside, and dragged the burning tapestry with me. It spat embers and sparks, catching the fine carpets that spanned the marble floors ablaze, as well.

At the intersection with the vestibule, I left the burning tapestry and drew my blades, watching as a herd of Tibran soldiers ran past. They didn't pay any attention to me, either. Not with a switchbeast galloping after them like the world's ugliest, most monstrous-looking cheetah chasing down startled gazelle.

Perfect for me, terrible for them.

Just the way I liked it.

Ducking into the vestibule, I took in the room and the utter chaos of the soldiers now locked in close-combat with two more of my unleashed, sort-of allies. Men shouted and screamed. The switchbeasts howled and screeched. Blood splashed over the marble. Flames roared in the hallway behind me, sending thick black smoke boiling up into the air.

Through the mayhem, the ripple of that red cloak and feather-crested helm caught my eye. High General Crassus moved with brisk, sharp efficiency, ducking around his panicking men out a doorway on the other side of the room.

And Sanja was right on his heels.

My smirk widened. The hunt was on.

I bolted forward into the room, ignoring the flare of agony in my leg as a fresh burst of rage pushed everything else from my mind. There was no pain. No fatigue. Nothing but the burn of fury like coals in my throat as I forged forward, dipping and ducking through the frantic Tibran soldiers and raging switchbeasts.

I followed the High General and Sanja out that door barely a minute later—just in time to see them angrily barking orders at a small group of bronze-armored men.

Dropping into another crouch beside the door, I kept my head down and hood low as I watched from a distance.

"No excuses! You *will* fetch the beasts and load the wagons immediately! We leave nothing behind!" High General Crassus snarled over them.

One of the soldiers began to protest, but he barely got his mouth open before the High General rammed him through with his longsword all the way to the hilt. Ripping the blade free, he kicked the man to the floor and glowered at the rest of them.

"Would anyone else like to argue with their superior?" Crassus seethed.

They didn't. Or rather, none of them said a word as they scrambled away into the manor.

"You think so few can manage his cage?" Sanja scoffed as she nudged the fallen Tibran soldier with one of her dainty feet. "He is not a normal bear, remember."

"Go and help them, if you're so concerned." High General Crassus cast her an icy sideways glare as he stormed past her, stepping over his fallen underling on the way.

Her mouth twisted to the side bitterly, but she followed along after her general instead.

I waited a beat, then rose and pursued again. When I reached the fallen Tibran soldier, I did him the service of cutting his throat rather than leaving him to slowly bleed out on the floor. More mercy than his own commanding officer had shown him.

He didn't thank me, though. And I took his crossbow and quiver of bolts as payment for services rendered.

I hobbled past him, following the rest of his cowering comrades deeper into the manor. The High General and Sanja would have to wait. They would wait—especially since I was going after the very things they wouldn't want to leave without.

A bear in a cage? My heart surged with hope. My eyes welled and I bit down hard to keep a wild, desperate sob of relief from leaking past my lips.

I'd been right. Roxus *was* here. And I was going to find him.

Even if I couldn't get the staff, I would get him out of here. I'd save the only person who truly mattered. The person I couldn't live without.

Or we'd die in the flames, fangs, and claws that would consume this place together.

FIFTY-ONE

I heard him first.

The rumble of Roxus's roar shook the walls of the manor as I chased after the Tibrans. That cry, like a clap of thunder, hit my chest and snatched all the breath from my lungs. He was alive. And he sounded ... okay. Angry, but okay.

Er, well, as okay as a furious bear can sound, I guess.

I'd take any noise as proof that he was at least not on the verge of death, which was more than I'd even dared to hope for.

Rounding a corner, I skidded to a halt before the company of soldiers as they worked together, trying to roll a massive cage through a doorway on a series of long poles. I guess that was the only way they could work out moving it from the room where it had been before to the wagon that was already waiting at the other end of the passage.

The armored wagon had been backed in through a large opening, likely originally intended for unloading deliveries to the kitchens. With its back doors open wide, ready to receive cargo, several soldiers were already setting out a loading ramp for the rest of them to move the cage into place.

They all looked up as I flailed my arms a little, barely stopping without faltering and falling on my injured leg. Whoops.

From within his cage, Roxus's massive furry head whipped around to consider me with familiar, warm, light brown eyes. He bellowed again, slamming his bulky body against the bars. All the soldiers around him cringed back, glancing between us as though they weren't sure what to do. Clearly, they hadn't been expecting me. But who was I? Just another Viperi fleeing the burning manor?

I didn't give them the chance to work it out.

I opened fire with the crossbow, aiming at the nearest two Tibrans and dropping them immediately. By the time I had to pause to reload, the rest of them had come to the conclusion that I was, in fact, not an ally and had drawn their own weapons.

I managed another shot, dropping another soldier with a well-aimed bolt to the forehead, as I dashed to the side and closed the distance to the wagon. Within his cage, Roxus bucked and roared. He slammed himself to one side so hard that the entire cage teetered, then crashed down sideways on top of two more soldiers, who were immediately crushed underneath it.

Then it was chaos.

Arrows flew, zipping all around me as the soldiers panicked, apparently torn between dispensing with me and righting the cage to get out of here as soon as possible. The split effort cost them, and I dove at another soldier as he stepped into my radius, dagger already whirling.

Nearby, another scream of panic ripped through the hall as Roxus caught one of the soldiers who had come too close to his cage. The soldier wailed and panicked as Roxus dragged him in close enough for his powerful jaws to finish the job.

That must have been enough to rip what remained of the loyalty and morale from the four or five soldiers remaining.

They instantly gave up the effort. I watched, dagger still clenched in my hand, as the Tibran soldiers clambered onto their wagon—without the angry caged bear—and took off away from the manor.

I watched the wagon rattle away, chest heaving and pain flaring through my leg so badly I couldn't hold it in anymore. I let out a strangled cry and sank slowly to my rear, body shaking and blood seeping through the bandaging Axien had wrapped around it. I'd reopened it, or made it worse.

"VIOLET!" Roxus yelled suddenly.

I flinched, instinctively curling up as his human voice startled me. Then I turned, slipping my dagger back into its sheath on my thigh, and started crawling for his cage.

"R-Roxus," I whimpered through my teeth.

He crouched before the cage door, once again a human-looking man, his clothes tattered and bloody. His body was mottled with cuts, gashes, and slashes. Blood slicked nearly every inch of him. But he stared at me as he gripped the cage bars, desperation twisting his features as he reached out for me as soon as I was close enough.

I grabbed his hand, unable to hold back a sob as he all but dragged me in closer and hugged me through the bars. Suddenly, I was encased in his strength. His familiar smell filled my noise, and the steady thump of his heart was pure bliss against my ear.

I was safe. Safe with him. Always.

"I thought you were dead." He breathed shakily, his broken words murmured right against my hair. "Gods, I thought I lost you, girl."

I gripped him as hard as I could, still on my knees, body shaking as I buried my face in his shoulder. "W-We have to get you out," I wheezed. "Now. We have to go. Before they realize what's going on."

"What *is* going on?" he demanded, pulling back when I began shifting away.

I had to use the bars to drag myself back upright so I could start working on the first of the three locks that held his cage closed.

"I let some of the switchbeasts out," I explained as I worked. "Then I started a fire. They're evacuating the manor. I don't think they know it was me. Not yet. But they will soon."

"They will?" he pressed, watching me work until the last lock popped free. Then he pushed the door open and stepped out.

A free man.

"I have a feeling I was one of the beasts High General Crassus ordered his men to load onto that wagon with you. I imagine they're discovering my cage is already empty right about now," I muttered, not expecting him to fully under-stand. There would be time to explain everything later on.

Right now, we just had to run.

Only ... I couldn't.

As soon as Roxus stepped free of his cage, my leg buckled and I fell. He caught me just before I hit the ground, sweeping his arms under me and holding me against his chest. My head lolled into him, and he sucked in a sharp breath.

I guess he had noticed my leg.

"You're hurt," he growled ominously.

"No worse than usual." I forced a twitching, agonized smile. "And so are you."

"Not nearly as badly. Come on, I'm carrying you," he insisted, and immediately dropped down to a knee so I could shakily climb onto his back like a child with my arms around his neck.

As embarrassing as it was to be hauled out of here clinging to his back like a scared baby monkey, I knew my leg would only slow him down otherwise. He'd be more vulnerable if he had to wait for me to hobble along after him.

This was the only way.

So I swallowed my dignity and held on tight as he ran out the same open corridor the wagon had taken.

We fled the burning manor, delving immediately into the streets of the city. Screams and shouts echoed down every street. Ash and cinders floated in the air, lighting the way and swirling around us like a million fireflies. The echoes of clashing swords, screeching of animals, and wailing of panicked women seemed to come from everywhere at once.

CRACK—BOOM!

Something thundered through the cavern like an explosion, making rocks and debris shower down from overhead. I didn't dare look to see how many of those massive, building-sized stalactites were dangling over us.

Too many.

"What was that?" I yelped in Roxus's ear as another explosion made him stagger.

"Catapults! They're firing the war machines!" he yelled back over the noise.

My blood went cold.

Why would the Tibrans do that? Didn't they realize doing that put everyone, even their own men, at risk? And for what? What were they even firing at? The switchbeasts?

Roxus skidded to a halt as he rounded a corner, nearly tripping as we came face to face with the answer.

Tibrans and Viperi filled the streets, locked in combat. They bashed with their round bronze shields, their blades flashing and howling with every strike. Crossbow strings cracked, firing a hailstorm of bolts that zipped in every direction. Men shouted, wailed, rallied, and fell in tangled masses. Switchbeasts circled, picking off anyone who strayed too far from the thick of the battle.

Why ... why were they fighting each other?!

"Gods and Fates, what is happening?" Roxus snarled in horror, taking an uncertain step back. "What exactly did you do?!"

I had no idea. At least, not when it came to all this.

Stealing a glance back over my shoulder, my mouth fell open when I saw the manor. Flames belched out of every window on nearly all ten floors as though it were a massive furnace. Even the banners were ablaze, and people were trying to climb down the walls to escape the inferno.

"I-I ..." My voice died in my throat when a few of the Tibrans noticed us standing there and began advancing.

Roxus growled and spun on a heel, bolting away down a side street and leaving that part of the battle behind. I didn't dare look back again to see if we were being pursued.

"We need a way out of here!" he yelled back.

"There!" I pointed over his shoulder to the northern end of the city, far in the distance, but elevated enough that we could see the exit tunnel. "It goes to the surface!"

"You're sure?" He gripped me harder, lowering his head as he ran faster.

I squeezed my arms around his neck tighter, hanging on for dear life. "Yes!"

Another beastly growl left his lips as his body warped beneath me, growing and changing into something monstrous and furry. He hit the ground on all four bear paws and ran, moving a lot faster than I'd ever thought a bear could.

Much faster than a human, anyway.

With my fingers twisted into his dense, coarse brown fur, I hunkered down and tried to hold on as he charged onward. Blood matted places in his back—places where he'd taken crossbow bolts or sword slashes previously. But if any of those injuries bothered him now, it didn't show.

We galloped through the city, dodging the areas choked

thick with combat and trying to keep out of sight. It didn't take long for a pair of switchbeasts to fall in pursuit behind us, their jaws open wide and their powerful legs stretching for each bounding leap. They were much faster and gaining, but I still had my stolen crossbow.

Whipping around, I kept one hand gripped tight into Roxus's furry scruff as I leveled the crossbow back at the nearest of the two beasts. My hand shook with every move Roxus made, but it couldn't be helped. I had to do this. Now.

Sucking in a breath, I led the creature by a foot and squeezed the trigger. The crossbow flinched in my hand, the string snapping with a sharp report. The black bolt fired, ripping through the distance and landing square in the switch-beast's skull with a *crunch*.

It fell immediately, straight into its partner's path. The second switchbeast bounded over the tumbling body without missing a beat, hissing in dismay, and pouring on more speed.

Curse it, it'd be on us in seconds.

I floundered, scrambling to reload my weapon. I had to grip Roxus's furry waist with my thighs while I did, my stomach in my throat as I fought not to tumble off backward. My hands slipped. The thick resin string resisted as I dragged it back into place and spun around to fire again.

Too late.

The switchbeast was right in my face, jaws open, ready to clamp onto my neck. On instinct, I rammed the entire crossbow into its open mouth and fired. The monster's yowl of pain became a dying gurgle as the bolt ripped through its mouth and out of the back of its throat.

Blood spatter filled the air, and the switchbeast fell, rolling to a halt far behind us with my crossbow still lodged in its jaws.

So much for that. I was down a weapon, but at least we weren't about to get mauled.

Wiping switchbeast blood from my face, I hunkered back down against Roxus's back just in time to see the next, much bigger problem rising before us like a roiling bronze sea.

More Tibran soldiers—hundreds of them—choked an entire open square dead ahead. They rallied around their ballistas and trebuchets, barely holding off an invading wave of black armor and silver-dipped weapons in much faster, well-trained hands.

Viperi guards were not to be taken lightly, and they were in their element here, on their home turf. They used smoke bombs to confuse and blind the Tibran ranks, converging on them using their heat-vision instead.

I clenched my teeth, swallowing against the coppery tang of bloody vapor in the air as we dove headlong into the fray. There was no time to look for another path forward. We had to push through somehow.

I would have to be his eyes.

With a hard blink, I swapped to my heat-vision as we forged headlong into the smoke. Leaning forward, I seized Roxus's little furry ears and used them like reins on a horse, steering him around throngs of enemies. He seemed to pick up on my cues right away, lowering his big head and pouring on the speed. I gave him a little kick and nudge, urging him to jump over heaps of fallen bodies.

"On your left!" I screamed as someone drove in with a halberd, the weapon aimed right for his side.

Roxus sidestepped, narrowly dodging the strike with a defiant growl. The soldier floundered back with a cry of alarm. I guess he hadn't anticipated the sheer size of the beast he'd swung at.

But we didn't stick around to finish that fight.

Roxus let out a victorious cry as we burst out of the curling, dense cloud of black smoke on the other side. I let go of his ears and dared to take a breath, to hope for the smallest instant that we might actually do this. The tunnel wasn't far now. I could see it through the tangled chaos of burning war machines, wandering banks of black smoke, and heaps of bronze-armored corpses.

We *would* make it.

Arrows whizzed past my head from the guards atop the ramparts as we charged through the arched entrance in the city wall. Roxus let out a roar of pain as a few caught him in the flank, but he didn't falter. He didn't stop. He couldn't. Not now.

Not when we were *so* close.

I dared to let out a screaming cry of relief as we sprang into the tunnel, diving headlong into the eerie dimness of the passage and leaving the battle behind. Behind us, the rumble of battle faded. Before us, strange silver light seemed to ebb in from somewhere just out of sight.

Was that ... moonlight?

The tunnel had almost been cleared out, with no war machines or wagons left in sight, so I caught a blast of fresh, cool, free-flowing air straight to the face. Air from the surface. It hit me like a slap, startling me and wringing another agonized cry from my lips.

Tears welled in my eyes. I gripped Roxus fiercely, my knuckles white and my whole body shaking.

Free. Gods, we were free! We were—

Roxus lurched to a halt so suddenly I nearly tumbled right over his head. His immense body went tense beneath me, as solid as iron under all that shaggy fur, and a rumbling growl kindled in his throat.

I stared, mouth open, as all the wind tore from my chest at once.

My ears rang. My blood went cold.

No. This couldn't be happening. Not now. Not when we

were so close I could taste the brine of the desert's salty sand on my tongue.

But there they were—gathered around a large, armored wagon that seemed to have been damaged by falling debris shaken loose from the tunnel's ceiling.

Sanja, Axien, and General Crassus stood before us not thirty feet away, flanked by a dozen Tibran soldiers.

And there was no way around them.

FIFTY-TWO

There was nowhere to hide.

Nowhere else to run or retreat to. No other path I knew of to get out of this nightmare other than the one in front of us—the one they were blocking.

I was all out of ideas and clever tricks. I didn't even have a ranged weapon now that my crossbow was gone. Fates, I didn't even know if I could stand.

My heart pounded in my throat, and my stomach sank somewhere down to the soles of my boots as my gaze flashed across the three of them.

Sanja clutched something long wrapped up in white cloth —something suspiciously staff-shaped—as she gaped back at us. All her pretty painted features were drawn tense in a look of wild-eyed panic, almost like she was desperate for *something* in her plan to go right for once.

Beside her, Axien stood with his back rigidly straight and his shoulders braced like he'd been petrified on the spot, not even blinking as he kept his gaze fixed squarely on me. All the color drained from his handsome features, and his lips parted slightly.

And High General Crassus ...

The big, armor-clad man glowered at us with his nostrils flared and face turning a startling shade of red. He shouted at his men, barking orders that sent half of them scurrying around the wagon as they struggled to dig the front wheels out of the fallen rubble. The other six turned on us and formed ranks, swords drawn and shields at the ready.

Fantastic.

"I have to get off," I whispered down to Roxus. "I can't fight, and I'm just slowing you down."

He snapped his jaws, growling his disapproval.

"I'll be fine, you stubborn furry idiot," I hissed as I released my hold on his scruff and prepared to slide off his back. "By now you should know I can handle myself just fine."

His big head turned just enough for me to catch a glimpse of one big, very worried brown eye studying me. Then he made a deep chuffing sound and widened his stance, claws raking over the stone as though he were steeling himself for what came next.

The fight.

The one that would decide our fate.

I took in a shaky breath, never taking my eyes off the advancing Tibran soldiers as I slipped off Roxus's back. I hit the ground with my good foot, using my injured one only for balance as I hopped away from him.

The instant he was free of my weight, Roxus took off like a thundering mountain of muscle. He roared and stood up on his hind legs, diving headlong into the soldiers without any hesitation.

CRUNCH!

I grimaced, waving my arms to steady myself when he slammed into them, grabbing the closest man's head in his powerful jaws and slinging him aside like a child's toy. The soldier's body slammed into the stone wall of the tunnel and hit the ground with a *thud*.

He didn't move again.

One down. Five to go.

None of them seemed all that interested in me—which was good. I had other problems to deal with.

My body spasmed and shook as I forced my injured leg to straighten, to take my weight. Just this last time. That's all I needed. A few minutes to end this once and for all.

Tears filled my vision. My jaw ached as I clenched my teeth, feeling every torn muscle and ligament light up with white-hot agony all at once.

But I didn't make a sound. No screaming. No wailing. Not when my gaze was fixed on Axien, Sanja, and that staff. The High General was a problem, but he wasn't my main concern.

Not yet, anyway.

My sweaty, trembling hands slid around the hilts of my daggers, finding that perfect fit where hours of relentless training and sweat had made the leather grips form to the shapes of my fingers. Like slipping on a pair of well broken-in shoes, it felt right to pull them free of their sheaths, the silver metal singing its familiar deadly tune as I whirled them over my hands one at a time and took a slow, calculated step forward.

Sanja spat a vicious curse and spun on Axien, shoving the staff at him so hard he stumbled back a step.

"Deal with her!" she screamed right in his face and thrust a finger in my direction. "Use whatever pitiful magic you have left in that useless body and end her! NOW!"

Axien blinked at her owlishly, as though he were still trying to work through the shock of seeing Roxus and me emerging from the battle-torn city. Maybe he hadn't really expected me to survive, even after giving me that key.

Or, more likely, he assumed I'd take the opportunity to flee into the caverns and leave Roxus and everyone else behind to burn. Any other Viperi probably would have.

But I was not just a Viperi. I had become so much more.

I was Zenith's Call now.

I had taken my oath and accepted their mark. I had sworn myself to this purpose, and even if every other part of me was twisted, wicked, dangerous, and strange—my word was my bond. I would not betray it.

I would not turn my back on what I'd sworn in the moonlight of Arx Eburna because, like it or not ... the order might not like me, but by all the gods, they *needed* me.

Right now.

My lip curled in a snarl as I swung my daggers wide, slowly shaking my head from side to side as Axien locked eyes with me again. I slid my stance into a formal opening maneuver and held it, poised and waiting—daring him to follow that order.

His brows skewed upward, expression fracturing as he glanced between us and then down at the long bundle of cloth in his arms. He opened his mouth as though he were going to speak.

Sanja slapped him.

His head snapped to the side and he staggered back again, nearly dropping the staff.

"You see this?" Her whole body twitched with wild, manic fury as she drew something out from inside her belt and held it up right in front of his face.

A tiny, thumb-sized glass vial shaped like a teardrop. It hung on a glittering silver chain that matched the adornments that seemed to make that vial more like a stopper or a strange locket. Inside, a dark red liquid swirled as the pendant swung slowly back and forth right in front of Axien's nose.

No. It couldn't be.

Could it?

Was that tiny glass and silver vial ... his phialim?

He'd mentioned the device only once, and even then, it wasn't something he'd seemed all that delighted to discuss. Basically, as far as I could understand, it somehow bound him to whoever owned him in the eyes of the Aurati. He'd mentioned that it gave them control over him.

He just hadn't explained exactly *how*.

A cold knot of dread twisted up in my stomach and I narrowed my eyes, watching as his eyes widened and the glowing, magical blue of them seemed to flicker and intensify for a second. Not good.

"I own you. You do as I say, wretch, or you will suffer," Sanja commanded and clenched the vial in her fist. "You will dispense with that insufferable piece of Viperi scum and bring me her head!"

Axien's body jerked at the gesture, his jaw clenching and all the muscles of his neck tensing so the veins stood out against his skin. He shifted his grip on the staff, hand sliding down the length and ripping the fabric wrappings away. The long, tri-tipped dagger on one end glinted with brutal, breathtaking beauty. One blow from that would punch a fist-sized hole through armor, flesh, and bone as easy as slicing warm butter.

But that wasn't the end that worried me.

As Axien's strange blue eyes gleamed, the magic in them seeming to wax and wane, flickering in and out like a candle sputtering in the wind, the crystal on the other end of the staff sparked to life. It glowed weakly, crackling with raw power that filled the air with an electric radiant buzz as Axien stepped away from Sanja—right toward me.

His expression emptied as his chin lowered, as though all sense of himself had gone. Like he was no longer in control of himself.

Fear surged up my spine, digging its claws in deep and raking them down all the walls of my sanity.

I-I didn't want this.

I didn't want to fight him—and not just because he was a sorcerer.

He'd risked a lot to slip me that key and my weapons. He'd risked even more stealing me away from the temple when Sanja had taken the Moonscape staff in the first place. Again and again, Axien had put himself to the hazard for my sake. He'd never wanted to hurt me, even in that stupid fighting pit.

He was an idiot. He was mouthy, cunning, and way too full of himself. But deep down, where it really mattered, Axien was ... good.

And he deserved far better than this.

With the battle between Roxus and the Tibran soldiers still raging around us, bodies slamming into the stone and swords slashing, I watched Axien prowl toward me. Magic rolled off the staff like ripples of blue light spreading outward in a pond, hitting me and sending tingling chills scurrying over my skin.

"Axien," I gasped, squeezing my daggers tighter.

His face twitched slightly, but he didn't stop—not until he stood before me, staff swung wide and expression agonizingly empty. Seeing but not seeing.

Out of control.

"I'll kill you if I have to," I promised, the words burning like acid on my lips.

His expression seized again, eyes squeezing shut for a second.

I held my breath.

"I know," he murmured back, his eyes reopening to reveal nothing but radiant magic so intense it made them shine completely white. "I'm counting on it."

FIFTY-THREE

Axien was going to kill me.

I screamed as I threw up block after block, barely matching his speed as he whirled and spun that staff as though it were an extension of his will. My leg faltered, throbbing with agony. I was too slow. Too exhausted. Too injured.

I couldn't win.

BAM!

I feinted too far, whirling right into the crystalline end of the staff that smacked me across the face and sent my entire body spinning. I hit the ground, my vision swimming and breath scraping in frantic gasps.

Blood filled my mouth and I spat, arms shaking as I coiled my legs beneath me and willed my body to stand—just as Axien sent another bolt of power straight at me.

I cried out again, throwing up a desperate parry with my daggers crossed before me. As if it would help. As if mere metal could do anything against power like that.

His magic crackled in the air like lightning, stinging at my skin but never seeming to touch me fully. Instead, it seemed to arc around me, whirling and spinning like a globe of sizzling light, but never reaching me.

And my daggers, they ... *glowed*.

What the—?!

Gods and Fates, it was almost like my daggers were deflecting Axien's magic.

My pulse skipped. No—not deflecting. They were *absorbing* it.

Spelldrinkers—that was what Roxus and Axien had called them. I'd nearly forgotten.

The Vordegans had forged these blades for a fight exactly like this.

Rushing forward, I surged through the current of power flowing off that staff, parting it like a curtain.

Axien let out a shout of frustration and pressed in harder. But it didn't work. Every spell, every wave of power, made my daggers glow as bright as two silver flames in my hands. Magical power sang through the shining metal, leaving trails of white in the air like ribbons of glittering mist with every movement.

I whipped in close, beating him across the face with the hilts and forcing him to stagger back. He shouted again, bellowing something in Avoran I couldn't make out over the blistering hum of energy around us.

Behind him, Sanja screamed in frustrated fury. I chanced a glance at her, barely glimpsing her holding that phialim up again like a threat.

Or just a means of control. A way to keep him from resisting her orders.

That was my target—not him. Somehow, I had to destroy the phialim. I had to set him free.

Baring my blunted teeth, I dove past Axien, my gaze narrowed on her. On the silver vial in her hand. The solution.

Pain exploded through my already injured leg. My vision went white. My ears rang with a screeching, high-pitched note, and the entire world seemed to tilt sideways.

No, not the world. Me.

I hit the ground with my cheek against the cold stone floor of the tunnel, my breath a scraping crackle and my body shaking out of control.

M-My leg. He'd ... gods, I didn't even know. Had he kicked my injured knee? Or stabbed it with the dagger end of that staff?

Rolling onto my back, my hands smacked uselessly across the ground. Empty. I'd dropped my daggers somewhere. I needed them. I was defenseless without them.

My vision swerved and tunneled, barely giving me glimpses of a dark figure standing over me. They crouched down, the outline of a head and shoulders moving as though the figure was considering me. Watching me writhe. Waiting for me to die.

I recognized the shape of his sharp jawline and pointed, half-elven ears through the haze.

Axien.

He was right there, so close I could have reached out to touch him. His eyes still glowed, but with the power of that staff coursing through him, they looked white and far too bright. Divine. Unfeeling.

As though the Axien I knew was gone.

"Axien, p-please," I begged, my voice hoarse and weak. "Please, I know you're scared. You've been at the mercy of people like her your entire life. B-But I'm right here. I will fight alongside you. Just ... please ... please choose something different. Choose yourself. Choose freedom. And fight for it ... with me."

I reached for him, stretching out a trembling hand toward that blurry figure, shutting my eyes tightly. Whatever came next, I didn't want to see it coming. If he ran me through with that staff's blade. If he started cutting my head off to deliver it to Sanja, just as she'd ordered.

I didn't want my last memory in this world to be the look on his face when he realized what she'd made him do.

"She winds the threads of my soul as ribbons in her hair," he murmured so quietly I barely heard him over the surging of power and battle around us.

W-What?

"She wears my heart as a jewel at her throat. And I am lost," he spoke again, louder this time. Stronger. Clearer.

My eyes flew open. Those words, like a poem or a song, resonated deep in my chest like the toll of a bell. They rang clear and loud and pure through my brain. Through my heart.

Through my soul.

Axien stared down at me, blue eyes shining and mouth bent in that familiar, roguish smile. *"I am lost to her unto the end of days."*

A strong, steady hand appeared before me. His hand.

I seized it.

Strength surged through my body, filling me from my toes all the way to the tip of my nose. My spine curled, muscles spasming as tingling heat spread out through every muscle fiber and nerve. My vision cleared. The ringing in my ears stopped. Breath filled my lungs like I'd broken the surface of a bottomless dark void.

I stood up in one fluid, painless motion.

"Don't let go of me," Axien warned, his body still thrumming with that radiant divine power as he held onto the staff with his other hand.

I nodded. "Same to you."

His smile widened slightly, tinged with a hint of sadness I didn't understand.

There wasn't time to work it out now, though.

Together, we turned toward Sanja and the High General, who had noticed the tide of the battle was turning. The earth shook beneath us as Roxus's massive bear form galloped past us, barreling into the group of Tibran soldiers still fussing with their trapped wagon. They abandoned the task immediately, frantically drawing arms as the giant, furious bear tore into them.

We ran right behind him, still hand-in-hand, and sprinted past the wagon.

High General Crassus let out a roaring string of curses as he spotted us running past, turning from where he'd been advancing with his own weapon in hand, ready to deal with the giant angry bear that was ripping through his ranks like straw practice dummies.

"YOU!" He whirled on Sanja suddenly, longsword clenched in his shaking fist.

"Don't blame me, you fool!" she screamed back. "Do somethi—"

The High General moved like a phantom, so fast I hardly saw him move. One instant, he was facing her with his entire head now purple with rage. The next, he seized Sanja by the back of her hair and rammed his sword through her body to the hilt.

Just like he had his own soldier.

Her expression went white, mouth open and eyes bulging in shock.

My legs turned to jelly, and I staggered to a halt, dragging Axien with me until we both stood, gaping in horror.

"Useless whore," High General Crassus seethed through gritted teeth as he twisted his sword and jerked it free of her body, flinging her to the ground at his feet. "You've failed me for the last time."

G-Gods. Dead. Sanja was dead. He'd killed her.

And now he—

My breath caught in my throat as High General Crassus bent down, grabbing the silver chain from her belt and yanking it free. He held Axien's phialim up and turned toward us, eyes utterly black with hate beneath that red-crested helm.

Oh no.

"You will *not* defy *me*, slave," he rumbled as he held it up, Sanja's blood drizzling down the chain and dripping from the tip of the glass vial.

Axien's hand clamped down onto mine tighter. His entire body went rigid like he'd been struck. Over the edge of his tunic's collar, I saw dark veins spreading up his throat. They snaked across his face, around his eyes, and even across the top of his hand that still gripped mine.

"You will obey, or I will take it all away. I'll drain you of every drop of that magic like a suckling piglet, and your head will be my footstool for all your little friends to witness in my court," Crassus promised. "Give me that staff. *Now.*"

Axien let out a strangled cry and doubled over, his hand ripping free of mine.

Instantly, all the pain flooded back into my system like a mudslide, crushing down on my body from all sides. My legs buckled. I hit the ground and the world spun out of focus again.

He ... he had been using his magic to keep me going. To dull the pain. To help me stand.

Without it, I could barely force myself onto my side. My lungs squeezed and spasmed, fighting for breath as I watched Axien stagger toward the High General.

One step. Two. Farther away from me.

"AXIEN!" His name tore from my throat in a wild sob.

He froze with his back to me. His body jerked, shoulders shaking.

"You *will* obey!" High General Crassus bellowed again.

His knuckles blanched as he clenched the phialim, as though pouring every ounce of his malice into it.

Foul power wafted off that glittering glass vial—so strong I could practically taste it like a coppery film in my mouth. I could almost hear the whisper of High General Crassus's thoughts, whispering every cruel, twisted, vile thing he would do to drag Axien closer to him.

Torture me. Let his men have me while he was forced to watch. Kill me. Then move on to anyone else Axien ever cared for. Anyone he'd even glanced at would suffer.

Fury lit the fuse deep in my chest. It crackled and popped, sizzling down as something shining caught my attention not two feet from me.

My daggers. I'd dropped them, or maybe flung them, as I fell before.

But there they were. So close.

Just out of reach.

I crawled for them, dragging the dead weight of my injured leg. With a ragged shout, I flung myself as far as I could, both my arms out.

It wasn't far enough. My outstretched hands fell inches short of the hilts, my palms slapping against nothing but cold stone.

No. Gods, no! I-I needed something—anything. Now!

My body jerked as realization hit like a punch to the chest. And I knew what I had to do.

Axien staggered another step closer to the High General, dragging the staff behind him and gripping the side of his head with his free hand. He yelled and groaned, those black veins spreading like dark spiderwebs over his skin.

"Bring it to me!" the High General ordered again, his voice like the crack of a whip over Axien's back.

He lurched another step. Almost too far.

I reached into the inside of my boot and drew out the little

Avoran kitchen knife. It was small. Light. It would fly far—farther than my spelldrinkers. It had to.

I threw both of my arms back, silver knife poised in my fingers as I sucked in one final, desperate breath and took aim.

Then I screamed and let it fly.

"ROXUS, RUN!"

FIFTY-FOUR

Seconds melted into centuries as all time seemed to slow around me.

My stolen kitchen knife swirled in the air, spinning like a little silvery-white hurricane, straight at the High General. At the last second, he ducked to the side as fast as a blur.

But not quite fast enough.

The blade flew true. It caught the chain of the phialim. It snapped, sending the little glass vial falling ... down, down, down.

It shattered on the stone ground into a million tiny shards.

But it didn't stop there. The blade continued on, too late to hit the High General's head as he dodged. He let out a furious shout as it lodged deep in the meat of his shoulder, right by his neck, instead. It sliced his ear and pinned him to the side of that gods-cursed wagon.

My vision swerved, turning dark around the edges as I toppled sideways—but my head never met the stone. Strong arms swept under me, snatching me up off the ground and running as a crack like a bolt of lightning burst in the air.

"RUN!" Axien shouted as he hugged me tight against his chest.

My vision went white as power exploded through the tunnel, shaking the entire tunnel. Somewhere nearby, a familiar beastly roar answered.

Roxus.

Moving—we were moving. Running. Going fast as smaller explosions rumbled all around us. Rocks and sheets of dust and grit fell over us. I couldn't see. The falling debris choked out all my senses.

All I could do was cling to Axien as he forged forward, relentless. His heartbeat hammered like mad in my ear. The skin of his neck was clammy against my arms, and he seemed to fight for every scraping breath. Gods only knew how much longer he could keep this up.

But the world was falling down around us.

Suddenly, light bloomed through the haze of dust. Warm, beckoning light that was only eclipsed by rocks shaking loose from the tunnel ceiling and falling like meteors around us.

Almost there.

Axien yelled again, a pleading Avoran curse as he flung himself forward with all his strength. He dove into the light with me gripped tight in his arms, and he hit the ground—the warm, soft, sandy ground—and started rolling.

We tumbled like freshly cut timber down a steep dune, landing in a heap somewhere under the glow of a brilliant red sunset. Roxus rolled to a halt right beside us, back in his human form, and lay flat on his back, gasping for breath.

He had the Moonscape staff clenched in one hand and what might have been a pair of small blades in the other. Were those ... my daggers? I couldn't tell. I could barely see with my vision still slowly fading to shades of gray.

My head throbbed. My leg—I-I couldn't even feel it

anymore. It was nothing except raw, unending pain from the hip down.

"A-Are we safe?" Axien gasped between pants as he sat back on his knees and stared at the mouth of the cavern. His skin was a sickly, ashen gray hue, although I couldn't tell whether it was from using too much of his magic or just the dust sticking to the sweat on his face and neck.

Roxus pushed himself onto his elbows with a grunt and a curse, and squinted at the cavern's opening, too ... just as it completely crumbled and collapsed with a low, rumbling *BOOM*.

In a matter of seconds, it was nothing but a heap of rubble in the side of the golden dune.

"Yep," Roxus wheezed as he flopped back down with his arms and legs spread like a starfish. "I'd say we're good, so long as there's no other Tibrans around."

Axien frowned, squinting around with the warm, fierce desert wind snagging through his locks of long, dark hair. He said something else, and his tone was tight with alarm. But the ringing was so loud in my ears. I couldn't make it out. All his handsome features had gone blurry, too, and my eyes wouldn't clear no matter how hard I blinked.

My limbs were numb. My head, gods, it hurt so much. Even my teeth seemed to throb. My thoughts turned to mush as the darkness crept in, growing thicker and thicker around the edges of my vision until I couldn't see anything but smears of shadows.

Was I ... dying?

I didn't know.

Everything hurt so much. My ribs ached and each breath was a fight, as though there were a weight sitting on my chest, trying to crush all the air out of me. I was drowning from within, unable to even cry out for help.

But as the sound of the wild, desert wind filled my ears, a

symphony of a million golden grains swishing over each other, I could have sworn I heard her.

My mother's voice, now forever part of this place, whispered soft and gentle. She sounded so close, as though she were breathing each word right against the shell of my ear.

Her voice was nothing but a single grain amidst the thousands, but the only grain that was solely mine.

"You must live, Visha. You must rise and fight again."

FIFTY-FIVE

I f this wasn't death, it must have been something close.

I was drifting, numb and weightless, alone in the dark. Flecks of light sailed past silently, distant and well out of reach. Stars like diamonds that sang glassy songs to an ever-spinning universe.

And somewhere in the eternal sea, I floated like a passing memory. No voices. No dreams or nightmares. Nothing but the void before me and a sense of peace like cool water poured over a raw, burning wound.

Then a hand closed around mine, tight and strong. Smooth, slender fingers wove through mine, so cold they seemed to have been cut from glass.

I turned to look, my hair swirling like waves of silvery-white around my shoulders. And there she was—someone else floating there with me. A young woman with skin as dark as the night. Robes of purest white draped over her slim, willowy form, revealing in crisp contrast how her ebony skin was flecked with thousands of spots of glittering light like freckles.

As though she were made of the night sky itself.

Her eyes shone like rings of silver, gleaming and crinkling

at the corners as she smiled. She brushed her other hand over my cheek, tracing the contour all the way to my chin.

"There you are, dear one." She breathed the words, and the universe around us seemed to shiver and echo her with a chorus of a thousand whispers.

I blinked owlishly, my brain working frantically to understand. Who was she? What did this mean? Why were we here?

"You will not carry the curse of your forebears," she murmured, her voice gentle and motherly as she combed those chilled fingers through my hair, pushing it away from my face. *"Henceforth, you will bear my mark. You will be mine. And I will not forsake you."*

My entire being—body and soul—seemed to sigh at those words. As though they'd released some deep, groaning tension I'd never known was there. I leaned into her touch, eyes rolling closed. My arms and legs hung limp, floating freely.

Then falling.

Not fast, though. I felt the pull of gravity like a nagging little tug as I floated down, down, down. Falling away from that endless sea of stars toward a great light. Warmth hit my back like the glare of the morning sun, and I opened my eyes.

I needed one last look—a final glimpse of her.

But there was only those boundless, glittering stars ...

... and a magnificent, perfect, silvery full moon.

---- ·+ ⊢ ⟩⟩ ✳ ⟨⟨ ⊣ +⎯⎯

My body was one giant, throbbing bruise.

Or, that's how it felt, anyway.

I groaned and shifted on a bed, making its rickety wooden frame creak in protest. The sharp, herbal aroma of healing salves stung at my nose, and my eyes were sore and itchy, like I'd grit trapped in them for days. When I finally pried them open and squinted around the sparse, narrow room, it took a few blinks to clear things up.

Not that there was much to see. Other than my little bed, a washstand, and a faded wool rug, the narrow room was nearly bare and empty.

It made the elegant woman perched in the chair beside my bed stick out like a perfectly manicured sore thumb.

I stiffened, my body cringing up involuntarily at the sight of her. That's all it took for every inch of my body to thrum with a shock of pain that forced a whimper through my teeth. My eyes welled, and my hands fisted in the threadbare sheets.

"Hush, child," Curator Vanora said quietly as she leaned forward in her chair, combing her fingers through my hair the same way the woman in my dream had. "You're safe. Everything is all right now."

I'd never heard her sound so ... worried.

Curator Vanora was always concise. Always composed and perfect, right down to even the tiniest gestures.

But as I lay there, staring at her through the tears that welled in my eyes, I watched her brow crinkle in distress and her red-painted lips press into a thin, worried frown. There was quiet earnestness in her multihued eyes that sparkled in the weak light of the room as she let a palm rest against my forehead as though testing me for fever.

"Wh ... What ...?" I tried to ask, but my throat was raw. Every sound burned as though I'd swallowed a mouthful of crushed glass.

"What happened?" she guessed.

I managed a shaking nod.

Vanora's gaze drifted down, her expression dimming as she seemed to contemplate her next words carefully. "I overstepped my bounds, I suppose. After you departed, I worried knowing you would be going away with Sanja—especially given how Roxus had apparently welcomed her back with open arms. I did a bit of digging about her past, where she'd been before returning to Arx Eburna. So much of her story about how she'd spent her last few years made no sense."

I held my breath as a sick feeling swirled in my stomach. I had a pretty good idea of what she'd uncovered.

"She'd spent a lot of her time in Tibrus, under the guise of surveilling Lord Argonox's growing interest in divine artifacts. I suppose that part wasn't entirely a lie, though. She had been observing it ... and assisting him," she said. "She had been corresponding with that Tibran High General, sending him letters and feeding him information on locations of our strongholds, locations of divine artifacts that might be of interest, and much more."

My face contorted, twisting in disgust as I looked away. Unbelievable. Or, rather, all too believable.

Curator Vanora's chair creaked as she scooted to the edge of it, moving closer to my bedside and grasping my hand in a gentle squeeze. "I need to know everything that happened, Violet. As much as you can remember, from the very beginning, when you all left Arx Eburna. Mistress Orvana is very reluctant to accept any accusations against our own ranks, especially after what happened with Domitri."

I dared to flash her a heated look. "Wh-Why?"

"Another betrayal might fracture the order and call her leadership into question, if she's allowed not one but two traitors to move through our midst," Vanora replied. "But we cannot afford to turn a blind eye. And it might be possible that Sanja was the root of both incidents. She might have paved the way for the situation with Domitri, giving those agents information on how to infiltrate Arx Eburna to begin with. But I need to know everything—as much as you can remember, if I'm to build that case."

Right. Because Mistress Orvana would probably find it much more palatable if both incidents were related, two halves of one bigger plot, rather than the idea that she'd fallen for the same trick twice and welcomed wolves into her sheep's pen.

It made sense.

So I swallowed hard, trying to soothe the burning ache in my throat, and began at the beginning. I told her everything. About the mercenaries who had attacked us after leaving the bathhouse. About the tagged switchbeasts. About the attack on the Levanurith temple.

About how Axien had saved me.

Curator Vanora sat quietly the entire time, her expression a perfect mask of intense thought that didn't betray any emotion. She kept her hold on my hand, rubbing the back of it on occasion when I had to stop to let my burning throat rest. And when I'd finished, she simply nodded and looked down at my bandage-wrapped body that had been covered with a few white sheets.

"I-Is ... is Roxus ...?" The words died, strangled by a sob that threatened to break past the pain in my throat before I could finish.

Vanora met my gaze again, giving me a faint smile that never reached her shimmering, opaline eyes. "He's alive and well, recovering in the next room. He's been asking about you constantly."

Warm tears slipped from the corners of my eyes and ran down the sides of my face. Thank the gods.

Or, maybe, one goddess in particular.

"That stubborn, reckless man ... he managed to carry both of you and the staff all the way to the city gates here before he collapsed. The order's agents posted at our stronghold here received word from the city guard that two of their own had been found in a poor state, and they contacted Arx Eburna immediately," she explained, her tone touched with something warmer when she mentioned Roxus.

It almost sounded like *affection*.

But I didn't dare read too much into that.

Besides, something else she'd said stuck in my mind like a thorn. I had to know—had to ask. "B-Both of us?"

"That boy, the one who posed as Sanja's tandem, is still alive. Granted, he may not be for much longer. He's in poor shape after using so much magic," she answered. "The healer calls it spell sickness and claims it is an affliction that those blessed with magic often experience when they call upon more power than their bodies can withstand. There's no cure for it, other than time and patience."

Panic coursed through my body like a shiver, making my skin go cold with a chill and my pulse immediately quicken.

Axien was barely alive. He'd nearly killed himself using that staff. Was ... was that the explosion that had brought down the tunnel? Had he caused it to give us a chance to escape?

I couldn't remember. Everything had been such a hazy, tangled mess in my head by that point. I hadn't seen the cause of the explosion, only the aftermath.

Only the three of us, running for our lives while the tunnel caved in around us.

"I-I need to see him," I whimpered. "I need to t-tell him—"

"You need to rest, Violet," Curator Vanora scolded firmly. "I'm not sure if you've noticed, but there's not much of you that isn't wrapped in bandaging. Your knee was in poor shape, and the healer is worried you'll have a limp from now on if you don't take the time to let it heal properly."

I scowled at her, face burning and tears still making warm trails down my face as I sucked in shallow, ragged breaths. "Wh-What if he dies b-before ...?"

Her eyes narrowed, head tilting to the side slightly so that her silvery-white hair slid over her shoulders like sheets of white satin while she studied my face. Reading my mind, or rather, my expressions.

I couldn't even try to hide my emotions as I lay there, glaring at her defiantly, while my entire body trembled with panic and frustration. I *needed* to see Axien. Just once, just for a minute. I needed to tell him, to beg him, not to die.

We weren't finished.

He didn't get to just leave. Not when we still had a lot to settle between us. Not when there was so much I still needed to tell him.

"You care for him." She said it almost like an accusation.

I flinched—*hard*.

"No," I snapped back.

But it didn't matter. She'd seen it. There was no lying to her, especially when my own body seemed determined to betray me. My chin wouldn't stop trembling. My body shuddered with a sob, and I glared up at the ceiling, refusing to look at her again.

"Oh, Violet," Vanora breathed in a deep, resigned sigh. Like she pitied me. Like she was watching me burn myself alive, and there was nothing she could do.

"He's n-not what he seems," I gritted out, my voice catching as I bit back more sobs. "He's a g-good person. He doesn't d-deserve this. He should get another ch-chance."

"Another chance at what?" I could hear the sharp, almost accusing curiosity in her voice.

I shut my eyes tightly; the words leaving me like a desperate prayer. "Freedom."

I'd broken his phialim—the chain that bound him to the Aurati. This was his chance, wasn't it? To finally live for himself? He couldn't die.

Not before he'd actually gotten to live.

Silence rushed into the stillness between us, so deep I could hear the faint sounds of bustling city life somewhere beyond that one window. Voices and the baying of cattle in the street. Rattling wagon wheels. Merchants calling wares.

Vanora's chair creaked again as she stood. The lengths of her long, pale green dress unfurled with a rustle and swished when she moved away. Then her footsteps paused, as though she'd stopped in the doorway.

"Rest, Violet," she murmured again, her tone much quieter and gentler than before. "Rest and trust that the gods are often far kinder than we deserve. I believe their work has only just begun when it comes to you."

I wanted to laugh. To scoff. The gods didn't work through Viperi. We had been created to defy and destroy them. Why would they ever choose to do anything but despise me?

"You will bear my mark. You will be mine. And I will not forsake you." The words shivered through my brain, leaving trails of cold, prickly tingles behind that spread slowly through every tired, aching muscle.

Maybe Curator Vanora was right. Maybe the gods had been kind to me. Maybe they had heard my prayers and shown me mercy by letting me survive all of this.

Now, I just had to hope they'd do the same for Axien.

FIFTY-SIX

I was going to smash this bed to splinters.

There was no getting comfortable in it, not with the awful trench that had been worn right down the middle of the mattress. I wasn't sure if the dull ache in my hips and lower back was coming from my injuries or how long I'd been lying there.

Either way, I couldn't wait to get up.

But after three excruciating days of being force-fed rice porridge laced with healing tonics, rubbed down with herbal salves, and warned that any attempts to get up would leave me with a lifelong limp ... I couldn't take it.

Limp or not, I had to move. To stand and feel blood flowing through my legs again.

I waited until nightfall, when the healer's assistants finished their rounds of last-minute checks on every room, before I threw back the sheets and swung my legs over the edge of the bed. My back cracked and throbbed, every muscle up and down my spine screaming in protest.

But not moving was much worse.

My bare feet met the cool, worn wooden floorboards, and

I let out a deep, relieved sigh. My knee was wrapped in a thick cast to hold it at an angle, so I could only touch the floor with the toes on my right foot. It was enough, though.

Enough to convince me I could do this.

Using the headboard to steady my wobbling, I slowly pushed myself up to stand. My good leg burned, muscles stretching and trembling at first. Then, little by little, they seemed to remember their strength. I flexed my good foot and wiggled my toes, breathing deeply as the tingles in my heel subsided.

My bad leg was a problem, though. Not one I was completely unfamiliar with, thanks to the last time I'd been this injured. I'd gotten pretty good at hopping around Roxus's house then. I'd just have to reuse those skills.

And not get caught by any of the healer's staff that might still be up monitoring all his patients.

I used the chair by the bed to balance myself as I wobbled a few steps, careful not to put any weight on my bad leg while I hopped back and forth between the bed and the wall.

By the third trip, I felt good about trusting the strength of my good leg. I'd just have to take things one step at a time and keep my right side against the wall for balance. Nice and easy, slow and steady.

I inched toward the door of my room, wincing at every groan of the old floorboards under my weight. The doorknob clunked too loudly when I twisted it, and I held still for a few seconds, holding my breath as I waited for the flurry of footsteps from one of the healer's assistants rushing up to see what was happening.

But there was nothing. Just silence filled with the hiss and crackle of the sconces burning in the hallway outside.

Whew.

I slowly pressed the door ajar just far enough that I could slip through, then hedged out into the hall. With half my weight leaning onto the wall so I didn't have to use my right leg, I hopped along. After a few yards, sweat ran from my forehead and made my hair stick to my neck.

Curse it, I might have some strength back, but my stamina was still shot.

The first room I passed was empty, with just a single, unoccupied bed, chair, and washstand exactly like mine. The next, however, had a young woman stretched in it with a small cot placed beside her where a *very* new-looking baby wriggled and fussed.

I closed her door quietly, careful not to disturb either of them, before I hobbled away.

By the time I reached the third door, my good leg shook uncontrollably with fatigue. I wheezed and wiped the sweat away from my face on the sleeve of my thin chemise. No point in stopping now, though. I didn't know if I had the strength to get all the way back to my room, and if I was going to get caught, I might as well see this through.

The third door creaked as I pushed it open, revealing a tall figure stretched out on the bed. The figure shivered under two heavy-looking quilts that had been tucked around it, and a washbasin sat at the bedside with a rag folded neatly over the rim. Moonlight poured through a crack in the drapes over the window, casting a ghostly silver beam right across the pallid face of the young man lying there.

Axien.

My heart dropped to the pit of my stomach as I stared at him from the doorway—at how pale he was. He shivered and shook, his skin glistening with a sheen of sweat, and there were heavy dark circles under his eyes. Everything about him looked sunken and ashen, as though his soul had already left him.

I rushed to him, ignoring the flare of agony up my bad leg as I pushed away from the doorway and crossed the distance to his bedside. I practically fell into the bed, forcing my body to cooperate so I could sit right beside him. I seized one of his hands, biting back a gasp at how cold it was against mine.

"Axien?" I whispered as loudly as I dared. "Axien, can you hear me?"

No response.

His expression stayed frozen in a faint frown, brow slightly furrowed, as though beneath this catatonic state, he was in pain.

Gods, what was happening to him? Was this really because he'd used too much of his magic? Granted, Sanja had forced him to take that staff and use it—a staff intended for a godling. Based on what I'd read of them, those born as godlings had incredible amounts of divine power coursing through them. They were, after all, gods cursed into mortal form.

A half-Avoran couldn't hope to stand before that kind of power and walk away clean.

But he'd not only stood—he'd gripped it with both hands and fought with it.

I gripped his hand tighter and leaned down, whispering right against one of his pointed ears. "You can't give up, do you hear me? You keep fighting. You come back to me. Understand? I ... I ... won't forgive you otherwise."

One of his eyes twitched. My pulse skipped, and I pulled back slightly. Seconds passed, but he didn't move again except for the shallow, almost forced rise and fall of his chest as he breathed.

So I leaned down and pressed my forehead against his. "I think I saw a goddess, Axien. I think Adiana came to me in a dream."

Tears pricked in my eyes as the memory replayed, so clear it felt like she might be standing right there behind me, with all the night sky painted on her beautiful ebony skin. If she was ... if she'd meant what she said ... did that mean she could hear me now? That she would listen to my prayers?

I didn't know. But, gods, I had to try.

"Give him back to me," I begged. "Please. Just this once. I know I have no right to ask you for anything, but I will do whatever you want—serve you until the end of my days, just let him have another chance."

A sudden, eerie chill passed over my skin, like frosty breath had puffed across the nape of my neck. I shivered. Every tiny hair on my body prickled.

But I didn't dare to move.

Not until I felt Axien's hand twitch ...

... and faintly squeeze mine back.

FIFTY-SEVEN

"Delthene will never forgive me," Roxus sighed.

He stood alongside a small covered wagon, arms crossed as he watched me limp out of the healing house's front door with a crutch under my right arm.

"For what?" I glared at him, ready to whack him if he made another comment about my lack of speediness.

"For letting you get injured. Fates, preserve me," he said, then slid me one of his devious little smirks. "At least the stairs at home ought to keep you contained to your room, eh?"

I gave him a rude gesture. Jerk.

It had been almost a week of being trapped with his nonsense now. I'd have preferred an asylum. But after the healer's assistants had caught me sneaking out to visit Axien, they'd wasted no time moving me down to one of the lower floors, where I got to share a community room with a few other patients—including Roxus.

All so he could *keep an eye on me*. Ugh. Fussing, overprotective, nosey bear-man.

"I won't need the stupid crutch by the time we get home," I reminded him as I wobbled to the back of the wagon and sat down on it, glaring at my bandaged knee. Ridiculous. I could put weight on my foot without much pain now, so why couldn't I just walk on my own?

Because healers were fussy and way too cautious and Roxus believed anything they said, that's why.

"Just see that you don't fall off the back while we're moving, eh?" Roxus jabbed playfully as he swaggered past, making his way up to the driver's seat.

"Fine speech coming from you. We all know where she gets the stubbornness from," Curator Vanora quipped as she breezed past, carrying the Staff of Adiana in her arms as though it were made of glass.

We'd wrapped it up in many layers of clean white blankets and tied it off with twine, disguising the shape and protecting it as best we could. I guess that wasn't enough to soothe her worries, though, because she carefully laid it in the back of the wagon and covered it with more blankets, then motioned for me to scoot farther in.

Right. I was on guard duty.

Roxus's gaze followed Vanora like a spotlight, always seeming to lock onto her whenever her back was turned. He probably thought he was being sneaky about it—but I'd picked up on it right away. The way his brow would furrow slightly, almost like he was right on the verge of saying something important to her.

He never did, though. At least, not where I could hear it. And if she'd noticed the tension in his demeanor, or the way he stood back and gave her lots of space whenever she moved into the vicinity, she didn't acknowledge it. Strange.

Just what, exactly, had gone down between the two of them? Obviously, she'd known him before—when they were all young tandems, like me. I got the feeling a *lot* had transpired between Roxus, Sanja, and her, though.

Maybe I'd wheedle it out of her while we made this final

little trek to deliver the staff to the Temple of Adiana. Granted, calling it a trek was a bit of a stretch. It should only take a few hours, since the priestesses had agreed to meet us on the edge of the city. With so many Tibrans in the area, looking for temples to raze and loot, they didn't want to risk drawing any more attention to their very secluded location.

I couldn't exactly blame them for that.

After we handed off the staff, however, our mission would be complete. We could go home, and Vanora had already secured us a spot on a merchant caravan heading back west toward Rienka. Thankfully, this time, we wouldn't be acting as guards—just fellow passengers.

Not that I was in any shape to be fighting off Tibrans, switchbeasts, or any of the dangers the open desert had thrown at us so far.

"Should I sit on the front?" Axien called from the doorway of the healing house.

His voice made my stomach flutter strangely, and I was suddenly thrilled to be hidden away in the back of the wagon, well out of his line of sight. My stupid face must have betrayed all the tangled-up embarrassment that still twisted my brains around in knots, because Vanora cleared her throat.

I flashed her a glare of warning.

She just arched one of her slender dark brows, looking wholly exasperated, before rolling her eyes and answering him. "I'm riding in the front. You'll ride back here."

Great. She was definitely onto me—and conspiring against me. Just freaking great.

Axien did a superb job of avoiding even glancing my way as he tossed a heavy bag of gear into the back of the wagon and climbed inside and sat down beside me. The whole wagon jostled as Roxus snapped the reins on our one small olifant, and I immediately lost my balance.

"Easy, there," Axien murmured, catching me by the shoulders as I nearly toppled sideways.

I tensed in his grasp, every muscle locking up solid.

He immediately let me go, his expression falling. He rubbed at the back of his neck as we sat quietly, nothing but the rattling of the wagon and the chattering of the crowds on the street to fill the tension.

Awkward.

Gods, it had been like this ever since he'd woken up a few days ago. He wouldn't speak to me—not really. Not more than a few words. He wouldn't look me in the eye. If I entered a room, he found an excuse to leave.

It hurt, and I had absolutely no idea why. Something about it stung so deep, like he might as well have slapped me across the face.

I just wasn't sure how to even begin dealing with it. Did I talk to him? Ask him what was wrong? Sure, things were ... different now. But Roxus and Vanora had sat him down and talked over everything. They seemed to be all right. At least he'd talk to and look at both of them, now.

So why not me?

I gnawed on the inside of my cheek, mulling it over and scouring every dusty corner of my brain to find something—anything—to say to him. A place to begin so we could figure this out.

There was plenty I wanted to know and ask him about. Had he had any strange dreams about goddesses while he was asleep? Did anything feel different about his magic now that his phialim was gone? What was he going to do with himself now? Was he coming back to Arx Eburna? Or had he figured out something else he wanted to do with his freedom?

"Violet?"

I almost jumped right of my own skin as he said my name.

I coughed and sputtered, choking on my spit before I wheezed out a frazzled, "Yes?"

Smooth.

"I've wanted to say ... that is, I've been trying to find the right time to tell you ..." He faltered, stumbling over his words. "I am so sorry for my part in what happened. For deceiving you. For ... allowing you to be injured, and then with the staff, I—"

"I don't blame you for any of that, Axien," I interrupted, forcing myself to look up at him.

He gaped down at me, eyes wide in shock. "You don't? But I—"

"You did what you felt you had to do," I cut him off again before he could roll into another apology, or worse, an excuse. "I can't imagine what you've gone through, being bound to someone like Sanja and that High General. I know you didn't have a choice. I know you tried to help me when you could. I also know none of us would be here right now if it weren't for the things you did, even while you were bound to them. You saved us, Axien."

His mouth slowly closed, and he seemed to shrink before me, his broad shoulders drawing up around his ears and his mouth mashing up into a bitter, uncomfortable line.

"What matters to me is what you choose to do now that you have your freedom," I added quickly. "I want, er, I mean, I *hope* you'll choose to stay with us. To join the Zenith's Call properly."

Axien shifted and went back to scratching at the back of his neck and fiddling with one of the leather straps that held a new sword sheathed across his back. "Curator Vanora asked me to," he admitted. "She offered to be my patron."

"She did?" I sat up a little straighter, watching his demeanor for the smallest clue about whether or not he'd taken her up on it.

His mouth pinched to one side, his features tense with uncertainty, as he dropped his gaze to his lap. "I ... haven't given her an answer yet."

"O-Oh." I did a truly horrible job hiding my disappointment.

He must have noticed, too, because he forced one of those thin smiles and a weak, hollow chuckle. "I'm not sure how I could ever be trusted by anyone else in the order now that they know what happened—what I was before."

A loud, barking laugh broke out of me before I could stop it.

Axien cringed back, eyeing me like he wasn't sure if he should be offended or scared that I'd finally lost my mind.

"I'm a *Viperi*, in case you forgot. They let me in. Why, by all things divine, wouldn't they let you join? Especially since Vanora has volunteered to be your patron," I asked.

He seemed to deflate at that, head hanging some. "It's complicated," he muttered.

A pitiful excuse.

"It always is," I countered. "But in case you hadn't noticed, not many of us in the order are there because we were shining examples of chivalry, honor, and success. Roxus was exiled from Vordega. Vanora was a courtesan. I'm pretty sure Mistress Orvana is secretly a demon in disguise."

One corner of his mouth quirked upward, as though he were fighting a real smile.

"Why wouldn't we want an ex-Tibran, half-Avoran sorcerer to join us?" I insisted as I gave one of his knees a reassuring pat. "Even if he is a really terrible kisser."

Axien froze. His eyes looked like they might roll right out of their sockets as he stared down at me.

"Horrible, actually. Truly the worst," I went on and gave him another consoling pat. "Honestly, I finally understand why you had to use a wager to get one. So sad. But I'm sure you can work on that. There's no shame in admitting you need a little practice. Maybe you can ask Varren if he'll—"

Axien seized the back of my head so suddenly, I didn't even have time to gasp. Or blink. Or do anything except realize that his lips were against mine, capturing mine with ravenous hunger.

Like he'd dreamt of doing this, of kissing me, a thousand times.

FIFTY-EIGHT

Gods—Axien was ... he was *kissing* me!

One moment I was paralyzed, stiff, and stunned.

The next, my body was melting into his as he put his arms around me.

My heartbeat rushed as he drew me closer, ensnaring me against the solid strength of his chest. The warmth of his lips welcomed me in, soft and confident as they moved against mine. Tempting me in deeper. Capturing me completely.

My hands went to his hair, twining my fingers through those soft brown locks. His rich scent saturated every breath I took. And I was lost, instantly and entirely.

Every inch of my body was on high-alert, wildly sensitive to the brush of his calloused fingers and the puffs of his deep, ragged sighs against my cheek. His mouth opened slowly, gradually, for a swipe of his tongue that turned everything inside me to tingling jelly.

A deep, aching heat rose in my belly, and I arched into him, my body moving on its own. Pleading for more.

Desperate for it. Wanting to shatter every tiny shred of distance between us.

Axien sucked in a sharp breath. He tensed, every muscle suddenly going solid under my touch.

I hesitated.

He slowly, carefully, withdrew. His hands stayed on my face, cradling my jaw with his thumbs brushing my cheeks. He held me as though I were fragile—something precious he might shatter by accident. His eyes searched mine, so close and bright I could pick out every tiny fleck of light in them, like shards of starlight amidst the shimmering blue.

But his expression—gods, why did he look so ... *terrified?* His brow skewed, jaw clenched tight, gaze darting across my face as though he were bracing for something awful. Was he waiting for me to slap him? Shove him away?

I didn't want that. I wanted *more.* More of him touching me, kissing me, and holding me close.

No one had ever touched me that way.

"Axien?" I whispered shakily, now acutely aware of how my whole body was trembling against him.

"I ... I owed you that," he murmured, his tone tight and almost frantic. Like he was scrambling for any excuse he could come up with in that instant.

I frowned. "For what?"

"Giving away your secret," he said. "About your runesight. I know you've been hiding it. And I am sorry for that, as well. I just didn't know any other way to ensure they wouldn't kill you right away. If you were valuable, if you had something more they wanted, I knew they'd keep you alive. I-I—"

I pulled away slightly, searching his fractured expression for some sign that he was joking.

He wasn't.

Wow. He'd done *that* as an apology? Really? Like it was some sort of payment or transaction?

For whatever reason, knowing that made me feel ... *dirty*. Dirty—and humiliated.

Of course he wouldn't do it for any other reason. Who would want to kiss a Viperi unless they felt like they had to?

My chest throbbed with a sudden, terrible heaviness. A pain I'd never felt before. My face burned, and I looked away and wiped my mouth on the back of my hand.

"Violet?" Axien's voice was tinged with uneasiness. "What's wrong? I didn't mean to—"

"It's nothing," I snapped, and I kept my face angled away as I scooted a little farther from him. "I guess I should be grateful you did tell them, then. I didn't realize anyone else even knew what runesight was. Thanks, I guess."

He was silent for a beat, his gaze sliding slowly over me as though he were trying to figure out why the mood between us had shifted and gone so sour.

Gods, was he really that dense? I had no experience with men, but that part should have been obvious, right?

"You said the Aurati look for people with runesight? Was that part true?" I had to change the subject. To stop him from pushing the issue, otherwise I'd snap. I'd say things I'd regret. Things he didn't deserve to know.

Like how much he'd just hurt me.

"The Aurati always look for rarities when they breed their products," he replied, his tone quieter. More careful. "That is one quality they've wanted for a long time. I heard them discuss it quite often. I suspected you might have some hidden talent when you were able to pick out that man in the market with the enchanted cloak. It wasn't until you mentioned my eyes glowing blue that I was certain, though."

"Why would calling your eyes blue tip you off?" I asked, my words clipped with irritation.

"There are ancient stories about magic glowing blue before the eyes of ancient human sorcerers," he answered.

Something about the way he phrased it, so cautiously, made me pause. It almost seemed like he was choosing his words *too* carefully now.

Like he was hiding something.

"Which ancient human sorcerers?" I demanded.

Axien's eyes darkened as he flicked me a quick glance, almost like he was warning me about what the answer would be. That I wouldn't like it.

I didn't care. I needed to know. We were so far beyond this nonsense of him hiding things and keeping secrets.

He *would* tell me, one way or another.

"Specifically, it's found only in descendants of Emperor Zarexius," he said flatly, like I'd just asked him to spit in my face.

He might as well have.

My pulse seemed to slowly and achingly thud to a halt. Crippling, soul-crushing cold spread through my veins, freezing every part of me until all I could do was sit there, gaping back at him.

It was a lie. It had to be.

Curator Faera had hinted at something like that before, but only in passing. Only as though it were a slim, unlikely chance. This—that look in his eyes like somber regret—was too much. Too real.

I wouldn't believe it. Not yet.

There was no way that I ... had a gift that came from the bloodline of the Foul Father.

That would make me his heir. And there was nothing in the entire world that could be worse than that.

A deep, stabbing, wrenching pain burrowed deep into my chest, digging through me like a worm into an apple. A secret I could never tell. One that would destroy me and everyone else standing too close.

The Zenith's Call might reluctantly tolerate the fact that I was Viperi. They might be able to stomach having one of Vescor's abominations slithering around in their midst, as long as I kept my blades aimed at the things they wanted.

But I knew, the same way Curator Faera must have known, that they would never allow this. If they found out my blood ran thick with the traitor who had almost destroyed the world, they would see that not a single drop of it endured any further.

I would have to be exterminated rather than risk having his namesake ever rise and take up his cause again.

I swallowed, pressing a hand to my heart, right where that deep, aching pain thrummed sharply.

"You can't tell anyone else that, Axien," I said, my voice snagging in my throat. "They will kill me if they find out. It won't matter what oath I took or what marks I have branded on my skin. No one can know—especially not Mistress Orvana."

The wagon jostled, the rattling of the wheels filling the iron-heavy silence between us before Axien reached over, putting his hand over mine, against my heart. Every one of his handsome, sharply refined elven features had gone stern and utterly resolute.

"I will cut out my own tongue before I tell anyone else, Violet," he swore. "On that, you have my word."

FIFTY-NINE

I shouldn't have believed him.

I should have stabbed him through with the nearest pointy object and kicked his corpse off the back of the wagon. Where did Axien go? No idea. Guess he thought better of joining the Zenith's Call and decided to run away.

Ugggh.

It was stupid to trust anyone with a secret like mine, let alone a guy who had already lied to and betrayed me several times over.

But I did.

There was something in the way he leveled that resolved, relentless look on me that sent chills out through all my extremities. Like this might be the first true thing he'd ever said to me.

Gods, I just prayed he didn't make me regret this. Again.

The mood between us stayed stiff and strange as I withdrew from his touch, giving him a small nod that I hoped he'd take for an answer without pushing the issue any further. I hedged my way to the very back of the wagon, letting my legs dangle off the end as I sat and watched the world slowly grind past.

Dumathis rose around us like a manmade reef of shaped sandstone buildings. Remnants of Avoran ruins peeked through some of the gold-toned structures, as though years of the relentless desert winds had stripped away the sandy exterior to reveal the treasures buried beneath.

A striking contrast of earthy simplicity and complex, orchestrated beauty—Roxus had explained that Dumathis was one of the oldest cities in all the Southern Kingdoms. It was the place in the lush plains where the Avoran elves had built a magnificent, glittering heart for their empire. Their royal city, with only one other to rival it that lay far to the north.

No wonder there were so many ruins beneath it. Gods, Axien and I might have been lost in that ancient warren forever if we hadn't stumbled into that armory. I couldn't decide if that had been divine intervention, or sheer dumb luck.

Regardless, it had saved us.

According to Roxus, the buried portions of Dumathis stretched on for a fifty-mile radius in every direction, with countless entry and exit points that made charting them a nightmare. Even worse, it made all the treasures that lay below easy pickings for looters ... and an ideal place for some of my kin to build a flourishing little empire of their own.

Part of me wondered just how many Viperi cities like that were hidden away under the sand as our wagon rattled out into the outskirts of Dumathis. Hundreds. Maybe even thousands. And each one was sure to have its own little king—a Brood Father—who always thought he was the most powerful Viperi ruler to ever live.

Ridiculous. And almost sad, honestly. I'd never considered how very small their view of the world really was until now, as my eyes tracked the vast horizon that rippled and wavered under the heat of the setting sun.

Here, the sand seemed to be swallowing more and more of the buildings built farther out, like a sea slowly corroding away the shore. What had been a boundless fertile valley thousands of years ago had been scorched to nothing by the War of the Stones, leaving behind bones, ruins, and sand.

All because of an emperor's vicious greed.

The same sorcerer who might also be my ancestor.

That thought made my stomach go queasy again. I grimaced and let out a deep breath. If it really was true, there was nothing I could do about it. I couldn't change who or what I was.

Even if I desperately wanted to.

My pulse skipped, snatching me from my whirling thoughts, as the wagon finally lurched to a halt. Looking up, I searched the horizon with a hand up to shade my eyes from the intense glare of the massive, red swollen sun that was slowly sailing westward.

And I saw them.

A line of dark figures steadily approaching from the southeast. Five riders sat astride dunestriders that moved across the dunes in smooth, dynamic leaps. The silver-scaled beasts ran like sighthounds, long and slender, with large feet that didn't sink into the sand. Everything about them was built for speed and cutting through the fierce winds, and they didn't seem at all bothered by their riders.

Magnificent.

Envy twisted in my chest like a live eel. I still hadn't gotten to ride one. Hopefully someday.

"Better get ready," Axien muttered as he shuffled around in the wagon behind me. "This is sure to be interesting."

I cast him a knowing, sideways look. "Only if it goes exactly how the rest of this mission has gone," I said dryly.

"At least it won't be boring." He cracked a smirk and tossed me a length of airy, dark purple linen cloth so I could wrap myself up and cover my face and hair—just in case our visitors didn't take kindly to seeing a Viperi handing off their most sacred artifact.

"No," I murmured as I pulled the shawl over my nose and mouth, making sure to tuck all my hair into it before I dared to stick my head back out of the wagon to watch. "It definitely won't be."

——+ ❁))✳((❁ +——

They couldn't be human.

The five priestesses that dismounted from their dunestriders before us moved like mirages, the desert wind catching in the lengths of their black and purple robes. They covered their faces just like the ones in the last temple, only their eyes peering at us through masks of flawless silver.

Somehow, out here on the edge of Dumathis, with nothing but the open expanse of the desert behind them, they didn't appear haunting and ghostly like the priests in the temple had. They were ethereally powerful, their robes whipping around them like dark flames against the molten glare of the setting sun.

It made my stomach flutter as I peered out of the back of the wagon, watching from afar, one hand clutching my shawl around my face so the wind didn't snatch it away and blow my cover.

One of the priestesses stepped forward ahead of the others as Roxus and Vanora approached, her arms outstretched in greeting. She wore a delicate headdress of glittering crystals that tinkled musically when she moved, each bead glittering like a tiny fragment of pure starlight. Vanora clasped hands with her in some sort of greeting, but Roxus only bowed low.

Strange. But then again, these were not merely temple-keepers. They lived with a godling. An embodiment of the goddess they served. Maybe that came with a different set of rules and traditions?

I'd have to research it later.

"Look," Axien gasped, his face way too close to mine as he crouched beside me to watch.

Vanora had already started unwrapping the staff, and as soon as the light touched it, the crystal tip of it shone and sparkled like a hunk of pure diamond. The group of priest-esses bowed low, kissing their palms and raising them skyward as though in thanks.

All save for one.

The smallest of the group couldn't have been much older than me, or maybe younger. Her body was slimmer and smaller, but curved with hard, sculpted muscle. Her dark skin and long, pointed ears betrayed her as a Lunostri elf even before she took the silver mask off her face and handed it over to her headdress-wearing companion.

I sucked in a sharp breath as a strange little chill rushed over my body. A sense of knowing. As though I had seen her somewhere before.

Impossible—it wasn't possible. I didn't know her. I'd never met any other priestesses of Adiana, and certainly not one my age.

She strode forward on bare feet, approaching Vanora with her shoulders back and head held high, the desert wind teasing in her finely woven braids. The swirling runes adorning her brow shimmered as she considered the staff, strange yellow-green gradient eyes narrowing on the crystal before she reached out to grasp it firmly by the shaft.

Immediately, the crystal glowed brightly. It filled the air with a radiant internal light, so clean and pure I had to shade my eyes for a moment.

Gods and Fates, that young priestess ... she was the one. The godling.

She was Adiana's essence in mortal form.

A goddess.

Her brow furrowed slightly as though in concentration as she lifted the staff from Vanora's grasp and stepped back, still studying it. Then her gaze snapped to the side—straight to where Axien and I were definitely snooping.

Oh, gods.

I snatched back, ducking into the cover of the wagon with a gasp.

"She saw you," Axien snorted like he found it hilarious.

I shot him a glare. "How do you know?"

"Because she's smiling," he chuckled. "Oh, and now she's saying something to Roxus."

"What? She is?!" I scrambled back to the edge of the wagon to see. Oh, gods, had she noticed what I was?

Sure enough, Roxus had bent over and turned his head so the young priestess could whisper into his ear. She grinned broadly and gave a little nod before she stepped back again, rejoining her sisters.

Then they all gave a parting bow.

Roxus and Vanora mirrored the gesture and stood watching while all five of them glided away to where they had dunestriders waiting to carry them back across the dunes. Back to their hidden temple, somewhere far in the distance.

Mission accomplished.

I chewed at my thumbnail, bouncing my good leg while I waited for Roxus and Vanora to make their way back to the wagon. Only when I felt the whole rig lurch as they climbed back onto the driver's seat did I dare to poke my head out of the front flap, like a prairie dog popping out of its hole.

"That was really her, wasn't it? The godling?" I questioned, glancing between Roxus and Vanora for some clue. "What did she say to you?"

My scruffy tandem scratched at his chin, smirking deviously. "Well now, let's see. She said many things."

JERK.

"She whispered to you!" I hissed and poked at the back of his head. "I saw it! What did she say?"

"She warned me that you'd be causing me a lot more trouble very soon, so I'd better watch myself," he laughed. "I guess she's talking about our next mission, eh?"

What? Really? That was it?

"You're terrible," I grumbled, scowling at the back of his arrogant head.

"Then she made me promise I'd take good care of you," he added at last, giving me that familiar, warm, almost fatherly smile over his shoulder. The one that always squeezed at my heart and made me feel seen, safe, and wanted.

I smiled back, wrinkled my nose, and flicked his ear before I ducked back down into the wagon again. He really was the worst.

And also the best.

Roxus just laughed and snapped the reins, urging our juvenile olifant to start trundling back in the direction of Dumathis. Back to the west, where the sun was already sinking slowly beyond the distant mountains.

Back home.

"It's a long way back," Axien sighed as I settled into the back of the wagon across from him. He'd stretched out on his back with his hands behind his head, using our pile of bedrolls as a pillow.

The atmosphere between us still felt off. Tense, but only if we got too close. I'd just have to watch myself from now on. I'd have to make sure to keep that distance well established.

Otherwise, things might get *complicated*.

"I know." I rubbed at my injured leg, tracing my fingers over the bandaging as I lost myself to the jostle, lurch, and rattle of the wagon. "I think that's a good thing, though. I'm not quite ready to be back yet."

Axien cracked an eye open to steal a glance my way. "Oh?"

"It'll be complicated when we get there," I said. "Mistress Orvana will want to know everything that happened, too. She's not going to like it when I tell her about going through the Viperi city. She'll probably accuse me of being a double agent for them or something. It always causes a lot of stress for Roxus."

The godling girl had been absolutely right about me causing him trouble—more so than he probably realized. Oops.

Now both of Axien's eyes were open. He leveled a worried frown in my direction as he asked, "You really think Mistress Orvana would go that far?"

I shrugged. "Probably. It doesn't matter, though."

He arched an eyebrow. "Why not?"

I smiled down into my lap, to where the buckles on my new hip-sheath sparkled. I'd given up my Spelldrinkers as lost —something I'd sacrificed to give Axien his freedom. But Roxus had come into my room at the healer's house and set them, new sheath, belt, and all, on the bed beside me.

Roxus had grabbed them along with the staff on his way out of the collapsing tunnel. He'd risked his life in those seconds—all for me. I probably looked like a madwoman crying over daggers, but Roxus had just petted my hair, smiling as though he understood.

Not that I'd be able to use them anytime soon, thanks to my stupid leg. But maybe that was for the best. I didn't plan on fighting any more sorcerers if I could help it. So long as Axien behaved himself, anyway.

"I know who I am," I replied at last. "Even if Mistress

Orvana or none of the other elders believe it, I swore myself to this life. To being a member of the Zenith's Call. And now I'm sure, whatever happens, this is what I'm meant to do."

"Even if they curse you? Distrust you? Ostracize you?" Axien's frown deepened, becoming thoughtful. As though he were no longer asking just about me.

"Some of them will. Some always have." I lifted my gaze to him, my smile more real, more certain, than it had ever been. "But the ones that matter don't, and that's all I need."

Axien didn't reply. He panned that deep, pensive frown away and stared out of the back of our small wagon without another word.

I stared, too, watching the landscape slowly slip by as the sun sank lower and lower, turning the swirling dunes and sandstone buildings of Dumathis shades of fluorescent red and vivid purple.

And for a moment, I could almost hear her again—my mother's voice whispering to me. Calling for me. Beckoning me back to that wild, arid land.

"You must live, Visha."

And for the first time in my life, I closed my eyes, took a deep breath, and sent my own thoughts back across that restless, wind-torn landscape.

"I am living, Mother. Your daughter is finally free."

———+ ⟨ ⟩⟩ ＊ ⟨⟨ ⟩ +———

GLOSSARY
OF TERMS

ADIANA – Goddess (or godling, specifically) of the Moon. She is considered a young goddess and is highly revered by the Lunostri elves. Symbolized by the panther.

ARX EBURNA – A prominent stronghold of the Zenith's Call located on the island of Sol'Karr in the small kingdom of Rienka, where the Mistress of the Call resides.

AVORA – Once a powerful empire of divinely-touched elves that stretched over the majority of Reatia. Their beauty and magical power was considered unrivaled, and they were the children of Enais. They fell from power after the War of Falling Stars, and now has limited territory in the north that is strictly guarded from outsiders.

CLYSIROS – Goddess of Death. She is revered as the guardian over the realm of the dead, judge of souls, and the prison of stars. Symbolized by the jackal.

CURATOR – Zenith's Call agents who specialize in dealing with ancient artifacts and texts.

DAMARIA – A vast human kingdom that specializes in agriculture and mining of precious gems. It was once a part of Nar'Haleen, but was divided and developed into a separate kingdom at the behest of Emperor Tashaar to appease his twin sons who did not want to share the throne upon his death. Since that time, Damaria has been fiercely independent and refuses to merge with Nar'Haleen once again. This refusal sparked the War of the Stones, which saw Nar'Haleen mount massive military efforts and enlist several of the gods to try to reclaim the land.

DEXTRUM – Active Zenith's Call agents who are sent out on missions, usually with a combat threat. They must be skilled in all areas, but may choose a specialization that makes them better suited for certain missions.

ENAIS – Foregod of Present. Symbolized by a golden three-pointed star.

ETERNAL HALL – A specialized area of Arx Eburna reserved for training and testing new prospects for the Zenith's Call.

HOLVRADIX – A race of hardy, war-like elves from the north known for their immense stature and physical strength. They have long warred against the Avoran elves, and care little for the world beyond their icy homeland.
ITANUS – Foregod of Past. Symbolized by a right hand.

KRIN'MOIR – The main hall of Arx Eburna. It features a

large ancient fountain depicting the two Fates, or Viepol. The waters of this fountain are considered highly sacred.

LUNOSTRI – A race of elves from Nar'Haleen who roam the vast desert in nomadic tribes. They are considered fierce warriors and keepers of ancient religious rites and knowledge that predate the War of the Stones.

MAGISTER – A senior agent of the Zenith's Call with greater than twenty years of experience.

MILONTOS – Foregod of Future. Symbolized by a golden eye.

MISTRESS (OR MASTER) OF THE CALL – The elected leader of the Zenith's Call who makes all major decisions regarding the order. He or she rules with the help of a council of six elder magisters from strongholds throughout the world.

NAI'POL – A large joint-temple complex on the island of Sol'Karr that houses prominent priests and priestesses and is dedicated to the entire pantheon of Reatia.

NAR'HALEEN – A vast kingdom to the east that once spanned the entirety of the southern region and was rivaled only by the Avoran Empire. It was divided into two halves (Damaria and Nar'Haleen) by former Emperor Tashaar to appease his twin sons. It remains the prominent power in the south, boasting military might and a rich mining industry of precious metals, but continues seeking to regain its lost territories through brute force.

PALIGNO – God of Life. He is known as a benevolent but

mysterious god, who first seeded life upon Reatia and often referred to as the shepherd of the wild. Symbolized by the stag.

PATRON – Dextrum agents of the Zenith's Call who are actively training new recruits, referred to as prospects, and overseeing their education.

PITATHI – A slur word used to refer to Viperi. In Nar'Haleenan, it translates literally as "dirty snake."

PROLEUS – God of War. He is a stern but fair god who values justice, mental and physical fortitude, and honor. He is often referred to as the father of humankind. Symbolized by the wolf.

PROSPECTS – New recruits still going through their training and trials to join the Zenith's Call. These may be children or young adults, but seldom are older than eighteen years of age.

RAJINNA – An ancient humanoid race highly gifted in magic. They are said to have been the first children of the goddess Astaris, making them one of the five peoples first created by the gods. Their skin colors are diverse, but all have shared features of horns, fang-like incisors, and tails. Their lifespan is far longer than the average human, ranging between 1,000 to 3,000 years.

REATIA – The known world (see map at the beginning of this book).

RIENKA – A small, newly-formed kingdom that has declared its independence from Damaria. Ruled over by five merchant lords who call themselves the Trader's Guild, it is known for its many islands, rich trade ports, and vibrant tapestry of cultures from throughout the world.

SIVANTH – A magical boundary wall created after the War of the Stones by the gods to separate the divine and mortal realms.

STEMMA – Ancient Avoran currency touched with magic. They are frequently used by the Zenith's Call as calling cards or identification markers.

SUROTRIX – The "Keeper of Whispers" that resides in the Vault of Whispers at Arx Eburna, overseeing the most volatile and secret archived documents and items for the Zenith's Call. This is considered a high honor that demands a lifetime of loyalty, and chosen candidates must have their tongues removed.

TANDEM – Pairs or partners of dextrum agents within the Zenith's Call that work side-by-side on missions.

UNDAE – Goddess of the Sea. Often referred to as the great mother, she is known for her changeable moods, love for adventurous souls, and beauty. Symbolized by the hippocampus.

URSINAAR – Bloodline of ancient Vordegan warriors who have the inborn magical ability to transform into a large bear. They are considered the most powerful and brutal of all Vordegan fighters.

VESCOR – God of the Void. Symbolized by a black spiral.

VIDRATHIAN STEEL – A prized and rare metal mined by

the dwarves of the Whitecrown Mountains and forged by the Vordegans into weapons. The metal has the unique ability to absorb magical energy, sparing the user from its effects if wielded in the right way. Vordegan warriors train their entire lives with these mystical weapons, learning to deflect or even redirect magical assaults with them.

VIEPOL – A pair of powerful god-like beings said to embody fragments of Avgior's shattered essence. They guard the boundary of the Sivanth, judge the souls of the mortal world, and take on the appearance of dragons. They are also known as the Fates.

VINDEXORI – Agents of the Zenith's Call who specialize in combat and are used as guardians or foot soldiers to protect certain sites, temples, or artifacts.

VIPERI – The ill-regarded offspring of Vescor. They are an ancient humanoid race that dwells in the caverns, cave systems, and long-forgotten ruins of ancient cities far below the surface world. They are vicious, highly skilled fighters and have no love for anything outside their subterranean realm. They are known to have pallid complexions, pale hair, red eyes, and fang-like incisors.

VORDEGA – A small, isolated kingdom to the west that is ruled by brutal, warlike tribes of humans said to be gifted at thwarting magic. They were known as the most efficient forces against the Avoran elves during the War of Falling Stars, but rarely deal with other kingdoms.

WAR OF FALLING STARS – An ancient war between the Avoran elves and the human kingdoms of Tibrus, Vordega, and Nar'Haleen. As the Avoran Empire expanded across

Reatia, it absorbed and enslaved a great many other kingdoms, showing particular hatred and disgust for humans. The human kingdoms allied against them, resulting in a brutal conflict that lasted nearly 800 years. The human kingdoms managed to drive back the Avoran Empire in a costly victory that left both nations forever diminished and broken.

WAR OF THE STONES – An ancient war between Nar'Haleen and Damaria that became interwoven with the affairs of the gods thanks to Emperor Zarexius's blood pact with Vescor. Many of the gods chose sides, and the result was catastrophic. The war left the landscape eternally scarred, many races of peoples nearly extinct, and two of the gods themselves were destroyed. To see that no such war ever took place again, the gods all made a pact to seal their power behind a mystical barrier called the Sivanth. Their influence would be tempered through sacred stones with a mortal individual acting as their mouthpiece.

ZAREXIUS – Emperor of Damaria during the War of the Stones who made a deal with Vescor, the God of the Void. He is also known as the father of the Viperi, as he was given leadership over them after the fall of Vescor.

ZENITH'S CALL – A secret society of scholars, assassins, mercenaries, historians, and priests that formed after the War of the Stones. They are sworn to protect the secrets and artifacts of the gods and those who worship them.

A Special Thanks To ...

My husband, Keith, who takes the time to read every book I write. He's my number #1 fan, and I am eternally grateful for a partner who not only supports my journey, but takes my hand and walks alongside me through it. I love you so much!

Heather, Khara, Emily, Alicia, Ashlee, Richard, and all of my author friends who have been so amazingly supportive through the ups and downs of the past year. You guys embody the kind of author I want to become — positive, encouraging, passionate, and too stubborn to quit!

My AMAZING Beta team!!! Thank you so much for taking the time to make sure these books are ready for the world. I couldn't do it without you!

My lovely artist, Lulybot, who has created such wonderful pieces for these books! Thank you!

Philippians 4:13

Books from
Nicole Conway

THE DRAGONRIDER CHRONICLES
Fledgling
Avian
Traitor
Immortal

THE DRAGONRIDER LEGACY
Savage
Harbinger
Legend

THE DRAGONRIDER HERITAGE
Hunter
Betrayer
Successor
Godling
Sojourner
Pathfinder
Paladin
Eternal

MAD MAGIC
Mad Magic
Vicious Vows
Wicked Ways

SPIRITS OF CHAOS
Scales
Wings
Hearts

EMPIRE OF BLADES
Born of Shadow
Oath of Moonlight
Cage of Secrets
Curse of Thorns

www.ingramcontent.com/pod-product-compliance
Lightning Source LLC
Chambersburg PA
CBHW020824030726
47496CB00001B/75